NO ONE KNOWS

"I can stand anything now. You're here with me," he said.
"In our Lost Boys' House."

NO ONE KNOWS

A Novel by
NANCY PRICE

A Malmarie Press Book
St. Cloud, Florida

This book is a work of fiction. Names, incidents, places and characters
are products of the author's imagination, or are used fictitiously. Any
resemblance to actual events, locales, or persons alive or dead, is completely coincidental.

First Printing

Malmarie Press and colophon are registered trademarks of
Malmarie Press, Inc.
Manufactured in the United States of America

ISBN: 0-9744818-0-7

Library of Congress Catalog Card Number: 2003113201

First Malmarie Press hardcover printing June 2004

Illustrated by the author

This book appeared in 2001 in a French translation titled *Un Écart de
Jeunesse*, published by Presses de la Cité, Paris, France.

ATTENTION UNIVERSITIES, COLLEGES, SCHOOLS AND
ORGANIZATIONS: Quantity discounts are available on bulk purchases
of this book for educational use, gift purchases, or as premiums for
increasing magazine subscriptions and renewals. Please contact Malmarie
Press, Inc., 4387 Rummell Road, St. Cloud, Florida 34769.
E-mail: nancypricebooks@aol.com Fax: 407-891-9001
Phone 800-509-4905

For
David, John, Catherine and Charlotte

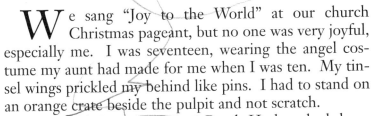

1

We sang "Joy to the World" at our church Christmas pageant, but no one was very joyful, especially me. I was seventeen, wearing the angel costume my aunt had made for me when I was ten. My tinsel wings prickled my behind like pins. I had to stand on an orange crate beside the pulpit and not scratch.

It was Christmas 1941. Pearl Harbor had been attacked. We were sure America had already lost the war – Hitler and Mussolini had grabbed whole countries and nobody stopped them. Nobody could. So the congregation was hardly in the Christmas spirit, and neither was I. If those prickling tinsel wings had been the real thing, I'd have flown out of Iowa the first time I tied them on.

But that was the night that Conrad Raymond Beale noticed me. I didn't think I was very pretty, especially as an angel, but the fact was that my costume was made of a few layers of awfully sleazy white cheesecloth. Every December I had to loop scratchy tinsel around my neck, cross it under my breasts and tie it in back. I'd always worn a little cheesecloth jacket over the whole thing, but this year I discovered (dressing in the church choir room) that I couldn't even get that jacket on, and I didn't have time to go home and get my bra. Since the last Christmas I'd developed what was politely called "a nice figure."

My aunt was having a baby at the time, or she'd have snatched me right off my orange crate. But I stood there and said my angel speech, lit up by the janitor's flashlight. I knew my words by heart, so I had time to notice that most of the boys and men weren't looking at pretty Anne Majors, who was playing Mary in a blue blanket. They were watching the lit-up angel in cheesecloth. Even handsome Robert Laird in the back row of the choir was looking at me.

Then the pageant was over. I stepped down from the orange crate, hurrying to get that tinsel off, and there was Conrad Raymond Beale. He took my hands and said, "Miranda Letty, you're the most beautiful angel God ever made."

I smiled back at him. Con wasn't handsome like Robert Laird, but I knew something about Con that most people didn't. My uncle was a minister, so he often talked about money, and I'd heard him say, "Conrad Beale is rising in the world. He's the richest man in the church, believe it or not. He's running his father's company and getting war contracts already."

I smiled at Con. I'm sneaky, and I was getting pretty smart, too, because I read so much. I got more fun from reading than I got from anything else at seventeen, and I was trying to read right through our school library, shelf by shelf, not even skipping the bottom rows where the big, thick books were.

We called those books "mailboxes" because when the librarian wasn't looking, you could stick love notes in them. Then you just whispered "Spencer" or "Milton" to somebody you had a crush on, and they knew where to look.

No boy had ever whispered "Spencer" or "Milton" to me, but I read those books. I read Spencer's *The Faerie Queene*. It's four hundred years old. Canto One starts out, "A gentle knight was pricking on the plaine," and if that won't make you laugh when you're low, I don't know what will. But it's magical, too, and sort of touching. Who's seen a gentle knight lately?

I thought maybe Con Beale might be one. He was tall; he had to bend a little like a giraffe to look into my eyes, and he had eyelashes almost as long as a giraffe's –they were the prettiest thing about him. They made him look gentle, the way giraffes look.

So I smiled at Con, but I didn't let him hold my hands for more than a few seconds, there in front of everybody in church. A girl had to think about her reputation – it came first, even when a boy said everything you wanted to hear and promised marriage. Maybe you were pretty sure he meant it, and you'd spend the rest of your life getting his meals and washing his clothes, but you kept his hands above your bra and below your knees and said "No!"

And of course the boy knew exactly what you were thinking when you said No – he wouldn't make the mistake of supposing you really meant Yes. If the boy didn't "score" with you, that meant that you were a "nice girl" he could marry, and he told the other town boys that you were "hard to get," and was proud of it. If "he lost control of himself" he'd be robbing you of all you had to barter with in life, because nobody – not even him – wanted "damaged goods."

You couldn't even *look* like you might be damaged. In movies, what was the first thing Katherine Hepburn or Claudette Colbert or Jeannette MacDonald did when they met Clark Gable or Nelson Eddy or Spencer Tracy? Those gorgeous girls stuck their noses in the air and froze over; that's what they did. They acted as if the handsomest men in Hollywood were nothing but traps full of moldy cheese that any girl could smell a mile off.

So I didn't let Con Beale hold my hands more than a few seconds there in front of the whole congregation. Con's mother was dead; he lived with his father and was in church every Sunday, and no one had ever seen him with a girl. I told him how kind he was to say I looked like an angel, and Con said he meant it, and I said, "How sweet of you," and smiled some more, and went to the choir room to get that cheesecloth and tinsel off.

The next week my aunt came home with my baby cousin. I'd lived with my aunt and uncle and cousins since I was nine, and I soon found out the new baby was mine to take care of, most of the time. I almost forgot Con Beale. The baby cried and spit up and filled diapers – he was a regular diaper-filling machine. One of my jobs was to keep the diapers coming: I rinsed them in the toilet, washed them, boiled them, put them through three rinses, and hung them on clothes racks (since it was the dead of winter) where they dried as stiff as if they'd been starched. I hardly got one batch folded before the diaper pail was full again.

New Year's Day came and went and it was 1942. One cold afternoon the parsonage doorbell rang. I heard my aunt answer it, then say in her sweetest voice, "I'm so sorry, Mr. Beale, but Reverend Letty is at the church. I'm sure he'll be so pleased to see you."

I came to watch from the back hall. Conrad Raymond Beale stood on the doorstep without a word, letting the winter wind whip in, until he finally brought his other hand from behind his back, and it had a box of chocolates in it.

A man who brought chocolates to a house did not do it lightly. A box of chocolates meant business. I saw Aunt Gertrude's head jerk back: Mr. Beale's business wasn't lost on her. An eligible man was standing on her doorstep with a box of chocolates – but who for?

At first I simply stared at Con – were the chocolates for my cousin Betty, the "daughter of the house"? Then Con's eyes met mine over my aunt's shoulder with a look I recognized, though I'd never seen it before. I had my apron on and my new cousin in my arms, but that look brought me to the door to stand beside my aunt and say sweetly, "Why, Mr. Beale! Do come in," though I was quivering all over. My astonished aunt had to take the baby and my apron while Mr. Beale handed the box of chocolates to me and wiped his shoes thoroughly on the doormat. I was too dumbfounded to say a word or look at him, but I hung up his hat and coat, and off we went to the parlor, which I hardly ever saw except when I cleaned it.

Aunt Gertrude was not dumb. She got rid of the baby and brought coffee so fast that Con and I hadn't said more than ten sentences about the weather before there she was with a tray. This was hospitable, but it also told this eligible bachelor that I was being watched, and would be watched, diligently. I'd come to myself by that time: I opened my box of chocolates and begged my aunt to have one in a very ladylike manner, and she helped herself and thanked me politely and smiled at Con and went out, leaving the parlor door wide open, of course.

"Now you must have one," I said to Con, holding out my box of chocolates to tease him. "I'll be able to tell what kind of man you are by which one you choose."

It amazed me then, and it amazes me now, thinking how quickly you can become someone else. There I was – astounded as I was – flirting with a man like the heroine in one of the books I'd read. And there was Aunt Gertrude playing an absolutely new character, too: the polite aunt thanking me for one of my chocolates and guarding me as if I had never been anything but her very attractive, dangerously desirable niece. And we did it in a couple of seconds.

Con didn't stay long, which was part of the game, too. Neither of us could think of much to say – the fact that he was there said more than enough. I was desperately fishing in very empty waters for pleasant topics when he stood up.

I told him how glad I was to see him. I helped him on with his coat, and noticed it was new and expensive, like his suit. While he was putting on his snap-brim felt hat, I whispered, "Do come again."

When Con stepped off our porch, Aunt Gertrude was beside me in a second, looking through the front door curtain at Con's back. "Well," she remarked in a tone that said that miracles were very scarce events.

But I was holding a box of chocolates. I gave her a look that said miracles were quite easily repeated if you were a girl of seventeen, not a woman almost forty with a wet diaper in her hand.

2

"C onrad Beale comes *every afternoon*," I heard my
cousin Betty say to my aunt after a week.

"Never mind," Aunt Gertrude said. "You're only sixteen."

"Roses ... candy ... and she's not even *eighteen*."

"That just shows it'll be your turn pretty soon," my
aunt said.

I heard the envy in their voices. As the days passed and
Conrad progressed from a chair across the parlor to the
sofa close beside me, I sometimes wondered: could he be
that unbelievable thing, The Just Reward, sent as com-
pensation for my first seventeen years?

Some of those seventeen years had been speckled with
happy times, but mostly there weren't any. When I was
little, my father worked nights in Chicago and wasn't
home much; finally he wasn't there at all. My mother said
he'd gone to another town to find work. The two of us
stayed alone in our rented room, and he sent us money.
My mother told me he'd come back, but one day a letter
came instead. "It's from a hospital," my mother told me.
Tears were running down her face. "Your daddy's dead."

We cried together for a while. "He's gone...he's
gone," she kept whispering. "He was so good, and we
loved him so..."

She cried at night, too. I heard her. But in the daytime
she said, "We'll get along somehow. At least it's spring.
We won't be cold." I watched her count the money in our
money box over and over. There wasn't much left.

And then another letter came, and my mother cried
again. When she could stop crying, she said, "It's from

your daddy's brother. He's invited us to visit him, and sends money for the train. We're being given a home in Cedar Falls, Iowa."

I was only nine, and I took that literally: we would be given a house.

A house. The only house I'd ever had was the doll-house I made from cigar boxes I found in an alley. Nobody I knew lived in a house. Our friends were like us: they had a room or two in buildings of sooty brick. Out-of-work men slept in abandoned cars through bitter winters at the bottom of the Depression. Those hard times killed my father, I suppose: I think of him as one more man without a job on the streets of some other town.

But I was only nine then, and it seemed to me that my father had died to give us our new home in Iowa. I thought it was something a loving father might do. "I'm going to have my own house in Cedar Falls, Iowa," I told my playmates.

I asked my mother and asked my mother, but she wouldn't say another word about Cedar Falls, Iowa. "I can't think about anything but getting ready to go," she told me. "You'll see your new home soon enough."

Years before my mother had bought enough material to make curtains for our windows. Now she took them down and cut out dresses for us both. She lay on our day bed to sew, and when she was too tired, she went to sleep. I tiptoed around our room, or ran down three flights of stairs to play with my friends on the apartment house stoop. School was out and summer was growing hot.

"You'll have to give most of your toys away," Mother told me when it was almost time to leave. "We've only got one suitcase."

I cried, but I had to part with my blocks, and a Parcheesi game that had almost all the pieces, and my

When I was little, my father worked nights in Chicago and
wasn't home much; finally he wasn't there at all. My mother
said he'd gone to another town to find work. The two of us
stayed alone in our rented room.

cigar-box dollhouse. I could only keep three toys small enough to carry in my pocket.

My mother and I ate the last of our food before we took the train from Chicago to Iowa. The May morning was hot, and windows were open in every car, so locomotive smoke blew in and speckled our white gloves my mother had made. You couldn't rub the specks or wash them off: we had to spread our gloves in our laps and not touch them. I'd never had white gloves before. I wore a hat my mother had made from one of hers. A little girl in the same car didn't have gloves or a hat; I walked by her slowly several times with a paper cup from the water cooler, bringing my mother a drink.

After a while city streets were behind us, and I saw row after row of suburban bungalows. Houses! Would ours have a bedroom for each of us? A bathroom? A real kitchen like the pictures in magazines?

Before long we passed through small towns whose houses had lawns and flower gardens. I'd never imagined a garden. Only half awake, I added a garden and a lawn to the house I was dreaming for us.

A man came through the train with sandwiches, but Mother said we didn't have any money. I went to sleep and dreamed of houses, and was hardly awake when I felt my hat tied under my chin. I followed Mother down steps, and then a portly man was saying very loudly over the hiss of the locomotive's steam: "Hello, Alice. And this must be Miranda." He leaned down to look at me.

I nodded. "She's still half asleep," my mother said. "Say 'How do you do?' to your Uncle Boyd."

I said "How do you do?" to the watch chain looping across his middle, and entered another dream, because Uncle Boyd opened a door for me, and I climbed into a automobile. I had never ridden in one. I sat on the black leather seat like a princess, my white gloves spread on my knees.

It was an old, battered car, but I didn't notice. My uncle's red face appeared and reappeared above its radiator in rhythm with a cranking noise. I was proud to think that I was a city girl and knew what he was doing. Then the car sputtered and putted, he climbed in, and off we went.

Cedar Falls wasn't a city like Chicago. It was a town. It had a few blocks of high-fronted stores, but no tall buildings at all – only houses, houses and more houses standing by themselves in hot green yards. Picket fences ... gardens ... porches with cool shade and wicker swings. As we rattled along every block, I thought, "Is this where we stop? Is this the house they're giving us?"

"We call Cedar Falls the 'Lawn City,'" my uncle told my mother sitting beside him in the front seat.

"It's lovely," my mother said in a faint voice. Then we turned into a part of town where the houses were smaller and closer together.

We stopped in front of one. It had a porch and a small lawn. The thin woman in the doorway wore a housedress and had dark hair, and she wasn't smiling. Neither were the three children with her. I had only time to see that the children were smaller than I was before Uncle Boyd helped my mother from the automobile and she fell on the grass and lay still.

My uncle shouted. The woman and the children came running. Mother wasn't very heavy; my aunt and uncle carried her into the house and put her on a couch. Her eyes stayed shut. I stood beside her and held her hand tight, but I couldn't help looking around me at our new house.

It had at least three rooms downstairs, and there were steps climbing to more rooms. I'd never seen so much furniture – every room was full. There were curtains, too, and rugs on the floors. The front door had an oval window with shiny flowers and leaves cut into it. A dining-room table showed through an archway, circled by its chairs. Such riches! "Wake up!" I wanted to tell my mother. "Wake up and see!"

The children and I were locking stares. No polite talk for us: we were sizing each other up. The girl wasn't as old as I was, and the boys were smaller yet, so I stared right back. I was bigger than any of them, and this was my house. They didn't look friendly, being children. They looked natural. My aunt and uncle gave me friendly glances, but I held tight to my mother's hand, because their voices had an angry worry in them, and the sound was truer than their looks. "Your mother's tired from the long train trip," my aunt said to me.

"I'll call Dr. Horton," my uncle said, and went to a telephone on our hall table just under the stairs. Our house had a telephone!

I wished they wouldn't call more people in. There were too many already. Why didn't they go home? Then my mother could wake up and we would explore our whole house.

Waiting for the doctor, my aunt took my mother's gloves and hat away and bathed my mother's face. My uncle smiled at me. "Here are your cousins," he said. "Betty is the oldest – she's eight – and Benjy is six, and Bernard is almost five."

"How do you do?" I said as I had been taught. "I'm Miranda."

"This is Miranda," my uncle said to Betty. "Why don't you take Miranda to the bathroom so she can wash up after her long ride." He came to me. "Shall we take off your hat and gloves? It's such a hot day."

I let him take them off. I followed my cousin Betty, anxious to see more of my house. I caught sight of a stove through the hall door; then we went upstairs to a whole new floor of rooms.

The bathroom had a big bathtub with lion's paws at each corner. I tried not to look at it. Although it was my bathtub, I was sure I would never in my whole life crawl naked into something with claws on it.

I washed my hands and face in my own bathroom, and asked Betty to wait outside while I went to the toilet. I suppose I used a bossy voice, but I was older than she was, and it was my toilet.

Then I explored the upstairs of my house while Betty trailed behind. There was a little room full of junk next to the bathroom, and then a fine big bedroom that would be my mother's. Mother's bed had shining spikes sticking up at the corners, and a fringed and beaded lamp beside it. I imagined her so warm and comfortable there, not in the cot we had dragged every night from under our daybed. My father had done all this for us. And there were other rooms...

"Come on," Betty said, yanking at my arm, so I followed her to another bedroom filled with narrow beds. "You're going to sleep in that corner in that old cot," she said. "The one Bernard wet on."

I must have turned red in the face and glared, because she backed away when I yelled, "I'm going to have a room of my own!"

"You are not!" Betty yelled back. "You're a *poor relation*. We have to take you in, and we don't want to, but it's *Christian charity!*"

"I'm not!" I cried. "It is not!" But I knew she couldn't have thought of those words herself – they hit me like stones. They were grown-up words, said so many times that she could parrot them. I didn't know exactly what "Christian charity" meant, but I understood "poor" and "take you in" and "don't want to."

Betty was grinning as if she knew my happiness was shrinking and drying up like dead mice I'd found under our stairs in Chicago. What could I do but slap her hard? She clattered downstairs wailing for her mother, and I followed and grabbed my mother's cold hand where she lay on the couch asleep.

I got as close to Mother as I could. Everyone in the room was scowling. My aunt was awake and big and angry, advancing on me. "You are not to slap your cousin ever again," she said to me. "You and your mother are going to live in our house because your father is gone and you haven't any home. You remember that. Do as you are told."

My cousins stared at me in triumph. I held tight to my mother's hand and would not cry one tear. The rooms around me had been magical; they were rich with wood and carpet and glass, book bindings, framed pictures of Christ – all ours. Now I knew my mother and I were like Hansel and Gretel in the house of the wicked witch. I held Mother's hand very hard and glared at everyone and changed, then and there, into somebody who had the world pretty well figured out.

3

The doctor came, and then they carried my mother to her bed: a couch in a little room at the back of the house.

I couldn't eat any supper; I drank a glass of milk and didn't look at anybody, and then ran to find my mother and hold her hand. But after a while my aunt made me put on my nightgown and lie on Bernard's cot in a corner of a hot bedroom.

After they said their prayers, my cousins chattered about all their friends and the wonderful things they were going to do. I pulled my sheet over my head and lay in sweaty darkness in a corner of a strange house. My mother had always sung songs with me at night if I was afraid.

My cousins fell asleep. I heard my aunt and uncle come upstairs to bed with a creaking of floors and thump and gush of running water.

At last the house was still. I took my pillow and crept between the children's beds, step by step. The door squeaked, and so did the stairs. I tiptoed down and lay on the floor beside my mother, holding her hand.

The windows of the little back room were open, but the roar of the city was gone – those sounds of car engines and horns, shouts and sirens that I had always thought belonged to the night. Instead I heard what seemed to be birds or bugs: cheeps, clicks, hums and buzzes that filled the night air around us without a second's rest, ringing like small bells, chirping like birds, or grating like files, metal on metal.

I could hardly hear my mother's slow breathing. I stared into the dark rooms I had thought were ours. When I squeezed my mother's fingers, she didn't squeeze back, and even when I crawled up to lie against her, she never moved. But I hid my face against her neck to smell the nice smell that only she had, and fell asleep.

When I woke, my mother was gone.

I sat up. I was in my cot in the children's room again. My aunt and uncle were bending over me in the morning sunshine. "Your dear mother has left us," Uncle Boyd said.

"She is in heaven," Aunt Gertrude said.

"No!" I yelled at them. "No!" I jumped up and raced downstairs. My mother's bed was empty. There was nothing in the little back room to show she had ever been there. I ran from room to room looking for her, though my aunt and uncle tried to catch me, tried to talk to me.

I stopped at last in the front hall, jammed in a corner, hiding my face.

My mother had gone away. Uncle Boyd put his arms around me, lifted me although I was kicking, and carried me to a rocking chair to rock with me until breakfast was ready.

I wanted to bite him. I would not sit at the table. I would not eat.

Mother had gone away like my father without a single word, not even "Goodbye."

My aunt made me wear a black dress that was too small for me. I watched a long box lowered into a hole in the graveyard grass. I didn't cry a single tear. I wouldn't sleep in the cot Bernard had wet on; I slept under it. I wouldn't say one word.

For a week or so I was left to myself. I wandered the house that wasn't mine. The Letty home was a shabby, thin-walled parsonage in hard depression times, but it didn't seem that way to me. Everything in it was rich and strange, and every object was unfriendly. Even the cream-colored stove glared at me with its row of enamel tulips, as if to say, "So you thought we belonged to you!" But I had to eat. I had to sleep in the corner of the children's room. In a week or two I couldn't recognize my dream house: it was a den of three shrieking, slapping, teasing children who guarded their places and toys, as sharp-eyed and unforgiving as tigers. If I shut myself in the bathroom or wouldn't get out of bed, their mother would be told.

Aunt Gertrude was the ruler of that den. My uncle could disappear into his study when he wasn't at his church a block away. Everything that made up my life would come through the sharp-nailed hands and sharper voice of Aunt Gertrude. I was not – as she would remind me often through the years – any relation of hers whatsoever.

When Uncle Boyd was home and among us, I didn't think he missed very much. The very blue eyes in his fat face were often on me. Even the shiny back of his bald head seemed to be watching between his large, alert ears.

We went to Sunday school and then church every Sunday. My cousins had a few different things to wear, but I always went in the one good dress I had – the "curtain dress" I wore on the train. It was only plain blue cotton, but my mother had embroidered daisies on the collar and down the front, because my middle name was "Daisy." Miranda Daisy Letty.

My uncle stood in his pulpit in his long black dress with the white scarf hanging around his neck and down past his knees. A big gold cross shone just where his fat stomach started to stick out, and his church voice reached the farthest balcony corners. Everybody's money was brought to the front of the church in big plates and put down in front of him. Nobody left until he said the final blessing, unless they had to go to the toilet or were sick or their baby cried. Afterwards he stood with Aunt Gertrude in the hall, shaking hands with everybody when they left, while my cousins and I stood behind them in a corner and were not allowed to fight, or even fidget.

I came to know every dent and stain and splinter of that parsonage. We had cupboards we threw junk into when the doorbell rang, and my aunt kept a "good dress" behind the pantry door to put on in a hurry while Betty or I showed the caller to the parlor or the study. The world outside that house, I learned, was a merciless judge of ministers' wives who wore aprons or left dust on the top of the china cabinet or let children speak when not spoken to.

We had to be "presentable." June was so hot that my aunt spread sheets on the downstairs carpets for a few nights, and we slept beside and under the furniture to the back-and-forth rattle of an electric fan. But we had to be up by dawn, trailing our sheets upstairs, for "someone might come."

The Chicago room where I'd lived with my mother had been small, but it was our own. Now I didn't even have my own bed – my cousins sat on it or tore off the covers or turned it upside down. Betty had long brown hair that my fingers itched to pull. Her face was sharp-nosed and pinched looking, and she didn't miss a thing I did. Benjy's big ears stuck out like his father's ears; he was even more sharp and thin than Betty. Bernard was plump and sulky. His brother and sister were mean to him, too, so he watched the world sidewise and kept his head down, and picked on me whenever they were tired of doing it.

I had nothing left of Chicago but a few clothes and the three hidden treasures I had brought in my pocket to Cedar Falls. The first was a wooden church an inch square with an open door, so that I could put my eye to it and imagine a wedding inside, or Easter, or Christmas. The second was a tiny celluloid doll with arms and legs that moved. The third was a real book no bigger than the church, with tiny pictures of kittens on every page.

My cousins had never seen my treasures. I kept the three little toys in my bloomers: the puffy underpants with elastic around the waist and legs that small girls wore.

When I sat down, I sat down carefully. In bed I put my treasures on my stomach and slept on my back all night.

But one Friday night I forgot to wear my bloomers to bed, and Aunt Gertrude shook out my toys when she gathered up the washing. I stood before her, my eyes on the three precious objects in her hand.

"She's been running around with these in her bloomers!" my aunt said to my uncle, who was passing in the hall.

Uncle Boyd looked at the doll, the church and the book. Then I felt him looking at me. He said, "You don't have any place to keep your belongings, do you, Miranda?"

I couldn't even shake my head.

"Shall I keep them for you?" he asked me. "Come down to my study. We'll find a place to put them, and you can play with them when you ask."

He took my treasures from my aunt, and I followed him, my eyes on my shoes. He shut his study door behind us, gave me my church and doll and book, and asked me to sit down.

"Your father and I were brothers – you know that, don't you?" he asked. I only looked at my treasures.

"Did he ever tell you how we grew up?"

I wouldn't look at him. I counted the ticks of his study clock: one, two...

"We grew up in Chicago, like you did," my uncle said. "And we were really poor. We had to beg for food. Your father and I went out on the streets and begged when we weren't any older than you are."

Betty had told me over and over how my family was "so poor." I scowled at the study rug.

"Then we grew up enough to get jobs. Your dad went to work in a canning factory, but I was lucky – I met a minister who took me in and sent me to school." My uncle leaned down to look into my face. "So I've been taken into someone's house when I didn't have any place to go. I was just like you."

I had to look at him then. His voice was kind.

"I hated it," my uncle said. "Having to live like that and take charity – but I knew what it was like to live on the streets in Chicago. Have you seen people begging in Chicago?"

I certainly had.

"Even little children?"

I nodded. Dirty children had stood on the stoop of our apartment house, begging when my mother and I went in or out. We couldn't feed them or take them in, my mother said. We only had enough for ourselves.

"Then you know I had to stay with the minister's family and get an education – but your father wasn't so lucky. The canning factory closed, and he couldn't keep a job after that – not for long. You were just a baby, and he had to come home and see your mother and you with hardly enough to eat. That's a terrible thing for a father to see."

I'd never thought about that. Not once.

"What could he do?" Uncle Boyd asked. "Of course he had me. He could ask me for help, couldn't he? Wasn't I his brother?"

I didn't know how to answer that. It seemed to me that if you had a brother he would help.

"And I would have helped him," Uncle Boyd said. His voice wasn't his prayer voice; it was a real voice now, and so sad I stared at him. There were tears in his eyes; he was a big fat man in black with a white collar and a gold watch chain and eyes brimming with tears. "But he wouldn't come. He wouldn't ask. He was too proud to ask for help. Just like you. You're too proud to ask for help, aren't you?"

I could hardly nod. I was like my father?

"I'm like him, too," Uncle Boyd said. "We're both like him. That's because your dad and I had the same father and mother. They were your grandfather and grandmother. We're all the same family."

We were. I hadn't felt what it meant.

"Now, what could your father do to save you and your mother, who was sick?" Uncle Boyd said softly. "He knew what it was like to beg for your food on the street – he didn't want you or your mother to live like that, did he?"

"No," I said in a whisper.

"He wouldn't ask me for help, but he could write me a letter and tell me where you and your mother were, and say he was leaving. He knew I would send money for her to come here with you."

I could hardly say "Yes." I had thought I knew what my world was like.

"I suppose you wonder why your mother wasn't too proud to come here with you," Uncle Boyd said. I hadn't thought of that, but I thought about it now.

"Let me tell you about a cat I knew once," Uncle Boyd said. "She had just one kitten, and *how* she took care of that kitten. She hid her kitten in an old shed and brought food to it and slept curled around it to keep it warm. Mothers do that. She certainly was too proud to bring it in the house and let us feed it – it was hers and the only one she had. But the shed she kept her kitten in caught fire while she was out hunting for food. We tried to stop her when she came back, but she ran right past us and into that burning shed and dragged that kitten out by the scruff of its neck. She saved it. She died, but she saved her kitten."

I was crying. I couldn't help it. Uncle Boyd had tears on his fat face. "That's what mothers do," he said. He sat beside me and put his arms around me and I cried and cried. "Mothers are proud," he said, smoothing my hair.

"But they're mothers first. She had just enough strength to get you here to a safe place. Remember the last words she said: *It's lovely*. You've had a proud father and a strong mother. You can stand anything."

My parents had loved me after all. Uncle Boyd and I were family. He'd been poor and alone like me, and understood, and kept my treasures safe in a drawer in his desk.

All Uncle Boyd had said was very comforting, but nevertheless I had to come out of his study and live with Aunt Gertrude and Betty and Benjy and Bernard. Maybe Uncle Boyd had been a poor little boy, but now he was a big man, and he could go into his study and shut the door, or go off to his church. He didn't find spiders in his bed. Nobody stirred the food on his plate into one big mess when Aunt Gertrude wasn't looking.

I thought about my father and mother. I wondered if they knew what had happened to me – and that made me think of Alibi Ritter back in Chicago.

Alibi Ritter called herself a "witch woman," and she slept in parks in the summer and a railroad shed in winter. We children asked her how she stayed so fat. She told us she could eat anything, like a goat, and had died nine times and always come back.

The neighborhood children sat on a Chicago stoop on hot summer nights and listened to Alibi's stories of the dead. She had songs about graves and being buried, and how "your body turns an ugly green and foam runs out like thick whip cream." We listened to her – we couldn't *not* listen – and then we went to bed and woke up screaming, because we figured she was right.

Alibi Ritter said, "When people die, they never leave you if they've loved you a lot. They pick out a room in your house that nobody uses much, and they stay there. You'll hear the floor creak at night, and that's them. You'll go in that room and feel like somebody opened the icebox door – that's them. Sometimes they sit by your bed at night to keep you safe. If your enemies try to hurt you, your enemies will have terrible bad luck and die a slow, horrible death, and never know why."

I remembered Alibi Ritter.

That night when I crawled into my cot, I waited until Aunt Gertrude had heard the four of us chant "If I should die before I wake, I pray the Lord my soul to take," and had shut off the light and gone downstairs. Then I crept into the storeroom next to the bathroom. It was almost dark except for a little gleam from the streetlight on the corner. I shut the door and sat on a box, and wondered if my mother and father might have moved in there.

After a while my cousins opened the door. "What are you doing in here?" Betty said.

"I can't tell you. You'll tell Aunt Gertrude and Uncle Boyd, and terrible things will happen to you," I said.

"She's peeing," Benjy said.

"She can't find the bathroom – poor people don't have bathrooms," Betty said.

"Be careful," I said.

"Careful of what?" Betty said, and pushed her way in. "There's nothing in here but old boxes."

"Back up," I said. "You're standing too close to my mother. Can't you feel her? She died in this house."

Betty jumped and looked at the dark behind her. "What?"

"My mother and my father – he's come to take care of me, too. Don't you hear them at night, walking around in here? But you can't tell grownups about them, or you'll get awful sick." I looked very sad and shook my head. "I shouldn't have told you. I didn't mean to. But I thought maybe you've seen them, standing by my bed at night."

Betty got out of the room fast with Benjy and Bernard hanging on to her nightgown, but I stayed where I was, sitting on my box in the dark. "They take care of me," I said through the open door. "When people are mean to me, they keep score, and then those people get sick, or they're unlucky, or they die." I spread my hands in the gleam from the streetlight. "See? My father's holding one of my hands and my mother's holding the other. Can't you see them?"

My cousins were backing down the hall by this time, so I followed them with my hands held out. "They're coming, too," I said happily. "They'll watch by my bed. If you tell any grownup about them, my ghosts'll come after you at night, and you'll be sorry. My ghosts take care of me."

By that time we were in our dark bedroom, and I could hear Betty and Benjy and Bernard jumping into bed under sheets, though it was a hot summer night.

"Are they here?" Bernard said in a shaky little voice. Nobody answered him. I got into bed. In a little while I started to hum.

"Who's that humming?" Benjy said.

"It's just Mandy," Betty said, but she didn't sound very sure.

"It's me," I said. "Mother and Father say they don't like the way you call me 'Mandy' instead of the real name they gave me. I'm *Miranda*. They *especially* don't like the way the children in this house are treating me, but they're going to give you one last chance. They could kill you, or make you real sick, but tonight you're only going to get bad dreams. You watch. You're going to wake up and scream and run to your mother."

"You're crazy," Betty said in a small voice.

"And I was humming because my mother's teaching me a song," I said. "She wanted me to know what it's like when you die and get buried in the graveyard in a box."

The bedroom was very quiet for a while. Finally Bernard said in a whisper, "What's it like?"

I spread my hands in the gleam from the streetlight. "See? My father's holding one of my hands and my mother's holding the other. Can't you see them?"

.

He was a stupid little kid, all right – because I sang all the verses of Alibi Ritter's song, right through the draining your blood so you won't decay, and the coffin leaking, and the foam like thick whipped cream, and the worms playing pinochle on your snout. I sang it slowly, with real feeling, and then I rolled over and went to sleep.

Sometime in the night, I heard Benjy sobbing, and then Bernard chimed in. I heard them banging on my aunt and uncle's bedroom door, and then I heard Betty running down the hall, too.

I lay in the dark wondering if my mother and father were really there. If they were, my cousins wouldn't say one word about why they woke up with such bad dreams.

I waited for them to tattle. Aunt Gertrude would come in and yell at me.

Aunt Gertrude came. She whispered to my cousins and tucked them in. They sniffed and snuffled in the dark when she was gone. I heard her shut the store-room door.

I waited and waited until they were asleep. Then I crept between their beds and opened the storeroom door and stood inside it for a minute, whispering to the dark: "I know you're here. I know you're helping me."

I left the storeroom door open and went back to bed, the only one awake in the still house. I listened. I held my breath. The bedroom door might open. If I held out my hands in the dark, would two other hands be there?

When I woke the next morning, it seemed as if Betty and Benjy and Bernard had changed a little. They fought with each other as usual, but they circled me just an arm's length away, as if I had something catching.

"What was the matter with you children last night?" Aunt Gertrude asked them at breakfast. They said they didn't know, and sneaked looks at me.

After a few days, I saw what their habits were going to be. They sneered at me and whispered about me to each other, but there was nothing nasty hidden in my bed at night. My shoestrings weren't tied in a row of knots, or missing. If I braided a clover braid and wore it around my neck, nobody yanked it off. And, best of all, they called me "Miranda."

They wanted to hear, over and over, about being buried in a grave. At night, lying in the dark, they begged. "Sing us the worm song."

I'd been reading books since I was six; my mother taught me to read, and took books out of the library for me. In a week or two I started telling my cousins Grimm's fairytales (the grimmest ones). Aunt Gertrude was pleased with how willingly we went upstairs to bed. It was fun to tell stories from *The Wonder Clock* and the *Joy Street* books. Betty was reading at the "see Spot run" level, and my younger cousins hardly knew the alphabet. The only stories they had heard at home were Bible stories, and those didn't count.

So I was the storyteller in the dark. It wasn't long before I got smart, and gave them only a piece of a story, stopping at crucial places, like the moment when Beauty first sees her Beast, for instance, or just as the biggest Billy Goat Gruff goes over the troll's bridge. Then if any of my cousins called me "Mandy," or "accidently" dropped my toothbrush in the toilet, or told friends that I was scared of their bathtub and wouldn't sit down in it, I was silent as the grave when we climbed in our beds, and talked to nobody but my mother and father, who came from the storeroom at such times.

After a few weeks we were sitting at breakfast. Aunt Gertrude and Uncle Boyd ate at the big table, and we children sat at the drop leaf one by the door. Aunt Gertrude looked around at us all and said, "Somebody leaves the storeroom door open every night, and it's dangerous – if you go to the bathroom in the dark, you could walk into it. Every night when I go to bed, I close it, but every morning it's open again."

My cousins stopped chewing. They looked at each other. They looked at me, but not for long.

"Ghosts," Uncle Boyd said, and chuckled. The thought seemed to tickle him. "The Wesleys had a ghost in their house," he said. "Imagine it – the founders of the Methodist Church couldn't get rid of their ghost! They called him 'Old Jeffery.'"

The children stared at him. He laughed to see the look on their faces. "So we have ghosts?" he said. "Have you seen them, children?"

Nobody answered him. Nobody thought it was funny but him. And me.

"Go out and play with your cousins," my aunt told me on those summer mornings. What could I do? After breakfast I had to leave the house to trail behind Betty, Benjy and Bernard, pretending that nothing I saw was equal to the smallest charm of Chicago.

The truth was that I had never dreamed of anything like Iowa. Chicago streets were dark canyons between brick walls. Chicago skies were only a glimpse of blue or gray. But Iowa houses and trees and barns were small under a sky I had hardly known was there: clouds, lightning, thunder, stars, moonrise, sunrise, sunset. It made me feel small. It made me feel free.

And there was Iowa's black dirt, so dark that I wondered at first if it had been burned. A hundred shades of green gushed from it, unless the green gave way to flowers, or the purple-black of shaded streets, or the blues of far-off farmland.

When I could, I escaped from my squabbling cousins to the highest branch of an apple tree behind the house. Birds called and answered around me – real birds, not chittering city sparrows. A constant weave of insect voices spread on every side. A car passed now and then. A bicycle whirred. Mothers called their children, or talked in backyards. And all day long the trains went through, trailing their long, lamenting voices behind them like blue scarves.

Every week I put flowers from the woods on my mother's grave. I dreamed sometimes of the pieces of sod that covered her; they were seamed with dirt. In my dream I pulled them away and there was a stair leading down to my mother. For years I never knew why she had died. Finally my aunt said in a whisper, "It was cancer." That was a word to whisper: "cancer."

My mother's small gray stone wasn't far from old ones that tipped sidewise, and among them was a stone lamb. Its pedestal read: "Matilda Benson Aged Eight And A Little Child Shall Lead Them." I don't think I'd realized that children could die. I thought they were just scared of doing it.

The last of June was dry and hot. The slabs of sod on my mother's grave turned to yellow patches on the cemetery's green carpet.

The parsonage smelled of old wood, furniture polish and yesterday's supper, but out in the summer air we children traveled from one interesting scent to another, especially in the alleys. Those wide and shady lanes were hardly visible from a single house because of high fences and lilac hedges and garages that had once been barns. Clinkers from the winter's coal furnaces gave off a scent all their own, and so did garbage cans, tomato plants in the sun, and drowned kittens we sometimes found bobbing in a pail. We buried the kittens with dead squirrels and birds in our pet graveyard under the parsonage's back porch, and dug them up later to see if Alibi Ritter was right about the foam and worms.

My cousins and I were out of doors from dawn until the noon whistle signaled lunch time, and from lunch until the setting sun warned us that supper would be ready. The Cedar River ran between muddy banks that sucked our bare feet with indecent sounds – we laughed till our stomachs hurt. Trains rumbled over the railroad bridge while we crouched beneath it, our fingers stuck in our ears, shivering under that weight and thunder.

"C'mon in the dry goods store," Betty said, and pulled me inside to stand in a corner. "Now watch." I watched: a clerk was putting money and a receipt in a cylinder.

Suddenly it flew from her hands on an overhead wire to a balcony office, and then, in a moment or two, shot back with receipt and change, skimming above counters and shoppers.

If we ever had pennies to spend, we bought bubblegum, licorice sticks, ribbon candy, jawbreakers or jellybeans from the druggist's big jars. We loved to make our tongues licorice-black, and we stuck the candy on our front teeth to give ourselves toothless smiles. But so many times the druggist's licorice jar was empty. "Why don't you ever have licorice?" I asked him once.

"Can't keep it in stock," he said.

Cedar Falls stores faced each other across a few blocks of Main Street. They wore false fronts to make them look two stories high, though anyone could see their low roofs crouching behind. The square-block park had a dwarf Statue of Liberty, and concerts by the Cedar Falls Municipal Band. Their uniforms were heavy and hot, but the men tooted and drummed, row upon brass-sparkling row, while their faces grew as red as their red pants.

Every weekday we burned in the sun at the town swimming pool that was too big to pretend it was concrete. It had a sand bottom and grass banks and was next to the power plant, so we swam in water from the plant's condensers, blissfully. I wore an old swimsuit of Betty's; the scratchy wool dried on me as we ran home, trailing water.

Patty Hayes lived on a corner near the parsonage, but she couldn't go swimming with us – she had red hair and a pearly white skin and a mother who yelled, "Stay out of the sun now, Patty – you hear?" We teased her, of course, but sometimes we braided clover chains on a blanket under her hackberry tree – the town lawns were snowy and sweet-smelling with clover.

Patty was nine, like me, and so was Sonia Jensen, a tall, leggy, awkward, silvery blonde. "You know so many games and tricks," she said one morning, watching me fold chewing gum tinfoil. I turned the notched tinfoil edges to the center to make long, narrow strips and laid them one by one on Patty's shady blanket. "Now," I said, showing off my big-city knowledge, "you fold both ends to the center so they're loops, then hook the loops of another one through the new loops..."

"They stay!" Sonia said.

"A silver necklace," I said. "Can you make peach-stone rings?"

They'd never heard of them. So they collected peach stones, and sneaked files from their fathers' tool chests, and one hot morning we settled down on Patty's blanket to begin the long process.

"What're you girls doing?" Robert Laird and Joe Stepler dumped their bicycles on the grass and came to see.

"Making peach-stone rings," Patty Hayes said. Robert lived across from the parsonage, and was handsome enough to make the three of us stop filing our peach stones, though we wouldn't have admitted it.

"They look like peach stones, that's all," Robert said.

Joe Stepler bent to look at mine. "It gets smooth like wood. You're making a hole in it?"

"To fit my finger," I said. "Then you pick out the kernel and file the outside down and carve the stone, and you're done, if it doesn't break."

The rings broke, of course, sometimes when we were filing them and sometimes when we wore them. After a while we were tired of filing, so we built an orange crate stage with a curtain and put it on Sonia's wagon. Our puppets were characters traced from books and pasted on sticks so we could make them walk around in front of the sets we drew. In cool summer mornings we went from door to door ringing doorbells and asking for "the lady of the house." The ladies of the houses said our puppet show was wonderful and gave us pennies.

Patty Hayes and Sonia Jensen had little brothers and sisters who tagged after us. My boy cousins tried to do it, too, but all I had to say to them was "Bluebeard" or "Sara and Clara" – names of stories I was telling them at night – and they went home. Patty and Sonia couldn't figure out how I did it, and they pestered me to tell them, but I wouldn't, and neither would Betty, so they teased me about boyfriends when we jumped rope, singing, "Manda, Manda dressed in yella went upstairs to kiss her fella. How many kisses did she give him? One ... two..."

We parsonage children weren't allowed to listen to radio shows, but we did whenever we got the chance. Joe Stepler would whisper, "C'mon," and we'd creep into the Stepler living room to listen to "Jack Armstrong" or "The Lone Ranger" or "Little Orphan Annie" in the close, hot hours of late afternoons. Then we sneaked home and never told, so Jack and the Lone Ranger and Annie were tinged for us with a delightful sinfulness that would have astonished their sponsors.

Joe Stepler was a quiet, blond, wide-mouthed, wide-faced boy. His living room had a thick rug patterned with curling ferns, there were real ferns in wicker stands, and the huge radio console brought in shortwave from other countries, trolling the air for crackling voices of the deep, wide world.

Robert Laird was Joe's best friend, and the two of them took the rest of us to Mr. Calvinhorn's farm just out of town on a dusty road. Mr. Calvinhorn was a relative of Robert's mother, and he let us play with kittens in his huge, densely scented, shadowy barn.

Early one morning Robert and I were the only ones who wanted to go to the farm. "C'mon," he said to me.

"All right," I said. I didn't care if the girls were giggling and whispering: "Go on – give him a kiss." I'd pay them back later.

We scowled at the others and walked off: Robert in his old shirt and worn knickers, me in a letdown dress. Our socks drooped above our scuffed shoes. We were full of breakfast and comfortable.

"I've just read *Peter and Wendy*," I said, showing off.

"What's that?" Robert said.

"A book about Peter Pan, a boy who can fly," I said, and started the story as we took the gravel road, kicking stones ahead of us.

I hadn't finished the story of Peter Pan when we got to the barn. Mr. Calvinhorn's kittens were growing up to be wild, bigheaded, long-legged adolescents: we chased them around the barn until we caught one apiece. If we sat in the hay and held them down in our laps with one hand, we could pet them with the other.

The hay beneath us prickled and rustled; we could hear crows screaming over the cornfields and smell clover through the wide barn door.

I took us through *Peter Pan and Wendy*: Captain Hook and the crocodile, Tiger Lily, Tinker Bell and the Lost Boys.

Robert listened, his dark head bowed over his kitten. When I came to the end, he said, "An underground house – we can make one!"

"Dig?" I said.

"There's a hole out there in the woods." Robert nodded toward a wall of trees beyond the barn door. "C'mon!" We let the kittens go, and they shot into dark corners as we ran into the light.

It was an early summer morning: the woodland was blurry with mist, and smelled of earth and decaying leaves. At the edge of the trees we came to a sudden stop: a buck and a doe stood belly-deep in that mist, their big ears unfurled to face us. Then they snorted and leaped away, hardly stirring the ferns and grasses.

"Those deer are always up here somewhere," Robert said. Now he was showing off. "I see them lots. Last year there was a fawn."

Sunlight from farmland beyond the woods fanned through the trees in long streamers. Robert left the path to push his way through a thicket. Mosquitoes had whined around us in the woods, but as we stopped among weeds and bushes, a breeze from the cornfield blew them away. "Here's the hole," Robert said.

I stood on the brink, peering down. It was deep: a huge tree had fallen years before, ripping its roots out of the earth. The tree and roots had rotted away above it on the forest floor. Other roots had grown across the hole, laced together a foot or so from the top.

"We've got to hide it," I said. Robert jumped in and looked up at me through the gnarled roots. "Like the Lost Boys," I said.

Robert grabbed a root, swung his legs over another one, and pulled himself out. "How?" He jumped up and down on the roots, but they hardly gave at all.

"Planks," I said.

"Over the roots?"

"We could put dirt on top."

"And plant grass! Perfect," Robert said. "All we need's a couple of shovels from the barn – "

"But it's got to be secret," I said. "From everybody. We have to mix our blood and swear."

"Huh?" Robert said.

"Don't you read anything?" I said.

"I do!" he said indignantly. "Lots."

I explained about the finger pricking and the blood mixing. "Great!" Robert said.

I had a pin in my bloomers because the elastic had given out. "Ow," Robert said when I pricked his thumb. He didn't want to look at the blood, but I mixed mine with his, finger to finger, and then we hunted for a shovel in the barn.

"It's too big," Robert said, dragging the only one we'd found into the light.

"Here's a little one," I said. I'd found a rusty trowel.

The trowel made slow work, but we took turns and kept at it: one of us down in the hole filling barn pails halfway with dirt, the other piling it beside the hole to cover the planks later.

We dug every morning, ran home for lunch when we heard the town's noon whistle, then hurried back to the woods to work until suppertime. The Lost Boys' house grew until it was much deeper than we were high, and about seven feet square. Sometimes I read to Robert from *Peter Pan and Wendy*.

Day by day we dug our Lost Boys' House deeper and deeper under old boards and summer grass. "What are you doing to get your clothes so dirty?" Aunt Gertrude said when she saw my bloomers and my old dress. I couldn't help my clothes, but I'd worked barefooted, so at least my socks and shoes were clean, and Robert and I washed off in Mr. Calvinhorn's cattle trough before we went home.

We were as careful as spies not to be followed. "Where do you go all the time?" Betty asked me.

"Just off by myself," I said. "To the cemetery." That usually shut her up. Robert and I took different routes through town alleys and sneaked one by one to the woods.

There were planks in the barn, high in the loft. We waited until Mr. Calvinhorn drove away in his truck, then threw the boards down and lugged them through the trees. We laid a board floor at the bottom of the hole, then began to fit pieces of plank together for the roof. "They've got to be real close to each other so the dirt won't fall through," Robert said.

It worked. The roots held up our plank roof. It was the door that was difficult. Finally we found two boards about the right length and width, and Robert brought a hammer and some nails and fastened the boards together with laths underneath. We tied a few thick slabs of sod on top. Now we could lay our trapdoor to one side and jump down to an old box and then to the floor of our secret den.

We hurried to dump dirt on the planks – all we had, then more from the cornfield. At last the hole disappeared: it was nothing but a flat scar in the floor of the woods. We planted it with transplanted weeds and big hunks of rooted meadow grass. "We've got to have a secret mailbox," I said.

"We do?" Robert said.

"To put messages to each other in. 'I can't come today,' or 'Will bring cookies tomorrow' – like that."

Robert looked up. "We could stick a bottle with a lid there in that knothole," he said, peering up at a big oak tree. "Notes wouldn't get wet that way, and who'd ever see it up there?"

So he brought a mason jar from home. When he pushed it into the knothole it was hidden, and we only had to step up on a few lower branches to unscrew the lid.

One morning we found there was nothing more to do: we sat in our hole and looked at each other. "We have to have a housewarming," I said. My voice sounded trapped in the small darkness, like an animal trying to get out. "A real party."

"I'll bring doughnuts," Robert said. His mother was a widow with an only child, and he had an allowance.

"I'll bring milk," I said. At the parsonage there was always plenty of milk, delivered in clinking, paper-capped bottles before dawn.

We had to wait for our housewarming: rain kept us home for most of a week – a pouring rain that carried lightning and thunder in black banks of clouds, jarring the parsonage and flicking bright tongues through every window.

Finally I woke to a perfect summer morning, and sneaked a bottle of milk and two jelly glasses – stuck them in the dirty-clothes basket by the basement stairs when

I read to Robert from *Peter Pan and Wendy*. Day by day we dug our Lost Boys' House deeper and deeper under old boards and summer grass.

Aunt Gertrude wasn't looking, and retrieved them later. When I came to the farm road, there was Robert with a grease-spotted paper sack.

We'd made a habit of sneaking from the road through the cornfield to the woods. Coming out of the bright light into the shade of the trees, I stopped, confused. Rain had soaked the woods and pounded earth flat and turned our transplanted weeds and grass into a green floor scattered with dead twigs.

"Perfect," Robert said.

"Absolutely perfect," I said.

"Wait a minute," Robert said, pulling a bundle of rope from his greasy sack. He laid the sod-covered door aside and knelt to tie ropes to a root at the hole's edge. In a minute the rope unraveled and bounced below. "A ladder," Robert said. "Ladies first."

Challenged by that "Ladies," I put my milk bottle and jelly glasses near the hole and descended the rope ladder with as much dignity as a rope ladder will allow. At least I had tied my long hair back with two pink bows, and my socks matched. "Perfect," I said from the depths of the hole. Robert handed me the milk, glasses and doughnuts and climbed down, too, with a slap of the board floor underfoot.

Damp earth has a smell of its own, pungent and pleasing. Our board ceiling slanted a bit to the east, so rainwater had reached our house at only one corner, where it ran down a wall and away. We sat in the square of light from above and ate our housewarming feast, and said it was our secret house and we'd never tell, never, never, never.

6

"S chool starts in a month," Aunt Gertrude said to me
one day. "We can't buy dresses for you, but your
mother left some clothes of hers with enough material –
Betty has dresses made from some of mine. You can rip
the seams, and then Miss Kline will do the sewing. She
charges fifty cents to make a dress."

My aunt told me to sit in a dining room chair and gave
me a small scissor. "Rip every seam," she said, snipping
one open to show me how. "Don't get pieces of thread all
over – put them in your mouth to throw away when
you're done. Remember: if you make any holes, you'll
have to wear them later."

I hardly heard her. It was my mother's rose-flowered
dress, and I could smell my mother in the folds of it: the
scent of her skin and hair. Tears spurted into my eyes.
When Aunt Gertrude left, I held the dress against my face
and sobbed softly so no one would hear.

Betty was in the hail, and she heard. "What are you
crying for?" she said, coming to me and grinning.

I glared at her and said, "It's my mother's ghost."

"Here?" Betty said, looking around.

"She's everywhere. I was smelling this dress because it
was her dress, and it's the way her ghost smells." I stuck
the dress under Betty's chin. "Here. Smell it. Then
you'll recognize it when the ghosts come at night."

Betty didn't dare smell the dress, let alone touch it –
she gave me one scared look and ran away.

I took up the scissors and began to rip a seam. Tears
blurred the roses. I felt as if I were taking my mother

apart, not a dress. The sleeves came away like her arms. The waist seams broke her body in two as I snipped them open. Finally her dress was only pieces of cloth in my lap.

I started on the other dress. I knew the flower patterns of both of them by heart – my mother hadn't had many dresses. Standing beside her or sitting on her lap, I'd found parts of people among the flowers. The rose dress had the beautiful lips of a woman in one of the rose buds, and a leaf with a spot like an eye. The daisy print had a blank space along a stem that was a huge white grin with crooked teeth. Shopping with my mother, I had stood so close to her – so close – and found the roseleaf eye looking at me. My mother had been with me on the streetcar, her arm around me, her skirt touching mine, with the big grin smiling at me among her daisies. How could she be gone and her dresses still be there? Sometimes I stopped ripping to sob softly and wipe my face on daisies or roses.

Aunt Gertrude was upstairs in her room with the spike-cornered bed and the beaded lamp. "All right," she said when I brought the pieces to her. "Put hot water in the kitchen sink with some shaved Fels Naptha that's in a cup underneath – dissolve it in the hot water first. Then add some cold water and wash those pieces, but don't rub them hard, and rinse them three times, and then roll them up in a clean kitchen towel. They'll have to be ironed."

I found the soap. Its overpowering smell of naphtha rose from the hot water, waiting for my mother's dresses.

I couldn't put the dresses in the sink. I hid in a corner, my face in the cloth, breathing in and breathing in until the delicate scent of my mother disappeared in my wild sniffing and I heard my aunt coming downstairs.

"The soap's dissolved," she said, stirring the hot water with a finger. She mixed it and added some cold water. "Put the pieces in."

So I had to put my mother's arms in, and her neck...
the smell of her was never there again, no matter how
often I smelled the dresses Miss Kline made for me.

The dresses would cost money. Perhaps that was why
I had to begin work around the house that day. I was
trained that afternoon in the exacting job of washing dishes, scalding dishes, draining dishes, wiping dishes, and
putting dishes away without a clatter or thump.

In a week or two, when I'd mastered the art of dish-
washing to suit my aunt, I was expected to clear the dining room tables after each meal, wash the kitchen table
and stove, do the dishes, put them away, take out the
garbage and sweep the floor.

I don't recall that Aunt Gertrude ever hit a child, but
she had a way of hovering. I suppose she was quite pretty then, but to me she was only someone big who was able
to see in all directions. Before you knew it, you were in
her shadow.

"Never mind," I told my cousins one night in the dark.
Aunt Gertrude had added washing the kitchen floor on
my hands and knees to my list of chores, and Betty was
whistling through her teeth, which was her way of making fun of me.

"Don't, Betty," Benjy pleaded. "I want to know what
happened to the seven swans."

"Besides," Bernard said, anxious to be on my side,
"Ma said you're going to do what Miranda's doing
when you're nine."

"Your mother isn't my relative, and my ghosts know it,"
I said. "They are keeping a list. She will not have a happy
life."

My almost-free days of summer would end in a month.
Town lawns were brown with the summer's heat, and
trees looked tired and dusty when I walked in their shade
to Victoria Kline's with the pieces of my mother's dresses.

Miss Kline lived in two basement rooms at the Atwood
house with her father and a Minnesota sewing machine

she called "Minnie." She and her father used the twin stationary tubs in the Atwood laundry room for all their washing. Victoria did the Atwood's cleaning to pay the rent. She made enough money sewing to buy food, because people want to have clothes made over when it's a depression.

I thought Victoria was old, but she was only thirty. Perhaps she seemed old because she looked like a monkey. Her face was long and narrow, her ears stuck out, she had little bright eyes, and her lips were very thin and usually clamped on pins.

There was a small, elegantly lettered sign in a corner of the Atwood's basement door: VICTORIA KLINE, SEAMSTRESS, PLEASE WALK IN. I heard a sewing machine as I hesitated on the landing, and then went down steep stairs. The sound of the machine came from around a corner where there was no door, so I knocked on the wall.

"Come in," Victoria said, and there she was, lifting her foot from "Minnie's" pedal and smiling at me. Behind her, where sunshine fell in a patch from the high basement window, an old man in a rocking chair was reading *The Saturday Evening Post* aloud. *The Post* was a big magazine; one of Norman Rockwell's covers hid half of Mr. Kline. I liked those covers because sometimes there were girls my age on them, dressed like me in oxfords and ankle sox and cotton dresses and hairbows, only neater.

"Avoid lordosis," Mr. Kline said, rocking and reading. "Wear the girdle that realigns the spine." It seemed like a strange "hello" to me.

"I'm Miss Kline, and who may you be?" Miss Kline said.

"How do you do?" I said. "I'm Miranda Letty."

"Reverend Letty's niece," Victoria said in a very pleasant, approving tone. "And how do you do?"

"I can't complain," I said. That was what ladies at church often said, and it had struck me with its truthfulness.

Miss Kline laughed. When she laughed, her very large teeth made her look like a horse. When she pulled her thin lips over her teeth again, she only smiled like a mischievous monkey. "I imagine you can't," she said in a very kind tone.

"Lady Astor, preparing for a gala at her Fifth Avenue residence, says, 'I rely on Pond's for smooth skin,'" Mr. Kline read in his singsong voice. I was beginning to be able to treat him as background noise the way Miss Kline did.

"Not when your aunt is around, anyway," Miss Kline said. "What kind of work have you brought for me?"

"It's some dresses I've ripped," I said, handing her my brown paper package. "I need dresses for school."

"President Roosevelt states that two hundred thousand certified teachers are unemployed," Mr. Kline said.

Miss Kline unrolled my package and said, "Your mother's dresses?"

I nodded, and Miss Kline saw something in my face, I think, for she got up, package and all, and put an arm around me. "Come closer so I can see you better," she said. "And you'll have your mother with you when you go to school the first day – that's wonderful. I wish I had some of my own mother's things to wear, but they're all gone." She sat down again at the machine with me close beside her, and measured me here and there as she said, "There's plenty of material. I expect you'd like puffed sleeves?"

"Oh, yes," I said.

"And lace," she said, "and maybe some blue rickrack on the daisy one to bring out the blue in your very pretty eyes? I could make a wide ribbon sash, and you could put the same ribbon around that wonderful, long blonde hair?"

"Is the League of Nations Dead?" Mr. Kline asked.

Miss Kline said, "Now the rose material – how about some ruffles around the neck, with lace, of course, and

some just above the hem? It's a charming color for you –
brings out the pink in your cheeks. We women have to
work with our best points, don't we?"

I said we certainly did. I remember wondering what
hers were, but feeling that hers were better than "best,"
because I didn't want to leave her – that homely, homely
woman some people called "Old Maid Kline." There she
sat with pieces of my mother's dresses in her lap and her
father droning in the sunshine.

She'd said I had very pretty eyes and wonderful hair
and pink cheeks. Think of it. The thought of it was like
a new possession that I carried home. We women certainly did have to work with our best points, and I'd do
my best, especially since I would have two new dresses at
once.

August in Iowa was blazing hot, of course, but cooler
than the concrete-and-brick griddle of Chicago. On
Sunday the church pews were busy with discreet fanning;
from the balcony they looked like an aspen tree in a
breeze. Iowa State Teachers College on "The Hill" had
big revolving fans in the ceiling of the Reading Room.
We sneaked in to watch future teachers study at library
tables in still rows. And you could stay cool in the swimming pool all day if you didn't mind your skin wrinkling,
then turning hot and red until it peeled off.

We had band concerts in Overman Park, wafting the
scent of citronella to surrounding streets. We had the
cool, shivery sigh of lawn mowers, and the airy twang of
cicadas in the elms that made a cathedral aisle of Main
Street. We had the ice cold water of garden sprinklers to
run under until we were sure we'd never be hot again.

Every morning when I'd washed the breakfast dishes
and cleaned up the kitchen, I escaped to the library (I
went there nearly every day), or followed the ice wagon,
sneaking bits of ice to suck, or met my friends. We never
went to our playmates' houses and rang the doorbell;
doorbells were for grownups. We yelled "Patty!" or

"Miranda!" or "Sonia!" in our friends' front yard or back yard until they heard us and came out. That was the polite way.

Sometimes Robert and I met to have cookies or dough-nuts at our underground house, or sneaked out, one by one, to get notes from the mason jar and leave notes there. What else could we do with our hideout? Show it to our friends? Of course not. Play house? "Ladies first," Robert had said, and like the grown-up Wendy who sees Peter Pan once more, I'd realized that moment that play-ing house was not what we could do.

So we had dreamed the house and finished it, that was all, and soon the summer of 1933 was finished, too: a few months that set my mother's death at a little distance under the great blue sky of Iowa.

Then school began.

I loved school at first. Miss Kline had made my two new dresses as wonderfully frilly as the ones Shirley Temple wore, and I had Sonia Jensen and Patty Hayes as friends in my class, and Robert Laird and Joe Stepler were there, too. The boys wore knickers tucked into leather boots as high as their knees, and the boots had a pocket for a knife. The pockets were empty, but those flaps of leather seemed as virile to me as the sword scabbard of a knight errant, whatever a knight errant was. (My vocab-ulary was an astonishment to my teachers. It came from reading everything in sight.)

My uncle was proud of me. I worked hard and won as many prizes as I could: gold stars on my papers, a piece of candy for the best art project, a Perry Picture for never being late. Perry Pictures were small black-and-white copies of famous paintings, and they were our trophies.

Winning prizes at school doesn't make you popular, except with the teachers. I found that out. Still, I made good friends in school; we played together in the after-noons and on Saturdays, for a while.

But Saturdays were washdays at the parsonage, and that fall Aunt Gertrude took Betty and me down to the cellar where the Maytag wringer washer and two stationary tubs gathered around a drain in the light of one small cellar window and a naked bulb. Betty was supposed to watch while I learned to do the white loads first while the soap was strongest and the water hottest. The wringer shuddered and creaked through the Saturday morning hours, turning between the washer and the rinse tubs, between the rinse tubs and the bluing tub, shooting the intimate garments of the Letty family through its toothless gums.

At last the clothing, sheets and towels dropped— wringer wide and mashed flat – into the clothesbasket. The three of us lugged them upstairs to the clotheslines in the yard. By lunchtime those flat lumps of cloth had unfurled to their square corners in the breeze, or become bloomers and drawers, dresses and shirts, plumping with air until they seemed to be a headless, bobbing, unbelievably fat family.

That winter the wash froze, and my uncle's long underwear could stand alone in a kitchen corner until its knees buckled. Betty was supposed to know how to wash by then, but when I was sick with a cold before Christmas, she didn't get all the dark socks out of a white load. Our sheets and pillowcases were a sickish shade of lavender for weeks. My uncle wouldn't wear his lavender shirts. My aunt bleached and bleached and scolded Betty, and that was the last time Betty was allowed to touch the washing.

By spring I had learned to fold the clean wash exactly right or dampen pieces for ironing. There was a trick to taming the great white, snapping sheets to a pile in a laundry basket. Iowa air came in with the clothes: the kitchen filled with that scent no perfume has ever caught, and our beds held it for a single night. Sometimes my aunt and I had to race the rain, and if we won, we could laugh for a moment, watching bare clotheslines swinging like jump ropes in the storm.

Aunt Gertrude began her work before dawn. She was expected to be in the church kitchen for every tea, charity dinner, funeral and wedding, and help to keep the church clean, too. She began to take Betty and me with her at night or on weekends to run errands and carry food and wash dishes.

I was ten that spring. My cousins and I were sent out to our big vegetable garden to clear and dig and plant and water. We worked while Aunt Gertrude watched, and squabbled when she didn't. "Absolutely nothing gets done in the garden if I don't stand over the children every minute," she told my uncle at supper one night. "Every summer it's the same."

She threatened. She punished. She watched, and nothing seemed to escape her. She must have noticed that I didn't step on seedlings, and that I remembered what weeds looked like after she had pulled up specimens of the most important ones and told us to memorize them. I didn't scream like Betty did if a bug crawled on her; I didn't start fights and knock my cousin into the blackberry bushes the way Benjy did. I was, in short, the one who could be entrusted with the vegetable garden, little by little.

So on many summer mornings I couldn't go to the library or play, because the weeds had grown overnight in the vegetable garden just for me. My aunt made sure I learned when cucumbers were small enough to pickle and carrots were large enough to pull, but many mornings she left me alone with the morning bird song and "my" vegetables. I called them that. They grew for me. I grubbed among them in crumbling dirt, and ate my own vegetables on my dinner plate: buttery parsnips, crunchy white turnips, the sweet, folded-tight packages of Brussel sprouts, and broccoli and cauliflower like nosegays ringed with leaves.

My aunt was proud of her blackberry bushes, and her blackberry jam and jelly that she said were often "remarked upon." Blackberry bushes froze back every winter for other town gardeners, but in the fall my aunt wrapped her bushes in straw and then burlap against the cold, so that in summer fat blackberries hung from their arching, wicked, thorny canes.

One summer morning I was down on my knees picking bush beans. Across a stretch of grass the first blackberries were ripening under leaves wet from a night rain.

I was happy there by myself. I heard a cardinal in the apple tree. He called, listened for an answering echo, then called again.

Suddenly – almost under my hand – the bean bushes stirred, tossed...

The long snake slithered sidewise at the grass edge. Fluttering leaves brushed along his scales as he came, his back stripe a yellow S above his spotted sides, his tongue flicking, flicking – I jumped up, jumped backward, my eyes on the coils circling my basket. Then the snake rippled across the grass and under the arching blackberry bushes, a scaly whip that undulated here and there under thorns and berries, then vanished.

It was only a garter snake. It had only startled me. After a while I knelt to pick again, but the memory of it, sly and glistening, snaked through my summer morning.

When the blackberries ripened, we picked them cautiously, a thick glove on one hand to guard us from thorns and spiny leaves. I watched for the snake. Ripe berries dropped into our hands, but we picked not-quite-ripe ones as well – Aunt Gertrude knew the secret of mixing the two kinds in her blackberry jelly to make it set. All summer and into the fall we made preserves, and canned tomatoes, green beans, lima beans, peaches, pears, cherries, applesauce, apple butter... our fruit cellar shelves bowed under the weight.

Year by year, I was thoroughly trained in the "putting up" that took days of work with kettles and mason jars, rubber rings and paraffin and jelly glasses. Betty "helped," boiling jars dry until they cracked, and frying dozens of rubber rings. Finally Aunt Gertrude sent her out of the sweltering kitchen and the hot breath of the electric fan and told her: "Go pick beans! You can't hurt beans!"

Housework never ended. When I was a freshman in high school, Betty and I began to do the ironing every Monday after school. Anything cotton or linen that would be visible to the world had to be starched, dampened, ironed, and hung to dry on racks that filled the kitchen. Moisture ran like tears down the windows.

Betty and I learned to make boiled starch. We learned to cook. By the time I was a junior in high school I could make gravy without lumps. Betty always curdled her boiled custard, but I didn't. Miss Kline taught me to sew my own dresses, except for a beautiful one she made me for the first day of school every year. Most of the girls wore new dresses the first day, and year by year I noticed that Joe Stepler always told me that he liked mine. He'd smile his wide smile and say, "Your prettiest dress yet," and he never forgot.

Those first-day dresses were special: they always had a piece of my mother's dresses in them somewhere. At first they might have sleeves and a yoke made from my mother's cloth. Later on Miss Kline used pieces for a collar and cuffs, and later, resurrecting pieces from my old dresses, she could make just a pocket and belt from the rose print or the daisy one. Finally my high school dresses were without any of my mother's cloth, except for pieces I hunted for and always found: the lining of a pocket, or the facing of a waistband. "You must take your mother with you," she always told me, and was my dearest friend.

But year by year I saw less and less of my school friends. It wasn't so much that I got A's, or had so few dresses and only one pair of shoes at a time. Day by day and year by year I turned into someone like "the farmies." Those students came to school by bus, and afterwards they went home to do farm chores while the rest of the students had hours to spend with each other. "Farmies" were left out of almost everything.

Slowly but steadily I found I didn't have time to go to my friends' houses after school. I was like the "farmies." My friends stopped asking me – they knew I couldn't go – so I missed the birthday parties and slumber parties, school dances, high school ball games, double dates. Sometimes I heard my cousins call me "the hired girl" at school; they didn't dare do it at home.

I worked beside Aunt Gertrude until I was as tall as she was: we were a smooth housekeeping machine. I was no relative of hers; she gave me her grudging approval some-times, that was all. Yet she taught me everything I know about housekeeping and babies, entertaining and man-ners. By the time I was a senior in high school I could have run that parsonage as well as my aunt did.

My cousin Betty never learned. She managed to bun-gle and rip and batter and break until Aunt Gertrude said to me, "She's an absolute trial," but it seemed to me, too late, that Betty was an absolute genius.

"You've been given such a good home," people often told me when they saw me working beside my aunt at church socials and weddings and funerals and Ladies Aid meetings. Every time I heard those words, I remembered my mother saying: "We're going to be given a home in Cedar Falls, Iowa," and I saw for a second the parsonage as it had seemed to me that first afternoon: a gilded, glow-ing, rich, enormous gift that my father had given my mother and me.

And yet by that time I knew what had happened to homeless people in the Great Depression. I smiled and said, "Yes, they've given me a good home."

But what would happen to me when high school was over? As my senior year began, Hitler and Mussolini invaded country after country. Roosevelt ordered our ships and planes to attack on sight if German or Italian ships were found in our waters. The Germans sank our destroyer Reuben James off the coast of Iceland. We heard the sounds of the Battle of Britain on the parlor radio: explosions and sirens and cries that made us stare at each other. Would our country be next?

Late that December of 1941, I walked to the Iowa State Teachers College campus to look at red brick buildings that would never open their doors to me.

Snow was falling that afternoon. Somebody came up behind me on a college walk, and I heard Joe Stepler say, "Hi."

I turned and said "Hi" back, and we walked along together. "You're going to T.C. next year?" he asked. Snowflakes starred his blond hair – he was as fair as Robert Laird was dark, and nowhere near as handsome.

"College? Me?" I said. "Where would the money come from?"

Joe nodded and looked away.

"No – I'll have to find a job," I said. "Clerk. Secretary. My uncle can't go on feeding me forever."

Joe must have noticed the misery in my voice. The campanile bells dropped their tunes on us. Coeds wearing carriage boots and long, colored stockings ran through the snow in a college world I could hardly imagine. "What'll you be doing?" I asked to be polite, not really aware of anything but misery.

"The Marines," Joe said. "We're going to be in the war."

I gasped and stopped, so he had to stop, too. Falling snow stuck to his blond eyelashes. "Joe!" I cried. "And I've been feeling sorry for myself!"

"I'll be all right. So will you."

"You will! You will!" I said. "You've been so nice to me, Joe. Ever since I was an orphan and new in town.

Saturdays were washdays at the parsonage. Housework never
ended. I couldn't go to birthday parties, school dances,
high school ball games, double dates.

Remember how we'd sneak in to listen to Jack Armstrong and the Lone Ranger in your living room? Remember Mr. Calvinhorn's barn, and our animal graveyard, and the time you found Sonia when she got lost in the cornfield? Nothing bad can ever happen to somebody as kind as you! You should be the captain of the football team – or class president!"

We knew who was both of those things: Robert Laird. And Robert Laird – not Joe Stepler – had dated and then dropped the prettiest girls in our high school, too, until some of them wouldn't speak to each other, and certainly wouldn't speak to him. When he graduated, he'd go to Iowa State Teachers College and start dating the coeds; I thought it would take him a while to try them all.

"Thanks," Joe said. "I didn't do anything special." I told him he certainly had, and said goodbye.

The Lettys were trimming their Christmas tree when I got home, and listening to war news on the parlor radio. We hung the battered, fragile bells and balls and icicles as we listened to the sound of Hitler bombing London.

Then the Japanese bombed Pearl Harbor, and I wore my scratchy tinsel Christmas wings, and Conrad Beale said, "Miranda Letty, you're the most beautiful angel God ever made."

7

C onrad Beale rang our front door bell almost every cold January afternoon. At first Aunt Gertrude kept me busy after school taking care of the new baby, but at four-thirty, day after day, there I was, running upstairs to put my school clothes back on while Aunt Gertrude showed Conrad into the parlor. Finally she looked exasperated and said, "I'll certainly expect you to wash up after supper, but when school's over, you'd better stay dressed up and do your homework in the parlor so you'll be presentable." For the first time in years I had the hours before dinner to myself.

Conrad came in the new Cadillac he'd bought just before no one could buy a new car any more. Women in the church kitchen had discussed that Cadillac and Conrad at the last Thanksgiving dinner. I'd listened to the talk while I peeled potatoes – but what had Conrad Beale to do with me?

"Nobody's ever seen Conrad with a girl," Mrs. Valey had said as she stuffed deviled eggs. "Runs his father's factory, my Burt says. Does a lot of traveling – maybe that's where he kicks up his heels."

"Won't kick them up at home," Mrs. Newton said. "His father rules the roost."

"How old's Conrad? Twenty three? Isn't he? Nearly?"

"Wears those expensive suits."

"Dressed up like Robert Laird." Mrs. Valey sniffed, looking around to be sure that Robert's mother wasn't within earshot.

"Robert brings a different girl to church every month, I swear," Mrs. Palmer said.

My ears had burned the way they did when people talked about Robert Laird. I'd seen him at church with every one of his girls; they sat alone while he sang in the choir. He wore nice suits his mother managed to buy him somehow – she didn't have much, the women said. Robert's tenor was easy to find in any anthem: a rich, vibrating thread above the basses. I could look at him in the choir during a whole hour every Sunday, and I did. I'd watched him for years at school. I'd watched his house across the street from our parlor window.

"Conrad Beale and Robert Laird are cousins," Mrs. Newton said.

"Cousins?" Mrs. Valey stopped halfway to the icebox with the deviled eggs. "Really?"

"Really. You wouldn't remember. You're too young, and you weren't in town when the Beale brothers had such a fight. Robert's really Robert Beale."

"Adele Webster was supposed to marry S.C. Beale," Mrs. Carey said.

"Conrad's father," Mrs. Palmer said.

"But she changed her mind on her very wedding day and wouldn't marry S.C.! She married his brother Henry!"

"Robert's father," Mrs. Palmer said.

"Can you imagine? S.C. wouldn't speak to Adele or his brother ever again."

"My, my," Mrs. Valey said.

"Adele and Henry had Robert after two little girls that died."

"S.C. married Lillian McCutcheon pretty fast and had Conrad."

"But even after Adele was Mrs. Laird and widowed, S.C. wouldn't have a thing to do with her."

The women spoke in low voices in a kitchen corner. "I guess that's why Adele changed Robert's name from Beale to Laird," Mrs. Carey said. As I dug eyes out of potatoes, I was thinking: *Poor Robert. He lost two fathers, and even lost his own father's name.*

Robert's mother was in the community room next door setting tables: a thin, quivery-looking lady who very seldom spoke. But two brothers had fought over her. How romantic. It was hard to imagine, except that Robert had girls fighting over him at school. Being fought-over must run in his family.

"S.C. won't even come to church – Adele might be there," Mrs. Carey said.

It was only gossip, I thought as I finished the potatoes. I couldn't have guessed that a few months later the gossipers would have something new to talk about: me.

And they talked. Of course they did. Wasn't Conrad Beale's new Cadillac at the parsonage curb most afternoons, and didn't he escort me to the one movie theater in town on Saturday nights? I caught a particular look in people's eyes, as if I were as conspicuous as an angel on an orange crate, and had – all at once – possibilities. Even my cousins gave me a new kind of respect, and it wasn't because of ghosts. While other girls in my class were weeping at the thought of their boyfriends going off to war, Aunt Gertrude was moving the best china to a lower cupboard where she could reach it every afternoon, and making Betty help with supper and the new baby after school, while I sat dressed up and waited for Con.

My aunt and Betty had no choice about it. A girl's chief purpose in life was to "marry well," and a man was courting me – the richest bachelor in our church. Aunt Gertrude was warm and welcoming to "Mr. Beale," but afterward she often remarked to me that there was many a slip between cup and lip. She said that wise people didn't count their unhatched chicks.

But I was the one in the parlor with Con. He'd grown bold enough to take my hand, and since I didn't slap him, he held it every afternoon.

I hadn't done any of this before. In a few days I said, "Do you like to dance?"

"I'm not very good at it," Con said.

"Neither am I," I said. "Would you like to practice?" I found some swing music on the parlor radio, and when I went right up to him and put my hand on his shoulder, all ready to go, he had to put his arm around me or else stand there like a trellis with a vine on it.

He was so gentlemanly. We proceeded, bit by bit, from hand holding to dancing, from dancing to hugging, from hugging to kissing. Finally it seemed almost natural to me to sit on his lap ruining the crease in his trousers. And every Sunday Con's eyes followed me in church like two faithful dogs. The minute I appeared, I could feel even his clothes and his shoes and every hair on his head coming to attention.

How could I know about sex? Any available book jumped straight from the wedding to the happy couple eating breakfast the next morning. If I'd had a man like Robert Laird for a boyfriend – someone who'd tried his hand with all kinds of girls and had just about every possibility in mind – I'd have found out what I was doing pretty fast. But the really basic facts weren't in any of my books, and any adult I knew seemed to be as seamlessly sexless as cherubim and seraphim. I knew only one girl who talked about sex, and later I found out she had it wrong.

I'd never been kissed since my mother died. There I was after all those years, held and stroked and cuddled by someone who cared about me. Sex? It was something a man did and then you had a baby. It would have to happen to me, I supposed, but who'd want to think about it?

What I thought about was how gentlemanly Con was, and how I fascinated him. I couldn't understand it. I was the Lettys' orphan niece in old clothes, the "hired girl" who had chapped hands and was always reading books. Then – in a week or two – I turned into a magnet so powerful that I could pull a grown man to my doorstep every afternoon. I looked in every mirror at my amazing self, and kept trying out my new power like a bow-and-arrow hunter who's been handed a machine gun.

It gave me a certain swagger. I'm ashamed to say it and I tried to hide it, but it was a swagger. Somebody wanted me. Conrad Beale found me before church in the vestibule. He waited for me after church, and talked to me in the hall while the choir rustled by on their way to the choir room. I never once looked at that choir, but Robert Laird swept so close beside me that his choir robe brushed me and his eyes were on me – I felt it. Con said, "Hi" to Robert because Robert was his cousin, but I pretended not to see Robert and kept my eyes on Con.

And that was when I began to feel a change. I'd watched Robert Laird for years, but he'd stayed about as far from me as a classmate can get. But now I noticed that he often stood by my school locker – and my locker wasn't in the main hallway. "Hi," he said, or "Nice morning." Next I realized that several times a week Robert was in the lunch line behind me: the hairs on the back of my neck told me so.

February was coming, and the yearly operetta: it was *The Gypsy Girl* this time. Our school wasn't big, so if you could sing at all, you sang in the operetta chorus, packed with the other peasants or courtiers or gypsies on the little school stage. Robert was sure to have the male lead. He was the best tenor we had.

I went to the first rehearsal, along with most of the junior and senior class. Miss Harmon, the music teacher, said, "There are plenty of chorus roles in gypsy dress," so the girls were planning costumes while Miss Harmon passed out the music. She said, "Robert Laird will have the male lead," which didn't surprise anyone, but when she came to me, she said, "And I want you for the female lead, Miranda."

"Me?" I said. "But I've always been in the chorus – I wouldn't know – "

"You can learn," Miss Harmon said. "You sing in your church choir, don't you?"

So that was it. I'd substituted in our church choir when two of the sopranos had the flu. The girls sitting with me giggled. "You get married to Robert – see?" Patty Hayes whispered. "On page forty-five."

Marry Robert? In front of everybody? I went out the door looking at page forty-five and almost ran into Robert. "Heard you in church," he said. "Nice soprano. Perfect Gypsy Girl."

"You told her," I said, scowling at him. "Thanks a lot. It's work."

"It's fun," he said. "And the orchestra's so bad they'll drown us out – they always do."

"There's so much of it," I said, riffling through the music so I wouldn't have to look at him.

"I can help you after school," Robert said. "Every day I don't have basketball practice. Meet me in the music room tomorrow. It's old stuff to me – you'll learn fast."

Meet me in the music room.

I went home to sit on Con's lap and think: *Meet me in the music room.* I dreamed *Meet me in the music room* and *You'll learn fast*, and had those words for breakfast the next morning, since I couldn't eat.

I wore my best sweater and skirt to school. After the last class, I beat Robert to the music room and found a chair among bristling music stands – good, heavy music stands.

There he was in a minute or two, half shutting the door and leaning against a chalk rail: Robert Laird. He was grinning.

That grin of his was Con's big grin: I'd noticed that lately, because I'd seen Con at such close quarters. Robert had Con's wandering eyebrows, too, and the brown eyes that were almost black, and the same big nose. Of course. They were cousins.

I didn't smile back at Robert. I opened my music and said, "Where are we going to start? I can't stay too long. Someone's waiting for me." Someone was: Con would pay his usual afternoon visit. Robert had trapped me into this, my tone said, so he'd better get to work and stop grinning.

Our first duet was some inane song about the weather. Robert sang as he played it on the clunky old piano. I stayed where I was. But when we started through it the second time, Robert left the piano and began to move the music stands one by one while he sang, getting nearer with every page we turned, until I got up and slid behind the teacher's desk, still warbling about "a beautiful morning in May."

"We have to stand *together* to sing a duet," Robert said. He was smiling again. "We have to *blend*."

I knew he was right; I had to let him come very close, especially when he tossed his music away and read from mine. His sweatered chest was against my pink wool arm; I could have counted his eyelashes, and he looked as if he were counting mine. Had I put too much perfume on? Were bobby pins sliding out of my hair? Whenever we came to a measure or two of rests, we could hear the schoolrooms around us growing quiet. The halls echoed a last few footsteps.

I was trying to follow the music (the asinine lyrics were full of "thous" and "thys"), and not shiver or perspire. Finally Robert had to go back to the piano to pick out parts we couldn't get right. That wasn't a smart move for him: I had time to catch my breath.

We practiced some more. Now the school was silent and empty, and Robert's lips were getting closer and closer to mine. He sang, "Thou art my love, my only love," looking as if he meant it, and then I felt his arm slide around me –

"Don't!" I snapped, and pushed him away so hard a music stand went over, taking others with it in a clanging tangle. "I have to be going!" I said, glaring into his angry eyes, and grabbed my coat and books and left.

Cold January air felt good on my hot face. I'd heard girls tell how "smooth" Robert was, and he'd dated about every girl in our class except me – think of that – I was the absolute bottom of the barrel. For all those years I might as well have been one of the stone ladies holding lamps above the school door for all he'd cared.

So every day in that music room I was a stone lady, an alabaster Gypsy Girl. The looks I gave Robert said that he'd get slapped against walls and chalk boards if he tried anything with me.

He kept trying, of course. I think he couldn't imagine a minister's poor niece playing hard-to-get with the football captain and class president. He progressed from lightweight flirting to heavyweight appeals: "We're supposed to be lovers."

"That's right," I said in a cold voice. "Supposed to be."

"You're supposed to be crazy about me," he yelled – he'd just tried to grab me and kiss me, but all he'd got was a slap. He was really mad. His face was flushed and his eyes sparkled in the light from the music room windows.

Robert Laird! I was mad, and he kept getting madder, and I'd run home hugging myself with the deliciousness of it. I can't lie: I was in heaven that January, necking with one man and knowing what the other man wanted.

But I wasn't a stone lady. Not inside. On the afternoons when I practiced love songs with Robert, I went home and kissed Con in my aunt's parlor until we were both out of breath. How happy Con was, and it made me feel better, seeing Con smile. He was so gentlemanly and kind, and I liked him so much, and I hadn't done anything

wrong.   What girl wouldn't think about kissing Robert
Laird when he was inches away and willing?

Not that I was fooling Robert. I was too jittery and
skittery, and his brown eyes glittered as if he liked that
game. And so I knew that I could have – there at the very
end of my high school days – the stolen kisses, the rose in
my desk, the candy in my locker, and more than once
those old signals: "Spenser." "Milton."

8

The cast and orchestra of *The Gypsy Girl* went through the dress rehearsal without too many mistakes. Miss Harmon directed us from center stage, bouncing and waving. She was a large, broad-beamed lady, and the imposing shift of that beam from one foot to the other had, through the years, given her the nickname of "Hippo Harmon." She yelled, "Tempo!" as she waved her small arms. "Keep the tempo! One... two..."

During a song by the chorus, Robert leaned over a fake bush and whispered, "How about being my date at the strike party?"

I stared at him, tongue-tied.

A date?

He'd been after me for weeks. He'd been so mad he wouldn't even speak to me, and he'd certainly never asked for a date. A date would be official: Robert Laird is dating Miranda Letty. I found my voice and whispered back, "All right."

It was certainly all right, Oh, yes. I can't pretend I wasn't proud of myself. I'd played hard to get, and look what I'd got: it worked.

I didn't have a single dress good enough for a party, but I was lucky – the cast always wore their costumes to Arlene Brown's house to have cocoa and cookies, then went back in old clothes to demolish the stage set.

I couldn't keep the date to myself, I was so stupid. I had this delightful picture in my mind: Robert sitting with his Gypsy Girl bride in Arlene Brown's parlor for the whole cast to see. "Who're you going to the strike party with?" I asked Mary Hogan, who'd been Robert's last girl. "Joe Stepler," she said. "Who're you?" She had a condescending look in her eye.

"Oh, just Robert," I said, and walked off, and of course everybody knew ten minutes later. I didn't care. It was my first triumph in an awfully long time.

Then February thirteenth and the opening night of the operetta came. I had to marry Robert on stage in front of everyone, including Con. My wedding veil was cheesecloth, anchored by a wreath of paper roses, and my gown was somebody's mother's long formal slip of white satin hung round with more cheesecloth. It seemed to me that I was fated to wear cheesecloth in public every year of my life.

I had to keep up with the orchestra, the chorus and Robert. I had to remember the silly words, most of them about undying love. Worst of all, I had to look at Robert, who kept gazing at me with the most convincing undying love possible to a Prince in a hot wool World War I uniform and a heavily starched collar. And I had to kiss him. Everybody in the cast was waiting for that kiss – we'd skipped the kiss in rehearsals.

We did it for two nights, and Con was in the front row both times. Con tried his best to say he liked it, but after the first night he said, "Does he have to kiss you?"

"Yes, he does," I said, more truthfully than Con could imagine, because if Robert Laird wanted to kiss me at all, he'd have to wear that starched collar and hot wool and kiss the Gypsy Girl on stage in front of everybody.

I had to try to seem unenthusiastic about that stage kiss, but I don't think I fooled Con, or Robert. Part of me was praying that my veil wouldn't fall off or Robert wouldn't get his sword tangled in cheesecloth, but when his arms were around me, I sort of melted into that kiss, and both of us caught up with the music a beat or two late.

Of course Con didn't like it much. He was more unhappy than ever when I told him I had a date with his cousin. But Con was just one of my boyfriends, not my fiance, so all he could do was to look sad, and order a dozen red roses brought to me for my curtain calls. The last night I stood there in front of what seemed like the whole town, dressed as a bride, of all things, with an armful of roses, one boyfriend in the front row looking sad, and another one beside me, about to take me on a date. If that wasn't triumph, what was? Even Aunt Gertrude was impressed when I told her I was dating Robert, and she talked about a little competition being a good thing.

The last curtain had hardly come down when the cast rushed into the dressing rooms to take off makeup. I had my train and veil and pinned-tight wreath to keep out of my way, so I was the last girl out of there, and had my mouth open ready to tell Robert I was sorry to be late.

Robert wasn't there.

I waited by the boys' dressing room, but no one came out.

I looked through the curtain to see a few groups of people still talking here and there in the auditorium.

The half-lit stage was so quiet: just a collection of fake trees, fake bushes, a fake rose arbor, and a fake bride who'd stood there not fifteen minutes before with her arms full of roses and a triumphant smile on her face.

Her stupid, stupid face. I waited a little, my head buzzing and ringing the way it does when it collides with a horrible choice: I could go home alone, or I could go to the party alone.

I went to the party alone. I was too mad and too proud to go home. I trailed my veil over snow and slush to Arlene Brown's house across the street and tried to sneak in the kitchen door, which was hard when I was swaddled in cheesecloth.

Arlene's mother caught me yanking my veil inside. I tried to stop her, but she was too quick for me: she hurried in to announce to the whole cast in the parlor, "Here's the Gypsy Girl!" And there was Robert, cuddled up on a sofa in his World War I uniform with Mary Hogan in a red skirt and a gypsy blouse. Mary had hardly waited for the last curtain before she untied that blouse and made it off-the-shoulder and low enough for Robert to look down it, which he was doing.

All I wanted to do was leave, but Arlene's mother was saying, "Would you like some refreshments, dear?" She led me into her dining room and held out a plate of frosted cupcakes. "You did such a fine job tonight. Here, honey, have one."

There were tears in my eyes by then. I kept "taking one" with a blind politeness, saying "Thank you" and "Thank you" and then: "I have to go home. Thank you for the party."

I went out the back door I'd come in by, hired girl that I was. Only when I got to the street did I notice that I was holding not only my veil but three cupcakes and a half-dozen cookies.

It was cold February, with slushy snow underfoot, and I'd left my coat and boots across the street. Home was eight blocks away. What would people think if they looked out a window and saw a sobbing bride dodging puddles from streetlight to streetlight, her hands full of cheesecloth, cookies and cupcakes?

They'd think, "Left at the altar," I supposed: I was crying my head off. I needed a place to go where someone would hug me and kiss me and say, "Never mind," and "He's not worth a single tear," and "Men are such beasts," and so on.

Then, as I ran across Fifth Street, I saw a light shining from a basement window. I trailed down a flight of stairs and threw myself, sobbing, into Victoria Kline's arms, veil, cupcakes, cookies and all.

"It was so awful," I howled. "I was so happy, and then it was so awful! I wouldn't kiss him, and he was getting

What would people think if they looked out a window and saw
a sobbing bride dodging puddles from streetlight to streetlight?

even!" I told her everything, sniveling and sniffing, and she held me tight and said, "Never mind," and "Robert Laird is a stupid, silly boy," and put my cakes and cookies on a plate.

"Now," she said, delicately taking the bobby pins out of my wreath, "we'll just put you into something warm and cozy, and then we'll have a party all by ourselves."

Her father had gone to bed, and her small sewing room was warm. She found a flannel robe and some socks for me, and we sat in lamplight eating Mrs. Brown's cupcakes and cookies, drinking hot chocolate and talking about comforting things.

I hid all evening with Victoria, until I could go home in my dried-out wedding gown as if my date were over. I said, "Fine," when Aunt Gertrude asked how my date had gone, and escaped to bed because I was "tired." I lay thinking of Victoria, and friendship that's the lifelong kind.

I would hate operettas the rest of my life, of course. And yet *The Gypsy Girl* turned out to be helpful after all. Con had watched me being kissed by somebody else two nights in a row. He'd had to imagine me dating his cousin.

Con couldn't stand it. "Marry me," Con begged the very next afternoon.

How heartless I was. "But I've only known you six weeks!" I told him, and rumpled his silk tie and his thick, nicely-combed hair – his hair was pretty.

I wouldn't do anything as stupid as answering Yes right away, of course, but I kissed him and kissed him, because he couldn't have said anything that was more comforting, and I couldn't help but compare him with Robert. Con was... grown up. Yes. He was kind. And he was the marrying kind, too – not somebody who picked up and dropped girls as if he were a shopper at a sale. I went to school on Monday with Con's proposal like a suit of armor between me and the sight of Robert and Mary Hogan holding hands in the hall.

"Aren't you being awfully cold with Mr. Beale?" my aunt asked that week. I don't know how warm she thought I could get in a parlor with the door open, but she never caught us near each other when she came in, because the hall floor squeaked.

Four days seemed like a decent time to keep saying, "Maybe," and "We'll see," and "Let me think about it." How did I know how long I should treat Con like that? It seemed cruel. "It's just that I'm so young," I told him the fourth day. "If I marry, I can't work and make money enough to go to college."

"You want to go to college?" Con said, letting me go enough to look in my eyes. "You can go even if you're married. We've got a college right here in town. Will that do?"

"Oh, yes," I breathed, amazed and awed, and I gave Con such a smile that he batted his long eyelashes.

"I need you so much," he said.

"Do you?" I said. I was on his lap with my arms around his neck.

"More than anything in the world."

"I'm the most ordinary girl in Cedar Falls," I said. "You're such a kind person – "

"Ordinary!" Con cried. "I've never known anyone like you. You're beautiful, but it's more than that – you're so bright and warm – you light up everything wherever you are."

I hugged and kissed him. His brown eyes were so earnest, looking into mine. "Like somebody in cheese-cloth and tinsel, standing on an orange crate?" I said to tease him.

"Just exactly like an angel."

He meant it. He saw me like that. "Conrad Raymond Beale," I said solemnly, because it was a solemn moment, "I'm nothing like an angel, and never will be, but if you can stand to marry ordinary Miranda Daisy Letty, she'll be very proud to marry you."

How Con's face lit up! He grabbed me and set me on my feet and hugged me and kissed me and looked dazed with happiness; I felt awed, seeing what I'd done. He wouldn't wait one minute – he'd seen my uncle pass by outside the parlor window and come in the house.

Con bent down to our little parlor mirror to comb his hair and check for lipstick and straighten his tie, and off he went to knock on my uncle's study door.

I put more lipstick on – my hands were trembling – and combed my hair, while the thought of dear Con filled my head, the parlor, the house, the years ahead – big and safe, and peaceful. I couldn't stay in the parlor: it seemed as tiny as a birdcage. I waited in the hall.

When Con came from the study, Aunt Gertrude was halfway downstairs, staring at us. "I've asked your uncle," Con said to me, and my aunt's mouth started to fall open before she caught it and shut it – I saw her. "I'd like you to be present, too."

So Con and I went into the study and shut the door behind us.

"Mr. Beale has told me that you've agreed to marry him," Uncle Boyd said to me, looking stern.

"Yes," I said, smiling up at Con.

"Well," my uncle said in a thoughtful voice.

We waited.

My uncle said, "Hmm." He was a minister, but he knew how to discuss such things, since he'd gone through them himself, and was a businessman with a church to run.

"If I were volunteering for the war, sir, I'd ask Miranda to wait for me," Con said. "But my father can't run the Beale Company. If I enlist, there's no one to do it. We've got important war contracts already, and we'll have more. I'll just be another serviceman if I volunteer, but if I stay home I can keep the plant going so local people won't lose their jobs, and the armed forces will get years of our fighting materiel. And the draft board won't let me enlist, of course. I don't like it, but that's the way it is."

"Not going to war with your friends?" my uncle said, peering up at Con. "Not being able to say later that you fought? They might even call you a profiteer."

"Yes, sir," Con said. "Some people probably will."

I heard admiration in my uncle's voice. "You haven't had an easy choice to make. What does your father say?"

"He doesn't like it. He says people will look down on us if I'm a 'draft dodger.' He fought in the first world war. He thinks he can run the Beale Company if I volunteer."

"But he can't?"

"No, sir. He's in great pain – has been ever since his accident. He insists on going to the plant every day, but he hasn't been able to do the work for years."

The two men looked at each other for a moment in silence.

"I know I'm five years older than Miranda," Con said.

"You are indeed," Uncle Boyd said, and frowned as if five years were five feet of solid rock between Con and me.

"She won't want for a thing," Con said. "Though we will have to live with my father for a while. She plans to go to I.S.T.C., and I'll be glad to pay her college expenses. And I'll settle ten thousand dollars on her, too. In the bank. Under her own name."

My uncle's study suddenly wore that amazing look that surroundings have when a miracle occurs. I stared at Con's highly polished shoes as if they were the only thing that kept the house from blowing away.

"That's...fair," Uncle Boyd managed to say after a pause. You could buy a big house for ten thousand dollars. I felt dizzy. All I could think of was: *College. Ten thousand dollars.* My uncle said a prayer for us, Con went home, and I came out of that parlor an absolutely new person, carrying my happiness as if it were a wild bird that might escape from me and spread its huge wings.

Aunt Gertrude was waiting in the hall. "Did Con ask?" she said, jiggling the baby in her arms so he wouldn't fuss.

"Of course he did. He's going to pay for my college too," I said, and opened the icebox door.

My aunt had been making little bitty tea sandwiches for the Ladies Relief Society that afternoon. Each quartet of crustless triangles was wrapped in waxed paper, and nobody – not even my uncle – would dare touch one. I took out a package, unwrapped it, and ate all four quarters.

I still remember the taste of that egg salad on white bread, and the expression on Aunt Gertrude's face. Have you ever seen a dog making for you across a yard, determined to chew your leg off, until he's suddenly yanked back by his chain?

That's the way Aunt Gertrude looked. She was stopped in her tracks. She couldn't save those sandwiches – she was vibrating all over, speechless. I had more amazing secrets – she could feel it – but I wasn't going to tell.

I licked egg salad off my finger. "Awfully salty," I said, and went upstairs without another word.

9

Uncle Boyd didn't waste any time telling my aunt everything. I knew, because at supper we stood for our usual prayer, but then Aunt Gertrude said, "Betty, you're in charge of the small table. Stop the boys from fighting and keep an eye on the baby, and clear up after supper."

"Mandy – " Betty began, but my aunt said, "Miranda is engaged to be married to Mr. Beale. She'll sit at the large table from now on." Five pairs of eyes looked at me; then all of us looked at the large table and, sure enough, my aunt had set a third place just like the other two, with real china and the second-best silverware.

So I sat down calmly, like an honored guest. When the baby spit up and Betty wailed, "Oh, ick!" I wore a detached look and paid attention to my uncle's discussion of the fall of Manilla, like a woman soon to enter the larger world.

It was glorious. I knew that old, dark kitchen by heart: every chipped place on the dishpan and every bare spot in the table oilcloth and how to get through the pantry's swinging door with a full tray of dishes. And there was Betty loading the tray and backing through the swinging door and washing up on that oilcloth, while I drank coffee with my aunt and uncle in the parlor and listened to bad news on the radio: MacArthur was retreating to the Bataan peninsula.

The next day was Saturday, and Betty and Benjy and Bernard spent most of the morning taking storeroom junk to the basement and moving Betty's junk into the storeroom. "Miranda needs a room for herself," my aunt told Betty.

"It's not fair!" Betty wailed. We'd shared a room since the boys got into their teens and moved to the sleeping porch. "It's not fair!" Betty said when I got her bed and she got my cot, but I figured it was very fair, if unbelievable.

At lunch, sitting with my aunt and uncle, I asked, "Does the door to my room have a key?"

There was silence for a moment: no one in that house had locked a door in years – not even the front and back doors. Nobody locked their houses in Cedar Falls unless they went out of town, or died.

"Of course Miranda will want a key," my uncle said. "There's a bunch of keys in my study in the bottom drawer." He found them and gave them to me, and once more I had the pleasure of leaving the table without touching dirty dishes. I went upstairs and tried each key in my door while Betty clattered china to set my aunt's teeth on edge.

After a while I heard the baby yell in his crib down the hall. I didn't go to pick him up; I was exploring how far miracles extended. When my aunt came upstairs to get him, I discovered they extended even farther than I'd thought...and all in one afternoon.

I found a key that fit my door, and I hung it around my neck to wear day and night. To me that key was gold, not brass. A room of my own. A lock on my door. I'd probably never have such things again; I'd figured that out. When I was married, I couldn't lock a man out of a room in his own house, could I – supposing I even had a room that was all mine? Husbands in Cedar Falls had their "studies" or "libraries" or that fashionable new thing: a "den." I'd never heard of a married woman with a den.

Snug in my locked room, I lay on my new bed and listened to the thump-thump of the old Maytag in the basement. No loud voice came up the stairs, telling me to get down there and help with the wash. I felt like an invalid, but it was only Con, coming between me and eight years of housework. The old house leaked sound like the sieve it was: I could hear Aunt Gertrude yelling at Betty, and the clang of pails set on the basement stove to heat water.

I lay on my new bed and planned. I'd put beautiful magazine pictures on my bedroom walls – not pictures of Frank Sinatra like other girls had. But my most important plan of all was to stay engaged as long as possible.

I'd learned a lot, listening to women in the church kitchen. I knew you said "I do" for keeps. Cedar Falls was a college town, which made it a little more liberal, but the church women talked about one of the professors who'd been divorced – he'd said he knew that publicity about it would harm the college, so he resigned.

A divorced woman didn't appear much in polite company. There were a few of them, and they were watched. People were never quite sure what a divorced woman would do, since she had nothing to lose, so to speak. She wasn't a widow. She wasn't even "damaged goods." She was rejected damaged goods, like junk left after a rummage sale.

You got married for keeps. There wasn't much else you could do, if you were a girl. You could be a teacher or a nurse or a secretary. We saw women like that in Cedar Falls. They usually wore the same hat to church every Sunday, and lived in some widow's furnished room with "kitchen privileges."

So I was going to get an education and get married too. I'd have a long engagement "because I was still so young." That would take care of the baby problem – a serious problem, because nobody pregnant could go to college. I wouldn't date another man, supposing that the war left a single eligible man in town, because I'd be expected to "save myself" for Con Beale, as if I were a savings account with Con's name on it.

My uncle said Con was growing richer fast; the Beale Equipment Company had good war contracts, and went full blast around the clock. But Con had still found time to come to the parsonage every day, and take me to a movie Saturday nights.

The next Monday after school I sat in my room, polishing my fingernails and waiting for Con. When I looked at my nice smooth hands, I knew I wasn't dreaming: Betty was doing most of my work. I heard Aunt Gertrude shouting at Betty – Betty had ironed a good sheet and scorched it black so it would have to be mended. Betty had said she wouldn't – no, she would not – rinse diapers in the toilet. But of course she had to, and had to find time to do her homework while supper was cooking, without letting the schoolwork – or the cooking – distract her. I knew how that went.

Con came, and when we'd spent an hour hugging and kissing, he asked Aunt Gertrude if he could have a short visit with her before supper. They stayed in the parlor for quite a while; then Con left and Aunt Gertrude came upstairs and knocked on my door. She always knocked now.

"Come in," I said. I hadn't wasted any time. I'd changed to old clothes, and was tacking a beautiful Rembrandt painting from the *Ladies Home Journal* on my wall.

"Mr. Beale is so thoughtful," Aunt Gertrude said, sitting on my bed. "He's given me so much money for you! He wants you to have some nice clothes for school now, and summer, and college in the fall – after your engagement comes out in the paper, of course. He wants to take you and me to Chicago the end of March, and we'll stay at the Palmer House and go to the Empire Room and he'll give you your diamond..."

"Yes," I said smugly at the top of my ladder. "That's what he said he wanted to do. 'Nothing but the best,' he told me." Aunt Gertrude was amazed and excited. She was trying to hide it, but I could tell.

"You'll need sweaters and skirts and dresses and a formal and shoes and hats, and a suitcase. So next Saturday we'll go to Black's."

Shopping? Shopping at Black's? We'd never done that. The Letty family bought clothes from the thick Sears Roebuck catalog when we bought clothes at all. Betty and I could describe every girl's outfit in it, including available colors. That catalog sold everything in the world, it seemed to us – even live monkeys, and baby alligators that were "harmless when small." We loved that animal page. When a new catalog came, we children got the old one to cut up for puppet shows and paper dolls – how we hated it when the illustrations of ladies in underwear or bathing suits cut them off at the ankles. Even when the catalog was gutted, it was still thick enough for a child to sit on at the table.

"Shopping," I said in a calm voice, tapping in another tack.

"In Waterloo," Aunt Gertrude said, looking up at her niece on a stepladder who was lifted far above anybody's expectations, especially hers.

Shopping in Waterloo meant that you wore your best girdle and bra and slip and dress, and had your hair "set." It was like going to church, except that you were a lot more careful about your underwear. You wore gloves that were never warm, and a hat always, though winter winds might be at gale force. The hats had narrow, round elastic sewed on the band behind your ears. When you slid the elastic under your back hair, you had a fighting chance of grabbing your hat before the wind did. To make it even safer, you put a long hatpin through the front along your scalp.

Pinned and gloved and girdled and curled, Aunt Gertrude and I walked along snowy Cedar Falls streets the next Saturday afternoon, and climbed on the interurban car that rattled along Rainbow Drive. When the car reached Waterloo, the motorman flipped the seat backs so that passengers could face the other way on the return trip – flip, flip, flip – and it seemed to me that Aunt Gertrude had flipped over and was facing in the opposite direction, too. I hardly recognized her. She wore her one shabby coat, and her gloves were mended, but I was used to that. It was her new voice that I didn't know, and the look in her eye, and the astonishing way we talked so pleasantly as we swayed side by side, while snowy bushes whacked the sides of the car as it passed cornfield thickets.

Waterloo streets were half slush, half ice as we walked to Black's Department Store to spend Con's money. Black's Department Store had a "mezzanine." I loved that word, and I loved the lending library there with just-printed books that smelled of ink and glue and still wore their glossy dust jackets. You paid so many pennies a week to borrow a book, and that seemed the height of extravagance to me: paying money for a book you couldn't keep. The railing of the mezzanine was lined with chairs where old people spent the day watching shoppers below.

"What colors does Con like best?" my aunt asked as we entered the ladies' wear department.

"Blue and pink," I said, not telling how I knew. I loved teasing Con, and one day I pulled my blouse open a little so he could just see a blue bow on my slip, and I asked him, "When I buy under things for my trousseau, what colors do you like best?"

The poor man. He didn't know what to say. But the bow was blue and the slip was pink, so he said, "Pink and blue" in desperation. Luckily, both colors looked good on me.

Aunt Gertrude and I didn't pick an armful of clothes off the racks and drag them to a dressing room. A genteel lady installed us in a room with upholstered chairs and a view of the city below, and brought the clothes to us, and helped me try them on. This was the reason I'd worn my absolutely best underwear.

What clothes she brought! College girls wore loafers or saddle shoes with ankle sox to show they weren't their mothers' generation, but above those chunky feet the rich girls wore pleated wool skirts, thick and luscious, and lambs wool or angora sweaters that itched, so they put rayon shirts underneath whose collars folded over the sweater necks. Sometimes they wore ruffled blouses and jumpers, or rayon dresses that wrinkled, and cotton dresses when it was warm in the spring.

The clothes were so beautiful. The clothes were so expensive. To peel money off Con Beale's roll of bills felt as if we were peeling off our skin. We kept looking for ways to economize, whispering to each other while the saleslady was gone. Couldn't Victoria Kline make a skirt like that for half the money? Couldn't we get blouses cheaper at Sears?

No, Aunt Gertrude said. Con had specified that I was to go to Black's and get the very best of everything, and Miss Kline and Sears were not, were they, the best?

How could I choose? I wanted everything the saleslady brought, and Aunt Gertrude couldn't hide the wistful look in her eye. Somehow we managed to outfit me for the trip to Chicago, and the last months of high school, and summer, and college in the fall. Con said he wanted to see me dressed up for school and church, "just like an angel," he said.

I felt like an angel in the beautiful, beautiful blue net formal the saleslady brought: a dream dress with rosebuds at the shoulders and rosebuds on the skirt, all lined in rustling taffeta, and even a little blue purse to carry on my arm. I wasn't too far away from the fairytales I'd whispered to my cousins in the dark. I remembered Cinderella. I remembered Beauty and her Beast. Beauty and Cinderella both got the king's son at the end of their stories, and if Con wasn't as handsome as a prince, he was certainly as rich.

"Can I see what you bought?" Betty said wistfully when Black's delivered my new clothes that afternoon. Aunt Gertrude came upstairs, too, and they stood in my doorway and watched me shake out the contents of each suit box and spread the beautiful clothes on my bed.

"Oh!" Betty kept saying, "Oh, look at that sweater! And a skirt to match. Oh! And that beautiful, beautiful velveteen dress, and shoes, and another sweater and skirt! And that coat! A whole new wardrobe! She's got *everything*."

"Mr. Beale wants Miranda to dress nicely when she appears with him in public, of course," my aunt said, trying to sound matter-of-fact.

A sudden slither of sweet revenge snaked through me. Who else in that house could have such clothes? That was the question in their eyes as they looked at me across the riches on my bed.

10

M y father wants to meet you," Con said the next Friday. "On Sunday afternoon."

I was sitting on Con's lap, and I turned as cold as the snow falling outside. I was scared. The look in Con's eye told me he felt the same way.

My only pleasant thought was that I could wear some of my new clothes for the first time, since nobody would see them but Con and his father. I could choose. Which ones? A man could give his fiancée clothes, but until our engagement was made public and official by appearing on the town's society page, I had to stay a poor niece and my finery had to stay hidden, except that Sunday afternoon.

So there I was after dinner that Sunday, coming down the parsonage stairs in a blue velveteen dress with little rhinestone buttons, and gleaming, high-heeled pumps. My hair had been set, my fingernails were polished, and I could see by the looks on every face in the hall below that I was somebody new. Maybe a butterfly feels that way when it manages to drag itself out of its mummy wrappings and pump up the bags on its back until they are wings. I put on my blue velvet hat that matched my new winter coat with the beaver collar, and Betty and my aunt could hardly bear to look, but couldn't bear not to.

There is something about having brand-new clothes slipping so silkily against your skin that's very reassuring. Con escorted me down our rickety parsonage steps, opened the door of his Cadillac for me, and shut me carefully inside. I didn't even look to see if the whole Letty family was watching through the parlor windows. I knew they were.

While we drove I watched Con's profile, which would have looked at home on the range under a ten-gallon hat. His eyebrows wandered up and down, thick here and thin there, as if they'd lost directions, but his nose was big enough to know what to do: it stuck out. He had a nice square chin. His hair was dark brown like his eyes, and thick, and his teeth were white when he smiled, which wasn't often because he was so shy.

He didn't look at me or smile. I wondered if he'd be more relaxed in his own house. It had only been nine weeks since he'd brought that first box of chocolates to our door, and he hadn't seen me anywhere but at church or at the movies or in my aunt's parlor. Movies and church are so public, and lots of people get tongue-tied at a parsonage, as if God might drop in, I suppose.

"I'm scared," I said.

"Scared of seeing your new house?" Con said. "It'll be yours when Dad moves out. He planned to build a house, but the war put a stop to that."

Your new house. For a minute I was nine years old again, being driven to the place where I'd turn into a homeless orphan in a few hours. "Scared of seeing your father," I said.

"We call him 'S.C.,'" Con said.

We'd been traveling the grid of old Cedar Falls streets that were names if they ran north-south and numbers if they ran east-west. Now Con turned off Eighteenth to "The Knolls," which lots of people called "Snob Hill." Big houses were being built there, new "ranch houses." Cedar Falls didn't know quite what to think of them. We were used to two-story houses with gables and porches: upright affairs that looked you in the eye. A "ranch house" seemed furtive, flattened into rows of rooms and garages hugging the ground or half-buried in it, like a sod hut.

Con turned up a new street. I'd often taken that street lately, walking fast and looking out of the corner of my eye at the Beales' almost-new ranch house built into a snow-covered hill.

The garage door was open, and it swallowed our car. I'd never driven into a garage before; my uncle's old Ford sat on the street over its oil blotches. This garage was painted like a room, and we didn't go out in the cold to the front door: we climbed steps beside the car, and there we were in a hallway, wiping our feet while I stared through a door at the fanciest kitchen I'd ever seen.

Nothing about this house was like the parsonage. It didn't smell like old wood and wet galoshes. Slabs of winter sunshine shimmered on beautiful furniture and deep rugs.

I'd walked past that house, but I'd never allowed myself to imagine living there. *Don't even try,* I told myself. *Learn from past mistakes.*

But Con didn't say, "We have to take you in." I wasn't going to sleep on a smelly cot in a corner. "This will be our room," he said, leading the way to a big bedroom that made me blush. He got red, too, helping me off with my coat. I hardly wanted to let Con put it on the bed, I was so proud of it, and Con's father wouldn't see it. But I was wearing the velveteen dress with my lovely hat to match, and of course I kept my white gloves on, and carried my new purse.

We left that bedroom fast by hurrying through the nearest door, and found ourselves in what he said would be our bathroom, which was as fancy as pictures in magazines. I admired the double sinks and the brass towel rods with lion-heads at the ends and the bathtub without any claws, and even a shower stall (I'd never taken a shower), until we had both stopped blushing and turned businesslike again.

"My father is waiting for us in the sun-room," Con said. I had to follow him back down the hall and into a very bright room half walled with glass. A man who seemed older than fifty sat looking at us, his wheel chair glinting and sparkling. His bald head shone like a marble knob in the sunlight.

He didn't wait for introductions. He stared at me side-wise over his glasses and long, thin nose and said in a loud voice, "So you're the parson's niece. The orphan."

"Yes, I'm Reverend Letty's niece, and I'm an orphan, sir," I said. "Miranda Daisy Letty."

He smiled a little, I thought. Maybe he didn't expect me to speak up like that. Maybe it was the "Daisy." I looked right back at him and saw his eyes moving up and down, taking me all in.

"Tell her," he said to Con.

Tell me what? I looked at Con and saw him turn red, then white, then a little gray.

"You've told her you're going to be a draft dodger and sit out this war, haven't you?" S.C. said. Con nodded. "Tell her the rest. Get it over with. Then she can leave if she wants to, before anything goes too far."

Con looked sick. All I could do was to put one of my gloved hands on his arm to comfort him a little, but he didn't seem to feel it. He didn't look at his father. He didn't look at me. He stood very still and straight, but his hands twisted around each other, white-knuckled. "I can't have children," he blurted out in a shaking voice. "We can't have a family."

"No children," his father said. "No family. No disease. He was born that way, we found out later. The doctor said, 'The plumbing works, but the pipes aren't connect-ed' – those were his very words – but don't worry, Con here can still..."

He stopped. They were both looking at me: Con through his long eyelashes, as if he could hardly bear it, and his father with a sidewise squint. It was so quiet that I could hear the clock on the wall.

Thoughts went through my head so fast that they couldn't have been thoughts – they were streamers of feelings from my seventeen years, faster than light, ending with Con laughing as he sneaked money into my pockets, and his miserable face beside me, and his twisting hands.

Then I said, "I love Con."

Nobody spoke for a moment. The clock ticked as if to underscore what I'd said with a dotted line.

"Would you love him if he were poor?" S.C. said.

I snatched in my breath at such a question. "I don't know," I said, and stared right back at that man. Was he trying to hurt Con more than he had? "It's not fair to ask."

S.C. laughed. "She's right," he said. "Con, ring for tea and pour me a drink. And you, Miranda Daisy, come here and tell me why you think you have to go to college before you can marry my son."

"When you're married, you're married," I said, sitting down in a chair Con brought for me and taking off my gloves. "I want to be a good wife for Con, and I'll be busy. There's the cleaning and the meals to get and laundry and gardening and entertaining – "

"You've done all that? You sound as if you have," S.C. interrupted.

"For my aunt," I said, with a little proud note in my voice.

"You won't have to do it here!" Con cried. "Not a thing. You can have your own room to study in, and the time." His head was up as he came with his father's drink; he stood over me with the happiest, proudest look on his face.

An older lady in a white dress brought a tray filled with tiny sandwiches and cakes and teacups as thin as paper. I'd heard that Mr. Beale had a full time housekeeper. I smiled at her, but no one introduced her before she turned and left.

Con ate almost nothing; he sat and looked at me while I tried to ask intelligent questions about Mr. Beale's manufacturing. My aunt had taught me to ask about other people's interests.

I didn't hear much of what S.C. answered; I was busy eating as much as I decently could while I smiled into Con's adoring eyes now and then. I remember the sensation of stowing away all that had happened in that house—packing it in my mind like papers in a pocket to read later. That was the only way I could manage to eat all the sandwiches and cake that I dared while I carried on polite conversation at the same time.

"Well, what are you waiting for?" S.C. asked Con the minute the woman took the dishes away. "Miranda Daisy needs a room to study in – let her pick one out and maybe she'll marry you."

So I thanked S.C. for his hospitality and shook his hand, and Con and I left that room and all we'd heard there behind us and went exploring.

Where could I study best? Con wanted to know. What room would make me feel at home? I realized, didn't I, that if I lived in his house, there was a full-time housekeeper, and Iowa State Teachers College just a few blocks away? He was thoughtful and kind. Of course I could have the back bedroom that looked out on the patio. Get rid of the bed, and the room would only need a desk and a good lamp and book shelves and a comfortable chair and a typewriter – plenty of heat in the winter, and cool air from the garden in the summer. He kissed me every minute or two while we were planning, and I kissed him back hard to show him I knew how awful the afternoon had been for him. "Marry me in June," he said, and I said, "June?"

"Why wait? You can study better here than you can at home." That was a peculiar reason for marrying, but Con had tried all the others.

"Let me think," I said. "I have to think."

So he took me back home to think.

Aunt Gertrude and Uncle Boyd went into the parlor with me the minute Con drove away. "Did you have a nice tea?" Aunt Gertrude wanted to know. She had Bruce in her arms, and he was fussing, so she put his face on a diaper on her shoulder and patted his back.

"Lovely," I said. "Cucumber sandwiches and little cakes."

"And you'll be living there when you're married?"

"We'll have our own bedroom and bath," I said. I took my white gloves off and smoothed them in my lap.

"Did his father mention Con's not enlisting?" Uncle Boyd asked.

"He wanted Con to tell me, but I knew it, of course – why does Mr. Beale keep after Con about it?"

"I don't know," Uncle Boyd said. "Con certainly wants to enlist, but I hear the draft board won't let him. They're local men – they know Con's running the Beale company. Every day he ships parts for mines and machine guns overseas."

"Was Mr. Beale friendly to you?" Aunt Gertrude said.

"Yes," I said, but I heard Mr. Beale's scornful voice: *Don't worry. Con can still...*

"That's nice," Aunt Gertrude said. Now Bruce wasn't fussing; he was screaming. That baby yelled in the middle of the night and was wet all the time and had to be fed and kept clean – why would I miss something like that? Wouldn't I give up children like Betty and Benjy and Bernard and Bruce if I could have a man who adored me, and four years of college, and a room of my own, and no housework?

I sighed and said I was tired and went upstairs just as if I were a guest. Betty was cooking supper, and the boys were setting the table and fighting.

I looked around the bedroom I'd been so proud of. It was a dark, cramped little hole. I hadn't sewed the bedspread or curtains yet, or chosen the wallpaper. Maybe I never would.

Maybe I'd consider marrying Con in June.

11

Nineteen forty-two had hardly begun when Conrad Beale changed my life with a box of chocolates. Before March he'd proposed. I couldn't believe my new life. Aunt Gertrude no longer yelled for me, or at me; she yelled at Betty and the boys instead, and gave them plenty to do. Sometimes I'd go downstairs when the baby was wet and howling or the dinner was burning, just to see if I was still invisible. I was. I could lock myself in my bedroom and try on my new clothes every day, and wear them when Con came.

But as those weeks passed with January thaws and February snowstorms, I had time to think. I had time to watch. Bernard and Benjy had tormented me; now they left me alone, so I saw how anxiously belligerent they were. They pummeled each other as they always had – big gangly boys getting pimples and shooting out of their clothes, who took the stairs three steps at a time and knocked holes in the woodwork when they wrestled. Benjy's ears still stuck out like my uncle's did, and he was still skinny. He couldn't pick on Bernard any more – Bernard was still sulky, but he outweighed Benjy, and was tall enough to look down on him, too. In a few years they would be drafted, and they were beginning to know it. We were sure that the war would go on for years and years. The Allies were not winning. America had lost Wake Island, and Manila.

If the boys were growing tall, it seemed to me that my uncle had shrunk. He sat at his desk in his study for hours, and every time I caught a glimpse of him, there were numbers on the paper before him, not words. I'd been another mouth to feed for eight years. Now there was the new baby.

"You're such a help to your aunt," Uncle Boyd said to me now and then. "I don't know what we'd do without you."

Aunt Gertrude had never said such things. I dressed up every afternoon and waited for Con to come with candy or flowers, while Aunt Gertrude and Betty and the boys wore old clothes and worked.

I'd had time to watch Betty, too. Being "Betty Letty" was bad enough, but the kids called her "Betty Boop," because she was nothing like bosomy Betty Boop, I guess. When she washed dishes, the kitchen apron didn't even touch her front on its way down, and she bobby-pinned her hair behind her ears as if nobody would want to look at it either.

On top of it all, Betty was a minister's daughter. The only thing worse was to be Charlotte Brewer, the undertaker's daughter, and have boys bring you home from a date and whisper on your doorstep, "Is there...you know...anybody in there?"

My imagination has always been a burden – there's too much of it. I started to imagine what it must be like to be Betty. And what would it be like to be Aunt Gertrude? I saw that my aunt was growing old, with wrinkles I hadn't noticed before, and a stomach that stuck out, even though she'd had the baby. She was up at dawn to feed Bruce and drag the boys out of bed, and make the big breakfasts: fried eggs, or pancakes, or oatmeal cooked in pans that had to be scoured clean. Three meals a day, and washing, ironing, mending, nursing the baby – and then she was expected to be at the church for circle meetings and group meals and weddings and funerals.

I saw her. I saw them all as if they were in a movie called *The Poor Minister's Family*, and I was enjoying myself in a dark theater, watching.

So after dinner one day I surprised everybody. I surprised myself most of all, because since January I'd been so blissfully free. I said, "I'll just help Betty in the kitchen." I picked up dirty dishes and went through the swinging door, and saw my uncle smile as I passed him.

I couldn't believe I'd done such a thing. There I was with Betty, scraping plates in the kitchen and stacking them in hot water to take the grease off. We put away the leftovers without saying much, and got down to the slow business of washing and scalding and drying.

I'm sure we both felt how odd it was to be working together, almost like sisters, while Aunt Gertrude and Uncle Boyd listened to war news in the parlor without me. I'd done the dishes alone in that kitchen for years.

"You and Mom are so lucky – going to Chicago, seeing the Palmer House and the Empire Room," Betty said. She even sounded like a sister. She handed me a glass to dry.

"Con said if he was going to give me a diamond, he wanted to make it a special occasion."

"You're so lucky," she said, not in a snarly way. She sounded wistful.

"He's nice. He says he wants to make me happy," I said.

We washed and dried for a while in a companionable sort of silence. Aunt Gertrude came into the kitchen, and I said to her, "Con wants me to start buying my trousseau, just in case we decide to get married in June. Could you find time to go shopping with me on Saturday? I really need your advice." I saw the look in her eyes – she'd have to watch me try on beautiful clothes again – and that old, sly thrill of revenge slithered through me. Hadn't she said for years that I was no relative of hers?

I don't like to think of that next Saturday when I sailed rather grandly into Black's Ladies' Wear again with Aunt Gertrude.

The salesladies recognized us, and had to step back and let "my saleslady" take charge. "We'd like to look at coats first," I told her.

"You've already got your new coat," Aunt Gertrude whispered. How she loved that coat. She couldn't imagine I'd want another one.

"I'd like another one," I told her.

What could she say? The saleslady brought coats, and I tried them on. There was a black one with a mink collar. "Such a lovely coat," Aunt Gertrude said. When I'd tried a half dozen, we came back to that one. It was my size.

"Is this collar real mink?" I asked the saleslady, who was hovering.

"Oh, yes." The saleslady's tone showed shock that anyone would ask. She removed the coat from its hanger with a practiced sweep that showed the coat's satin lining, jet black and shimmering.

The saleslady helped me into the coat again, using that reverent touch salesladies use, as if what you're trying on is really too precious for any perspiring, skin-shedding mortal woman. I told her I wanted to look at some dresses suitable for church or afternoon teas next, and she went off to get them.

"What do you think?" I asked Aunt Gertrude as I twirled in front of a wall of mirrors.

"It's so beautiful," she said.

"I really can't decide," I said, frowning.

"Look at that mink collar," Aunt Gertrude said. "All down the front... and the little mink tails."

I sighed. "It's so hard to make up my mind. Will you try it on? Let me see it on someone else."

We were the same size. Aunt Gertrude could hardly bring herself to put her arms in the sleeves. "My hands are so rough," she protested. "I'll snag the satin." But I put it on her anyway, and buttoned it. She looked at herself in the mirrors. She almost touched the mink collar, but she didn't. She turned around and around so I could see every side. The coat made her old shoes and hat so shabby: I saw her try not to look at anything but that beautiful mink and black wool.

"No..." I said. "No. I don't think so."

"You don't think so?" Aunt Gertrude breathed. "You really don't like it?" She was staring at herself, and I hardly knew the look on her face: she must have had that shy, proud expression when she was young, and Uncle Boyd told her she was pretty.

"No. I don't like it on me," I said. "I like it on you, though. It's just the kind of thing a minister's wife would wear to church." I actually said that.

Aunt Gertrude gave a dry little hopeless laugh. "I suppose so," she said. She took the coat off and hung it tenderly on its hanger.

The saleslady came back with an armload of dresses. "Do we like that coat?" she asked me.

"Yes," I said. "I'll take it. My aunt likes it."

Aunt Gertrude looked shocked. "But you said – "

"You said you liked it, didn't you?" I asked her.

"Well, yes. I did."

"Then she'll take the coat. We're staying in Chicago at the Palmer House in a week or two," I said. "And she'll want a dress to wear with it."

"Dear me," the saleslady said. "I was confused. I thought the young lady was the one—"

"No," I said. Aunt Gertrude looked very pale; I said to her, "Perhaps a dress with black in it, to go with the coat? With some color in it, too? Silk? Isn't red your favorite color?" I turned back to the saleslady. "And she'll need a formal, since we're going to the Empire Room for dancing."

The saleslady went out with her load of dresses. Aunt Gertrude sat there saying absolutely nothing, which was unusual for her.

"I'm...so sorry," I said, and I was. "I should have told you before that Con and I want you to have new clothes for the trip, and feel absolutely relaxed and carefree. It's time you had a vacation. I hope you don't mind."

Then I saw she had tears in her eyes. She put out her hand to barely touch the mink scarf of her coat. "It's too much," she said in such a faint voice that I could hardly hear her.

"I should have told you before we came," I said. "I'm truly sorry."

Then the saleslady rustled in with a new load of dresses. I hadn't warned Aunt Gertrude about underwear; I was relieved to see that she was wearing her best slip – one I'd sewed new lace on when I waited in the parlor for Con one afternoon. She was thin, but she'd lost some of the stomach from having the baby, and she'd put on her tight girdle, so she looked pretty good for being almost forty. She kept her hands in fists so she wouldn't hurt the silk dress as she disappeared in it and then came out at the top and looked at herself as the saleslady zipped her in.

It was a beautiful dress – black with small red flowers. "I doubt if we'll see silk like that again until the war's over," the saleslady said. "Schiaparelli's colors...in Paris, you know. She's using black this season, with red, shocking pink, Chinese yellow, lime green..."

We'd heard of Schiaparelli. We read copies of *The Ladies Home Journal* that were passed around in the Ladies Aid Society. Aunt Gertrude stood there like a paper doll, arms out so she wouldn't touch the dress. Schiaparelli. There was a rapt look in her eyes and relief in her voice – what would she have worn to Chicago, trailing after me in my beautiful new clothes? And I'd let her worry about that for weeks. I was ashamed.

"Now a nice formal," I said. "You can't go to the Empire Room without it."

Aunt Gertrude in a long dress! She loved every evening dress the saleslady brought, especially one that was two shades of beige – a "dinner suit," it was called. She couldn't hide her delight, but she said, when the saleslady was out of hearing: "I can shorten the skirt after Chicago, and it'll be a perfectly good suit."

"Keep it long a little longer," I said. "You'll have to be 'mother of the bride' – I don't have any other mother." And, do you know, Aunt Gertrude put her arms around me.

"We're suggesting to our customers that they buy stockings now, if they're needed," the saleslady said, coming in. "There may not be any more."

We bought stockings. We bought Aunt Gertrude shoes and gloves. Our last stop was the hat department.

Hats were uncomfortable and perishable, but necessary, and they could be magical. If you wore exactly the right hat – the hat that had been made for you, fated for you – you had a right to expect extraordinary events to occur.

Aunt Gertrude tried on hats in that spirit. She sat at one of the little polished tables that had large mirrors attached to them, and the saleslady, with proper reverence, lowered a hat upon her head: it was allowed to settle, like a butterfly. Then – when the veil was pulled down and arranged – Aunt Gertrude picked up a mirror, turned from one side to the other, and regarded the east and west of her reflection with the required sober, slightly haughty look, as if no hat could be as charming as her own unadorned head.

Aunt Gertrude prolonged the pleasure of it. The saleslady brought butterfly after butterfly; only a few of them were allowed to settle very long. At last my aunt chose two, and rose from the little velvet-upholstered chair with a certain air of triumph. Her cheeks were pink, her eyes sparkled, and I hardly knew her.

12

To drive to Chicago...to stay at the Palmer House...Aunt Gertrude and I talked about it every day when the rest of the family couldn't hear us. Con had said: "We might as well drive to Chicago while we can, before gas is rationed."

At last the morning of March twenty-eighth came. Aunt Gertrude and I put on our new clothes. Then Con appeared, and my aunt and I hurried as fast as we decently could to climb in his Cadillac and hide our beautiful hats and coats from the neighbors, though it was barely dawn. Bernard and Benjy put our new suitcase in the trunk.

Aunt Gertrude settled herself grandly in the back seat. I sat in the front seat beside Con, looking as nonchalant as possible – hadn't I been in that car before? The boys eyed it with the ravenous look they gave to pictures of Betty Grable in a swimsuit.

As we drove through town, Aunt Gertrude and I tried our best to carry on a polite conversation, as if we weren't almost too excited to make sense.

Aunt Gertrude admired the car. I admired the weather: "Not too cold for the end of March." Con recited a list of the highways he intended to take. "We'll have lunch in a restaurant in Galena, Illinois," he said, turning his head and raising his voice so that Aunt Gertrude could hear. "It's a nice place. If that's not too long for you ladies to wait."

"Oh, no," my aunt said.

"Not at all," I said.

Suddenly, watching Con out of the corner of my eye, I was as scared as I'd ever been. I was on my way to be engaged. Married. I was barely eighteen. I didn't have much faith in my good judgment – how could my aunt and uncle let me...

I stole glances at Con. Did I know him at all? I'd kissed him a lot. I'd sat on his lap. How different he seemed now, driving his big car down strange highways and through strange towns to pull smoothly into the parking lot of the restaurant he had chosen for us.

It was such an expensive restaurant. Con talked to the waiter, then seated us. He discussed the menu with us: two flustered women who had never chosen from such an array of delectibles, or seen such prices. He ordered what we decided upon: "The lady across from me will have... the lady on my right would like..."

And when we came into Chicago – that huge city, that confusing welter of people and cars and buses and taxis – Con drove straight to the Palmer House. He knew how to sign a hotel register and find our rooms and tip the bellboy. Aunt Gertrude and I followed him like those little fish you see following a big one. We swam through the glitter of the Palmer House trying not to stare at anything, even the women's clothes, but when Con finally left us alone in our wonderful two rooms and bath, we sat down in chairs and looked at each other for a while.

Aunt Gertrude came to herself first. "We've got to hang up our clothes," she said.

Maybe we had to do it, but it was a pleasure. How different our dresses looked, shaken out and hung by themselves in a wallpapered closet that was prettier than any room in the Letty house. It seemed to me that my new clothes had a slightly disdainful look: they belonged in such a closet, they implied with every seam and pleat. They had endured being hung in an Iowa parsonage for weeks by mistake.

Then my aunt and I explored our living room, and our bedroom with twin beds, and our bathroom, and we made little crooning noises at the satin bedspreads and the view of the city from our living room window. I was back in Chicago; I looked down at grimy streets and wondered where, in that sea of roofs, my family's one small room had been.

"Such stacks of towels!" Aunt Gertrude said from the bathroom. We admired the clean glasses wrapped in paper, soap wrapped in paper, and even the toilet seat wrapped in paper. Tissues – such a luxury – waited to be plucked from the bathroom wall. There were lamps everywhere for us to turn on and leave on, and we did. We read the list of services that would be available to us the minute we picked up our telephone. In such a strange new world we had nothing to do but explore, and the only familiar thing we found was a Bible in a bureau.

Then Con knocked and Aunt Gertrude let him in. "We won't dress formally until nine tonight," he said. "But I've reserved our table for dinner in half an hour, if that won't rush you." He'd changed his suit, and he had such a pleasant, confident air, even when he looked at me.

The restaurant lunch had been formidable. Dinner in the hotel dining room was scary. Silverware was marshaled before us in ranks we had only seen in Emily Post, and the waiters covered our table with enough china to serve the Letty family a day's meals. There was a wine list. There were finger bowls. Con knew what to do; we watched him from the corners of our eyes.

"May I have the salt?" I asked Aunt Gertrude in a bored voice.

"Of course," she said, lifting it languidly, as if salt was too common for words. What a day we were having. We'd talk about it for weeks.

But the Empire Room was the pinnacle of our trip. We were going to wear our long dresses in public, and sometime that evening Con would give me my diamond. We helped each other dress, and finally there we were in a full-length mirror: Mrs. Letty and Miss Letty. Just then a bellboy knocked on the door and handed in two beautiful rose corsages from Con.

We pinned on the corsages and looked at ourselves in the mirror. We knew we were gorgeous, and were trying to look as if we always had been. We practiced that look for at least ten minutes, wandering around our two rooms with a luxurious rustling of our taffeta petticoats, stealing glances at ourselves in any reflecting surface, hardly saying a word.

Then Con knocked, and there he was, as handsome as he'd ever be in his life in a jet-black, double-breasted, peaked-lapel tuxedo. I probably turned pale: I felt the seriousness of it. I'd only seen one man in a tuxedo in my life, and that had been at a wedding. To add to the solemnity, I knew that somewhere in that tuxedo was a diamond ring. I went down to the Empire Room on Con's arm as ceremoniously as a queen opening a parliament.

The huge room was "jumping." The first swing band I'd ever heard in the flesh was making it impossible to talk; Con found a chair for Aunt Gertrude and then took me out on the floor.

No one on that dance floor was dancing; they were packed so tight that they could only sway together, like corn stalks in a stiff breeze, and they were as still as corn, too, because trumpets and saxophones were wailing about sleepy lagoons and one dozen roses and Johnny Doughboy finding a rose in Ireland. We had to let go of each other when they started "Deep In the Heart of Texas," and clap four times at the right spots along with everyone else. When there were patriotic songs, everyone looked solemn: we were fighting a war.

Con held me tight. I liked the smell of the after-shave he was wearing – he always smelled good. His shirtfront was stiff and gleaming. He was tall enough so that the carnation in his buttonhole was right under my nose.

As the band ended a song, he kissed my forehead and whispered, "Did you mean what you told my father? Do you love me?"

Did I? I'd told his father I did – but I was afraid I'd only said it to stop him from hurting Con any more. I blushed a guilty red. To be honest, I should have told Con that I didn't know whether I loved him, but I liked him and admired...

The band saved me with a beginning blast of "The Hut-sut Song." Drowned out, I squeezed his hand and kissed it and looked up at him with what I hoped was an absolutely loving glance, and it must have been, because he blushed, too, and laughed, showing all his white teeth, and squeezed me.

We had ginger ale at Aunt Gertrude's little table, and then Con asked her to dance. Who could have dreamed of such a thing? There was Con dancing with Aunt Gertrude, while I sat in that splendid room in a perfectly beautiful new formal, watching.

About ten-thirty Aunt Gertrude said she thought we had better go up to bed after such a long day. When Con opened our hotel door for us, she thanked Con again for a perfectly beautiful evening, said goodnight and disappeared into the bedroom, but she left the door ajar.

Con and I couldn't go to bed yet, obviously; we had to sit down on the living-room couch to talk self-consciously about what we found in the newspapers on the table. After a while Con said, "Pictures of American Japanese leaving their homes. Having to live in camps."

"There isn't going to be any more rubber for civilian car tires," I said from behind my section of the paper.

Finally Aunt Gertrude caroled, "Good night, you two – I'm in bed and almost asleep already. Don't stay up too long."

I was on Con's lap before she stopped talking – all of me: rosebuds and blue net ruffles and rustling petticoats, and we kissed and kissed and whispered the words that sound so new and daring when you first say them to someone, even though they're just dog-eared old clichés. When Con finally left, his hair was a mess and there was lipstick on his chin, and I was wearing a one-carat diamond.

That diamond scared me to death. It was worth so much money! How could I go to bed wearing it – but if I didn't, wouldn't someone steal it? How could I wash my face and hands or take a bath – what if it dropped from its setting and went down a drain? The responsibility of it was fairly equal to the pleasure of it, it seemed to me, and was that the way expensive things always made you feel?

I hung up my beautiful formal and shut myself in the bathroom. No matter how late it was, I couldn't go home the next day without finding out what a shower felt like.

It felt heavenly. No waiting for the tub to fill, no soap scum and dead skin keeping you company while the water cooled, no ring to scrub, and no climbing over slippery enamel. Only warm, clean water carrying your day's dirt down the drain, and a step out on a fluffy rug and into a fluffy towel. Heavenly – and I'd have a shower of my own in June!

I put up my hair, slid into my twin bed and said my prayers, which were nothing but Thank-yous, of course. I lay warm and sleepy, and the sounds of Chicago filled the room with car horns and motors, squealing brakes, and the sirens of ambulances or fire trucks: sounds of the city where I had been born. Somewhere out there my mother and I had shivered on our narrow cots, holding

As the band ended a song, he kissed my forehead and whispered, "Did you mean what you told my father? Do you love me?"

hands while she told me stories until we fell asleep in this same March cold.

"Mom," I whispered. "I'm back in Chicago. I wish you were here with me. I'm so happy – I'm engaged and I'm going to be all right. I love you, Mom. Sleep warm under the snow."

We drove home from Chicago Saturday afternoon, and news of the engagement was in the Sunday *Waterloo Courier*. "Reverend and Mrs. Boyd S. Letty of Cedar Falls announce the engagement and approaching marriage of their niece, Miss Miranda Daisy Letty, to Mr. Conrad Raymond Beale of that city." People read the *Courier* before they went to church, so our news was out.

After breakfast on Sunday morning I came downstairs from my very own room, dressed in the beautiful new clothes I could finally wear to church. Con came to the door, escorted me to his Cadillac, and off we drove, though the church was only a block away.

For years I'd worked in that church. There wasn't a cake pan or basting spoon in the basement kitchen I couldn't find. I'd rubbed polish into pews, gone through the hymnals for left-over Sunday programs, washed grape juice glasses after Communion, and mended the choir's robes so often that I could tell you which chorister was wearing the worst one, even if I was sitting in the very back behind a pillar.

But I couldn't slip into any old pew this Sunday. Con always sat three rows from the front, and that's where we went, with the usher going before us, and Robert Laird watching us from the choir. Con was trying to look natural and so was I, even though I'd never been escorted to my seat on anybody's arm before, and everything I had on was new, and my left hand's diamond ring was blazing like a Fourth of July sparkler on Con's sleeve.

I prayed the prayers beside Con and we sang from one hymnbook, but I didn't hear a word that was said or sung;

I was trembling inside with the power I had, from my waved blonde hair to my polished toenails. I'd made a grown man propose marriage and give me a diamond and a fortune. There he sat with me in front of the whole church to show he intended to make me into a settled, safe person who would be somebody: Mrs. Conrad Beale.

He would give me a home.

So I said a little prayer of thanks for such awesome power; I certainly wasn't responsible for it. The amazement was still in my head when the service ended and Con and I had to shake hands and shake hands and thank people for their congratulations and smile until our smiles were numb.

After church I didn't go home to get dinner: Con took me to Bishop's Cafeteria in Waterloo. We were free of Cedar Falls and everyone we knew, so we laughed together over our mashed potatoes and Swiss steak and chocolate pie, getting rid of that stiff church morning. Con seemed to like being giggly and young; maybe he never had been.

"I was so lonely," he said, holding my hand on the table. "You can't imagine how lonely I was, and you were, too." He squeezed my hand and said, "No more."

When Con took me home again and I was alone in my room, I planned the excitement of going to school. When you haven't had much chance to show off, you want to make it last.

So on Monday morning, there I was, "the Lettys' hired girl," taking my usual seat in school just before the bell rang. I hadn't worn new clothes – I didn't need to – so I settled myself among the others in my old sweater and skirt and saddle shoes. Then, in the most natural way possible, I reached up with my left hand to arrange the curls at the back of my neck, and heard a hiss of breath in the seat behind me, and then whispers. The room had six lights at the ceiling, and I knew how my diamond was breaking them into a rainbow dazzle. Then I opened my notebook – with my left hand, of course – and studied whatever page I'd turned to with a fake concentration worthy of a final exam.

How delicious it is to own something nicer than anyone else has – almost as if it makes you nicer, which of course it doesn't. "Let me see your ring," Sonia Jensen said after class. I held my hand out, and other girls crowded around me to look, too.

"Is it a whole carat?" Patty Hayes whispered.

I said it was, and noticed that three other engaged girls kept their tiny little quarter-carat stones out of sight; they just looked at mine.

That afternoon in the parlor Con and I started to plan our wedding. I had to keep him from making it the most expensive production the church had ever seen. "Uncle Boyd's the minister," I said. "And don't you know there's a war on? Orchids flown in? Champagne? That's almost immoral."

"I want you to have your absolute heart's desire," Con said.

I had a lot of absolute heart's desires. One of them was to get Victoria Kline out of the basement she lived in. The next day after school I dropped in to see her – I was always doing that – and I said, "I want you to make my wedding dress." I sat beside her at her sewing machine and waited until she said she would. Then I told her what I was going to pay.

"I couldn't take that much money for a dress!" she said.

Her father said, "Glamour girls, the Rose Bowl, the comic strips, a radio diet of soft soap, laxatives, pep talks and jazz – all conspire to keep millions of us insulated from reality for many hours in the day." He was reading from *Common Sense* in his rocking chair in the May sunshine. "We are up against two-ton bombs, fifty-ton tanks and sixteen-inch shells."

"You could take that much for a dress," I said firmly. "You are a designer, not a dressmaker. Designers get paid much more. I want you to design me a beautiful wedding gown, and then I want you to look for a nice, comfortable apartment with a real kitchen and bathroom for you and your father, and use the money for the first few years of rent."

"But I'd never make enough to keep living there," she said.

"'Lucy Carver Williams is a member of a distinguished Boston family and, through marriage, is connected with the Williams family of Rhode Island fame,'" read Mr. Kline. He was through with *Common Sense* and was starting a *Ladies Home Journal*. "'In the portrait, Mrs. Williams is shown wearing some of her family jewels.'"

"Wait and see," I told Victoria. "You're going to be so busy sewing that you'll have to hire an assistant. But get my gown done first."

Mr. Kline was reading about Lucy Carver Williams' travels. I jumped up and went over to him. He had never exchanged a word with me, so I wasn't surprised when he didn't even look up, but went on reading: "'Wherever I am,' she says, 'I make it a point to have plenty of Camel cigarettes on hand.'"

"May I have some of your *Ladies Home Journals*?" I said to Mr. Kline.

He had a pile of magazines beside his chair. The beauty shop in town kept only the newest ones and gave him the others, and some of Victoria's friends contributed more. He didn't like to lose his place, so he nodded and kept reading: "'Mary is a very careful mother. Not always, her bathroom paper is terrible.'"

"Look here," I said to Victoria, opening a magazine to the usual society lady in her wedding gown. "Can't you copy any kind of dress you see?"

"I think so," Victoria said, blinking her bright little monkey eyes.

"Then you're going to make my dress exactly like one of these rich Mrs. So-and-so-the-thirds," I said. "Why not?"

Victoria and I looked through all the recent women's magazines, and settled on Mrs. Ambrose Darcy Dumond II. She had a whole page of the magazine to herself: a haughty bride lit with what looked like moonlight, but you could see every thread of lace in her dress. "That's it," I said. Could Victoria make it by June fifteenth? Indeed she could.

I gave Mr. Kline his magazines and sat down again with Victoria. "I'm wearing my new clothes to school now," I said.

"You're happy?"

"Yes," I said, and then I said, "No."

"London During An Air Raid," Mr. Kline said.

"I used to be like the 'farmie' kids—the ones that everybody left out of things," I said. "Now, just because I have nice clothes and a big diamond, the most popular senior girls talk to me. They say, 'Where'd you get those dreamy shoes?' and 'What's your wedding gown going to be like?'"

Victoria laughed her large-toothed horselaugh. I could tell her anything.

"I'm not going to tell them about my dress," I said. "Not until they beg."

They begged.

"Tell us!" they said. "Tell us what your dress is like!"

Finally I said, "Well... a designer's making it for me. She's copying the beautiful gown Mrs. Ambrose Darcy Dumond II wore at her wedding in New York – you can see it in the February *Ladies Home Journal*.

"Ooooh," they said. Two of them were marrying in June before their boyfriends went into the service.

"Golly," Janet Woodruff said. "I bet that's expensive."

I smiled and whispered, "Not if you ask my designer nicely."

"Who?"

"She's very busy just now," I said in a low voice, "but I'll tell you – it's Victoria Kline. She can copy any dress you like— from the movies— your favorite star's. Or find a dress in *Harpers Bazaar* or *Vogue* or the *Journal* and she'll make it."

"From the *movies*," crooned Marie Ford.

"Gosh!" Janet said.

So before my dress was finished, Victoria had three more wedding gowns to do – at the same good prices – and the bridesmaids' too. She hardly had time to move herself and her father to a little house near the grade school, or put up a discreet sign beside her front door: "Victoria Kline, Designer of Ladies' Fashions."

How fast April went. Benjy and Bernard said they'd be ushers at my wedding. "Who'll be your best man?" I asked Con one afternoon.

"I don't have any relative except Robert," Con said. "I've already asked him, and he says he'll help us out. He won't be drafted for a while."

Robert? Our best man?

"He's just seventeen – skipped first grade because his mother taught him to read and write," Con said. "He won't be drafted until he's eighteen late this December. He can take some college classes."

Robert Laird. Robert Laird beside Con at our wedding. I tried not to think of that when I saw Robert every day at school. I wore my diamond and hardly ever looked at him. For years I'd kept track of him at a distance: a glimpse of his back in the hall as he talked to some girl, or times when his brown eyes looked a classroom over – brown eyes that had always passed over me. I noticed that now they didn't. Much good that would do him – let him stand church beside Con. Let him watch the Gypsy Girl in a real wedding gown marrying somebody who'd never leave her at the altar.

13

"If you're going to be my bridesmaid, you'll need a nice formal," I told Betty. "And let's get you a new hairdo first – that'll be fun."

I took Betty to Waterloo to a fancy beauty shop. She'd never been in one. They gave her a permanent "because the young lady's hair is so lovely and fine." If she wore a pageboy, they said (as they soaped and rinsed and snipped and divided her hair in sections and hooked her to clamps to cook), she'd look as lovely as a movie star – maybe Deanna Durbin?

And she did look quite pretty when they were done. The fashionable girls wore their hair in coils or sausages on top, and the rest curled almost to their shoulders. Betty had sausages, and then a long, shiny pageboy. The beauty operators taught her to make pin curls and use rollers and shape her eyebrows with pencil, and we bought the right shades of lipstick. When we walked out the beauty shop door, I caught her sneaking glances in every mirror and shop window we passed.

Our next stop was Black's Department Store, and "my saleslady" said to me, "How nice to meet your cousin," while she looked Betty over. "Young ladies develop their bosoms at different rates," she said, making Betty blush and fidget. "This young lady is going to have a fine figure before long, but we can enhance it just a little, can't we, until then? If your mother questions it, just tell her that the clothes don't fit right without it."

The feminine ideal was to look as if you were wearing two funnels on top, like pictures of Petty girls and Varga

girls that were hung in the boys' school lockers and painted on bombers. Our shoulders were padded, big and
broad, and we squeezed our stomachs and thighs into girdles that made us rush to our bedrooms when we got
home to *get them off*. The stomachs of movie stars were
practically concave. We yanked at our girdles when no
one was looking, and glanced backward and down at our
calves to check our stocking seams. Some girls took an
innocent-looking pair of bobby socks to school and put
one in each side of their bra when they got there, but it
was hard to get the pointy effect with socks.

Of course Betty couldn't "develop" all at once. We
bought three bras in graduated padding, so that she could
"enhance her bosom" a little more every few months. We
bought her a girdle, too, and nylons, and silver slippers,
and a pretty pink formal with puffed sleeves.

"Such a nice formal," Aunt Gertrude said when Betty
came home glowing with her new hairdo and bridesmaid dress. "Both of you will look lovely at the Junior-
Senior Prom."

Us? Betty and I looked at each other.

"You'll go with Mr. Beale, of course," my aunt said to
me. I stared at her and realized that I had a date at last –
a permanent date. "In your new blue formal."

The Junior-Senior Prom! "And Betty's bound to have
a date, too," I said. Betty giggled and patted her new
pageboy. "Doesn't she look pretty?"

The Junior-Senior Prom was the talk of the school
every spring. This year I didn't hover on the edges of that
talk – I had my new clothes and my big diamond. Arlene
Brown, the Homecoming Queen, said to me after history
class, "Come on down to the Women's Clubhouse
Saturday morning. The seniors with dates are building a
papier-mâché wishing well for the middle of the ballroom."

So there I was with the popular girls, soaking newspapers in paste and twisting crepe paper into flowers and

streamers. We talked while we worked – endless discussions of boys, formals, corsages, and hairdos.

"What's your dress like?" Mary Hogan asked me.

"It's one I wore in Chicago to dance in the Empire Room at the Palmer House," I said. "So it's not brandnew." I laughed a little as if I were confessing an embarrassment, when I knew they were all speechless with envy.

When prom night came, Con and I drove to the Cedar Falls Women's Clubhouse high on its green slope, a confection of white gingerbread porches. Con parked his Cadillac right in front, walked around it to open the car door for me, and offered me his arm. How nice he looked in his expensive suit. "I'm certainly going to show off tonight," he said. "I'm an old, confirmed bachelor, and I've won the most beautiful blonde in town."

So we entered that Clubhouse laughing, to be met at the door by Joe Stepler's parents, our formally dressed prom chaperons. They greeted the couple ahead of us with the usual indulgent smiles parents give the young, but I saw them rearrange their expressions instantly when they saw Con.

"Good evening, Mr. Beale," Mr. Stepler said with a deferential handshake. "We're so pleased you could come tonight." He remembered me. "And Miranda."

Mrs. Stepler's voice had a trace of indulgence in it again. "How pretty you look, dear."

"She's beautiful," Con said, towering over the Steplers.

"Oh, yes," Mr. Stepler said quickly. "Beautiful indeed." And I swept into the clubhouse on Con's arm, my blue dress rustling, Con's diamond flashing on my hand and my back very straight. No wonder I could meet Robert's dark eyes without flinching when he brought Mary Hogan into the ballroom a few minutes later.

"An orchid!" Sonia Jensen said, staring at Con's corsage on my shoulder.

"It's real!" Patty Hayes touched one of its white petals.

"Hi," Betty said, coming up on Bill Jensen's arm. She looked very pretty in her bridesmaid dress, and she had on her second largest bra; I could tell. The boys were signing the girls' dance programs, and in a little while Betty whispered, "My program's *all full!*" It dangled from her wrist, and she'd hang it on her bedroom mirror later: a trophy. She was going to have a wonderful time.

"Every dance for me," Con said, and signed my program: C. Beale, C. Beale, C. Beale. "You're mine."

Con could dance – he was good at it now. We didn't jitterbug at proms: we danced to records of wartime songs that reminded us how soon most of the boys would be overseas: "He Wears a Pair of Silver Wings" and "Kiss the Boys Goodbye" and "This Is My Country" and "The White Cliffs of Dover." Con and I danced close together like the other engaged couples, and toasted each other in ginger ale punch, and laughed at our own jokes. The ballroom's tall French doors stood open to spring air, and I was so happy I never even looked to see where Robert Laird was.

But suddenly Robert was beside me, his hand on Con's shoulder. "Cutting in," he said.

Con was going to let Robert dance with me. Robert was his cousin. I saw it in his eyes and felt his hand start to leave mine. In that split second I whispered, "No. I don't want to," and snatched Con's hand back, and turned us away. Robert was left by himself among the dancing couples for everyone to see, and the flash in his eyes said he wouldn't forget it.

My face was red, I knew it, and my hand was wet in Con's. "What's the matter?" he asked when we'd waltzed to the other side of the room. "You don't want to dance with him?"

"No," I said.

"Why not?" Con asked in his nice, gentle voice, bending down a little to hear what I said over the beat of "I Guess I'll Have To Dream the Rest."

"He's...not like you," I said, and knew I was right.

"A lot handsomer," Con said.

"He's mean," I said. "That's one reason I'm marrying you. You couldn't be mean to anybody."

"Not to you," Con said. "Not ever. I can't imagine any man with two eyes being mean to you."

"Robert was. We had a date when the play closed, and he stood me up. In front of all the people in *The Gypsy Girl*. I ran to Victoria's and cried on her shoulder until it was time to go home."

Con looked bewildered. "Why? Why would Robert do that?"

"I...wouldn't kiss him," I said. "Except in the play. He was mad. He was getting even." I looked Con in the eye. "But what did I care, after all? I had you to kiss."

Con's dark eyes glowed at me under their long lashes. His face turned pink, and I thought for a second he was going to kiss me in front of everybody, especially Robert Laird.

Graduation Day was a hot day; we could hardly wait to get our robes and mortarboards off. Robert and I took quite a few honors between us. After the photographs and Con's lovely present of my very own typewriter, I walked to the cemetery and took the gravel path among the stones.

The grass above my mother's grave matched the grass around her now; she had sunk into the quiet, smooth green.

I knelt at her stone with the gardenia corsage Con had given me, and put my graduation program there under the flowers. "I've graduated from high school, Mom," I whispered. "I wanted you to know. And I'm going to be married in a week to Conrad Raymond Beale. You'd like him. You'd have a son, if you were here." Tears came to my eyes and blurred the gardenias on the grass.

Red light from the setting sun cast the shadow of young leaves over us. I was sobbing, and didn't hear Robert Laird's step; he was beside me when I looked up. "I thought you'd be here," he said. "I came to my father's grave."

A breeze fluttered fern in the corsage at my feet. The Beale plot was hidden beyond a hedge; I'd seen his father's grave there, alone near the big granite slab that said "Beale," where S.C.'s wife, Lillian, was buried.

I got to my feet and turned to go.

"I thought I'd be starting college this summer, but I can't," Robert said. I turned back, though I hardly wanted to talk to him. "I've got to make some money working at the drugstore. You're starting in the fall, too?"

I nodded. We stood in silence among the gravestones.

Suddenly Robert said in a rough tone, "At the end of December I'll be called up."

"I know," I said. The setting sun picked out scarlet threads along the edge of his suit coat. "I'm sorry," I said.

He took a carnation out of his buttonhole and fiddled with it. "I'm the one who's sorry. Standing you up after *The Gypsy Girl*."

"It's turned out all right," I said. "I'm sorry I didn't dance with you."

He handed me his red carnation. "Then we're both sorry."

I smiled at him. "It's late. I have to go now," I said, and left him there among the graves.

When I was home again and in my room with the door shut, I sat on my bed and looked at Robert's red carnation, and thought of all the years I'd watched him, and all the years he'd never wanted me. Hidden under the paper in my dresser's bottom drawer were clippings about Robert Laird's winning debates, Robert Laird's football victories...

I tore them all into tiny bits and tossed them in my wastebasket. I couldn't throw away a fresh carnation – I put it in a jelly glass on my dresser. The only thing left under the drawer lining was what had been my most prized memento when I was nine: Robert's broken shoestring he'd left on the playground. I threw it away, too.

Someone knocked at my bedroom door, and I called, "Come in."

"I thought maybe we could have a little talk," Aunt Gertrude said, and settled on the other end of my bed, looking uncomfortable. "Since you'll be married in a week."

"Yes?" I said. We'd already practiced where I'd stand and what I'd say, and the march up the aisle – it wouldn't be easy with my long veil.

My aunt started picking at her cuticle; she did that when she was nervous. I had to look away because I never could stand to see her do it. "About what marriage is like," she said. "With your husband."

"Oh," I said. I blushed, and a kind of dread settled on me. If she had to talk about it, it must be worse than I thought. What I thought wasn't much. I simply had no idea of anything past kissing and "necking," and nobody I knew could tell me, or would. I'd seen cats at it once, I thought, acting as if they were playing leapfrog. What did people do?

"Your husband will expect it," my aunt said in a desperate voice, not looking at me. "It makes him happy and it's good for him. You just let him. It only hurts at first. I'll pack some little flannel squares in your suitcase, and you put two under your pillow."

To my relief, she didn't say anything more. She managed to smile at me and left the room fast. We'd had the same kind of short conversation when I got "the curse." The "curse" talk had been as unpleasant and vague as this one, and both dealt with matters I really didn't want to think about. So I lay on my bed and dreamed of my wedding gown and my wedding bouquet and the reception the church women would put on – all delightful things that stood between me and Aunt Gertrude's "little talk."

And then there was the pleasure of the rehearsal dinner at Con's house. If ever I'd felt the grandeur of my new life descending on me, it was that night. There I was, the soon-to-be Mrs. Conrad Beale, sitting at Mr. Beale's right hand in his beautiful house, with Conrad so in love that it was impossible to find a second when he wasn't looking at me, while Robert did the same whenever he could. My aunt and uncle and cousins were trying to pretend they often visited houses like that, but they were so quiet I hardly recognized them. They looked sidewise at everything when they could, including the housekeeper, Mrs. Pell, who looked sidewise right back at them.

But I smiled in everybody's face, happy as I was, and trained to be a hostess by my aunt, too. I persuaded Aunt Gertrude to talk about helping at the school when everybody was issued their War Ration Book One. She started very stiffly, but limbered up (she was wearing her beautiful silk dress) and made us laugh at fibs people told about hoarding sugar so they wouldn't have stamps torn out of their new ration books.

Betty could talk about the spelling bee. The boys could tell about the high school football team. I finally got Uncle Boyd and Mr. Beale talking about Dr. Price, president of the college. "What's he going to do to keep I.S.T.C. going?" Mr. Beale said. "Almost every male student will be gone soon. If you don't fill the classrooms, you can't pay professors."

"If you don't fill the dorms, you can't make payments on dorm loans," Uncle Boyd said. The older men would carry the conversation now; the rest of us could relax and enjoy the china and glassware and silver and all the food, (though the food wasn't very good), while I sat in the place of honor and enjoyed myself.

After dinner Uncle Boyd took us through the wedding rehearsal in the dim, empty church sanctuary. It would be beautifully decorated the next morning: Con was paying for the whole wedding and wouldn't hear of Uncle Boyd spending a cent.

My uncle talked about "the bride." "The bride stands here...the bride gives her bouquet..." What was so familiar about being put through those paces? *The Gypsy Girl*, of course: Miss Harmon yelling, "The bride paces slowly to center stage! Robert – keep up with the orchestra and for heaven's sake, *don't* step on her veil!"

My wedding dress was as beautiful as Mrs. Dumond II's. I'd modeled it as Victoria made it, but when Betty and I took it off its hanger on my wedding morning and I started to put it on, there was a surprise in it; I got tears in my eyes and gave a sob and had to stop.

"What's the matter?" Betty said.

"I miss my mother" was all I said. Betty hadn't seen what I saw. Inside the dress and right above where my heart would be, Victoria had put a small heart of my mother's rose-patterned cloth, sewn on the lining with beautiful little stitches.

Con had given me lovely pearls, and insisted on ordering real orange blossoms for the circlet on my hair – just like Mrs. Dumond II's. What a fragrance they had, along with more of them in my huge wedding bouquet. My veil was billowing tulle that followed me into the sanctuary like smoke.

Our organist began the wedding march. I paced slowly down the white-spread aisle on my uncle's arm, Betty before me in her pale pink formal with her own orange blossom wreath and big bouquet. Had there ever been such a beautiful wedding in that sanctuary, trimmed as it was with flowers at the end of every pew and great bouquet fans at either side of the ranks of candles?

I squeezed my uncle's arm, and he squeezed back as we passed all the profiles turned half our way, too polite to look over shoulders as we came. There was Con waiting beside the altar, his eyes on me as if there were no one else in the crowded church.

And there was Robert Laird. I tried not to look at him, but I did anyway, for a second. Oh, but he was handsome in his white tuxedo – so handsome that I suppose every woman there figured the best man was the best man.

I didn't look at Robert again; I kept my eyes on Con. I'd watched Robert Laird for years; now he could watch me.

He was doing it. Is there a woman in the world who isn't at her very best coming down the aisle as a bride? Every inch of her is as perfect as weeks of planning and hours of fussing can make it, and bridal gowns are so extravagantly virginal that a woman might as well be wearing one of those signs they put on new business buildings: "Soon to be..."

Uncle Boyd gave me away, and then a borrowed minister from another church took us through our vows. As I looked at Con, I had to see Robert at his elbow, and my ring went from Robert's hand to Con's hand, and from Con's hand to mine. I was numb, but I noticed that.

"I do," Con said, and so did I, and we kissed there between Betty and Robert, then trailed my veil down the aisle past the Letty family and Con's father in his wheelchair to stand in a line and shake hands with everyone and smile, smile, smile.

The church basement was as bright as a basement gets on a sunny June morning, but it smelled the way it always had. Church people had worked very hard on the refreshments and bowls of non-alcoholic punch. "How beautiful you look," people said to me. "What a lovely bride."

"It's your dress," I whispered to Victoria Kline who stood nearby.

"It's the bride," Victoria said, hugging me. "He'd better do his best to deserve you."

Uncle Boyd drove S.C. and his wheelchair home. After an hour or two Con left to bring his car to the church door – we'd change clothes at the parsonage and be on our way to Chicago. I escaped wedding guests for a moment in the vestibule between doors, watching for Con.

But Robert found me standing in that dim place. He shut himself in the vestibule with me and said, "The best man gets to kiss the bride," and squashed me and my satin and veil against his white tuxedo. His eyes were cool but his lips were hot – I had to push him away to catch my breath, and he laughed.

"Stand on the steps outside and let me take your picture," he said.

"Wipe the lipstick off," I said.

"Wipe off yours," he said, grinning. I rubbed my smeared lips with the back of my hand, and posed for him against the arched church door just as people burst through it with rice to throw. They shouted congratulations and good wishes as Con and I got my yards of white into the car.

When we left them behind, I put my head on Con's white wool shoulder, thankfully. The Cadillac was festooned with crepe paper. My cousins had scattered rice over the car seats and floor; cans and old shoes thumped and rattled behind us.

We changed our clothes at the parsonage, and ran another gauntlet of teasing and rice, thanks to my cousins. As we drove away from the parsonage and I waved goodbye to the Lettys, I had the feeling you get when a very long tunnel suddenly shoots you into sunlight.

I looked at Con beside me. We were alone. We'd be by ourselves the whole honeymoon. Once you were married, nobody had a right to watch the two of you night and day. I'd thought of that, but I hadn't felt it.

Now I could snuggle close to Con, even while we were driving through our hometown. If I liked, I could kiss him at every stop sign and red light all the way to our Chicago hotel. We acted like kids, stopping at a little roadside park to put our car's "Just Married" signs and crepe paper and the cans and old shoes in the trash bin there. We teased each other and made faces and giggled even while we ate lunch and dinner in fancy restaurants. When Con finally turned a key and we were alone in our hotel suite that night, we were floating on our jokes and the champagne we'd had, and liked each other a lot.

He'd managed to tell me he was a virgin, too. I suppose a pair of virgins trying to figure things out would be hilarious to most people. We took our clothes off in the dark and lay down together, and I probably felt as strange to him as he felt strange to me, since I'd never been skin-to-skin with anybody, except perhaps when I was a baby, and I didn't think he had, either. He maneuvered until I was under him in a face-to-face position, which seems very odd to a woman who's always been told to keep her knees together, and poor Con must have felt uncomfortable on his knees and elbows that way.

I didn't think I ought to be so bold as to touch him, but I could feel something, and wriggled in order to steer it in what I thought was the right direction. Since he started hurting me, I guessed I had the correct place, but I cringed and gave a little moan, and he stopped and slid over beside me.

"Go on," I said. "It has to hurt."

"I don't want to," Con said. I felt for him and he was lying face down. "I don't *want* to hurt you." His voice was muffled in a pillow. "And what good is it? We can't even have a baby."

Ah, now that was real hurting. I squirmed under him until his face was between my breasts, and I whispered, "We do it for *love*. Babies have nothing to do with it. Do you think I married you to have a baby?"

He kissed me and kissed me and tried it again, and we fitted together that time, hurting and all. How strange. So that was what people did. I could never have believed it. The two pieces of flannel under my pillow came in handy.

How relieved I was. I went to sleep in a few breaths.

But I had to wake up in the morning and remember everything. I sat up, found I was in bed with this hairy, large, strange person, and turned red with embarrassment. Con must have felt the same, because when I grabbed a sheet to wrap up in, he took a blanket. We didn't look at each other. We politely asked a mirror or a door, "Would you like to use the bathroom first" and "Are we going downstairs to breakfast?" We dressed by ourselves, each in a room, and what a relief it was to me when Con appeared in his clothes, and was the Con I recognized. I suppose he felt the same way about that girl in bed with him.

We sat across from each other at a little table in the coffee shop and ordered from a menu. While I ordered, Con watched me, and while Con ordered I watched him. It was so very adult to be a couple ordering breakfast. We were both wearing wedding rings. A touch of pride crept into our voices as we said, "Coffee please," and before the waiter had turned his back, we smiled into each other's eyes and were proud indeed, I think. We had done everything that was required of a wedding day and a wedding night, so now we could have fun, though Con could only be away from Beale Equipment on Saturday, Sunday and Monday.

It was Chicago, my native city. Dressed in my fine new clothes, I ate with my new husband in restaurants, danced in a nightclub – a nightclub! – as dazzling as a movie set. For the first time in my life I saw a real play in a real theater, with real actors becoming real people before my eyes, effortlessly and perfectly, the whole evening long.

I entered my first art museum whispering to Con, for I felt as if we were guests in an abandoned palace. The paintings and statues, room after room, seemed like riches left behind when some king packed up his household and fled, leaving no ordinary furniture but chairs where uniformed guards sat, yawning. Our footsteps and our whispers echoed in that silence.

When we went out to the city streets, uniforms were everywhere. I'm ashamed to say that a war seemed a romantic, thrilling business to me when I was eighteen. The boys one year ahead of me in high school were already in training; eighteen-year-olds seemed years older in their marine green, army khaki or navy blue, as if they were wearing their big brothers' clothes.

The girls seemed suddenly older, too. They were supposed to marry a soldier and send him off happy to fight. "Marry him, honey," a woman said to me in the theater lobby. "He'll need you at home when he's over there."

But Con wasn't going over there. One afternoon a man waiting beside us on a street corner said to Con, "When are you reporting for duty?"

Con said, "I – can't."

I hoped Con didn't hear what the man said as the light changed and we stepped off the curb: "Yellow belly!"

S.C. in his wheelchair met us at his door when we came back from our honeymoon and I was swept up to be carried over the threshold like a cave woman stolen in a raid. S.C. sat in the doorway with no expression on his face. For a moment I thought he wasn't going to let us in – then he rolled his chair back.

We retreated to our big bedroom and bath. When Con shut our door, we hugged and kissed, shut away from the world. "Do you like the house?" Con whispered in bed that night.

"I love it," I whispered back, "but not as much as I love you."

Con gave a happy little grunt. "You deserve every beautiful thing. When I saw you in that parsonage, I wanted to pile all the money I had in your lap."

"And my pockets, and my shoes, and down the front of my dress!" I said, and we laughed and squeezed each other and settled down "spoon-fashion." It's such a comfortable way to sleep – you either hug or are hugged all night long.

The bell for breakfast rang the next morning: a discreet ding-dong in the hall. I came to the table with Con, bringing my best manners, of course, smiling at Mrs. Pell and asking if S.C. had slept well.

Neither of them seemed to hear me. Mrs. Pell disappeared kitchen-ward without a sound; S.C. rattled his *Des Moines Register* as he folded it in quarters and propped it against his water glass.

Con gave me a contrite look; had he forgotten to tell me something? I ate my breakfast silently and so did he, but we managed to play footsie under the table and held hands there, too, when we could. Underhanded, you see, already.

"Dad likes to read at meals," Con told me before he left for work. "Meant to tell you. He likes it quiet."

I started to say, *Let him eat by himself then, so we can talk*, but I couldn't. I was a stranger in somebody else's house. I was lucky to be there.

When Con and his father left for work, I explored our big bedroom and bath, our private place. When I'd asked Aunt Gertrude what she thought of the Beale house, she looked down her sharp nose at me. "Not clean," she said. "And that dinner was hardly edible. Mrs. Pell's lazy. Had her way there for years, plain to see. You'll have to bring her up short."

My aunt was right. Though two busy men might not notice, there was dust in corners and dirt on the plumbing, and our breakfast eggs were like leather. Would I have to tell a woman old enough to be my grandmother...

I didn't want to think about it. I put my underwear and stockings in drawers Con had cleared for me. My clothes hung next to his in our closet, silent witnesses to marriage.

S.C. in his wheelchair met us at the door when we came back
from our honeymoon and I was swept up to be carried over the
threshold like a cave woman stolen in a raid. For a moment
I thought S.C. wasn't going to let us in.

Nothing I had brought in my luggage belonged to my hired-girl days, except a toy church, a small book with pictures of kittens, a celluloid doll, and a cloth heart sewed inside my wedding dress.

I went softly down the hall to a sunroom that was full of wicker and chintz, with a braided rug on the linoleum floor. The dining room's stiff mahogany stood ready for formal dinners, but the table wasn't polished, and the sheer curtains looked dingy.

Fashionable "earth tones" were in every room: cream, tan, beige, brown, gray or, for a bold touch, "dusty rose" or "rust." Con's bedroom was cream and brown, his father's room was tan, the bathrooms and kitchen were hospital white, and dusty roses spotted the living room carpet and bloomed in the drapes.

I'd never seen windows that cranked out and back and had rolling screens. I opened one in the living room and tried to pull the screen down, but it shot up again – zip, bang.

"You lock it at the bottom," the housekeeper said, giving me a start. Mrs. Pell moved through that house as if she didn't use her feet, but floated like an owl floats over a mouse: you never heard her until it was too late. "Push the triggers into the slots," she said, demonstrating.

"Thanks," I said. "It seemed a little close in here – I thought I'd get some air."

"Brings in the dust," she said, folding her hands over her ample stomach. She was a square Danish woman: square jaw, square hips, and low-heeled oxfords set squarely on the carpet. She was not about to smile. She was not about to leave. She watched until I rolled the screen up and closed the window.

When I turned back to her, she was gone. I didn't hear the kitchen door shut; only a rectangle of summer light blinked in the hall and vanished.

15

I should have been happy. My hours were my own. During the week I packed my lunch after breakfast and rode the bicycle Con had bought me into long and idle summer days that I hadn't had since I was nine.

Iowa State Teachers College was waiting for me. I went along the creaking, shining old floors of the Auditorium Building to find out what classes I would be taking my first quarter. Then I bought the textbooks.

"Look at you," Con said when he came home and found me in my "study." The bed was gone, the book-shelves and typewriter were installed, and I could sit at my desk, or in an easy chair, or bask outside on the patio in the summer breeze.

Con came to look over my shoulder. "I'm writing out the answers to the chapter questions," I said.

"You don't need college," Con said. "You're perfectly capable of educating yourself."

Most afternoons I went to the college library. Arlene Brown, the prettiest girl in my senior class, was there as much as I was; finally we laughed about it. "You're a book lover, too," she said one day.

"Devoted," I said.

"Eternally worshipful," Arlene said. "That's me." Our aim was to sound sophisticated and "with it" – a large vocabulary was sexy; it was the way Katherine Hepburn talked, or Claudette Colbert.

After that Arlene and I often met on her porch swing or my patio chairs to read the newest novels to each other and drink lemonade. We read *For Whom the Bell Tolls*, and both of us read pretty fast when we came to those parts where "the earth moved." Arlene didn't know what Hemingway had in mind, I don't think, but neither did I. The lovers rolled up in Robert Jordan's robe seemed to be having some kind of seizure. I certainly hadn't felt the earth move when I made love to Con, and I didn't think he had, either, no matter how much we loved each other. But the book's ending was wonderfully sad and valiant, and made Arlene and me cry into our lemonade.

Sometimes I had sodas with Patty Hayes and Sonia Jensen, who were going to ISTC in the fall, too. Sometimes I sewed for Victoria when she had a wedding deadline. I canned the summer's fruits and vegetables with Aunt Gertrude and Betty on the old cream-colored parsonage stove whose enamel tulips had seemed so luxurious to me once. When I came through the patched screen door of the parsonage kitchen, I was, for a second, my orphan self, washing pieces of my mother's dress, or doing the dishes alone. Then, magically, I was Mrs. Conrad Beale, "helping" my aunt and being thanked for it, too.

I could see the Letty family so clearly now – didn't I know every trick they had for looking neat and "respectable," though shabby? And didn't I have so much money to spend? "Go ahead," Con told me, "buy the Lettys some more decent clothes. They've looked forlorn for years, but I couldn't do much about it. Now you can."

So I took Betty to Black's again. "You'll need some summer outfits for dates," I told her, and she blushed, because Bill Jensen was taking her to the movies almost every week. "And let's buy you some sets of sweaters and skirts for fall, too, and shoes, and a winter coat – your old one's worn out – and hats."

When Uncle Boyd and Aunt Gertrude saw Betty's new wardrobe, they sat down in the parlor with me and told me I was spending too much.

"Perhaps you should save the money Mr. Beale gives you," Uncle Boyd said.

"He told me it would make him angry if I did," I said. "You've never had money for nice things,' he tells me. 'I want you to enjoy them now.'"

"It's for *you* to enjoy, you see?" Uncle Boyd said. "The money isn't for us. Not that we aren't grateful – "

"But Conrad knows how delighted I am to buy things for you," I said to my aunt. "Wouldn't you enjoy buying things for me if you had some money?"

"Well, I suppose..." Aunt Gertrude stopped, flustered.

"I hope we would," Uncle Boyd said.

"Didn't you take me in when I was just a heartsick, lost nine-year-old orphan who wasn't even any relation to Aunt Gertrude?" I said. "Didn't I cry every night because my whole world was gone, and didn't you comfort me?"

"I hope we did," Uncle Boyd said.

"You gave me a place to keep my three toys," I said to Uncle Boyd. "And you told me what kind of people my mother and father were. I'll never forget that."

"Yes," Uncle Boyd said.

"So I want you and the boys to have new clothes, too," I told him. "You need a new winter coat, Uncle Boyd, and you should have new shirts and two suits and shoes and ties, too. And the boys should have suits for dances at school – they're getting old enough to dance – and pants and sweaters and new coats for next winter. Get some summer things for the three of you – "

"I don't know," my uncle said, frowning at the rug. "What will people say?"

"They'll say our relative has helped us," Aunt Gertrude said. "That's all. The Greenlees got money from his brother, didn't they? Nobody thought that was odd. And the Bannings have nice clothes; they've got a rich grandfather."

So Uncle Boyd and Benjy and Bernard had their turn. Being male, they tried not to show how much they liked new clothes, but anybody could see it. And Aunt Gertrude and I went shopping for her, too, until she had a minister's-wife wardrobe that delighted her.

But the Lettys found that new clothes created a major problem. "It won't look right, will it?" my aunt said to my uncle one afternoon when all of us were having iced tea. "The whole family suddenly wearing new clothes?"

The six of us discussed it.

"We can't wear our winter coats," Benjy said. "It's July."

"Of course not," Aunt Gertrude said, no doubt thinking of mink collars. Betty said she wished she could wear her blue coat with the real seal buttons – maybe there'd be a cold wave?

Uncle Boyd said, "Remember, most people are having awfully lean times."

"They'll certainly notice," Aunt Gertrude said. "The minute we step out the door."

"Just one of us can wear something new to church each Sunday," Uncle Boyd said. "How about that? The rest of us will wear our old things. That way people can see that we may have nice clothes, but we don't intend to wear them all the time and show off."

"Who starts?" Bernard asked. "There's five of us."

"We can draw straws," Aunt Gertrude said.

"How many Sundays are there in July?" Benjy said. "Who's got a calendar?"

Uncle Boyd carried one in his billfold; he took it out and looked at it. "July, you'll be sad to hear, has only four Sundays," he said. "But this has to be the first time I've heard anybody in this house wish there were more Sundays in a month."

"I don't have to wear my new summer suit to church," Aunt Gertrude said. "I can wear it to the Ladies Aid."

"I can wear one of my suits to the church board meeting," Uncle Boyd said.

"Then we've got an extra July Sunday," Benjy said.

"And then can we begin with the other clothes?" Betty said. "Summer will be over before I get to wear my yellow cotton suit!"

"Maybe weekdays should be another case," Uncle Boyd said. "Maybe each of you can wear one new thing every week?"

"Looks like you've figured out what to do," I said. "I'll be going now – I told Victoria I'd help her with some sewing this afternoon. She's got three weddings this month."

I left them drawing straws in the parlor, and walked along streets where Monday afternoon washings hung in sunny rows from clothesline after clothesline. When I went up Victoria's porch stairs, I met Carol Jacobs going down.

"Another wedding?" I asked Victoria.

"Not until August," she said. "Thank goodness."

Victoria's electric fan rippled layers of chiffon spread on her cutting table as we settled down to hem two bridesmaids' dresses.

"'In the Battle of Midway we sank seventeen Japanese ships, including four aircraft carriers. Japan lost 275 planes and 4800 men,'" Mr. Kline said, reading a newspaper in his rocking chair by the window.

In a little while Victoria said to me, "You're not your usual cheerful self."

I sighed. "I hate having Mrs. Pell sneaking up on me. And I hate seeing that beautiful house so dirty. But S.C. pays her, and she won't change anything unless he tells her to. I asked her if Con and I could have breakfast in the sunroom, 'so we won't disturb Mr. Beale while he reads his paper.' She said she only took orders from S.C.."

"She's been there for years."

"She acts as if I'm some troublesome playmate of Con's she wishes would go home," I said. "And she's got Ironclad Rules. Dozens. Take napkins, now – they can't be folded in rectangles – she'll glare at you and snatch them if you put them down that way. They have to be folded in triangles. And the window shades. Every one is pulled exactly a foot down."

"In case anyone passing by has a yardstick and a ladder?"

"Towels," I said. "The minute you use one, it's unfolded, and that won't do. She's as quiet as a cat. You never know when you'll find her in your bathroom, folding your towels in thirds again. And garbage. It has to go in empty canned food cans. The minute you fix soup for yourself – and you must leave the can lid attached – she grabs the soup can, rinses it completely clean, and waits until there's garbage to put in it. We have the most immaculate garbage in the neighborhood – it's canned."

Victoria's homely face changed completely when she laughed – I loved to see her laugh.

"There's a rule for everything," I said. "She doesn't cook what S.C. and Con like – she cooks chicken a la king because it's Tuesday and scalloped potatoes and ham because it's Saturday, and you can hardly eat any of them. We have to leave the daily paper nicely folded on a certain table after we read it, or the world will end. We'll die of germs if she uses the dishwasher. We'll live in sin if any glass or cup sits on its rim in the cupboard. But the house is dirty."

"She's had the place to herself for so long."

"She doesn't have it to herself at night – she goes home," I said through clenched teeth. "And she doesn't have it on Thursday afternoons – it's her day off."

"Hmmm," was all Victoria said.

"I have to do something. I have to start somewhere. But Mrs. Pell isn't my worst problem – S.C. is."

"'The Sixth District of the American Legion has voted to urge the federal government to deport all Americans of Japanese descent to Japan when the war is over,'" Mr. Kline read.

"Supper time is torture-time for Con – I couldn't believe it at first," I said. "S.C.'s words flick across the table just like a toad's tongue and hit Con where it hurts the most. And Con just sits there."

Victoria took the pins from her mouth. "Why?"

"Why does he just sit there? I don't know. It makes me... not respect him – I hate it!"

"And he knows how you feel?"

"I try to hide it. I have to listen every night, and jam food in my mouth so I won't yell at S.C.."

"But Con must notice. Doesn't he care if you respect him – "

"He does!" I cried. "I know he does!"

"Then what's so important that he won't talk back to his father, even if he's losing your respect? He's a coward, maybe? Can't stand up for himself?"

"Oh, no!" I said. It wasn't any use trying to baste the dress hem – I dropped it on my knee and sat thinking instead. "He runs the company. Tells the men what to do, and women too, and goes traveling to get war contracts – works so hard. And people call him 'Yellow Belly' and 'War Profiteer' ! I thought we'd entertain, but we never do, except for the Lettys at Sunday dinner now and then, because he knows what people call him – and he's doing so much for the war effort!"

"He must need a lot of self-confidence." Victoria turned a satin sleeve inside out. "To stand against his father and the town. He's a strong man, I should think." She broke a thread with her large teeth. "Brave."

"'A new kind of correspondence called 'V-mail' has been sent from New York City to London,'" Mr. Kline read from the paper. "'It will soon be used for overseas mail. Letters are written on prescribed forms and micro-filmed.'"

I stared at Victoria. "Brave."

"He must love his father, mustn't he?" She smiled at me. "And knows he can count on you to understand?"

There she sat with her little bright eyes and her big ears and her kind smile. "Oh, Victoria!" was all I could say.

Con and his father worked late that night, their papers spread on a table in the sunroom. I heard S.C. shouting at Con, and Con's quiet voice answering, and knew Con wouldn't get any rest that evening.

When we could, Con and I escaped the house after supper to walk downtown to a movie, or hear a band concert in Overman Park, or dance at the Electric Park Ballroom. But most of our free evenings we simply walked the dark streets of town, passing older men watering their lawns, the fan of water glistening and hissing. Porch swings creaked at house after house in company with laughter and the chink of ice in glasses. Children played tag and Red Rover and Sardines under the streetlights until parents called them home to bed.

"I want to show you the Company," Con said the next night as we walked hand in hand. "It's the family business, and I'm proud of it."

I wanted to see it very much, I told him, so the next Wednesday morning I went with Con and S.C. to Beale Equipment Company. I'd passed it often in the last nine years: it was an ivy-covered brick building beside the river. Hundreds of women and middle-aged men worked there now; cafes and small shops clustered around it.

Con helped his father into his wheelchair, and I held the big door while Con rolled S.C. into a building that seemed to be all one room, alive with clanging and shouts. Sunlight streamed from high windows and a hole in the roof to light a railroad car on tracks in the floor. Men were hauling sheets of metal from it, loading them on wooden carts in the hot, dusty air.

We couldn't talk until Con pushed S.C. into a big office in one corner and shut the door. "Dad's office," Con told me, rolling his father behind a desk. "Mine's back here."

Con's office was small and dark, a warren of shelved papers and file cabinets, but it was quieter. We sat down on the only two chairs, and Con said, "We're lucky we laid that railroad spur right into the factory last year, just before the government said we could finish any products we'd already started, but we couldn't use any more steel. It was tough – Dad just about gave up. But he let me go to Washington, and we got contracts with the War Department, so we're making powder canisters and land mines and strap wenches."

I giggled. "Strapping wenches – no wonder you're never home."

"They're for unscrewing hot machine gun barrels," Con said, and then chuckled himself, and I laughed and he laughed, but we had to stop when a man appeared at the door. It was a foreman; Con introduced us. "Maybe you'll be more comfortable in Dad's office," Con said to me. "It's noisier, but there's more space."

I sat down near S.C.'s desk. His office was paneled in wood, with leather chairs and gold-framed pictures. S.C. read a newspaper at his desk; I watched a procession of men and women pass through the big office to the little one beyond. When the door opened, the sounds of motors and ringing metal filled the room. The workers nodded to S.C. as they passed, and looked me over, too: the boss's new daughter-in-law.

"Come out on the floor," Con said to me after a little while. "You won't see anything quite like this again. We're installing a new fifty-thousand-pound press, thanks to the government."

He wheeled S.C. out and I followed him. "We're bringing it through the roof," Con said. "Only way we can do it."

The great press was already dangling in air under the roof hole, unwieldy and gleaming. Workers retreated among the machines along the wall as it slowly descended. It came to rest exactly on a chalked rectangle on the floor, and the men and women cheered. "Now," Con said, grinning at me, "you've seen the event of the month, and I'll take you back home. It's going to be too hot to be comfortable in here pretty soon."

As we drove home I said, "It looks as if S.C. just sits there, and you keep the company going."

"Guess so," Con said.

"And you have to listen to him criticize you," I said. "It's not fair." I kept my eyes on the river as we crossed the bridge to town. "Could we ever move?"

Con didn't answer. I said, "Couldn't we find our own home right now? You work on business with your dad some nights, and take him to work, but Mrs. Pell runs his house, and we could live near him. He can stand, and he can walk a little. He can take care of himself."

"I want that, too," Con said. "But it's not that easy."

"Why?"

"Dad's...got the money," Con said. "That's it."

"He wants you to live with him?"

"He enjoys it," Con said in a bitter voice I hadn't heard before. "You can tell."

"Yes," I said.

"He hates everything," Con said. "I try to feel sorry for him. He hates not running the factory any more. He hates the way our workers come to me, not him. He hates not being able to walk or work much since his car accident. He hates not having grandchildren. I'm not going off to war, and the men at the factory let him know how they feel about that. He hates getting old. And he's always in pain – that's the worst part. I think that's what makes him mean."

When Con drove into the garage, we sat a moment there in the reflected light of a summer morning.

"Dad didn't get the family farm when his father died. He got money. He bought the old Blanchard Equipment Company and was just beginning to break even when he drove off the road in that rainstorm. Just beginning to succeed."

I put my arms around Con in the quiet garage. "You're a wonderful man," I said. "A wonderful son. I don't know how you stand the way your father treats you, but every time he's so mean to you, I admire you – I do! I do!"

16

The first day of the fall quarter I carried my new textbooks and notebooks to Iowa State Teachers College. I wore a fashionable cotton suit: red plaid, with a pleated skirt that had to be starched and took an hour to iron and less than a minute to wrinkle. My bobby sox were white, my loafers were polished, my hair had been set the day before. I was what I'd never thought I'd be: a college freshman taking her first class.

I didn't know that classrooms were open ten minutes before the hour. The room in the Auditorium Building was already full of strangers when I looked in, except for one familiar face: Robert Laird, pointing to the seat he'd saved for me. It was the only one left. I had to sit there, or stand.

I sat beside him. The chairs were the paddle-armed kind, crammed so close together that when I squeezed between them, my skirt pleats flipped over on Robert's nicely pressed trousers. I snatched my skirt back. "How did you know I was in this section?" I whispered as the professor shut the classroom door.

"I'm passing a seating chart around," the professor said. "Kindly write your name in your square, and keep these seats as your own." So I'd be next to Robert the whole quarter.

"Bribed the registrar," Robert said. I gave him and his joke one of the exasperated looks Katherine Hepburn gives to "fresh" Cary Grants or Spencer Tracys and opened my textbook.

I loved that textbook. It was like an enchanted road lined with bits of knowledge I already had, fitted together with new ones to make sense of the past. There were the masterly groundbreakers, the Greeks, and then the road-builders, the Romans. Hebrews opened the way to conscience, then came the Dark Ages that led to the Middle Ages, the Renaissance...

I found a hideaway in the library stacks: a table on a small balcony hidden behind bound periodicals no one ever read. Between classes I studied there, while a maple outside a small window turned from green to orange in the fall weather. If I was hiding from anybody in particular, I didn't want to think about it.

Dr. Price, the college president, called a special assembly in October to tell us about a new unit of the naval reserve, the Women Appointed for Voluntary Emergency Service, called the WAVES. "The Navy has asked to bring a thousand WAVES to the campus in December for training," he said, just as Robert slid into the seat beside me.

Arlene was sitting with me. She saw Robert and gave me a look.

"Our first objective is to do everything in any way and every way possible to win the war," Dr. Price said.

"Isn't he a dream boat?" Arlene whispered.

"Who?" I asked.

"Not the president." Arlene giggled. "Your best man."

"The women in Lawther Hall will need to live three to a room," Dr. Price said.

"Even if he plays around – dates every girl in sight," Arlene whispered. "And he does. I should know."

Students were clapping: residence hall rates would be reduced, and we were going to get more Thanksgiving vacation while the college got ready for the WAVES.

"How about a coke after?" Robert said in my ear.

He plays around. I knew Robert did. I started to say, "No, but thanks anyway," when I saw the look in his eyes.

He wasn't smiling. Something was wrong. I said, "Okay." I raised my hand with almost all the others when President Price asked if we were willing to have the WAVES come. Robert kept his hand down.

The Commons soda fountain was busy, but we got our cokes and found a table in the corner. "What's the matter?" I asked Robert as we sat down. "It's the math?"

"It's the war," Robert said. "A thousand *women* in uniform on campus?"

"You should be delighted," I said. "Absolutely radiant and ready to date them all. 'Line forms on the left.'"

"Me – date a WAVE? The first thing she'd say to me would be, 'Why aren't you in uniform? I'm supposed to take your place so you can fight.'"

"You're too young. You're not even eighteen."

"They're going to know that?"

"No," I said. "You're disgustingly adult. Fortyish, I think."

"It's not funny," Robert said. "Pretty soon there won't be a male student around who isn't 4-F." He was right, of course. Men were disappearing from the campus; classes were already rows of girls with only an occasional man.

I said, "Con's not happy either. Strangers ask him why he's not reporting for duty."

"Yes," Robert cried. "That's it. So you understand, don't you? How I feel? You're the only girl I know who can understand."

One of his hands suddenly closed around one of mine, the one without the rings. I didn't look at him. I snatched my hand away, grabbed my books and left him there.

October can be dreary in Iowa: no birds sing but cheeping sparrows, trees are stripping down for winter, and sunshine turns thin and doesn't stay long. Wind blew me home from college every weekday afternoon to no one but Mrs. Pell: Con was spending long hours at the Company with his father.

And yet all the help Con gave S.C. didn't seem to matter: his father made us dread every evening meal. Desperate, I threw conversational subjects into our supper hour the way you'd try to distract an attack dog with raw meat. I'd begin to discuss the sinking of our carrier Wasp or the Japanese attack on Henderson Field, or coffee rationing coming soon, but all S.C. would talk about was some mistake he was sure Con had made that day, or would make the next. And Mrs. Pell kept us trapped in her Ironclad Rules.

But Con and I had our room we called "Con's Castle." We talked in bed while wind rattled trees around our corner of the house and made our warm bed more of a hideaway than ever. We shared our life stories, little by little. One night I told him about Alibi Ritter and the parsonage ghosts, and we held each other and giggled under the covers.

"What about your years in Iowa City?" I asked him. "Did you stay in a dorm?"

"Lived in a dorm, went to classes, studied, graduated. That's about it."

"No fun?"

"Not much. Dad needed me here. He was so smashed up that for a while the doctors didn't think he'd live. I scheduled my classes Monday through Thursday, then came home to help him three days a week."

"You were like me. Living on the edges of school," I said. "Not really belonging."

"I belonged at the Company," Con said, stroking my hair. "It fascinated me – as long as I can remember, I've dreamed of what I'd do if I owned it. When I thought Dad was going to die..." he held a handful of my hair tight for a moment "...I don't like to think about that. It was like wishing him dead. Horrible."

"But all your dreams have to wait."

"The Company makes things – that's what I like. Useful things. So many men spend their whole working life shuffling paper, talking on the telephone, going to meetings – but at the Company I'm creating *vital objects.* Machines won't work without them. I like to hold them in my hands. They're real. They're even – " Con laughed a little in the dark. "Beautiful."

We lay quiet for a while, listening to the wind.

"Dad's had such a hard life," Con said. "I try to remember that when he goes after me. He went to war, and then had to put the Company back together when he was mustered out. He lost the girl he loved, lost her to his own brother, so he lost his brother, too. You give up a lot when you're unforgiving. I don't think he cared so much for my mother, and they were only married seven years."

"I'd think you and your father would have been close, left alone like that," I said.

"He worked so hard. I didn't see him at meals – he was gone before breakfast and came home too late for dinner. I always ate alone."

"Without even Mrs. Pell?"

"I don't think she likes children."

"So lonely," I said. "So lonely."

"And then Dad had the accident, and we moved here – built the house so he could use his wheelchair in every room and take the garage ramp to the car. But he's in constant pain... no one knows how much. I think he feels his life's been so unfair, and he envies me: the way I can move around, the way I can work at the Company..."

"He's just plain lucky you've stayed with him, taken care of him."

Con didn't answer. We lay in each other's arms. After a while, when Con was half asleep, I sighed. "What's the matter?" he said.

"Mrs. Pell," I said.

"You want to get rid of her?"

"Yes," I said. "But you should decide."

"It's not my house," Con said. "It's Dad's."

"She doesn't clean," I said. "The food is awful – except for that perfectly delicious tea she served the first day I came here."

"I bought it all at the bakery," Con said.

"You did?"

"I wanted absolutely nothing to scare you away."

I hugged him and said, "She won't help me make life easier for you. She's set like cement in her very, very peculiar ways."

"Dad's used to her."

"And he's paying her. We can't fire someone who's working for him."

We lay for a while, thinking.

"Would you mind if I tried getting rid of Mrs. Pell by underhanded methods I've been thinking of?" I said.

"How?"

"I'll be a good little wife, that's all," I said. "I'll just be trying to keep S.C.'s house clean and improve his meals. What's wrong with that?"

I waited. The next Thursday afternoon I'd just come home when I heard Mrs. Pell shut the front door. I looked out the window. She was leaving for her afternoon off.

I waited until she was out of sight, then went into the kitchen. Nobody was there to sniff at me or give me that I-smell-something-spoiled look.

It was a beautiful kitchen. When I turned on the gas stove, it lit all by itself. The new refrigerator had no coils on top, and inside was a little freezer compartment to keep ice cream or ice. I played with the spray faucet on the sink, and slid the never-used dishwasher trays in and out. I was wondering where to start.

I gritted my teeth and began with the spoons and knives and cooking pots: Mrs. Pell would certainly use them that night. They filled two big drawers and three cabinets that were lined with dirty oilcloth.

I felt like a burglar in my own kitchen, but in an hour or two not one cooking utensil was where Mrs. Pell kept it, because I had reorganized those cabinets and drawers to suit myself. I knew where I wanted the measuring cups and the spatula and the grater and the pressure cooker, and whose kitchen was it, anyway? At least it wasn't Mrs. Pell's.

I enjoyed myself, alone in the still house, scrubbing shelves that hadn't been cleaned for years. When I was done, I took a shower in my lovely bathroom that I kept spotless myself, and put on a fresh cotton dress and waited for suppertime.

S.C. sat in his place at the head of the table, his face as expressionless as usual. Con sat at the foot and I sat on one side. At the Letty house there was always plenty of talk at meals, even though there might not be plenty of food. Here at the Beale house there was plenty of food – poorly cooked as it was – but almost no talk, if Con and I were lucky. I kept one eye on S.C., dreading to see him open his mouth.

He kept his mouth closed at supper that night. So did Con and I. So did Mrs. Pell. But she looked as much like thunder and lightning as a square Danish woman could look. Every time she went into the kitchen through the swinging door, we heard clatters and thumps.

I told Con what I was doing. "You can chase her away if anyone can," he said, and laughed and kissed me and said he admired my war strategy.

The next afternoon while she shopped, I started on the dishes. I moved the cups and saucers and plates from a cupboard near the door to a cupboard over the dishwasher – anyone could see you'd want the dishes there when you put them away clean. I turned all the glasses and cups over so they stood on their rims, not their bases. I switched the kitchen towel drawer with the pot lid drawer, and found new places for the wastebasket and garbage can.

Nothing stayed where it was for very long in that kitchen: the kitchen table migrated from under the window to beside the stove, then in a day or two it roamed like a gypsy to the wall by the dining-room door. I started on the dining-room china cabinet and buffet, turning every goblet and sherbet over on its rim, and folding every clean napkin in rectangles, not triangles.

Con enjoyed it all; he said he felt like the wicked little boy he'd always wanted to be. He helped me pull shades up or down when Mrs. Pell wasn't looking, and one evening we dumped the newspaper on the couch twice and watched her fold it twice and put it on its appointed table. We never left our napkins in triangles, or hung our bathroom towels in thirds.

Mrs. Pell sniffed and glared and banged things in the kitchen, but she didn't complain to S.C.. And she didn't quit.

"It's not working," I told Con one night.

"What's your next plan of attack?" Con said.

"I kept hoping I wouldn't have to use it. It's not kind," I said, holding him tight in our dark, warm bed.

"Neither is she," Con said. "Never has been. Whenever I read about witches when I was a kid, I thought of her. It's not as if she has to work. She's saved her money, I bet, and she got money and a house from her father when he died."

"If there were any other way..."

"If we ask Dad to fire her, he'll keep her forever."

"She'll never leave unless she's...pushed?" I said.

So the next Thursday I dumped food scraps out of every opened can in the garbage. Coffee grounds and meat trimmings and leftover breakfast cereal dribbled to the bottom of the bin in a most satisfactory way. I put fresh meat in a pail in the broom closet, and a pound of butter in the refrigerator onion drawer. Soda and flour look a lot like each other, but when they're switched, your biscuits stay flat but your cream sauce foams.

Sugar in the saltshaker...tea mixed with dried chives...the food had always been bad, but that night it was perfectly awful. Even S.C. wouldn't eat it. He said he couldn't understand it.

Mrs. Pell had served the supper in ominous silence, putting down dishes with an exasperated thump before us. When she came to take away dessert plates and bring coffee, S.C. leaned back in his chair to look her in the eye. "What kind of dinner was this?" he said. "We couldn't eat it."

Mrs. Pell stopped in her tracks. She came back to the table to put her load of dirty dishes on it with a clatter. "What kind of dinner was it?" She glared at him. "That's what you want to know, is it? Well!"

"Well?" S.C. growled.

"Don't ask *me*. It's the kind of dinner you get when I can't cook it – that's what it is – the butter's missing. The pans keep moving."

"Moving?"

"Moving." Her voice went up an octave. "And the kitchen table! And meat in the broom closet in a pail...coffee grounds and breakfast cereal all over the bottom of the garbage can – "

"What's that got to do with sup – "

"Sugar in the saltshaker. Kitchen towels and lids over here – then they're over there."

Her yelling made S.C. wince. "What on earth are you talking about, woman?"

"Poison. That's what I'm talking about. Somebody's trying to poison us, and you think I don't know who it is?"

Her wild eyes were on me.

S.C. stared at her.

He turned to stare at me.

"Are you daring to imply," he said, turning back to Mrs. Pell with such absolute scorn that her face turned red, "that *Mrs. Beale* has been trying to poison this family?"

For a moment Mrs. Pell stood speechless, wringing her apron in her hands, opening and shutting her mouth. The three of us gave her three unbelieving stares.

"Oh," she cried. "Oh," and was gone into the kitchen, yelling as she went. The swinging pantry door chopped the sound of fierce Danish into bits as it slapped back and forth.

S.C. scowled after her. "Senile," he said. He snatched his napkin to swat crumbs on the tablecloth. "Crazy."

The next morning someone knocked on our bedroom door. When I put on my bathrobe and looked out, there was S.C. in his wheelchair, asking me if I could get breakfast. Mrs. Pell had called to say she'd have to care for a sick relative.

"She doesn't plan to come back," S.C. told us after we had eaten my good scrambled eggs and bacon in our usual silence. "She's gone for good after all these years. Senile. No help for it."

I watched Con try to keep his face straight and look suitably concerned. "We'll need a new housekeeper, I suppose," he said.

"I'll find one," I said. "The two of you are so busy – you shouldn't have to worry about it. Just tell me what you pay, and I'll see what I can do."

"Ten dollars a week and meals," S.C. said. "If she's a good cook and knows how to clean."

"I'll see that she does," I said, trying to sound obedient, not triumphant.

I knew exactly what housekeeper I wanted.

By supper that night Mig Swensen was installed in S.C.'s kitchen. Our staples had returned to their places. Dinner was on time. Not a single dish tasted odd. Even

S.C., putting down his napkin after supper, had to admit that Mig could cook. "Where'd she get that crazy name?" he said.

"It's really 'Mignon,'" I told him. "Her mother's French. 'Mignon' means 'dainty' and 'darling'." I'd looked it up.

Mig Swensen had been in my highschool class, and if I was a "hired girl" and lumped with the "farmies," she'd been even lower. Her father was dead. Her mother took in washings. After school Mig pulled an old wagon to houses in town, delivering clean laundry and picking up a dirty load.

When I went to Mig's house, it was dank with steam. I told her what I wanted. Mrs. Swensen left her ironing and came to us, wrapping her red hands in her apron. "Ten dollars!" she said. "Every week?"

"What made you think of me?" Mig said.

"Your good cooking," I said. "Haven't I eaten it at the church for years? I'd like you to live with us – you can have a bedroom and your own bathroom, and do your laundry there, and have your meals, and Thursday afternoons off."

"Oh, my," her mother said in a weak voice. She looked as if she would cry even while she was smiling.

I helped Mig with the supper that night, to get her started. "My father-in-law's cranky," I said.

"He is?"

"Don't let him scare you," I said. "He doesn't know yet what a cook he's getting."

S.C. ate everything on his plate that night, and Con ate more than usual, too, because Mig and I had cooked his favorite dishes. Mig served S.C. his dinner the way you'd serve a hungry tiger: very carefully and very fast. "She's what?" S.C. said, when I mentioned that she was staying nights.

"I saw that you had a place for her," I said. "This house was built with a room and bath off the kitchen for the help. And, of course, the wealthier people in town all have live-in maids."

S.C. snorted, but I had him there. He liked to think he was rich. He was rich.

So now I didn't have an enemy in the kitchen. S.C. left the housekeeping to me.

"Once before, I thought a house was mine," I told Con, "until Betty yelled, *You're a poor relation. We have to take you in.*"

"You're the woman of the house," Con said.

"You should see me roaming around the rooms, exploring, dancing little jigs all by myself." I snuggled close to Con in the dark. "And Mig and I are cleaning this house – chasing dirt like the girl on the Dutch Cleanser label. And tomorrow you and I start having our breakfasts together in the sunroom. We can go to the dining room later and have coffee in silence with S.C. and the *Des Moines Register*."

"I wouldn't want to be on any side but yours," Con said, kissing me. "If they made you Major General instead of Doolittle, the Pacific War'd be over in a week."

17

"Paris wronged Menelaos, king of Sparta," I scribbled in my notebook as Professor Lane lectured on Aeschylus and *Agamemnon* the next Monday morning. "He was the king's guest, but he enticed the queen, beautiful Helen, to go with him to Troy."

"Dramatis Personae," Professor Lane went on. I'd never heard those words said aloud. "Persaunee" I wrote in the margin of my book, then covered it with my ring hand: Robert was reading my notes again, close as we were, paddle-armed chair to paddle-armed chair. I often put my ring hand where he could see it. I liked to watch my two rings sparkle, and they served as a kind of reminder, too.

He needed it. He had an instinct for what turned girls weak-kneed and helpless, maybe because they tended to be that way around him. Why did he pick on me? He was surrounded by hundreds and hundreds of coeds, and there were fewer and fewer men.

"'I have learnt to know night's goodly company of stars, and those bright lords that deck the firmament,'" Professor Lane read from *Agamemnon* in his wonderful deep voice.

How about some reviewing together for the test tomorrow? Robert wrote in the corner of my notebook page.

I gave him a sidewise look. *In your secret place at the library*, he added.

Secret? He knew about it. I glared at him.

Sorry, he scribbled, and smiled.

What could I do? After lunch he brought another chair to my little table in the dusty stacks, and we drilled each other on Aristophanes and *The Frogs*. In an hour I got up and put on my coat. "I'll have to get home now," I said. "We've got a new cook and we've made plans for supper." That was to remind him that I was married and out of circulation.

"Don't go," Robert said. He was standing too, and very close, because there was so little room. I could feel his breath on my cheek – and then he kissed me before I could get away. It made me so mad. It made me dizzy. I don't know how many seconds went by before I shoved him into a shelf of *National Geographics* and grabbed my books and ran.

A cold wind cut across campus and tunneled down the town streets to cool my hot face. Who did he think he was? Who did he think I was? I was *married*. And I'd have to go to class and sit right beside him and take that test the next day.

I was grateful for the cold November wind. I was grateful for Mig greeting me in the kitchen: a clean, neat housekeeper with her dark hair pinned in a hygienic bun and her apron on. I went into the bedroom and shut the door and couldn't bear to lie down on our bed.

I washed off my lips. It didn't help.

S.C. had a scowl on his face when we sat down to dinner that night. "We'll have to work late every evening this week," he said to Con, making me cringe. He and Con would be in the sunroom past midnight. But the war hung over us, a constant black cloud. Our boys were dying.

Con and I sat very close together on the sunroom couch after dinner before S.C. came in. "You and Mig," Con said, hugging me. "This house is beginning to feel like home."

"It ought to," I said. "You work so hard all day – you should have a real home to welcome you."

He kissed me before I could get away. It made me so mad. It
made me dizzy. I shoved him into a shelf of *National
Geographics*, grabbed my books and ran.

"Home is where you are." Con looked at me with love in his eyes. I put my head on his shoulder and was miserable and told myself I hadn't done anything really wrong – Robert had.

Then S.C. wheeled himself into the sunroom, and I went to bed to listen to S.C. shout at Con in his high, thin voice, and hear Con's few words, or his silence.

I gave up my hideaway in the library. I sat stone-faced beside Robert in class and wouldn't answer his notes – I blanked them out with my pen so hard that the pen went through the paper.

Sorry, Robert wrote the next day at the edge of my notebook paper.

I scribbled his apology into a tangle of ink squiggles.

He kept at it. During the next class he wrote: *Should I throw away the paper rose I saved from your Gypsy Girl bouquet?*

I blotted out those words until they were a black puddle. I'd been the forsaken bride from that wedding, bawling and running to Victoria.

Robert was sitting so close to me. The professor was reading Ferdinand's love speech to Miranda from *The Tempest*, which didn't help. *After all*, Robert wrote at the bottom of the page. *You married me first.*

I can't pretend I'm not a pushover for romantic yearning. It *is* gratifying to have a spurned lover pining for you, especially if he's ignored you completely for years and years. All you have to do is enjoy that snaky little ripple of pure revenge while you look as beautifully inaccessible as possible, which I tried to do.

I *was* pretty inaccessible. Didn't I live with my own husband in my own nice house? And when I was on campus, I stayed with girls I knew. If I saw Robert I pretended I hadn't. Patty Hayes had put off marrying her boyfriend from Cedar Falls High, so she'd talked her father into letting her live in the dorm – married women couldn't live there. Arlene Brown and Sonia Jensen and I hung out in Patty's room when we had breaks in class schedules.

"It's going to be a ghost campus – no *freshmen!*" Patty wailed one November afternoon. She still had her bright red hair, and the white skin that kept her out of the sun. "What'll we do – dance with each other? Go to movies with 'the girls'?"

"Don't you miss the fellows' nice deep voices in class?"

"Those broad shoulders."

"All that shouting and pushing each other around."

"The war wasn't supposed to last this long – not after we got in it."

"Robert Laird's still here," Patty said. She'd dated him more than any of us.

"He doesn't look seventeen," Arlene said.

"He skipped first grade," Sonia said.

"Time for me to be home," I said. "See you." The dorm stairwell echoed as I went down. When I stepped into the cold wind, there was Robert waiting by the door.

"Hi," he said. "Saw you go in with Arlene."

I gave him a look and tried to pass him.

"It's Joe," he said, standing against the wind with his coat collar up and his dark hair blowing. "He's home."

"Home?" I said. "On leave?"

"He's hurt. One minute he was in the Pacific fighting and the next minute he's here."

"He's hurt?"

"Shot in the leg. It's starting to heal. He won't walk well enough to go back – he's out of the war. But the worst thing is that he's having some kind of mental trouble. He talked at first, but suddenly he stopped – he won't say a word, just eats and then lies on his bed in his uniform. Wants it dark. His mother hopes he'll talk to some of us. Can you go?"

I had to go. We fought the wind all the way downtown. I kept up with Robert's long stride, half-running. War had come home with Joe, as if something colder than November wind had blown through an opened door.

"I'm so glad you're here!" Joe's mother said when she saw us, and began to cry as we took off our coats. She didn't make a sound, hiding her face in her hands. I put my arms around her. "He's in his room," she said against my shoulder. "Maybe he'll talk to you." Mr. Stepler stood silently in the parlor doorway watching us.

We followed her into a small, dim bedroom. For a minute I couldn't see Joe; then a dull gleam of metal on his Marine uniform showed me where he lay on his back looking at the ceiling.

Robert and I tiptoed closer. "Joe?" Robert said in a low voice. "Joe? It's Robert. Robert and Miranda."

I could see Joe better as my eyes adjusted to the dimness. He was as blond and wide-mouthed as ever, but rigid, like a wooden carving of himself, dressed as a Marine.

"Joe?" I said, and leaned over him until my hair almost touched his face. "It's Miranda. Remember me?" I thought his eyes, for a second, twitched.

He would not move. He would not speak. His mother brought chairs, and Robert and I sat beside his narrow bed and tried to talk about the war effort and our college classes and the newest movies.

"What else can we do?" I asked Mrs. Stepler when we came into the front hall again.

"If you could visit every day for a little while?" she begged. "I asked Dr. Wilder when he came. He said that maybe Joe's friends could help, and Robert is certainly his best friend." She tried to smile at Robert. "And he's known you a long time, too, dear," she said to me.

We told her we'd be back, and went as quietly out of that house as if we'd been to a funeral.

"Come to my place," Robert said. "She was too upset to give us anything to warm us up – I'll make some hot chocolate."

"Is your mother – "

"She's at work, but my grandmother's there," Robert said.

It was all right then; I went with him down the block to his very small house. I was curious: I'd never been in Robert's house, even when I was a new orphan and lived across the street. No children ever went in and out but Robert. If you called for him in his yard, he'd come out to play, but you were never ever invited in. Our neighbors talked about it now and then: "People can certainly keep to themselves if they want to. It's a free country."

We went around the back to the kitchen door. I thought Robert hesitated before he turned the knob.

The moment I stepped in, I saw his grandmother in the parlor beyond the kitchen. "She doesn't like the draft from the front door, so we come in the back," Robert said, and I followed him into the parlor. "Grandma Laird, here's Miranda Letty."

She was tiny and stooped, and sat like a hibernating animal in a nest of odds and ends, all within reach of her bony hands. She didn't even look up; she was patting the sweater that covered her concave chest. "Where's my needle and thread?" she asked Robert in a voice like rustling paper, pawing among sacks and photographs and dog-eared magazines. "You've taken my needle and thread."

"It's stuck in your sweater," Robert said, trying to pull it out. The knot in the thread stopped him; he had to lean over and bite the thread free, his dark head under her indignant face. She looked at the needle and thread. "No knot," she said. He tied one for her, patiently, and helped her close her fingers around the needle.

I tried not to stare at her, or at the poor, threadbare house. There wasn't even a stove in the kitchen, or an icebox. Robert lit a gas plate with a match, put on a pan of milk and found some chipped cups and cocoa in a cup-

board. Waiting for the milk to heat, we heard the grandmother mumbling to herself.

I didn't look around the kitchen. I kept my eyes on
the chipped cups. Robert poured the hot chocolate with
care: he was wearing a thick white sweater; his shirt was
clean and starched. "There you are," he said, handing
me a cup.

I kept my eyes on the cup he gave me and said,
"Thanks." I was only a foot or two from Robert Laird.
There was that mouth of his. I'd kissed it, and I could do
it again. "It's such a cold day," I said, hoping he'd think I
was shivering because of the weather.

"And you've got a long walk to your house," Robert
said. "Wish I had a car – wish I had the gas. I'd bring you
to Joe's house every day and then take you home."

"I'm helping with the church supper tonight, anyway,"
I said. "And there's a war on."

"Joe's pretty bad," Robert said after a pause.

"Yes," I said.

"He's been at Guadalcanal. We wrote each other. His
letters stopped last month, and I was afraid..." Robert's
voice trailed off.

"But he's here," I said.

"Thank God," Robert said.

"Yes," I said, and turned away. "I'd better be going."

"Meet you at the library tomorrow to go to the
Steplers?" Robert said. "About four?"

I said yes and left him there in that small, dark kitchen.
Beyond him his grandmother was running the needle and
thread in and out of her sweater front.

The church smelled of onions cooking as I went down
to the basement kitchen. Less than a year before only a
few of the women would have noticed me. Now I met
smiles and greetings. Aunt Gertrude and Betty were hovering over cream sauce at the big stove, their cheeks pink
with the heat.

"Can I help?" I said. Oh, wasn't I the graceful and gracious young Mrs. Conrad Beale? Mrs. Lynch asked if I would mind putting napkins and silverware on the tables.

I said, "I'll be glad to," and gathered up handfuls of forks and spoons with such a feeling of smug delight. When I saw Robert's mother come from her grocery store job, slipping through the far dining-room door as quietly as always, I was the young society matron from head to foot, Oh yes. I went up to her with nothing but silly pride and affectation in my voice, I'm sure, and I stopped the poor woman and was all ready to say how I had enjoyed meeting her mother that afternoon, and what a nice cup of hot chocolate I'd had in her home...

"Mrs. Laird," I said, and then I remembered a shabby, hidden-away house. It saved me.

"Yes?" Mrs. Laird said. She was worried-looking and thin, wearing a hairnet and a middle-aged woman's dress of a dark, indefinite, serviceable color, like the suits men wore. I'd noticed her for years, and sometimes I thought she had been pretty enough, once, to be Robert's mother.

"Robert and I went to see Joe Stepler this afternoon," I said, wiping the young-society-matron smile off my face. "It's sad. He won't talk. He doesn't seem to know we're there; he lies on his bed in his uniform."

"He's their only child," Mrs. Laird said. She was turning her wedding ring around and around on her finger as if she could tighten her whole self down that way, and hang on.

There was nothing I could say; I watched her go into the kitchen; then I hid between coat racks in the hall for a minute, trying to think of anything but Robert.

I couldn't. When I went back to setting the tables, what I thought of was Robert bent over his shabby grandmother, and Robert stirring milk over an old hot plate.

Mrs. Laird stayed in the kitchen until the last dish towel was hung to dry, as usual. I watched her when I could, wanting to do some small thing – hug her, perhaps...tell her I knew how much she worried about Robert going to war. I didn't. I stayed until late at the church, too, putting off my long walk home when I'd have to think about the final and hardest thing: Robert Laird and his house. No one I knew had ever been in that place, not even my uncle, their minister. But Robert Laird had opened the door of his house that afternoon – for me.

18

November wind rattled the windows as I met
Robert at the library the next afternoon, and it
tried to push us off the campus sidewalks the minute we
stepped outside. "Let's get something hot to drink
first," Robert said, and we turned into the Commons.
"My treat."

I wished I were anywhere else. I followed Robert to
a table and watched him go to the counter for our hot
chocolate. It wasn't very good, because they had to
make it without sugar, but no one complained: we knew
there was a war on. A radio on a nearby table chattered
about hard fighting in North Africa and Pacific battles
island to island.

"Here," I said when Robert came back, "let's have a little bit of Mrs. Stepler's sugar." I took a package out of my
book bag. "I thought I'd bring her some of our ration,
because Joe likes her desserts, she says, but how many can
she make with just three ration books?" I put a spoonful
in Robert's cup, and one in mine. "And what else can she
do for him?"

"Nice," Robert said. "Do you know, you're not only
beautiful, you're nice." He put his hand over mine – not
the one with the rings. He never touched that one.

I snatched my hand back. He sat across from me, a
handsome sight that girls at other tables weren't missing:
I often noticed those small surrounding eye-gleams when
I was with him. What they couldn't see was what was
between the two of us at the table now, plain as our cups
and saucers.

Then he met my eyes, and I wanted to get up and run: he was going to talk about it – take me through another door into secrets I didn't really want to know, because secrets were like kisses: close.

"You're in the family now," Robert said. "Hasn't Con said anything to you about his father and my father?"

"That they quarreled?"

"They fought. Over Dad marrying my mother, because they both wanted her. Never spoke to each other again."

"That's terrible," I said.

"We never had much money, especially after Dad died. S.C. didn't want to give my mother a thing, ever. But he sent quite a bit each month for me, so I had good clothes, and a bicycle." Robert looked ashamed. "Mom wouldn't take a single penny of S.C.'s money. If I used it to buy anything for her or Grandma – even food – I had to take what I'd bought back to the store. I've had jobs since I was ten, but she never had enough to live decently, and my grandmother..." There was misery in his voice. "You've only seen her the way she is now. When I was little, she was so much fun – reading books to me, playing games, helping everybody in the neighborhood – and then, before I started school, it all ended. She wasn't really there, ever again, and my mother could never bear to have anyone come to the house and see her."

What could I say, except that I was so sorry?

"And I wouldn't be going to college without your father-in-law's money," Robert said.

"S.C.'s money?" I stared at him.

"Con didn't tell you? I didn't think he would."

"No," I said, while people I had thought I knew arranged themselves in astounding new patterns: S.C. supporting a child of the brother he'd hated? Adele Laird, refusing to take one cent from S.C. for herself? Robert spending S.C.'s money for years?

"It's been hard for me," Robert said, looking into his empty cup.

"But you had your mother, and your grandmother. You had your family," I said.

"Yes," Robert said.

"You had your own room, I bet."

"Yes. Always did."

"And you had new clothes and money for dates and school trips and class rings – "

"Yes," Robert said.

"And were popular. So popular," I said. "You dated any girl who was anybody, didn't you?"

I hadn't been one of those girls. He didn't know how to answer. He didn't understand quite how the conversation had come to where it was, and he'd caught the scorn in my voice.

I stood up and said, "We'd better be going. It's almost dark," and then saw the gleam in his eye: I'd given myself away. I flung on my coat, picked up my book bag and was out of there fast, but he was right behind me, catching me along a walk where evergreens closed the campus away. The first snow of the year starred the air around us.

"Sorry!" he cried. He hugged me tight and wouldn't let go, though I pushed against him, furious. "I'm sorry. I'm sorry," he kept saying in a voice he'd use to calm his child someday, supposing he had one, but I wasn't a child and I was ashamed, and so mad that I didn't feel the cold at all.

"You were an orphan," he said in my ear through my wildly-blowing hair. "Absolutely alone. Had to be a 'hired girl.' No nice clothes, no dates, no time – you think I didn't notice? And I made it worse. I'm still making it worse."

My eyes filled with tears. I sobbed against his shoulder, found a handkerchief in my coat pocket, and cried some more. I hadn't cried so hard for years, especially not with such pleasure and fear mixed, and I didn't know why I was doing it now. When he tried to kiss me, I got away from

"I'm sorry," he said, and hugged me tight. "I'm sorry. You were an orphan. Had to be the hired girl. You think I didn't notice? And I made it worse. I'm still making it worse." My eyes filled with tears.

him to tie my scarf and put on my mittens and walk to the Stepler house without feeling the blast of the wind or saying one word to Robert.

Gas rationing and cold weather kept the streets deserted that afternoon; only one car passed us as we covered our faces against the stinging snow and nearly blew away at the intersections.

"Oh, my," Mrs. Stepler cried, bracing her door against the wind as she let us in, "you came, and in such weather!"

"How's Joe?" asked Robert. His cheeks were pink and so was his nose. I looked in the hail mirror at my own pink and white face, and tried to smooth my hair a little.

"Not changed," Mrs. Stepler said. "Just the same."

Joe's room was as dark as before. We sat in our chairs and told Joe who we were. Then we looked at each other. "What'll we talk about?" Robert asked me.

"How about memories," I said. "When we were kids together that first summer I was in town. Joe was there most of the time. Remember the dead animal graveyard?"

"My pet rabbit," Robert said. "We buried him."

"In a shoebox. In tissue paper with a blue bow on it because he was a boy."

"You put 'R.I.P.' on the lath we used for a grave marker." Robert said. "I had to ask you what that meant, and you said, 'Rabbit In Paradise.'"

"I did?"

"You did, and I believed you. I loved that rabbit. It seemed to me that paradise was where my rabbit would go."

We both began to laugh, there beside the still body on the bed, and I hardly recognized myself – laughing as if I could laugh forever. What was the matter with me?

Then we remembered where we were, and stopped, and glanced toward the open door.

"Remember that rope in Mr. Calvinhorn's barn – swinging clear across from one loft to land in the other?" Robert said after a minute.

"Hay in your hair."

"Hay down your neck."

"It wouldn't seem so far to swing now."

"We'll go look at it," Robert said, talking to me, not silent Joe. "Next summer." Then I think he remembered there wouldn't be a summer at home for him; he looked down at Joe's hand on the bedspread.

"There was an owl in the barn," I said.

"And spiders. We poked flies in their webs."

"*You* did."

"You didn't?"

"Couldn't stand it," I said. "You boys pulled their wings off first."

"Sorry," Robert said, and memories of the times he'd said that word to me came back, and were changed, too.

"Remember when Sonia got lost in the cornfield?" I said.

"Joe found her," Robert said, and we looked at Joe as if we'd just remembered he was there.

"Remember when Patty's father took us to the circus?"

"The clowns!" I said. "The one with the yard-long shoes!"

"The bareback riders – those beautiful women!"

"The aerialists!" I said, so happy that I was on air, too, and felt that if I touched Joe, he would be filled with joy, like me. I don't know what I thought I was doing. I certainly wasn't thinking. "What would happen if I kissed Joe?" I asked Robert. "To wake him up, like the Sleeping Beauty."

"He wouldn't wake up," Robert said in a grim voice. "He'd probably drop dead."

That delighted me so! I leaned over Joe and slid my arms around him until my face was only inches from his. "Joe?" I whispered, "It's Miranda. Kiss me." What fun it was to have Robert sitting only a foot or two away, having to listen to my crooning voice, having to watch me stroke

Joe's face and run my fingers through his hair and then fit my lips to Joe's for a long kiss –

The next thing I knew I was on the floor and Joe was in a corner, screaming...screaming...screaming until his parents came running to the bedroom door and turned on the light.   There was Joe in his corner on all fours, screaming such terrible things that he couldn't hear us yelling, "Joe! Joe! It's us!" He crouched in that corner and spit out words as if he were vomiting huge chunks he couldn't swallow – "No legs! Billy! He'll walk again!"

"Joe!" His mother said, bending over him.

"You sonofabitch medic – I'll blow your head off! He's dead!" Joe was looking through his mother at something else. "Billy! Oh, Billy!"

"Joe! Listen to me! Joe!" His father knelt in front of him.

"Vernon!" Joe screamed.   He didn't seem to see his father. "Blow them up! Blow the fuckin' little yellow – "

I couldn't recognize the man in the marine uniform whose eyes bulged with terror, whose words –

"Dear!" Mrs. Stepler rushed to me. "You'd better cut your visit short today." Tears were streaming down her face. She snatched Robert's sweater sleeve with the other hand, and we went into the hall with her. We could barely hear what she said to us above Joe's shouting and his father's loud voice trying to calm him. "You've done so much good," she told us as we hurried to put on our wraps. "He's talking at last."

Talking? When the Steplers' door shut behind us, Robert and I stared at each other in a frozen world, while Joe's voice rose and fell, coming through the walls of the house like the barking of a dog.

We ran away. We ran to Robert's house where his grandmother sat fast asleep in her nest. We stood in a kitchen corner near the hot plate.

"Joe!" Robert said in a whisper.

"Yes," I said.

"They sent him home! No wonder!"

"Yes."

"War. That's where I'm going. In a month or so. And nobody understands how I feel. Nobody but you."

"Everybody's scared," I said. "They'd have to be."

"Everybody but Con!" Robert glared at me.

"Con has to – "

"He's got money in his pocket! He's got you! In his – "

Suddenly the door to the back yard opened, and Mrs. Laird came in, looking startled to see me. "Why, hello, Miranda. You two went to see Joe?"

"Yes," I said. Robert had turned his flushed face toward a cupboard; he brought cups and saucers to the table.

"I really must go," I said quickly. "Thanks for the offer of hot chocolate. I'm expected at home and I'm late now." Rattling off polite phrases, I managed to smile at Mrs. Laird and leave.

I ran down the street. I passed Victoria's house – I remembered that later. I never stopped. I ran on to my hill, my street, my house, my bedroom, and Con, who was in it.

"Con!" I said, not even taking off my boots or my coat. "Oh, Con!" I hugged him tight, giving off the cold of the cold day.

"Now, wait a minute, just hold on, what's the matter?" Con said. He took off my scarf and then my mittens and coat. Unwrapped, I began to cry, so Con took me on his lap as if I were a child, and muttered and whispered in my ear until I calmed down a little.

"Now tell me," he said. "Something terrible's happened?"

"I went to see Joe Stepler at his house – remember, I told you Robert and I went yesterday?"

"Yes, you did."

"And just now Joe...woke up. He got down in a corner of his bedroom and yelled the most terrible things. Somebody had lost his legs, and he was going to kill – "

"Battle fatigue," Con said. "There's a lot of it in the Pacific Theater, Ron Bailey told me. His son's home from there." Con held me tight and rocked me back and forth. "Sometimes it's real and sometimes they pretend."

"To get home?"

"To get out of that hell," Con said. "Any way they can, short of dying."

I went into the dining room with him in a little while, but I couldn't eat much supper. The men carried their coffee and pieces of Mig's good upside-down cake into the sunroom and began the evening's work.

I took my coffee to the living room and tried to read a magazine. I couldn't. I wandered back to the kitchen. Mig was scraping plates. I bent over the line of African violets I was growing on the windowsill and gave them a quarter turn, then picked off dead flowers. Mig watched me. After a while she said, "Aren't you feeling good?"

"We visited Joe again today."

"He's better?" Mig kept her eyes on a stack of dirty plates, but every inch of her, I thought, was listening.

"He talked, and that's good, but..."

"Oh!" Mig cried. "He's worse!"

"He's talking now, but he remembers such awful things. He can't stand them. Nobody could."

"But he's talking," Mig said. "He must be better, if he's talking! He has to be better!" Her eyes were filling with tears.

"Oh, Mig!" I said, putting my arms around her. "Don't cry!"

"It's just that he's a classmate, you know," Mig sobbed. "This awful war! This awful, awful war!"

"Maybe..." I said, looking into her wet eyes and smoothing her dark hair, "maybe you've watched him ever since you were in grade school?"

Mig tried to laugh shame-facedly, but sobbed instead.

"He's never known it? Never asked for a date?" I kissed her cheek. "And maybe you've kept little mementos and clippings, and if he ever did find out, you'd die of embarrassment – "

"Oh, yes!" Mig cried.

Suddenly I wasn't talking about her at all – words seemed forced out of me: "But then, what if he told you he was sorry he'd never asked you for a date?" My lips felt stiff, talking like that, but I couldn't stop. "What if he said he knew you'd had such a hard life so far...he'd been watching you all that time, and he loved you, and didn't want anyone else to have you – how would you feel?"

"Oh, in heaven!" Mig cried. "In heaven! In heaven! The whole past wouldn't matter, if he said he was sorry. If he loved me."

19

S aturdays were dreary at S.C.'s house: Con and S.C.
usually spent the day on accounts at the Company,
and I went to the parsonage. My smallest cousin, Bruce,
was still a diaper-filling machine, but he was a machine
that crawled on the floor now, eating anything he could
get in his mouth.

Benjy and Bernard were shoveling the parsonage sidewalk as I came along: big fellows kicking snow on each
other's cleared pavement. I left them wrestling in a snow-
drift and found Betty in the parlor with Bruce.

"Guess what!" Betty cried when she saw me. "You'll
never guess! I've got a date with Jack Southard tonight –
didn't I save that new sweater and skirt you gave me last
week, didn't I? Jack Southard! He asked me!"

No wonder she was thrilled – Jack was the Robert
Laird of her senior class. "It's those brassieres," I said,
scooping Bruce out of his playpen. "Bet you're wearing
the biggest one."

"It is not," Betty said, trying to sound mad, but she was
grinning. "Well, I am, but it's not – "

"Betty!" Aunt Gertrude called from the bottom of
the basement stairs. "Is that Miranda? If she's there,
can she watch Bruce? We've got the washing to finish
before lunch!"

Betty skipped off, too happy to mind even the washing.
I changed Bruce, put him in his playpen again, and there
I was – I couldn't believe it – going to stand a foot and a
half from the corner of the window, like an old horse that
follows a timeworn route. I'd stood in that place a thou-

sand times; it was the one spot in the Letty house where I could see Robert Laird's front door.

Betty's laughter echoed in the basement.

Robert would be in church the next day. He'd sit next to me in class on Monday.

But Robert wasn't at church.

At our Monday class his paddle-armed chair sat empty beside me. He wasn't there any day of that week, or the next.

On Thursday I went up to Patty's dorm room. Patty and Arlene and Naomi Winters were sitting on the bed and hugging Berniece Schuler, who was crying. When Berniece saw me, she gave me one look, sobbed, and ran out of the room.

"Her brother's been killed in the Pacific," Naomi said to me in a particularly hard tone.

What could I say? I was getting used to that look and that tone, and the questions when girls saw my wedding ring: "Where is your husband serving?"

"He's in supply," I said sometimes. "He makes land mines and the parts for machine guns." But they found out: I was the girl who had my husband with me, safe.

Arlene was my friend; she changed the subject. She said, "Anybody seen Robert lately?"

"Robert who?" Patty said, pretending she didn't know, even though she'd dated Robert more than anyone. She still pretended that he'd date her in a minute and would pine for her until he died.

"Laird, you dumbbell," Arlene said. "He hasn't enlisted, has he?"

"I wouldn't be surprised," Patty said in a knowing voice. "He's talked to me about it a lot – serving his country...doing his duty...he's very patriotic." She gave me a look, then sighed. "Before long he'll probably write me from some training camp or other. Robert and I were really close."

We sat in glum silence. "And a thousand WAVES coming to the campus!" Patty said. "So we'll be crammed in here, three to a room!"

"I'm so tired of this war already," Sonia said, coming in to help herself to Patty's cookies and join us on her bed. "We wear service pins and we jump up and down and squeal if there's a letter without postage in our mailbox – that's all! No hugs! No kisses! No necking, for Pete's sake! Might as well be eighty years old."

I felt them looking at me, because I wasn't going without lovemaking. I didn't look at any of them – I even smiled a little to myself, thinking – shameless as I was – that there were two men...

But where was Robert? When I went to help with the church supper that night, I stopped Mrs. Laird on her way to the kitchen. "How's Robert?" I asked her. "I haven't seen him in the choir or in class all week."

"I don't know," she said, stopping to stare at me. "I don't know. He isn't much interested in college, or church. He spends hours with Joe, and then he comes home and stays in his room."

"Do you think Joe would like to have me drop in with a friend some afternoon?" I said.

"I think so," Mrs. Laird said. "Robert says he's much better."

The next afternoon I ran home and found Mig ironing sheets. "Finish that sheet and put on your good clothes we bought," I said. "We're going on a visit in half an hour. Are there some of your oatmeal cookies left?"

There were. I packed a small basket full while she put on the new sweater and skirt, and makeup that made her look so pretty.

"Where are we going?" Mig asked as we started downtown along the wintry streets.

All I would say was: "Wait and see."

Finally, when we were only a half block from Joe's house, Mig stopped dead at a corner and said, "We're going to Joe's?" When she saw me smile, she wailed, "I can't! Let me go back home and you go! I can't – "

"Listen," I said, and looked her in the eye. "The boys have got to step up and ask us for a date – do you know how much gumption that takes? It's enough to make your heart stop – what if the girl says No Thank You, and you have to smile and walk away pretending you don't care? Aren't you as tough as a boy? Are you going to be a little limp violet wasting its sweetness on the desert air?"

"No," Mig said in a small voice.

"Then come on," I said, and we marched up to Joe's door and rang the bell.

"Good afternoon," I said when Mrs. Stepler opened the door. "I believe you know Mignon Swensen," I said. "She was in our high school class."

"I went to school with your mother," Mrs. Stepler told Mig. "She was such a good student, and I believe you take after her."

Mig blushed and stammered, but I said that Yes, indeed, Mig was an A student. "Is Joe feeling better?" I asked. "Would he like company?"

"Much better," Mrs. Stepler said. "Come in. Won't you hang up your coats? I'll tell him you're here."

While Mrs. Stepler was gone, I saw Mig looking so carefully at that house. Every door handle and drawer pull had been touched by Joe...he had walked across those floors thousands of times – I knew what she was feeling. And I was listening for Robert's voice, and looking for his coat in the hall. It wasn't there.

"Do come into the parlor," Mrs. Stepler said. Mig, jittery, hurried to hang up her coat, and I had the jitters, too: would Robert come? Mrs. Stepler couldn't guess what quivery females she was leading through her hall.

"Here are Miranda and Mignon," Mrs. Stepler said as we entered the room, and there was Joe, still in his uniform, sitting in the autumn sunshine. He was a good-looking specimen of a Marine, all right: Mig couldn't say one word.

"Mig baked you some cookies," I said, handing Joe the basket. Mig shot him one look and then kept her eyes down with such an embarrassed look that you'd have thought her slip was showing or her shoes were on the wrong feet.

"Goodness, we'll have to have some coffee to go with those cookies," Mrs. Stepler said. "People have been so good to us, bringing us coffee – and your sugar, Miranda! So neighborly. Do sit down."

I watched her go into the kitchen and said, "You're feeling better?" to Joe.

"I hope you are," Mig said in a shy voice.

"I'm much better," Joe said, and his eyes met Mig's: big blue eyes looking into pretty dark ones. "Thanks for the cookies."

"It's my mother's recipe," Mig said. "I hope you don't mind sweet things." I doubt if she knew what she was saying; her face looked so soft – there's no other word for it – like a picture a little out of focus. She was talking about a recipe, but that wasn't what her eyes said, and Joe kept looking. I'd heard that Marines were trained to be very observant. I hoped so.

"I like sweet things," Joe said, and Mig couldn't miss that, so she blushed. Joe was tall, but so was she; they made a charming couple, I was thinking – when suddenly I heard a familiar voice. In a split second I arranged my own face into calm friendliness, held my breath, and looked at the parlor door.

But in a few moments only Mrs. Stepler stood there, a tray in her hands. Joe said, "Was that Robert?"

"He said he couldn't stay," Mrs. Stepler said. "I told him the girls were here, but he said he had to go."

Joe never asked why. He didn't look surprised. We handed around coffee cups and ate Mig's cookies, but my mind was on Robert walking down a cold street alone.

"Such cookies!" Mrs. Stepler said to Mig. "Do you ever share your best recipes?"

"Oh, yes, I d-do," Mig said, so pleased that she stuttered a little. "If you have something I can write it on."

"Come into the kitchen – I've got recipe cards." Mrs. Stepler took Mig away with her.

I looked at Joe, expecting to make small talk. I was wrong – he was serious, and in a hurry. "Would you meet Robert at the college library – at your little studying place?"

"Well, yes, of course, I – "

"He's upset. He's really upset. He says he won't finish the quarter – won't go to classes – won't go anywhere. He'll lose credit for a whole quarter, and he won't even be called up until the end of this month. Who in their right mind would throw away a whole college quarter?"

"He's sure people think there's something wrong with him," I said. "But I think he's scared of going – "

"Yes!" Suddenly Joe's face was like the man crouched in a bedroom corner. "You aren't somebody who thinks war is a glorious patriotic duty, are you?"

"No," I said. "I'm not." Mig and Mrs. Stepler were laughing in the kitchen.

"Then be at the library at ten tomorrow morning, will you?" Joe said quickly: his mother and Mig were coming back. "You're the only one who can help him. I can't. I'm the last person he ought to see. Keep him away from here."

20

"You're the only one who can help him." I dragged those heavy words home from the Stepler house like a bag full of rocks, while Mig beside me nearly floated: a "hired girl" in pretty clothes whom someone had looked at, and looked at again, and called "a sweet thing."

One woman in the Beale house sang at her work that evening. One stayed awake half the night.

I had some persuasive arguments to keep Robert in college, I thought, as I walked to the campus the next morning. And I'd spent an hour on my face and hair and fingernails. I tiptoed through the library reading room past books in rows and coeds at work. My saddle shoes clanged on the metal stairs winding to the top of the stacks.

Robert was there, standing between the *National Geographics* and the *Atlantic Monthlies*. Maybe I had forgotten, after a week, what he looked like, or else he had changed: handsome, of course, but wearing a hungry look – he had me tight in his arms before I left the top step. I kept him from a kiss by jamming my face against his shoulder and my arms around his waist and giving him only a face full of my hair to talk to: he was whispering that he loved me, that he had to have me –

"Listen!" I hissed at him, face to face now but keeping one of my arms under his chin. "I'm not *yours*. I'm married to *your own cousin!*"

His angry eyes had turned from brown to almost black. "Can't you give me something to hang on to – someone at home – "

"What about all your girlfriends – what about Mary Hogan? Won't she give you something to hang on to?" I even laughed a little at that one. "How about Sonia Jensen or Arlene Brown?"

Robert couldn't look me in the eye – I knew how he'd treated those girls. He let me go and turned his back. I was ashamed. I wasn't the one who would have to go and fight.

"Robert," I said, "finish the quarter. Go to class, take the exams."

"Let somebody put another 'Yellow Belly' note on my desk?"

"What?" I said.

"Because I'm chicken, see? I don't go and fight like other men do."

"That's – awful! That's crazy! You aren't even eighteen until next month!"

"They don't know, they don't care."

"That's why you're hiding out?"

"They probably think I'm missing some...essential part. And I am. I'm scared. I'm supposed to be patriotic and fight for my country, but all I feel is scared." He swung around and grabbed me close again. "You're the only one! The only one who can understand, except Joe, and they drove him crazy."

"But now he's all right?"

"Maybe. I don't know. He'll walk with a limp, so he's out of the war. He fought on Guadalcanal. For weeks I've listened to him – he's imagined he's still there with his buddy in a hole. Billy somebody. One of them sleeps and the other watches, all the time, because the Japs never sleep, they creep in. One night a Jap threw a grenade in their hole, and Billy fell on Joe, got killed, got spread all over – "

"Don't!" I cried.

"And you get so you won't take prisoners, not even the wounded ones. You don't care – you loot their bodies, take their gold fillings out when maybe they're not even dead – use your K-bar. That's a seventeen-inch knife. And you don't let yourself get captured, either."

"Oh, Robert!"

"You know why? Nobody's told us about Bataan. We don't hear about the real war. We don't hear about our death march – sixty miles on one meal of rice, thousands and thousands of our men; anybody who stepped out of line was shot or bayoneted, and then they packed our men in boxcars in that heat. Thousands of our men died. That's why you don't get captured."

I couldn't say a word, standing there in his arms. Such horrors had never entered my mind, or my life, or even my imagination.

"And it's just as bad in North Africa. I listened to Joe all day long. What else could I do for him?" Robert said. "And that's where I'm going – to that kind of war. And you don't care."

"I do!" I cried. "You shouldn't ever say – "

He kissed me – another of those kisses that blew away that little cubbyhole in the library stacks: the rows of bound periodicals, the one light bulb, the little window. They went out like a snuffed candle, until I brought them back.

I yanked myself away from Robert and whispered to him from the safety of the steps, "You be in class Monday! I'll let you have my notes to catch up. You be in all your classes. You take the exams – all of them – or I'll – " I stopped. What would I do?

"You'll what?" Robert said. He hung over the stair rail above me, so close that I could almost feel that mouth I'd just kissed. His eyes, so like Con's, had little belligerent lights in them.

"I'll – never kiss you again!" I whispered, and tiptoed down the stairs, through the library, and into the cold wind, carrying every one of my reasonable, persuasive, unused arguments with me.

I spent the rest of the day at the parsonage. Night was coming early now. When I walked home, the lights of my house shone at the top of the hill. Even though it was Saturday, I didn't expect Con to be there; sometimes he didn't come back for supper at all. The Beale Company was brightly lit night and day. I was growing used to seeing him so seldom, except for the breakfasts he ate in a hurry. He fell asleep the minute we were in bed. I was growing used to that, too.

Robert smiled at me in church the next day: a wicked smile, I thought. And he was beside me in class on Monday. I slid through the narrow space between our two desks, not wanting to look at him. I opened my notebook and my textbook and took out my pen, very businesslike, but he was so close I could almost feel his breath in my hair as he wrote along the edge of my notebook page: "I'm here. You'll have to pay up."

I blushed. I couldn't write, "No. I won't," because I'd promised. My cheeks were hot and I knew he was grinning at me. But I'd done it. He was in class.

The bell hadn't rung yet. We were deep in the study of my old friend, *The Faerie Queene*, so instead of writing, "No. I won't," I opened my text and copied out below his "pay up": "For unto knight there is no greater shame, Than lightnesse and inconstancie in love."

He liked that game. Off he went in search of an answer, running his eyes down those old words from the fifteenth century, on a hunt among gentle Knights, royall Virgins, seven-headed Dragons and ramping Lyons. We looked as if we were deep in Spenser and taking notes, of course, and we were. Pretty soon he scribbled on my notebook page: "...her grace to have, Which of all earthly things he most did crave."

I gave him a look, and he laughed. But I'd seen another passage. I didn't know whether I dared write it, yet I wanted to show him I knew how he felt. At last I copied it out: "The danger hid, the place unknowne and wilde. Breedes dreadfull doubts."

I glanced at his handsome face as he read it. He was so close I saw where he'd cut himself a little, shaving. There was a white scar in the close-clipped hair behind his ear: he'd fallen on an upturned rake once in Mr. Calvinhorn's barn. Then his eyes met mine and he nodded with no more smiles.

The class hour began. We listened to Dr. Lane with serious faces, there side by side in our paddle-armed chairs. But as the class ended and students left the room with books and chatter, Robert wrote on my notebook: "Library. 4:00."

I went to my classes, I tried to study, but all I thought of was Robert at four o'clock. When I opened the door of Patty Hayes' dorm room after lunch, her bunk beds and chairs were full of coeds.

"Four girls to a room!" Patty wailed. "One sink!"

"And now the blackout," Helen Kapler cried. "Pull the shades if you turn on even one light."

"After eleven: no lights! Come from a study room after that, and you can put up your hair and wash your face in the dark!" Val Peters said.

"It's the WAVES coming," Patty said.

"And the boys going," Val said.

"Going?" Helen said. "They're practically gone."

I gave Patty the book she wanted and left. Boys gone? Not in my world. At four o'clock I climbed those little iron library stairs. I'd promised.

Robert was there. He was there every day at four o'clock. And now the war came so close. It shut us into a cramped space, like the rows of periodicals and the small library window. How could I not let him kiss me those few breathless December afternoons? He was going to war.

"I have to work with Robert at the library every afternoon this week," I told Con. "He's missed a lot, and has
to catch up." Con couldn't imagine how true that was.

"He hasn't been going to class?" Con said.

"No," I said. "He's been hiding out, because someone
put a note on his desk that called him 'Yellow belly' –
when he's not even eighteen."

"Yes. That's pretty hard to take," Con said, not looking at me.

"I told him people sometimes treated you that way. He
said you'd understand."

"Tell him I do," Con said, and I felt suddenly happy.
The two men were friends. Cousins. And I was only kissing Robert to make sure he finished the college quarter.

No one climbed to our hideout in the library stacks
those December afternoons – no one but us. "There go
the WAVES," Robert whispered the next day. We could
hear them below our small window: "Left, right, hup,
two, three, four" a marine sergeant barked.   Girls
marched in pairs down the walk to the gym. They didn't
have uniforms yet. I leaned from Robert's arms to watch
them: girls in cloth coats and fur coats, mittens, saddle
shoes – girls my age. War had already molded them into
stiff rows and lock step.

"Coeds talk to the WAVES when they can, asking to
buy their clothes when they get uniforms," I said.
"Maybe I should be a WAVE."

"No," Robert said against my lips. "You stay here. You
wait for me."

"Wait for you?"

"Don't I love you?" Robert said, drawing back so I
could see the anger in his eyes. "Don't you love me?"

"I'm *married*," I told him. "You were there at my *wedding*."

Robert seized his coat and his notes spread on the
little table, and clattered down the iron stairs without
a word.

Then the week was over. Exams were over. Grades came in, and Robert and I had all A's.

We were almost alone in the library that last afternoon. It was Robert's eighteenth birthday. At four o'clock I came with a little birthday cake and candles. When the candles were lit, we sat for a minute in their sparkling glow.

Robert blew them out. One stayed lit.

"That's the eighteenth one. That's the one that makes me report for duty," Robert said, pinching it out. "Monday. Train to Des Moines."

There were tears in my eyes; I stood up to hide them. "Don't," he whispered, getting up, too. "Don't cry." But I cried some more with my face against his neck, smelling the scent that was no one's but his, feeling his voice vibrate through his shirt and sweater to my skin. Then he let me go and sat at the table, staring at the little cake.

For a while we didn't speak a word. He wouldn't look at me. I cut the cake in half, and we ate it.

"Snow," Robert said. "The first real snow of the winter." Clustered flakes dotted the air beyond our little window. "Will you come and see my mother when I'm gone? She's all alone."

"Of course I will."

"Falling snow always makes me think of her. She's had such a hard life," Robert said. "She didn't have any brothers or sisters, and her mother died when Mom was barely thirteen. She'd run home from school to her father's farm to feed his hired men at noon – great meals of pork chops and potatoes and apple pie – they had to have that kind of food to keep going. She couldn't stay awake in the evening to do homework – she had to read while she was hurrying to school and back, and do her homework in her head, and write it down before she fell asleep."

Snowfall began to darken our small space. "Her school was a little country school with one teacher, and students seven years old all the way to grown-up. Sometimes the big boys would follow her home."

"She was pretty."

"Yes. She was. So she took the farm dog with her – a big mutt with a mouth full of sharp teeth. He'd lie under a tree by the school and wait for her, and if any of the fellows looked like they were going to try anything, she'd say, "Captain!" (That's what they called that dog), and he'd show all his teeth and growl."

We smiled at each other. "I could use a dog like that," I said. I expected him to look wicked, or grin.

His dark eyes gleamed with the snow-light, fixed on me. "You're beautiful," he said.

For a moment it was so quiet that we heard the campanile strike the hour through the thickening snowfall.

"Your mother lived all alone with her father?" I was asking the question to make him stop looking at me.

Finally he did. "Yes. They were happy together, especially in the winters when they didn't have to work so hard. After a snowstorm, they shoveled a path to the two barns and a path to the privy and a path to the pump, and in the very worst weather they were snowbound – shut away from everybody else in the world – no telephone. He taught her to play chess, and she taught him to crochet, and they read books to each other." Robert eyes were on the snow; he looked sad and withdrawn, as if I weren't there.

"Did you know him?"

"He died before I was born. Mom doesn't even have a picture of him, but she says he was a big man with the most beautiful green eyes – green as green. 'Weed-green,' he used to say, and laugh."

"What happened to him?"

"We can't imagine what it was like out there when they were snowbound in a blizzard – there's nothing to tell you where you are except a fence now and then – and whose fence is it? You don't know. You can't see any farther than the end of your arm. You can walk and walk until you freeze, and die just a field away from your own door."

"He went out there?"

"The blizzard was fierce. He was going to the old barn, he said, to get rope – they strung rope between the house and the barns when a storm like that came. Mom was shoveling a path to the pump and thought she heard him call, and yelled back, but there wasn't any answer she ever heard. She says the wind was howling in the wind-break and driving snow in her face – she could hardly see. She called, 'Dad! Dad!' until she was hoarse, running to the barn, and then to the 'old barn,' but he wasn't any-where. She found the rope he'd gone for: he'd tied it to a barn hook, and it led way out past the gate into the fields. She followed it as far as she could, calling him."

"He let go of the rope?"

"I don't know," Robert said. "Did he hear something, and go to see, and never find his way back? She never knew. She ran in the house and lit candles and put them in every window, and hung kerosene lanterns by the barn doors, and then stood out in the snow beating heavy iron saucepans together as long as she could make her arms work, hoping he'd hear. At dawn the snow stopped and she went out and called and called. There was nothing but snow as far as she could see. She said it seemed as if there was no one left in the world but her."

Again there was silence in our small space. The campus was turning white. "Did she ever find him?" I said at last.

"There was so much snow, and it drifted – it could cover a body for months until a spring thaw. She could-n't walk to town for help; the roads were drifted shut. It'd be days before anyone could get through. She did the chores and then started wading through that snow. It was up to her waist. Sometimes it was higher. She did it two days – poking drifts with a shovel handle and digging when it felt as if there could be something there."

"By herself," I said, my voice low with the horror of it. "Digging for her father."

"She found him. It was just luck. At sunset she poked in a drift along the pig lot fence, and felt something hard. She dug down, and there was her father's face looking up at her with his green, frozen eyes."

I covered my face with my hands. Robert went on as if he couldn't stop, had to tell it all. "She didn't know what to do. Shovel the snow over him and leave him? Go to bed that night with her father lying frozen in the snow? She wouldn't, not even if she had to work all night. She had a little kerosene left for the lantern, and she had the dog, and she had rope. She dragged the farm sled up the cornfield slope to the pig yard gate, and it wasn't much farther from there."

"She could lift him?"

"No. Captain was a smart dog. She tied a rope to his collar and the other end around my grandfather's waist, and they pulled until he rolled onto the sled. They dragged him home, and she said one of her father's arms was frozen straight out. She was afraid it would break off, frozen the way it was. They pulled him into the hall of the house, and she slept beside him holding his frozen hand. The next day when men dragged the road open, they brought a wagon and took her father away."

I had tears in my eyes. "And then she had to live alone?"

"They had only rented the farm. She couldn't work it by herself. She gave Captain to a neighbor and found a room in town, and was a waitress when both my father and his brother started courting her."

We sat for a little while without a word, holding hands across our little library desk. I heard the campanile chime again. It was late.

"I want to come and see Con and my uncle before I leave," Robert said. "When are they both home?"

She didn't know what to do. Go to bed that night with her
father lying frozen in the snow? She and the dog
dragged him home.

I thought a moment. "Sunday morning's the only time you can be sure of," I said. "Before church."

"I'll call them and be there," he said, and reached for his coat.

"We'll come to see you off Monday," I said with a little quiver in my voice.

He came very close to me, then turned to look at the table, the chairs, the light, the shelves, the window. He bent to kiss me one last time, a light kiss just brushing my lips, still flavored with birthday cake.

"Goodbye," he said. "Write me."

A few steps down the stairs, he turned back to look at me and whispered, "My love."

"Robert called," Con told me in bed that night. "He wants to drop in tomorrow morning to say goodbye to Dad and me. And you, of course."

"Your Dad and you are the only relatives he has, except his grandmother," I said, and waited. Con had never told me S.C. was supporting Robert. Did he know? He said nothing.

So there I was the next morning, dressed for church and standing between Con and Robert in our sun-room. S.C. sat in his wheel chair and scowled at Robert while we kept up a polite chatter about train schedules, the weather...

"So you're going to fight for your country," S.C. said. "Marines."

Robert said, "Yes, sir. I go to Des Moines to be sworn in, then to boot camp – I don't know where."

"At least there's one Beale the family can be proud of," S.C. said.

The room was still. Robert looked as if he hadn't heard what he'd heard, as if no father would say such a thing.

"I'll...write," Robert said, floundering in that awful silence.

"Good luck," S.C. said.

"Thank you, sir," Robert said. I thought he was going to shake S.C.'s hand, but I saw that he would not. He clapped Con on the back instead. "My mother will get my pay every month," he said, and his brown eyes glittered for a moment.

S.C. stared at him. "You look like your father," he said.

"That's what my mother says." Robert turned away. Con and I followed him to the front door and watched him go down the walk.

"His mother's poor," I said.

"Yes," Con said.

"She's your aunt," I said. "Couldn't you do something for her? Couldn't I?"

"You're a Beale now, too. She won't let us help her," Con said. He put his arms around me and rested his cheek on the top of my head. "Remember that mother cat with one kitten your uncle told you about once?" he said.

He wasn't going to tell me anything more, though we stood in each other's arms in the pale sunlight. "I wish I were going with him," Con said.

The station platform was cold next morning in spite of the sun. I stood beside Con among Robert's friends, and got only Robert's peck on the cheek that Mig and the other girls got. Robert hugged his mother and hugged Joe, too, who was there on crutches in his Marine uniform.

I hardly heard the lame jokes and sad banter. Robert and I were sending the strongest signal possible by agreeing without words to neither look at each other nor talk to each other. I hoped no one noticed. Then the train came in, relentless and thundering, and took Robert away.

"Can we drive you home?" I said to Mrs. Laird. Her face was very white, but she wasn't crying.

She glanced at Con. "No," she said. "No, thanks. It's only a little walk. It'll do me good."

Con's face took on the chilly, distant look he often wore in public now. People might not call him a draft-dodger to his face the way his father did, but they said it behind his back. "Let us know if you hear from Robert, and we'll tell you if we get a letter," Con called after her. "And if we can help you in any way..." She didn't turn and never answered.

21

"B ehold, I bring you good tidings of great joy," Betty
announced to the congregation the next Thursday
night. She was standing on my orange crate with the janitor's flashlight on her. My cheesecloth angel costume –
with the jacket – was draped on her, and the tinsel wings
were scratching her behind, no doubt. It was Christmas
1942, and after a year the church crowd was more cheerful: we thought we might win the war, even though it
seemed to be lasting forever.

"Unto you is born this day in the city of David..."

"You're the most beautiful angel God ever made,"
Con whispered.

I looked up at him with the same loving look he was
giving me. We sat in our usual pew, an old married couple. No Robert Laird watched me from the choir. Only
middle-aged men sang there now.

Betty climbed down and hid behind the pulpit until she
had to trail behind Mary and Joseph and a big baby doll
going off to Egypt. When the last hymn was sung, Con
and I went home to our first Christmas tree, expensive
gifts, and – the next day – Christmas day dinner with the
Letty family. Our holidays were as nice as Con could
make them, but then the long, cold winter settled in. All
I had to look forward to was college classes.

One afternoon I went up to Patty Hayes' dorm room.
She was sprawled on a dorm bed beside Sonia Jensen,
Arlene Brown and bags of popcorn. There was something new in her room: Robert's graduation picture stood
on the desk.

She'd seen me look at it. "Robert Laird's in marine boot camp," she said, passing a bag of popcorn to me. "San Diego."

I didn't even know where Robert had been sent. He'd written her. He had a perfect right to – she wasn't married. I tried to keep my expression disinterested, while the fickle, girl-chasing Robert Laird I had known in high school smiled at me from Patty's desk.

"So," Arlene said, teasing Patty. "You're getting love letters?"

"I'm not telling." Patty pulled her long red hair over her face for a moment. "We're such good friends."

"Where's he going to be sent?" I asked, calling her bluff, but she won.

"I've got his letter someplace," she said, pawing through junk beside Robert's picture. She found it, a single sheet of paper, but she wouldn't let us see it. "He doesn't talk about the *Marines*, she said, and giggled, running her eyes down her private note. "He's got some letters and numbers at the end – 'TFQ 1 22-23.' Maybe you can figure out where he's going from that?" She raised her eyebrows at me with a mock-innocent look. But don't tell. You know what they say: 'The slip of a lip can sink a ship.'"

"I've got to get home – suppertime," I said, hardly hearing their goodbyes, hardly seeing the dorm stairs, the students battling wind on the campus walks, or any of the streets on my way home. I found Mig in the kitchen looking just-kissed and blissful – it had been her afternoon off with Joe – but I hardly saw her, either. I mumbled hello, shut myself in my study and found my English textbook.

And there they were on the textbook page: *The Faerie Queene*, Canto One, lines 22-23: "...her grace to have, Which of all earthly things he most did crave."

I laughed out loud, there in my study. Had Robert taken his text with him? Torn out the pages? Clever-clever-clever. He was writing to me about love the only way he could: some letters and numbers across the miles. If Patty gloated, I could read his love letter to me, hidden in her note.

Which of all earthly things...I was so happy that I wanted everyone else in the world to be happy, too. TFQ 1 22-23.

But how could Con be happy? Evening after miserable evening Con had to listen to his father. Almost every night at supper S.C. told him he was no good.

I couldn't bear it.

One night before supper I went into the kitchen. "How's Joe?" I said to Mig.

"He's not...always himself," Mig said. "Sometimes terrible memories come over him, and I just hang on to him..." she blushed and started putting dirty dishes in the dishwasher to hide it.

I sat down to fold clean towels from the clothes dryer. "Con wishes he could fight," I said.

"I know," Mig said. "And the way Mr. Beale goes after him! The first time I heard him, I nearly came in the dining room to see if someone was having a fit. Such a lucky, rich man in such a house..." She stared at me. "What's the matter with him?"

"He's cruel. But I've got an idea," I said.

"Joe says you've got some of the best ideas in town." Mig grinned at me. "He says you got Robert to go back and finish the quarter. He'd tried and tried, with absolutely no success – he can't imagine how you did it."

I bent over the clean towels so Mig wouldn't see my face and changed the subject fast. "You can hear us from the kitchen when we have supper, can't you?"

"Every word," Mig said. "I bet the neighbors can, too."

"We've got to stop him," I said. "He doesn't do it every night, but the minute he starts, he gets that whine in his voice – have you heard it?"

"Think so," Mig said, her pretty dark eyes intent.

"Here's my idea," I said. "We'll find a half-dozen things that will suddenly call Con away from the table, and you can come in with one of them and shut S.C. up."

"Good!" Mig said and clapped her hands.

When Con and I were in bed that night, cuddled together in "Con's Castle," I told him my plan.

Con was quiet for a little while. I was afraid I'd hurt his feelings or gone too far. I put my cheek against his and said, "It's just that I can't bear to hear your father yell at you – he's cruel! He's a liar! And you have to sit and listen to it because you respect him and won't fight with him. It makes me so proud of you – and so mad at him!"

Con turned his face and kissed me hard. "You're a little fighter," he said.

"Maybe he can make us live with him, but we've got our Castle that no one comes into but us. We have our breakfasts together," I said. "We can't stop him from yelling while you're at the Company, or when you have to work with him in the evening, but you can watch him stopped in the middle of a sentence if he ever picks on you again at suppertime!"

Con was silent for a moment. I sighed. "I know it's sneaky."

When Con spoke again, his voice was so changed, there in the dark, that I hardly knew it. "But don't ever sneak with me, will you?" he said. "I couldn't bear it. Come talk to me. Tell me the truth."

Would the winter ever end? Would the war go on forever? Roosevelt traveled to Casablanca. Rommel's Afrika Korps drove our army back in Tunisia. Shoe rationing began – only three pairs a year for us. Dreary, dreary, dreary. I slogged back and forth to the campus in the snow and cold. And then, in a few days, there was a letter with no stamp among the letters stuffed through our front door slot.

Robert. I knew that handwriting – hadn't I seen it decorating the edges of my notebook? The envelope was addressed to S.C.. I had to put it beside his place at breakfast, and have my breakfast with Con in the sunroom.

We joined S.C. for our breakfast coffee as usual. Robert's envelope, slit open, lay beside S.C.'s plate. S.C. was silent, as usual, rustling the pages of his newspaper, and we had no choice but to drink and listen to our cups chinking on their saucers, or cars creaking past on the snowy street.

When Con and S.C. left for work, Con kissed me where I sat alone at the breakfast table, looking at Robert's letter beside S.C.'s crumpled napkin.

It wasn't my letter to read.

The telephone rang. Mig answered it and her voice grew soft and happy: she was talking to Joe, and would talk for a while. In a second I had Robert's letter out of the envelope.

He didn't say much. He was at boot camp in San Diego. He didn't know where they would be sent. He asked S.C. to give his regards to Con and me. And at the bottom of the letter: "TFQ 1 418-23."

I heard Mig saying goodbye and jammed the letter in its envelope, put it back and ran to my study. TFQ 1 418-23.

I found it. How I blushed, all by myself there, reading: "And made him dreame of loves and lustfull play, That nigh his manly hart did melt away, Bathed in wanton blis and wicked joy: Then seemed him his Lady by him lay, And to him playnd, how that false winged boy, Her chast hart had subdewd, to learne Dame Pleasures toy."

Professor Lane had read that passage in class. "The dream lady's complaining that her chaste heart has been subdued by a false boy with wings," Professor Lane said. "Now who could that boy be? How many of you girls have received a valentine with that false winged boy on it? What do we call him?"

"Cupid," somebody answered.

"Right," Professor Lane said. "But what's 'Dame Pleasures toy' that this lovestruck lady's going to learn? Well... every age has different words for that."

I'd giggled with the rest of the class then, not looking at Robert beside me. Now the dream of the "knight of the Redcrosse" came over the miles from a Marine boot camp, striking me with what Robert was dreaming of, and what he wanted, and what I couldn't give him.

So I wrote a letter to him. I could do that. No one would know. I could say one thing and mean another, and no one would know that, either. I sat down at my desk and began:

January 14, 1943

Dear Robert,

There in San Diego you can't be having the kind of cold, lonely weather we're having in Iowa. I sit in the library with a view of nothing but National Geographics *and a snowy campus, but there you are in sunny California in your "quarters." At least that's what Patty and S.C. think that "Q" means at the bottom of their letters. That's their best guess.*

Not much news. Does Joe tell you that he and Mig are coming very close to being engaged? His leg isn't healing as fast as it should, but the doctor believes it will just take time. Mig says Joe still has his scary spells sometimes, but he's soon himself again.

I wrote about my classes...the rationing...my letter sounded friendly, that was all. But when I finished, I opened *The Faerie Queene* looking and looking for lines that would tell him how much I...

Suddenly I closed my textbook with a snap. What was I doing?

Snow had begun to fall. I watched it settle on the dead garden beyond my window. I watched it for a long time. Then I opened Spenser again, and found the line I had to

write, and put it below my signature: TFQ VI 295.   I
mailed his letter before I could change my mind.

Coming back from the mailbox, I thought the below-
zero morning was warm compared to my letter.   Robert
would open it – I could see him in uniform with all the
others, running his brown eyes down that page.   Joe had
told me how hard Marine training was.   After a brutal day
preparing to kill or be killed, Robert could search at last
in *The Faerie Queene* for a single, hopeless line: "In vain he
seeks that having cannot hold."

The day dragged through classes and homework and
the cold walk home.   S.C. brought Robert's letter to supper that night.   "From Robert," he said, and read it to us.
We listened without a word.

S.C. pushed his glasses up his nose, staring at Robert's
letter.   "He's put 'TFQ 1 418-23' at the bottom.   His
quarters, probably.   'Federal quarters'?   'Field quarters'?"   S.C.'s voice went up.   "Serving his country!" he
snarled at Con.   "Doing his duty!   And I did my duty in
World War One!"

I saw Con brace himself, but I barely heard S.C. going
after Con.   I was listening to TFQ 1 418-23: *Then seemed
him his Lady by him lay...*

Lost in Spenser's words, I was as unprepared as S.C.
was to find Mig in the kitchen doorway saying,
"Telephone for you, Mr. Con."

"Phone?" S.C. snapped.   "I didn't hear any phone."

"Excuse me," Con said, and went into the hall.

I sat beside S.C. and ate my chocolate pudding, not
even tasting it.   *In vain he seeks that having cannot hold.*

"Who was it?" S.C. scowled at Con when he returned.

"Church business," Con said, smiling at me as he
wheeled his father away from the table and off to the sunroom where they worked evening after evening.   "Church

business" was a safe fib. S.C. never went to church: Robert's mother would be there.

Mig came to get the dirty dishes and grinned at me. "It worked," she said. "Maybe he won't try it again."

S.C. tried it again, of course. Every time his voice rose in its nasty whine over the supper table, there was Mig, informing Con that the kitchen faucet wouldn't turn off... the newspaper boy was at the back door...

It wasn't long before it seemed to us that S.C. had figured our trick out. "He'll go after Mig one of these days," Con said.

"I bet he won't," I said. "He'll be too ashamed. Haven't we told him – without a single word – that we all see how nasty he is to you, and we want him to stop?"

S.C. stopped, most of the time. He would hardly say a word to us at supper, but Con and I didn't mind. We could find plenty to say to each other after the long day.

Mig and I had made a habit of visiting the Steplers every Saturday afternoon. One snowy, wind-blown Saturday as we walked up to their door, Mig said, "Mr. Beale's stopped yelling. It's working."

"Thanks to you," I said. Joe opened the door, smiling into Mig's eyes, and I saw he had an envelope in his hand.

It was a service letter with no stamp. I knew that handwriting.

We took off our wraps. We talked to the Steplers and Joe. It seemed to me that Joe would never mention the letter – never read it. Our polite conversation began with the newest Abbott and Costello film, then we discussed whether *Mrs. Miniver* would sweep the Academy Awards, and talked forever, I thought, about rationing.

"A friend in Detroit wrote that the city's growing by hundreds of thousands," Mrs. Stepler said. "And the young teenagers!" She passed a plate of cookies. "They're leaving school in droves. Getting good jobs in the war plants."

I waited. I drank my hot chocolate. I fidgeted. Finally Joe said, "It sounds as if Robert's going into the Pacific theater before long."

Going to war. And there I sat with my cruel line from Spenser running through my head.

"I'll read you what he says." Joe unfolded the letter. Robert described preparations for overseas duty, and Joe stopped now and then to explain them to us. His face looked so much older, I thought, and very sad. "This will probably be his last letter from the States for a while."

We sat so quietly for a moment that we could hear a train going through town. Then Mrs. Stepler brought more hot chocolate. I drank mine without tasting it as I tried to see if there were letters and numbers on Robert's letter. Joe had put the letter down with the last page on top, but I was too far away to read it.

"Here's an interesting chart I was sent last week," Mr. Stepler said, passing it around. "For air raid protection. It's got the principal war planes – shows them from below." The names of the planes sounded in deadly earnest: "A-20A, Attack Bomber; Brewster Dive Bomber, SB2A-1; Grumman Fighter, F4F-3 ... "

Soon Mig and I would have to leave. "I wonder," I said idly, as if I really didn't care much, "does Robert's letter have numbers at the end? S.C.'s letter had them, and we didn't know what they meant."

Joe picked up Robert's letter again. "TFQ 1 466," he said. "I didn't notice it before. TFQ 1 466. Don't know – it might be the number of his quarters. They weren't using numbers like that when I was in camp."

How thankful I was that we had carried on enough polite conversation so that I could say, "I suppose we'd better be on our way home."

After long minutes, we left. I walked so fast that Mig could hardly keep up. "I'd better get some studying done before supper," I told her when we arrived, taking off my wraps as I disappeared down the hall. I shut my study door and *The Faerie Queene* flew open under my hands.

"1 466." I sat and looked at the line until I couldn't bear to look at it any more.

Let me not die in languor and long tears.

Robert had left the country, Joe told us. That was the reason no word came. His letters would take a long time now, Joe said, if Robert had been sent where he thought he'd been sent. Joe didn't want to talk about it.

That winter seemed to be two winters long. Thousands of older people moved to Washington to work in wartime offices. Canned goods were rationed, and then meat and fat and cheese, and all of them were scarce even if you had the coupons. But we won back the Kasserine Pass in Tunisia, and early in March we had a major victory: the Battle of the Bismarck Sea. We sank twenty-two Japanese ships – a whole convoy – and shot down fifty of their planes.

"It's a turning point," Joe said. "After New Guinea, and the Solomons, the Gilbert Islands...Bougainville... Tarawa..."

Now every young man was gone, except for the wounded, like Joe, and a few who were 4F, and a few, like Con, who were deferred. Servicemen in uniform came home on leave, but Cedar Falls was a town of the old, the middle-aged, and women and children. Con in his civilian clothes was stared at – we never got used to it. People bought war stamps, collected rubber...toothpaste tubes... grease...scrap metal.

Then four hundred Army Air Corps Cadets arrived on campus from Missouri.

"It's swell!" Sonia yelled, bouncing up and down on Patty's dorm bed. "Men!" She was wearing a man's suit coat, the newest fad. You wore your boyfriend's suit coat while he was in the service.

"Most of them are sick," Arlene said. "The first night they used up all the hot water in Baker Hall and Seerley Hall."

"Don't kiss 'em for a week, then," Patty said.

"I thought you were saving yourself for Robert Laird," Sonia said.

"Well, I am," Patty said, "but a girl has to have some fun. And it's almost April! It's almost spring!"

"Some spring," Arlene said. "The war in North Africa..."

"Every island in the Pacific," Patty said.

The three eyed me with expressions that said, "How would you know? What do you care?" I suppose it seemed strange to them that I kept coming to Patty's room when they gave me looks like that. Why would I want to be with girls who missed their men?

And then, one April afternoon, I climbed the dorm stairs and heard sobbing and cries from Patty's room. Patty was crumpled on her bed, red-faced and crying, and Arlene and Sonia were holding her hands and trying to calm her.

"Robert's been killed," Arlene said when she saw me.

I sat down at Patty's desk. Robert smiled from his picture frame.

"His mother just got the telegram," Sonia said. "Arlene's mother heard about it downtown."

"I loved him," Patty howled. "And he loved me." She sat up so suddenly that Arlene almost fell off the bed. "You were so mean to him!" she yelled at me. "Wouldn't even dance with him at the Junior-Senior Prom! Left him standing in the middle of the floor – I saw you!"

I couldn't say a word.

I walked to Seerley Park and sat on one of the swings for a long time. We'd played in that park, Robert and I, riding the merry-go-round faster and faster until we got dizzy, felt sick, and had to yell, "Stop!" and get off.

Dandelions bloomed at my feet. They knifed park grass with leaves as thin as saw blades.

His mother. At last I thought of his mother, and ran to her house through the warm spring sunshine.

No one answered my knock at the kitchen door. Was she home? Was she hidden away in a bedroom, crying by herself? The thought made me push the door open and call, "Mrs. Laird?"

There was old Mrs. Laird, asleep in her nest of shabby bits and pieces. She was wearing the same old sweater...Robert's dark head had bent over her ... I went to cry to myself in the kitchen corner by the old hot plate where Robert had shouted, "He's got money in his pocket. He's got you in his—"

Then I heard footsteps, and Robert's mother stood in the kitchen doorway. I couldn't say a word – I ran to throw my arms around her, and we cried and cried. "Gone," she kept whispering. "Nothing left. Gone. Nothing."

22

Robert's mother showed me the telegram. How many mothers had found a messenger at their doors that same day, delivering the envelope that held those final, dreadful, standard words:

The Secretary of War desires to express his deep regret that your son...

At first her doorbell rang: neighbors brought her food and flowers. But they were never invited in, not even my uncle. By the time the blue star in her window was changed to death's gold star, I was the only one who knocked on her door.

"She comes back to her poor little house about five every day," I told Con in bed one night. "And who does she have for company but an old lady who hardly says a word? I don't think she cares any more about whether I'm a Beale or not. I can make her tea and bring some cookies and listen to her talk."

"About Robert?" Con said.

"All the little things she remembers," I said. "She cries sometimes, but it does her good, I hope. I think she tells herself he's just gone somewhere..." Con could hear my voice change, gritty with sadness; he held me tight.

"She looks so thin and old now," I said, "but she must have been pretty once, with your father and his brother both wooing her, fighting over her."

"It was a battle," Con said. "Always is, if you find the one woman you can't live without, and somebody else wants her, too."

"There's no good way out of that," I said, thinking of myself.

"Except not to give up. Except to win." Con's voice was grave. "I think I'd have wanted to die if I'd lost."

"Die!"

Con didn't answer. We lay together in silence for a while, until I changed the subject. "She needs a lift. Something to cheer her up. There's nothing but that terrible old hot plate in her kitchen. I know you can't buy new stoves, but could we find a used one for her?"

"I'll find one," Con said. "You'll have to persuade her to take it."

I talked and talked to Adele. It was my present, I told her. At last she gave in. Con found a used refrigerator, too.

"Such luxury!" Adele said, and tried to pay Con and me.

"No, indeed not," Con said. "Your Robert fought for us – that's enough pay for anyone."

When I came after my afternoon class to admire her kitchen, she said, "You must have the first cup of hot chocolate from my new stove."

"Wish I'd stopped by the house and brought some of Mig's coffeecake," I said.

"Never mind – I've got cookies," Adele said, and we ate at her kitchen table by the shining refrigerator and stove. She wanted to hear what I'd studied that day. "I wish I could have gone to college," she said wistfully. "But Robert went, and got all A's, too. And you helped him when he wanted to give up and just wait to be drafted." Her eyes filled with tears. She couldn't say "Robert" yet without crying. I had a lump in my throat in that kitchen where Robert had stood so close to me and whispered, *Nobody understands how I feel. Nobody but you.*

"You should call me 'Aunt Adele,' dear," Adele said, looking at me over her cup. "That's what I am, after all, and you don't have many relatives."

So I called her "Aunt Adele," and one day I told her the story of how my mother had fallen on the parsonage grass and died that very night. I told her about Robert's rabbit: Rabbit In Paradise.

"And I liked Robert," I said. "Every girl did. I watched him – I even kept a shoestring of his for a long time." We smiled at each other. She looked younger when she smiled. Robert had had her beautiful lips, curved and sharply edged. If she'd have her hair set at the beauty shop and wear a little makeup, I thought, she'd still be pretty. But sadness seemed to dull her – eyes, hair, skin.

One day she said, "I've been wanting to show you some pictures of Robert ... and you, too," she said, and brought a photograph album to the table.

And there was Robert as a pretty baby, and Robert as I first remembered him, his brown hair combed straight across his forehead, his knickers tucked into knee-high leather boots with their knife pocket. And there was the Letty's orphan niece in old wash dresses and scuffed oxfords, hair bow wilted and long hair flying. "But some pictures are missing," Aunt Adele said, looking puzzled. "There were some of you right here – you with a pumpkin, and you with Robert, and you in your Gypsy Girl costume..." she leafed through the scrapbook.

"I'm a romantic," I told her. "I like love stories. Where did you first meet Robert's father? Was it love at first sight?"

"Oh," she said with a little tremor in her voice, "it was. I can't explain it. I was engaged to be married..." she hesitated. "To his older brother. I can't believe it yet. Engaged to be married to...your father-in-law. Think of it! I might have married Sam Beale! But Henry Beale was discharged and came home to help run the Equipment Company, and I simply couldn't help myself."

She got up from the table to put another album before me. "Look at them," she said. "Brothers. And I..."

I stared at the two handsome, broad-chested young men who had their arms around each other's shoulders. They were in army uniforms: the shining-booted, tight-coated look of the First World War. They smiled: a young Robert, a young Con—No. One was Robert's father. The other was sour, dour S.C. Beale.

Adele saw my confusion. "Good-looking, weren't they?" she said. "But they weren't at all alike. My Henry could charm you...charm you...so persistent, so deter-mined, and clever, too."

"Another Robert."

Adele shook her head, but she was smiling a little, too. "Robert broke some hearts, I'm afraid." She stopped smiling. "Henry and I broke your father-in-law's heart. There Sam Beale was, so proud of me, even though I was just a waitress at the hotel cafe, promising he'd give me everything I wanted someday when he'd made a success of the Beale Equipment Company – Oh, it was awful, what I did!" She put her thin hands over her face for a moment. "On our very wedding day! Everybody knew about it, and Sam..." Now she looked as if she would cry. "Poor Sam. He hated his own brother so. He hated me. He would-n't go in that church ever again, because there I was, com-ing down that aisle, going through the wedding we'd planned – the dress and the flowers and the minister and everything – marrying his own brother instead of him."

"But to marry the wrong man... "

"It filled Sam full of such hate," Adele said in a low, ashamed voice.

"But he helped Robert," I said. "He did do that."

"Yes. That made such a difference. But he wouldn't have Henry at the Company – we had to leave town. After that Henry could never seem to find the right job. Sam married Lillian McCutcheon not long afterward, and they had Conrad right away. But Henry and I had two lit-tle girls who died, and finally we had Robert, and then

Henry died in a flu epidemic. And then I married Charlie Laird, here in Cedar Falls, and he died, too."

"You've lost so many people you loved," I said.

"We both have," she said, making my heart ache, and got up to turn on the kitchen light. I told her it was about time for me to go.

"I have something...I didn't know whether to tell you..." she said. "I got a letter from Robert yesterday."

"Robert!"

"No...no...he wrote it before he...someone must have mailed it after he..." she couldn't finish her sentence but took the letter from her apron pocket and read it aloud: a short note that said the fighting was heavy, he was all right, he loved her and thought of home so many times a day.

"May I see it?" I said, and she gave me the letter. At the bottom of it he had written "TFQ 7 129."

I hugged Adele and said goodbye and didn't run to look in *The Faerie Queene*. Not this time. I walked home thinking that maybe I'd never open Spenser again, or read a single word of it.

I talked with Mig. I set the table for supper. I took a shower. I ate a few bites and said a few words to Con between his long evening with his father and his falling asleep beside me.

I lay wide awake. At last I slid from under Con's arm and tiptoed to my study.

The night was still. Only a train wailed through town in the dark. A spring moon was out, spreading white light on my desk and bookshelves. I opened Spenser and found Robert's last line, one line among all the other black letters in the moonlight. Canto seven, line 129:

So willingly she came into his armes.

Spring had never seemed sad to me before. Now it came without Robert, pushing its pretty buds and flowers in my face like a playful child at a funeral. I spent all the time I could at Robert's house, listening to Aunt Adele's stories of losing her little daughters, losing Henry, losing and losing.

I told her about my own life, not leaving out any of the bad parts when I'd lied about ghosts, or connived with Mig to make S.C. stop yelling at Con, or driven Mrs. Pell half crazy.

"I'm awful – I like to pay people back," I said. "Look how I treated Aunt Gertrude when I took her to Black's and didn't tell her the new clothes were for her."

"She deserved it," Adele said. "I watched the way she treated you – watched her for years. You were an orphan. Look how you helped Victoria, and Mig, and Robert, too, when people called him names and he stayed home and wasn't going to finish the quarter."

I couldn't answer that. "You need some new dishes," I said, changing the subject. "At least the war hasn't made china hard to get." War brides in town complained that everything they got at bridal showers was either china or glass.

Aunt Adele couldn't argue that her dishes weren't old and cracked. One day I bought her a new set, and sneaked in before she came home from work to put them in her cupboards.

Just as I finished, the doorbell rang. When I answered it, the boy put a telegram in my hand, jumped on his bicycle, and was off down the walk.

A telegram. No one I knew sent telegrams unless the message was death or destruction. I'd only seen one: the one saying Robert was dead. I put the telegram on the kitchen table. For a half hour it lay there like a grenade with the pin pulled.

At last Aunt Adele opened the kitchen door and said hello. She took off her hat and pushed her hair back from her thin face.

I held out the telegram. "It came just a little while ago," I said as she grabbed it with shaking hands and turned it over and over.

"Robert?" she said. "Robert?" She found a knife in a kitchen drawer and slit the top of the envelope as carefully as if the words inside might bleed. It only took her a few seconds to read them, and her face grew so white I thought she might faint.

"Robert's alive!" she cried. "He's alive! He's been wounded, but he's alive! He's coming home next Saturday! He's alive!"

I sat in a chair, weak-kneed. She wandered around her kitchen saying, "He's alive...he's alive..." and then hugged me and cried and cried, while I cried, too.

"I can't believe it," she said.

"I can't believe it," I said, and we went on repeating those four words, laughing and crying.

"Tell everyone!" she said, and I said I would. "You stay here and dance around and be happy," I said. "I'll run everywhere with the news!"

What an afternoon that was. "Robert's alive!" I cried when Joe answered his door. I laughed to see his astonishment, then his happiness, but all the while Robert was coming back to me: his voice, his kisses.

"He's been hurt but he'll be home Saturday!" I told the Lettys, and heard Robert say, *Wait for me.*

I told Mig. I told Con and S.C. when they came home. I was a real Christmas angel this time, even if it was May: "I bring good tidings of great joy."

There was no cold December wind on the station platform when Robert came home. No friends and family stood there with sad faces, trying to be cheerful. Robert had been dead to us, a gold star in his mother's window.

The train rumbled in, almost as loud as my heart. A tall Marine left the train and came toward us in the May sun: Robert.

"He can walk," I told myself in those seconds. Then I saw his empty sleeve. I saw the bandage covering half his face. He looked at me, and the expression in his one eye was so strange that I hardly knew him.

He had his right arm. He could shake hands with the men, and the women all kissed him, even me, on his unbandaged cheek. "We'd have had the town band out to welcome you home, but they're playing for Uncle Sam today," Joe said, and the rest of us laughed as if it were a good joke.

We said all the trite things people say at such times, and at last watched Robert walk away with his mother, his bandaged face bent to her happy one.

The next day in church his mother came alone. "How happy you must be," people told her after church. "How's Robert?"

"Tired," she said. "He wants to rest. He's not up to seeing people yet."

I talked to her in the church hall. "He's having a lot of pain," she said. "He wants to be alone, except for Joe Stepler. I wish you could come. Maybe in a little while."

Maybe never. Hadn't I written: *In vain he seeks that having cannot hold*?

I watched for him in church. I picked up the telephone, and put it down. I found excuses to go with Mig to Joe's house, and asked Joe, "How's Robert?"

"He's pretty bad yet," Joe said. "I'm spending a lot of time with him. He spent a lot of time with me."

Day by day Robert was in Cedar Falls. He was in his mother's house, hidden behind the front door that I watched from the Letty parlor. He seemed farther away from me than he'd been when I was the "hired girl."

I tried to keep busy. Housewives were constantly reminded that we had important jobs to do in wartime.

We saved fats – a pound of fat, they told us, had enough glycerin to make powder for six 75-mm shells or fifty 30-caliber bullets. Other ordinary household objects suddenly acquired lethal new personalities: razor blades could metamorphose into machine guns; 30 brass lipstick tubes would make twenty cartridges.

War Ration Book Two had come out in February with its rows of red and blue stamps marked A, B, C, D. Mig and I had to dole out the ones for processed foods, meat, cheese and fats. We could have twenty-eight ounces of meat a week for each of us, unless we wanted the best meat, which took more points. But Mig's relatives on a farm near town let us have something from their slaughtering every now and then.

We watched the newspaper for announcements: "Coffee coupon No. 25 expires. Last day to use No. 4 'A' coupon, good for four gallons of gasoline. Last day to use A, B, and C coupons for processed foods in Ration Book 2."

Our small ration of butter was never enough – everybody cooked and baked with it; there was nothing to take its place but lard. And four ounces of cheese for each of us a week? "Eggs," Mig often said resignedly. "It'll have to be eggs again." We washed empty food cans and soaked off the paper label, cut off both ends, mashed the cans flat with our foot, and turned them in to make tanks and ships.

I sold war savings stamps in the college union. Once a week I joined friends downtown at the Red Cross Center. We sat at long tables to fold bandages, measuring them against our rulers, listening to the war news and music.

"Robert's home, but I never see him," Patty Hayes said one night, sitting beside me at a Red Cross table. She was making sure that her diamond ring showed as she turned and folded the bandage gauze. Finally she said, "I'm engaged, you know. James Baker. In the Air Corps. He's from Texas – a cowboy." She giggled.

"Hope you'll be very happy," I said.

The Star Spangled Banner blared from the radio, and we all stood up. "I hear Robert looks awful," Patty said as we sat down again. "One arm gone – and an eye! I thought he'd at least call me."

"He doesn't even come to church," Sally Horton said. Robert didn't come to church. Nobody saw him, week after week. S.C. asked if we should have Robert to dinner, but his mother told me one Sunday that he wouldn't be able to come. Robert was avoiding almost everyone he knew, although they hadn't hurt him – except me.

Finally I went to see his mother, even though Robert shut himself in his room when I came. She made excuses for him: he was tired, he was sleeping. May went by. My college classes ended. It was summer vacation. It was June.

One morning Mig and I went out with the Steplers and Joe to admire neat rows of vegetables in their victory garden. I happened to be alone with Joe for a moment at the end of a line of green sprouts. "How's Robert?" I asked: the same old question I'd asked for weeks.

"Come to Overman Park this afternoon, will you? About one?" Joe said in a low voice the others couldn't hear, then left me, so I couldn't ask the one thing I wanted to know: would Robert be at the park? I hurried home to wash my hair, put on fresh makeup and a clean summer dress, and was so jumpy that Mig asked me what was the matter. I couldn't tell her.

But when I went to the park, no one was waiting by the little statue of Liberty but Joe.

He walked with a cane, and stretched his stiff leg before him as he sat beside me on a bench.

"It's about Robert?" I asked.

"He's not in so much pain any more," Joe said, "but I can't get through to him. I've tried everything, used every argument. But he's lost an arm. Worse yet, he's lost half a face. His eye's gone, and the cheek is mashed up – he won't even look at it – keeps a bandage on it."

"Have you seen it?"

Joe pressed his big hands between his knees. "Yes. It's not pretty. And he was always..." he glanced at me "...so good looking." He tried to chuckle. "Now, if it'd been me, nobody would notice."

"Mig would," I said, trying to keep my voice light. "Mig thinks you're the handsomest man who ever put on a Marine uniform, and I think she's not far wrong."

That almost made Joe smile, but not quite. "He's seen too much," he said. He began to rock back and forth a little, his hands between his knees. "He had buddies and saw them killed right in front of him. You can't bury them, or get them away. He tried to cover them with dirt, but shells came over and blew them apart..."

I put a hand on Joe's arm, as if I could bring him back from where he'd gone, but he cried, "You get like a tiger or a wolf – kill, kill, kill! And he got caught in mortar fire – I've been there." Joe put his face in his hands for a moment. Children were playing on a jungle gym nearby. "Ak-ak-ak-ak-ak" one boy yelled, machine-gunning his playmates with a dead stick.

Joe turned to me. "Go to his house, will you? He won't leave home. See what you can do. Talk to him alone, tell him he's got a long, good life ahead of him. He's alive, for Christ's sake! He won't have his left arm or his good looks, but he was supposed to be dead."

"If he doesn't want to see any – "

"You helped him once."

"Does he know I'm coming?"

"No. He won't like it. But you go tell him he's a fool! He's got everything to live for!"

I watched Joe limp away.

I hadn't said I'd go.

23

I sat alone on the park bench, staring at the grass. Robert's mother was at work.

I got up and examined the Statue of Liberty on her pedestal. Robert would be alone, except for his grandmother.

Finally I walked past the stores on Main Street and into the cool shade of arching elms.

Would I turn off Main Street to take the leafy alley block after block? Would I stop at Robert's house? Of course not.

But there I was a few minutes later, knocking softly on his kitchen door.

No one answered.

I knew every corner of that house now. I tiptoed into the kitchen. There was old Mrs. Laird asleep in the living room, her chin on her thread-stitched sweater, though the June day was hot. She had spilled tea from a cup on a tray, and the puddle glittered at her feet.

"Robert?" I called softly down the hall. "Are you here?"

I knew which tiny bedroom was his. I looked through the open door into his summer-hot, dim room.

Robert was there, lying so still in his bed that I thought perhaps he was asleep. His one eye was shut and the sheet was pulled halfway up his body; his bandaged face was hidden by his one arm. The stump of the other was buried under a pillow.

"Robert?" I whispered. "Are you asleep?"

He said nothing, but I felt that he was listening.

I whispered, "It's me. Miranda."

"Go away," he said.

I came closer. "Why?" I said. "Who's your best friend, except for your mother and Joe?"

He made a sound that was enough like a sob so that I couldn't bear it. I sat beside him, then bent to lay my head on his sweaty chest.

He kept his arm across his face. "Don't," he said.

"I will," I said.

"Will what?" His voice was so furious that I raised my head to look at him, and found his one eye glaring at me as if he would kill me if he could.

"Care about you," I said.

"Me?" he said, and laughed a horrible laugh. "You had your chance. Look at me now, lady. One arm. Half a face." His words were fierce, but his lips, free of the bandage, quivered. Suddenly a single tear broke from his one eye and streaked to the pillow.

I said his name over and over, not even hearing my own voice: "Oh, Robert...Robert..." I was crying myself, and trying to block his hopelessness any way I could think of, as if it were a wound and he would bleed to death. I shoved his arm away and kissed him.

Kisses weren't enough. Tears kept running from his eye to his pillow. Words weren't enough: I heard him sob. I yanked my clothes off, kicked them away, and pressed us together under his sheet, bare skin to bare skin. "Do you think I care about your arm?" I cried – I couldn't recognize my frantic voice, or believe what I was doing – "Do you think I care about your face?"

He groaned as I kissed him, and the stump of his arm slid from under the pillow, bandaged and dreadful. But his other arm was strong enough to roll him over me – his whole body was heavy on me as I kissed him; I smelled his bandage's adhesive tape and medicine. We were both sobbing, wet-eyed and wet-skinned, and suddenly I turned into someone new: a wild woman soaked in tears who moaned and gasped and couldn't help it, couldn't stop, didn't want to stop –

It scared me to death. I don't know how long I lay under him, his arm stump against me, my face against his bandaged face.

When I opened my eyes and stirred, he pulled himself up on his one arm. His bandaged face hung over me. I looked into his one dark eye and saw him on guard there, angry and hopeless.

Pity almost made me cry out, but not quite: I was too desperate for that. I smiled into his bleak, bandaged face. I kissed him. I laughed. I twined my arms around him, stump and all, and pressed myself close, and saw his eye widen, then deepen, then sparkle.

But I couldn't hide my shock very long; my thoughts staggered through my head. No, no, no, I said against his kisses, pushing him away, hurrying to dress.

What had we done? What had I done? We were as surrounded with wreckage as if the house had been bombed. Nothing was the same, not even my clothes: they felt like someone else's.

"Come tomorrow," Robert said. I couldn't look at him; I left him and tiptoed like a burglar down the hall, but I heard the happiness in his voice as he called after me: "My love."

It hadn't been an hour since I'd passed old Mrs. Laird. Her chin still rested on her shabby sweater. Spilled tea still gleamed at her feet. I closed Robert's kitchen door behind me and walked down the alley as if I weren't someone I didn't know.

It was Mig's afternoon off. Con's house was empty. I crept in like a stranger or a thief, threw my clothes in a corner, and scrubbed myself in the shower until my skin was red.

The garden patio lay cool and quiet in afternoon shade. "Your outside study," Con had said, and brought roses in planters from a nursery. "Your favorite flowers." I huddled in one corner of the garden swing he'd bought for me, surrounded by the scent of his roses.

I sat there until the men came home from the factory. At supper I ate almost nothing, and watched Con.

I had grown used to his eyes upon me; now I felt how sharp his awareness was. He watched me as I tried to eat, and afterwards, too, and after a few hours he said, "Are you feeling all right?"

"It's the heat," I said. "I think I'll go to bed early." I could hardly look at him, and he saw that, too. He came to bed when I did, and put his arms around me. Was I cool enough? he asked in his deep voice. Should he open another window?

I slid from his arms and hung over him, kissed him. He smiled at me in his gentle way and lifted my heavy, hot hair away from my face, but I was looking into his eyes. There was another man there – suddenly I saw him – a secret, hungry Con Beale, watching and waiting at the edges of what he wanted.

"Con," I almost groaned. "Oh, Con."

For a moment he couldn't believe it – couldn't imagine there was somebody so different in bed with him. I heard his gasps and choked half-words. He had two good hands, yes, ready to explore, and he had kisses he hadn't tried.

Where had we been keeping all Dame Pleasures toys? It took us a long, lovely time to get to that place where making love is as intense as a fight, but – lost as I was in that free-for-all – I felt Con's steady care, even while we were tearing up our bed and, no doubt, shaking the house.

Finally I got my breath back.

The day I had spent came back, too.

I couldn't look at Con. I stuck my head under my pillow: a woman who, all in a few short hours, had been in two beds with two...

Con must have thought it was womanly modesty, though how he could think that was hard to imagine. I was glad he couldn't hear me crying, and didn't take the pillow off my head. I lay there scarlet and wet with tears while he vibrated with happiness, murmuring how he loved me, rubbing my back and then, because I was so hot, stroking me with a cool, wet towel.

Finally he persuaded me to look at him, but I didn't look long at those two dark brown eyes glowing with love for me – me! He turned out the light and went to sleep in my arms, giving one last satisfied sigh.

I was left with my sleepless, horrified self. It seemed to me that hours went by before I crept from bed, dressed, and grabbed a shawl, for the hot day had cooled to a chilly night. No one was awake at my house. No one was on the streets. I went to my mother's grave.

The cemetery elms tossed heavy summer leaves in the wind. Their shadows broke a streetlight's lonely gleam into bits of pale gold streaming over the tombstones. I bent above my mother's grave. "Mom," I cried to no one but the wind blowing my shawl. "Mom—what can I do?"

The streetlight's broken glow flickered across her name. A train wailed, pounding beside the river.

Come tomorrow. Come to Robert's house? I woke beside Con in the morning and felt like a heap of dirty rags in his white bed. *Come tomorrow.*

I couldn't go to Robert's house. No.

Con at our breakfast table was so happy he couldn't hide it. He tried to read the war news aloud as he usually did, but he couldn't stop looking at me long enough to make any sense of the *Des Moines Register*. The headline said "Allies Conquer in North Africa," but it could have read "Love Conquers All," to judge from Con's tone of voice and the looks he gave me over the scrambled eggs.

He kissed me a last time and went to work with his father.

Of course I couldn't go to Robert's house. No. Robert wasn't dumb – he'd know we couldn't do that again ever.

The morning passed so slowly. I had bought the texts for my fall English course; I began to read one.

It was no use.

I ate only a few bites of lunch.

Robert was lying in his bed with his bandaged face and his stump of an arm.

The living room clock struck one. It crawled, ticking, through the quarter hours. Two o'clock. I went from window to window in Con's house, staring at the green and gold of hot June.

The telephone rang.

"It's for you," Mig said, coming to the living-room door.

"Hello?" I said into the black receiver.

Only one word came from it, and then the connection was broken.

My heart turned over. That was the exact sensation. I dropped the receiver in its hook.

What was I doing? Handsome Robert Laird wasn't pursuing the Lettys' hired girl just for fun, just because he could. He was a man with one arm and one eye, lying alone in his bed trying to hide his stump and half his face, more sure every minute that he was unloved. Unlovable.

And I had made him beg. I had made him say that one word: *Please.*

Please.

I walked to Robert's house.

I might as well have been wearing Hester Prynne's scarlet letter on my cotton dress.

Please.

It was the deepest, greenest summer time. I felt almost naked in thin cotton and sandals, the hot breeze running over me. Small girls played jacks on their front sidewalk: "Onesies...twosies...eggs in a basket...around the world." I remembered that game.

I bent above my mother's grave. "Mom," I cried to no one but
the wind blowing my shawl. "What can I do?"

I told myself: Robert and I would only talk. That was all. Just talk.

The alley to Robert's house was wide and shady, a tunnel of bushes and walls and ramshackle fences. The acrid smell of heaped lawn clippings crossed my path, then the reek of ripe garbage, then rose scent.

I hurried along the alley ruts. Robert ought to know we couldn't ever do that again.

I stopped at his kitchen door, but I didn't knock. I put my back to it instead, and looked down the quiet alley.

In a moment I was running away, running home, block after hot block, running into "Con's Castle" to throw myself on our big, smooth bed.

It wasn't even a half-hour before the telephone rang. Mig had gone shopping; I took the receiver off its hook and said, "Hello?" in a voice I hoped wasn't as guilty and belligerent as I felt.

"Come," was all Robert said.

"To the library this afternoon," I said. "Three o'clock." I hung up.

Maybe he wouldn't come. He hadn't been out of his house since the day he'd stepped off the train.

The telephone rang. I didn't answer. I rode my bicycle to the campus, left it in a library rack and tiptoed past summer school students at long tables under the whirr of fans. I had been to our hideout in the library stacks only once when I'd thought was Robert was dead. I'd cried and cried, and told myself I'd never go there again.

Now I climbed those familiar metal steps to the bound periodicals, the table and chairs, the small window whose view was quivering leaves, a sidewalk, a brick wall.

Robert had always been there first. He'd thrown his two good arms around me the moment I was hidden by the *National Geographics* and the *Atlantic Monthlies*. Not even a year before he had stood waiting for me, his eyes on me with that hungry look.

I sat in a chair and looked at the leaves, the walk, the wall.

When it was four o'clock, I went home.

"Somebody keeps phoning," Mig said when she saw me. "I answer it and they hang up."

"You're so busy – I'll go if they ring again," I said. Mig was making rolls for supper, and had flour up to her elbows. As if in answer, we heard the telephone.

I went into the little back hall and lifted the receiver slowly, as if some wild creature might leap from its black bell. "Hello?" I said.

"How can I have the courage to go out?" Robert said. "You give me everything, even courage, and then you take it away."

"The library at three tomorrow," I said very softly, then tapped the hook to break the connection. "Yes," I said in a normal voice. "Thank you. We'll pick them up."

Mig could hear me, there in the back hall. I went into the kitchen again. "Con's shoes are repaired and ready," I said. "That's all it was. I'm going to bike over to visit the Lairds for a little while."

"Joe says Robert won't go out at all." Mig stopped kneading, her face sad. "Just waits on his grandmother and roams the house for hours."

"Yes," I said. "Joe thought I could help a little, so I went over yesterday."

"He told Joe he'd been mean to you for so long," Mig said, "and he was – I remember that party after *The Gypsy Girl*." She slammed the dough on the table again, pummeling it. "Poor man. He was so good looking."

I took my bike from its hook in the garage and rode through the sun and shade of late afternoon. Old men, sleeves rolled up, were watering lawns before supper.

Aunt Adele would be home from work.

She was in her kitchen when I knocked on her back door. Robert was sitting at the table. His one eye gave me a godforsaken and furious look I hoped his mother didn't see; I didn't dare look at him again.

"How nice you've dropped in!" Adele said. "I told Joe it was time that some of Robert's friends visited – Robert's so much better." She smoothed his hair and I remembered how it felt – that dark and springy hair in my fingers while I kissed him. "He was just like his old self last night, laughing and joking, and this afternoon he's up and dressed."

"Hello, Robert," I said.

Aunt Adele pulled out a chair for me next to Robert. "Sit down, sit down – I've got some nice iced tea all ready to pour. How I do enjoy my new stove and refrigerator!"

"I can't stay long," I said. "We're trying a new meatless supper tonight." Why had I come – to make Robert imagine me in my own house with Con?

"No meat." Adele sighed. "Not even if you have the points. Maybe next week."

"Everything's rationed, or out of reach," Robert said in such a bitter voice that his mother said, "Oh, no! Everyone's so kind to us, bringing us sugar, and honey – "

"*Sometimes* they bring sugar and honey," Robert said. "Out of a sense of pity, I suppose." Before we could say a word, his chair banged against the wall and he was gone.

Adele looked after him, then turned her sad face to me. "He's so badly hurt," she said, close to tears. "Yesterday when I came home he was just like his old self, and this morning I actually heard him whistling the way he used to do. But now he's..." she raised her thin shoulders, and the corners of her mouth turned down.

"Come have your tea," I said. "It's so good."

She looked at the three glasses on the table. Robert had spilled his when he jumped up. "Your dear husband," she said in a low voice. "He called me at work today, and I know you've had something to do with it – he wonders if Robert would drive with him to Iowa City – he can get the gas – and let the doctors there take a look at his face and see what they can do. And maybe he can have an artificial arm."

"It was Con's idea," I said.

"Con's like his mother," she said. "Kind. Thoughtful. The older he gets, the more I see it. She was my best friend for years and years. I've never found another woman friend like her – at least, not until you came along, my dear. You're just like a daughter to me."

"And you're like my mother," I said, hating every word so sweetly dripping off my tongue. I couldn't stay. I thanked her for the tea and was gone with my bicycle to the parsonage across the street.

The Lettys were all at home. I went to the kitchen to peel potatoes for Aunt Gertrude.

"Didn't expect you," my aunt said.

"I stopped in at the Lairds'," I said.

"Oh?" Aunt Gertrude said, turning to look at me. "He's finally willing to see someone?"

"He saw me," I said, and felt an almost hysterical laugh at the back of my throat. All of me...he certainly had, the day before. "A little while," I said. "Then he went back in his room."

"Poor boy," she said. "But Adele's lucky to have him back. The Russells got one of those "The-Secretary of War desires to express his deep regret" telegrams yesterday. She's just gone to pieces."

I didn't answer. It wasn't conversation I wanted. I wanted to peel potatoes at that same old table. I wanted, just for a little while, to hear the cupboard door above the sink squeak as it always had, and smell the match as Aunt Gertrude lit the stove – that old stove with the enamel tulips on it. The crack in the linoleum floor comforted me. So did the familiar chipped bowl I held in my lap, and the tinny radio squawking war news in the parlor.

24

E very afternoon I went to the library. Robert never came. From the library I went to his house after his mother came home. Sometimes she could persuade him to join us in the kitchen, sometimes not. If he joined us, he sat at the table and said almost nothing and wouldn't look at me.

"Robert's not getting better," Joe said when he came to take Mig on a date one Thursday afternoon. "He won't leave the house, or say more than a few words." Joe looked at me with worried blue eyes. "Does he talk to you?"

"No," I said. "Not much."

"But he says he'll go on a picnic Saturday, if you girls are there," Joe said. "And Con, too, if he can come."

I told him Con had to work nearly every Saturday. There wasn't much enthusiasm in my voice; Mig stared at me and then said in a teasing tone, "Miranda's been as jittery as a cat with fleas lately – snapping at all of us, not hearing what we say, forgetting things."

"Then she needs to go on a picnic," Joe said. "Robert talks about Calvinhorn's farm sometimes. It's not very far. I don't think he wants to go where there'll be anybody but us."

"You fellows bring something to drink, and we'll bring the rest," Mig said. "Potato salad? Maybe chicken, if we can get any? Otherwise it'll have to be hard-boiled eggs."

"How about your chocolate cake?" Joe said.

"If we've got the sugar coupons, and the butter." They both grinned at me. I couldn't think of a single excuse for not going.

We had a coupon for sugar. We measured out a cup of it, and Mig traded some with a neighbor for butter. By the time we'd filled the picnic basket Saturday morning, it was too heavy for one of us to carry, so we packed two baskets instead, with red-checked napkins on top of one and a red-checked tablecloth on top of the other.

And then there they were: Joe and Robert walking up my front walk in the eleven o'clock sunshine: a blond man with a limp, and a dark-haired man with a bandaged face and a pinned-across shirtsleeve.

Joe and Robert took the baskets. Mig carried the lemonade, I carried the iced tea. We couldn't walk single-file, and there wasn't room to walk four abreast. Mig and Joe were a couple. Robert and I had to follow them, side by side.

Joe looked back at us. "I'm not as fast as I was," he said, and laughed at his own joke. "Mig's glad of that. You two go ahead at your own pace – we'll meet you there."

"Come on," Robert said in a harsh voice. "They want to be alone." We passed Mig and Joe, who were holding hands. Robert wouldn't slow down. We were out of their sight by the time we took the country road.

"Now," Robert said, "we can talk. Not that you want to. You talk to my mother. You won't come when she's not there. I can't say much on the telephone. You might as well be on the moon."

"You could come to the library," I said. "I'm there every day at three. Reading *Atlantic Monthlies* and *National Geographics*."

"I haven't got the guts to go there," Robert said. "What would you do if you had one arm and half a face?"

"I'm married!" I cried. "You have to forget me – forget any of this happened. You'll find someone else if you look. You won't remember – "

"I will remember! That's all I do: remember! I lie in my bed every night and remember!" He stepped in front of me so I had to stop. "What do you think I remember, there in my bed?"

I wouldn't look at him. "I can't help it," I said. "If I come to your house when your mother's not there, I might – "

"You might!" he cried. "Might what? Might give me a reason not to feel like half a man? That's what you might do if you came!"

I couldn't answer him. I walked on and he caught up with me, there by a line of fencerow trees dull with dust from the road. For a while we walked mute with only the cry of a meadowlark breaking our silence.

"Come to the library," I said.

"You sit at the kitchen table. You talk to my mother, and you try to talk to me. Do you know why I won't talk? I can't. There you are, so close I could touch you, with your beautiful cornsilk hair and blue eyes and those breasts of yours, and that voice, and that mouth – and you expect me to talk? You keep your whole self away from me, and I'm supposed to make conversation?"

I couldn't look at him; I looked at the cornrows beside us in the hot sun, and the ramshackle roof of Calvinhorn's barn beyond them. When I turned back, Robert had put down his basket inside an old gate. He took my load from me and set it down too. He pulled me into the cornfield where a thicket hid us from the road. "Now," he said. "Kiss me. I dare you."

I dare you. We'd yelled those words as children. *I dare you to climb to the loft of Calvinhorn's barn.* He grabbed me against him with his one good arm and said it again: "I dare you."

It wasn't like any kiss we'd ever kissed – I was back in his bed with him, bare and crying – my whole body remembered – it made him laugh as he pulled away. "See?" he said, triumph dancing in his eye. "You haven't forgotten! You won't! You want to come as much as I want you!"

"No!" I yelled at him. "Never. You're my dear friend. I'll do anything in the world for you." He took a step forward. "Anything but that."

I picked up the basket and the thermos of tea and left him there. I could feel his angry eyes on my back. I carried my load up the rutted farm path to the barn.

The old building leaned, turning one battered shoulder to the north, its bowels of hay spilled into the sun. I went into the barn's cool shade, wondering what I would do with an angry Robert when Joe and Mig came.

Clean hay was heaped under one of the windows; I spread the red-checked tablecloth on it, glad for ordinary things, listening for Robert. I unpacked the salad and fruit, and put out plates and cups. Then I sat on a barrel just inside the wide door, waiting.

Suddenly a shadow fell across me. It was Joe and Mig and their basket and thermos.

"Where's Robert?" Joe asked.

"Didn't you pass him?" I said. "I left him by the field gate."

"Then he'll be here pretty soon," Joe said. He helped Mig add her basket-full to mine on the checked tablecloth. There was nothing more to do for our lunch; we roamed the old barn. "I used to love swinging on that rope," Joe told Mig. "We climbed the loft ladder and grabbed it, flew over to kick the rail of the other loft and fly back, back and forth, back and forth, until some other kid took it away from us."

Mig smiled at him. The silence among us showed we were thinking of Robert. "You don't suppose he's gone home?" Mig said.

"Home?" Joe said.

"Maybe he wasn't feeling good," Mig said.

"Did he tell you there was anything wrong?" Joe asked me, and I might very well have said Yes, but I said, "No.

I just left him by the gate and brought the food here. I thought he'd be coming any minute."

"I'll go look," Joe said.

He went off down the farm path. Mig was smiling. "We talked all the way," she said. "We set the date!"

"Mig!" I cried. "I'm so happy! *You're* so happy, and so is he! When's it going to be?"

"October fifteenth," Mig said. "And guess what – Con has offered him a job at the Equipment Company! A good job!"

"Then you're all set. Con knows a good man when he sees one." I heard Joe calling, "Ro-bert! Ro-bert" somewhere out in the hot sunshine.

"We'll never be able to thank Con enough," Mig said. "He's the nicest man I know – except for my own man, of course." I heard her giggle, but my eyes were on the path winding downhill. Breeze from the cornfields stirred hay on the barn floor and set the loft rope swinging below its canopy of cobwebs.

Joe came back. "I found him. He says he's going back. I didn't want to ask him why. I suppose we'd better eat."

Joe and Mig were hungry and happy. I ate and tried not to think of the reason Robert wasn't there.

"You know," I said when we'd packed the baskets and folded the tablecloth, "three is a crowd. I'm going home – I've got some things I should do – and you two can take your time and enjoy yourselves."

They begged me politely to stay. Their hearts weren't in it. They walked along the path to say goodbye, but when I looked back at the field gate, they'd already disappeared in the barn's lopsided shade.

I swung my basket against the weeds along the road as I walked. A tractor somewhere buzzed like a distant bee.

Then I saw Robert. He was far away, coming through a cornfield. He didn't see me. He took one cornrow and I took another. Once on the road to the barn, he didn't look back. I ran softly behind him along the grass and reached him just as he came to the barn door. He turned, saw me, and gave me a furious look, and we both started into the barn.

We stopped. Joe and Mig were on the straw already, half naked and too much in love to see a shadow or hear a step.

Before I could touch him, Robert whirled and ran down the path, across the road, into the woods – he looked lopsided with only one arm to swing as he ran. I followed him and heard him crying, "Christ!" and again, "Christ!" Then he stopped and laid the good side of his face against a tree trunk as he flattened his body against the bark. "Oh, Christ!"

"Robert," I said, putting out a hand, but he ran away from me, ran through trees to the cornfield's edge. Then – so suddenly – he disappeared.

Of course. He'd dropped into the Lost Boys' House. It was still there.

Where? I couldn't see it. But I found the big oak tree with the jar still hidden in its hollow, and knew where the trap door was. "Robert?" I called.

"Go away!" His voice came from beneath the ground, eerie and disembodied, muffled by earth.

The door wasn't the flimsy one we had made long ago. I pulled it until it gave and folded back. The house below was dark. A well-made rope ladder dangled and disappeared in a hole that seemed deeper than it had ever been.

"Oh, Christ!" His voice was deep and despairing beneath me. "Oh, Christ!"

"Robert," I said, my throat thick with pity. I left my basket in the grass and took one step down the ladder, then another. The moment I reached the blanketed floor, Robert yanked a rope and the trap door closed over us.

Now there was only the blackness of deep earth, and Robert's hand pulling me down. I couldn't fight in darkness against his wounded stump of an arm and his bandaged face. We had left the summer afternoon with its bird song and rustling leaves, and were buried in darkness together as if, high above and far away, the world didn't matter.

Once Robert let me go long enough to ask, "Will Joe and Mig come looking for you?"

"I said I was going home."

"You are home," he murmured, his face between my breasts. "With me. In our house."

I lay under him in darkness, smelling the earth walls, almost tasting them in the dusty air. The blanketed floor beneath me was cool. Not a sound from the woods above reached us, not even the shrill cry of birds. My feet, my fingers, my hair spread on the blanket – was there any part of me unkissed? He said old, beautiful words to me – words we'd both memorized. My voice went softly along with his, and cried out and sighed along with his, too.

At last, tired and panting, he came to his knees and fumbled on the floor. He struck a match. The small light flared, flickering over our bare skins. He lit one candle stuck in the boards of a corner, and then another,

"Look," he said. "We're in our house. The house of Miranda. Wendy-Miranda."

My face was everywhere in photographs pinned on dirt walls: Miranda as a nine-year-old with a Halloween pumpkin, her hair stringy and her smile showing all her teeth. Miranda the Gypsy Girl in a school photo. Miranda at a Sunday school picnic. Miranda, a Robert-kissed, lipstick-smeared bride at the church door. A paper rose was pinned beneath it. "That's a rose from your *Gypsy Girl* bride's bouquet," he said.

I looked up. The hole was very deep now, and roofed with fresh wood planks; I had smelled their sappy fragrance the moment I left the light for the dark. We sat naked on a floor of blankets, my face smiling from every wall.

And there was Robert, his smooth, muscled body chopped off to a stump where an arm had been, a white bandage stuck over half his face. "What could I do last summer when you married Con?" he said. "I came out here. You were my 'blood brother.' We were Peter and Wendy."

He took the paper rose from the wall, and for a moment we both smiled as he looked for a place to put it on my bare skin. Then he tucked it in the tangled hair beside my ear. "I dug the house a lot deeper and brought new planks, built a new door, piled more dirt on top, put the blankets down, brought your pictures, spent hours down here while you..."

He stopped, but his one eye didn't look angry now; he lay close to me and shut his eye. "I can stand anything now. You're here with me," he said. "In our Lost Boys' House."

"I can't stay," I said, picking up my shirt.

"Yes, you can," Robert said, and blew the candles out. "*So willingly...*" he whispered against my mouth, "*so willingly she came into his arms.*"

But I got away at last, and put on my clothes in the darkness in spite of him, climbed the ladder in spite of him, flung back the wooden door to the late afternoon light, even though he begged me: "Stay."

The picnic basket I had left lay in the grass. I felt the paper rose rustling in my hair.

"Come tomorrow," he said, naked yet in the darkness of the Lost Boys' House. "Meet me here tomorrow. One o'clock."

I shook my head.

"Please," he said, his voice resonant with the empty hole he looked from. "Please."

I took the rose from my hair and laid it beside him in the dead leaves. "You ought to know we can't!" I cried. "I'm so sorry...I'm so sorry..."

I ran away through the sun-shot woods.

"I can stand anything now. You're here with me," he said.
"In our Lost Boys House."

25

The next day was Sunday. When I went down the church aisle with Con, there was Robert in his uniform, sitting beside his mother – he had come to church at last. I shook his one hand in the hall afterward, and so did almost everybody else – he was another brave American boy crippled for his country's sake. There were more and more of them, and more and more gold stars on the town memorial.

Robert watched me through the whole church service; I could feel it. We took communion at the rail, and as I knelt beside Con, I glanced along the half-moon row of worshippers to see Robert beside his mother. His perfect right side was toward me, and for a moment I was a high school girl again, stealthily watching Robert Laird. Then his one good eye gleamed across the little racks of wine glasses to me, and I wasn't the innocent Miranda Letty— I was Miranda Beale in such need of forgiveness that I shut my eyes and begged God: "Keep me away from him. Don't let me give in, even if I pity him so."

I didn't give in. Nothing he could say or do would bring me to him, except when his mother was at his house, or when I was surrounded and safe with other people. He called me on Mig's afternoons off, trying every word he could think of to make me come to the woods.

"Is Wendy there?" he asked if anyone answered the phone but me.

"You have the wrong number," Mig told him. He did.

When I visited his mother, he sat at the kitchen table, hardly speaking, reminding me silently of what he had said: *Do you know why I won't talk? There you are, so close I could touch you.*

Once it had been fun to keep him away, to kiss Con instead of him, and enjoy that snaky ripple of revenge. Now such pleasures were like a childhood playground you remember; when you go back, your shoes won't fit the steps of a tiny slide. The swing that seemed so big when you were small hangs only a foot from the ground.

In late July, Con said, "I've asked Robert about going to Iowa City and getting the opinion of specialists at the university hospitals. Maybe we should have him to dinner and talk about it. After church next Sunday? He's coming out of his shell, meeting people, back in the world. He won't feel self-conscious with us."

Robert came, wearing his Marine uniform, his bandage, his pinned sleeve, and his sullen look when he glanced at me. S.C. sat at the head of the table and said, "So they gave you up for dead, and you fooled them?"

"Yes, sir," Robert said. Mig smiled as she put his plate before him and he smiled back. "One of my friends came and found me and carried me behind the lines, but by that time I was an official statistic. It happens quite often when the battle's fierce and nobody's sure what happened. And even when I woke up in San Diego, people there didn't know I'd been listed as dead. I was almost ready to be discharged when I found out, and sent a telegram."

"Your mother nearly died from happiness," I said.

"Miranda went from one house to another telling everyone." Con smiled at me.

"She's been so good...to my mother," Robert said.

"So you're going to Iowa City with Con?" S.C. said. "Get them to patch you up?"

"I think I'll try. Maybe they can give me a hand." Robert didn't smile at his joke.

And Robert didn't smile when I saw him at church the next Sunday, either. Con had given me the bad news:

"The specialists told Robert his face was pretty hopeless. They could smooth out the scars a little, but there's no way to fix his cheek or ear, and his eye is gone for good. They'll give him a metal arm and hand."

"What can he do with half a face?" I asked.

Con shrugged. "Wear a bandage, or some kind of half-mask. Explain to every curious person. Learn to bear people staring at him. It'll be hard for him to get a job."

"Horrible," I said.

"I've spoken to him about a job at the Company," Con said. He looked at me with serious eyes. "You don't talk to Robert very much, I've noticed. It might hurt him. Try to be kind to him. Otherwise he'll imagine he's 'horrible' to you, and think you don't want to be with him."

"Con," I said. I couldn't say another word, but I ran my hands through his soft hair and looked in his dark brown eyes with all the love I felt for him.

It's hard to imagine how few of the facts of life I knew when I was nineteen. Once you learn those facts, they seem as commonplace as eggs for breakfast or leaves on trees, but when you don't know them, they're the last things you could have guessed. August came, and I decided the awful August heat was affecting me in a rather convenient and pleasant way, unless I was sick. I didn't feel sick.

But one Saturday morning, helping my aunt and Betty with the washing, I had to stop.

"I feel so awful," I wailed. "I must have eaten too many tomatoes yesterday."

My aunt waited while I threw up, and then asked me a few embarrassing questions as Betty stood there open-mouthed.

"Well," Aunt Gertrude said to me in a soothing sort of voice, "it's certainly not the tomatoes, and you're not sick. It's a baby coming. You have been married more than a year, you know. Two missed periods. Perfectly natural."

Perfect? Natural? I must have turned white, because my aunt put her arm around me. I hardly noticed such an unusual thing as a hug from her. I sat down in the nearest parlor chair and looked at Robert's house across the street.

"A baby?" Betty said. "Already?"

Her mother didn't set Betty straight, of course. She told her to go pick beans for supper. Then she brought me some tea and dry toast and made me lie down. "You must go to Dr. Horton and be sure everything is all right," she said. "Con will be so pleased. And his father, too."

I wouldn't believe her. Every other unpleasant thing she'd told me about my body had proved to be true, yet this one was simply not so.

But I believed her enough to throw up in secret every morning, which took some doing. Con caught me once or twice. I told him it was just something I'd eaten. "I feel fine now," I said.

I didn't feel fine. Every morning it happened. Every morning I began to believe Aunt Gertrude a little more. The more I believed her, the more the world became a terrifying place where you wanted to hold tight to your mother's hand and found she was gone.

A baby. I lay beside Con at night and poked around under my ribs. Where exactly was the baby? When would I start getting fat?

It was days before I believed Aunt Gertrude enough to lie in the dark and cry. I put my arms around sleeping Con and mouthed words against his warm back: "There's someone here with us – someone who doesn't belong here. Someone who's somebody else's."

Suddenly an explosion of feelings went off in me like fireworks. I saw Con's joyous face in our rumpled bed.

I saw Robert smiling in the candlelight of the Lost Boys' House.

Whose baby? It was *mine.* I doubled up, protecting my middle.

Con. Robert. What if I'd already hurt my baby, jumping in and out of beds the way I'd been doing? Not even a mother cat in a burning shed could have felt as fierce as I did.

Hurt my baby?

Oh, no. No more Robert. No more Con. Indeed not! Robert was still telephoning. "No," I said, and hung up. I said No to Con in bed the next night, and the next, and glared at Robert when I saw him in church.

Con was very kind, but puzzled. He hugged me and kissed me and drove me to Des Moines – he could buy gas for the Company – and we had a wonderful weekend, except that he got absolutely nowhere in bed.

Aunt Gertrude knew the baby was coming. Betty knew, too, but Aunt Gertrude would keep her quiet – she'd be waiting for me to tell Con.

As usual, my aunt had left me with a sharp little stone in my shoe: *You must go to Dr. Horton and be sure everything is all right.*

So I made an appointment and went to Dr. Horton's office one summer day.

I'd never had a man in a white coat poke and prod me and ask such questions before.

"You're in fine shape, young lady," he said. "How's S.C.? Is that husband of yours working too hard at the factory?"

I said "Fine" and "Sometimes," and he left me to put on my clothes again.

He'd never mentioned a baby. I looked at the shining, ominous equipment in his examining room the way someone saved from the gallows might look at the rope. Nothing had happened, after all. I was "in fine shape."

He was waiting for me in his office. "Get plenty of rest," he said. "Your baby ought to arrive about the middle of March." He smiled at me.

I must have looked as if he'd slapped my face. I left in a hurry, running down two flights of creaking old stairs to the sunlight of Main Street. Once in that sunlight, I didn't know where to go.

Go to Victoria and cry on her shoulder again, like a silly high-school girl in a cheesecloth wedding gown who'd thought the world was ending because Robert Laird stood her up? And now I'd go to Victoria and tell her that he – that Con couldn't –

No. Not even Victoria.

There was no one. I walked through the summer sunshine past houses of people who would turn their backs on me. I would be "that woman who..."

I'd have to take my bank money and leave. Even the Lettys wouldn't take me in with a...I could hardly face the words: "illegitimate child." I'd never known anyone who'd had that terrible thing.

I walked to the parsonage. Aunt Gertrude was canning tomatoes; the smell of them met me at the door: the acrid, comforting odor of past summers and the hot garden. I found an apron and began to peel a plump, scalded pile of them in the sink. "We're going to tell Con's father pretty soon," I said.

"I imagine he'll be very pleased." Aunt Gertrude dumped another load of tomatoes in the sink. "There's nobody but Con to carry on the Beale name – not that I know of. Robert's a Beale, of course, but he doesn't count since his mother changed him to a Laird."

I slipped the peel off a fat tomato and asked, "Will I be too fat to go to college in the fall?" and heard my new self, the one leaving town with her illegitimate child, snarl at me in my head: *You? Go to college? With a baby and no husband?*

"I shouldn't think you'll show too soon – not with your first. Con's awfully big-boned, so you'll probably have a big baby. But you can wear loose clothes and get by that long, I'd guess."

"Do you get sick?" *Sick all by yourself in some strange town.*

"Sick?" My aunt raised her eyebrows. "Not once you're over being sick in the morning. You get heavy and tired, and you're hungry for queer things sometimes, that's all."

She was putting mason jars in boiling water and had her back to me. I said, "Can you...will it hurt the baby if you...sleep with your husband, you know?"

Aunt Gertrude was kind enough not to turn around. "Never heard that it does," she said over the chinking of glass. "Don't let him the last month, maybe, just to be safe." And my snarling new self said: *Sleep with Con? After he knows? Never.*

Betty and Ben came through the back porch door with another bushel of just-picked tomatoes. How hot it was. The four of us canned the kettle-full that was ready, then went out to drink lemonade on the back porch.

"I hear Jack writes you nearly every day," I said to Betty. I was trying to act like the old Miranda Beale – the safe one, the happy one. It felt like carrying a heavy load up endless stairs.

Betty giggled and twisted her dirty apron in her lap.

"What else has he got to do?" Ben said. Bernard and Ben teased Betty every chance they got.

"Except fight a war," Betty said.

"When do you start work at Becket's?" I asked.

"Monday," Betty said.

"She's so lovesick she won't sell a single dress," Ben said. "Probably can't even make change."

"At least I'll be bringing more money home than you do," Betty said.

"Can't help it if I'm only sixteen!" Ben cried. "I'm almost seventeen and I'm big – maybe I should enlist. Tell them I'm eighteen. They won't care, if I can fight."

"Don't say that!" Aunt Gertrude cried with real despair in her voice. She sat with the cold lemonade pitcher against her hot front, tomato juice on her apron, her hair straggling down her cheek from the hair net. Bruce began fussing in his playpen; she gave me a You'll-be-doing-this-soon look, set the lemonade pitcher down beside me, and went in.

We canned tomatoes until the heat of the day was too much. I was grateful for the hot, sloppy, smelly work. It seemed to me that I was looking at that old parsonage for the last time. I would never eat the tomatoes on the kitchen table. They stood upside down in their mason jars, clean and bright and red as rubies.

I washed my sweaty self off in the old bathroom. The tub still squatted on its lion paws. I paused by the storeroom's open door. No ghosts were there, only afternoon sun lighting Ben and Bernard's football posters and tennis shoes.

"Thanks so much for helping with the tomatoes," Aunt Gertrude said, standing on her little front porch with me.

Someone called, "Hello."

It was Robert, coming across the street. He didn't look at me; he looked at my aunt. "Can you spare Miranda for a little while? My grandmother wants to talk to her."

"We're through with our canning for today," Aunt Gertrude said politely. "Thanks for the help, Miranda."

So I had to walk across the street with Robert and go in his front door.

His grandmother was asleep. His mother was at work. Robert pulled me down the hall and into his room – he was strong, even with one arm, and he was angry.

"Don't," I said. He was trying to unbutton my dress. "Let me go."

"Let you go!" Robert cried. "Why? What have I done?" He pushed me down on his bed, but I had two arms to keep him away. I said, "Listen to me. Sit down and listen."

He sat down so close to me that I could hear us both breathing hard. "I have to tell you," I said. "I'm going to have a baby."

It was so still for a moment that I could hear his grandmother's little bubbling snore from the living room. Robert's eye darkened almost to black, the way Con's eyes darkened.

"Mine!" he said. "It's what I wanted – it's what I prayed for – "

"What?" I said. "You what?"

"Prayed it would happen!" Robert's one eye was wide with delight and his half-face glowed.

"Why? Why in the world would you want – "

"Because now you're mine! You have to be – it's my baby!" He grabbed me to kiss me and hold me close with his one arm, his bandaged face catching in my hair.

"No!" I said, pushing him back. "No! How could I be yours? I'm married."

"Married?" Robert made the word sound detestible. "We'll go away, hide, just us and the baby. And we'll have more – a whole family – I love you so. I'll never let you – "

"Let me go!" I said.

But he wouldn't. He kissed me and then said against my mouth, "I'll teach you to fly."

Peter Pan, of course. But he couldn't make me smile. I got away and stood by the door. "I'm married," I said, just like a grown-up Wendy. "And there's a baby – "

"My baby!"

"No!"

"Mine!" Robert's one eye flashed. "Do you think I don't know? Con can't have children."

All I could do was stare at him.

"My mother knows that. She was the closest friend Con's mother had, and when Con was born..." He shrugged. "Nobody else here knows but Grandma, and me. I heard them talking once." He came very close, looking into my two eyes with his one. "You don't even know whose baby you've got? Didn't Con tell you? If he didn't, he's a coward. He's worse than that!"

I couldn't stand the contempt in his voice. "He told me," I said with scorn of my own. "Before we were married."

"Then why did you marry him?" Robert shouted.

"Because I love him."

Robert grabbed me against him and then flattened his one hand on me below my waist.

"You love *me*. It's *my baby*," he said. "*Mine*."

"No," I said. "Not unless I say so."

"Then say so!" he cried. "It is!"

"No."

"You can't take my own baby!" he cried.

"I have to. I can."

"You've told Con?"

"No."

"He won't want you!" There was scorn in his voice again. "He's not going to raise somebody else's child!"

My eyes suddenly filled with tears. It was very quiet in the small room. Then Robert let me go and sat on his bed. He put his one hand on his bandaged face. "He *will* want the baby." There was bleak despair in his voice. "He'll want you. He can't have a family of his own." I started toward him and put out my hand.

He leaped up to face me. "I'll fight him! I'll kill him! You think I don't know how to kill? He can't have you! He can't have the baby! He can't have *everything*!"

He meant it. "You wouldn't," I said, and tried to put my arms around him, but he shook me off. "Only a few of us know about Con," I said. "Isn't he as hurt as you are? You can have a wife and a family and be happy – "

"Not without you! Not without you! *Let me not die in languor and slow tears.*"

There was nothing I could say. I left him there by his narrow bed.

I had to tell Con.

By the time I climbed in bed with him that night, I was trembling and half-sick. For hours I'd been watching my safe, perfect life leaving me, the way a train station grows small and disappears as you're carried away.

"What's the matter?" Con said. "You're shivering. Are you cold? In this weather?" He pulled me close to him and wrapped his arms around me.

"I have something to tell you," I said.

"So important?" He smiled at me.

"Yes," I said. "Something I never thought I'd say." I was trying not to burst into tears.

"Oh, my dearest," Con said, "tell me anything. It's all right." He smoothed my hair with his big hand.

I took a deep breath as if it were my last before I stepped off a cliff or into an ocean. "I'm having a baby next March."

His surprise jerked his body in my arms. He said, "What?"

"A baby," I said.

I felt Con's eyes on me. I couldn't look at him. He let me go and sat on the edge of our bed with his back to me. His bare shoulders drooped there in the lamplight.

I didn't dare touch him, or say one word. He turned off the lamp. I felt him stretch out beside me.

A car went by on the street. Our windows were open, and leaves lifted and fell on a night breeze, rustling.

After long minutes, I heard him take a deep breath. "Are you sure?" he asked.

"I went to the doctor this morning," I said.

Again Con was still. Minutes went by.

"I prayed, you know," Con said. "I thought it was hopeless, and yet I've always prayed. Every night. But it's not mine, is it?"

My throat closed up; I could hardly whisper, "It's my fault. I was just so sorry – "

"So this is the answer to my prayer."

I couldn't see his face, but I heard the heavy pain in his voice. He was feeling his way through it blindly, step by step.

I don't know how long we lay there without a word, side by side like effigies on a tomb.

I couldn't bear the silence any longer. "You asked me once..." I could feel myself trembling, "...to always tell you the truth."

Con left our bed and stood by a window. I could see his dim profile against the dark wall. I hadn't told him the most wounding thing –

"I think I know the truth," he said. "If you want me to know. The child's a Beale – our family – because the war's hurt so many of us, ruined our lives, and you can't bear to see anyone suffer."

I pressed my hands against my mouth, trying not to cry.

"He loves you. Anyone can see it. And now he's so hurt and ugly. I think that's why..." he stopped, then suddenly hit the wall with his fist. "I think that's what the truth is," he said in a voice so low and strained that I could hardly hear him.

The night wind was rising. I listened to the trees toss. I'd hurt him so much – what did it matter if I told him one more thing? "Robert knows we can't have a family," I said. My voice trembled. "Your mother was Adele's best friend. He heard her talking to his grandmother about it once."

Con made a small, muffled sound. He leaned on the sill of our high window, a lonely, dark silhouette as far away from me as he could get.

"So he knows the baby is his," I said to the man alone at the window. "And he wants it. He wants me."

The curtain beside Con billowed toward me with the storm wind. Then the silence between us was filled with the rush of leaves in falling rain.

Con closed the windows and came to the bed to turn on the lamp again.

He leaned on the sill of our high window, a lonely, dark
shadow as far away from me as he could get. "He wants it,"
I said. "He wants me."

I was curled under the sheet, my face hidden, and felt the bed give under his weight as he sat on the edge.

"A little girl," he said softly. "A little girl, or a boy."

"Yes," I said, my face still hidden.

"Is it going to be his? Is it going to be mine? You haven't said."

I sat up, horrified. "Con! It's yours! Aren't both of us yours? Who else would I ever give it to?"

Con turned off the lamp. I felt him lie down again. The rain beat against our house corner. Once lightning showed me the room for a moment, and I saw Con turned my way, his eyes on me.

For a long while there was no sound but the rain. Then Con spoke beside me in the dark.

"I can't live without you," he said. "That's how it is."

26

When I woke at dawn, the windows shimmered with diamond drops. Con was asleep beside me. I sat up, staring around me. This was the day I would have to leave –

No! The life I'd thought I'd lost flowed back – it carried me like a warm, unbelievable wave. *I can't live without you.*

It was mine, still mine! I was Mrs. Conrad Raymond Beale, safe beside her husband at home, at church, in the town – no one but his unremarkably pregnant young wife.

I hurried to dress before Con woke – how could I look at him?

When he came to the breakfast table, so handsome in one of the business suits he always wore to work, I kept my eyes on a piece of toast I was buttering.

When I stole a look, he wasn't looking at me, either. After a while he said, "How are you feeling? Are you still sick in the morning?"

"No. Not any longer. I'm fine," I said.

"You've been so ... withdrawn..." he said. "But it was the baby coming, wasn't it?" I heard the relief in his voice.

I nodded. "I'm so happy," I said in a low voice. "To be with you. With the baby."

"Good," he said. I heard him put his coffee cup on the saucer. "We'll have to tell Dad."

We. That small word. We. "Yes," I said. "Before my aunt and uncle say something, or my cousins."

"We'd better tell him on Thursday," he said. "I'll bring him home early from work."

So he dreaded telling S.C. as much as I did. Mig would not be there on Thursday afternoon to hear.

We had our breakfast coffee with S.C. without a word, as usual, and for once I was glad of that silence. S.C. read the *Des Moines Register*. Con and I sat mute with a secret his father would have to know.

The men left for work. I walked from room to room. My clothes were in my closet, not in a suitcase. Textbooks for my fall classes lay on my desk.

The polished dining-room table glimmered with green from a window full of leaves. Sun gilded the silver tea set, the cut-glass bowl on the living-room sill, the perfume bottles on my dressing table. Mig was in the kitchen; I went in and nearly hugged her. How could she guess that planning the supper menu with her – such an ordinary thing – could make me want to cry?

I had to talk to someone. That night while Con went to a meeting at the church I walked to the cemetery. A full moon silvered my mother's gravestone and sparkled in night dew on the grass.

"Mom," I said. My voice was lost among the graves; nobody alive was there to hear me. "Oh, Mom – I'm having a baby, and it's not Con's."

Nothing answered me but a woman somewhere calling her child: "Joan! Come in! Right now!"

"But Con wants me," I said with a lump in my throat. I knelt by my mother's gravestone. "He wants me. He's piling everything he has around me, like a fortress he's going to defend."

That week of summer days crept toward the Thursday when we would have to tell S.C.. Each day was a week, a month, a year.

Robert was at church on Sunday, sitting with his mother across the aisle from us: I saw him as Con and I followed the usher to our usual place. There we were: Mr. and Mrs. Conrad Beale singing from one hymn book and praying side by side while my uncle smiled down at us from the pulpit: he certainly knew by then that I was "expecting."

I had heard Uncle Boyd preach every Sunday for ten years. Had I ever wondered how many in the congregation had hidden lives? Were there secret lovers there, like Robert and me, listening to Uncle Boyd talk about the bombing of Rome and the importance of forgiveness? Was there another husband there who had to look at the father of his wife's child?

We sang the closing hymn. Uncle Boyd prayed a last prayer for President Roosevelt, Winston Churchill and Joseph Stalin. The organ pealed as the congregation rose to leave. Coming from our pew, Con and I were face-to-face with Robert and his mother.

"Good morning," Adele said, smiling at us. "Your hat is so pretty, Miranda."

"Thank you," I said. Robert wasn't smiling. Neither was Con, looking for a second or two into Robert's single eye. Then Con took my hand and tucked my arm in his. We went together down the aisle.

Monday. Tuesday. The week would last forever. My only comfort would have been making love to Con – I loved him more than I'd ever thought I could.

He was so kind to me. He was so quiet. He was so polite.

"What did you expect?" I said to myself, lying beside him in our bed. "Would you want to touch him or kiss him if he told you he'd made love to another woman with that mouth of his, that body, those hands you'd thought were only yours – and she was having his baby when you couldn't have one?"

Sometimes I was sure Con wasn't asleep: he was lying beside me, hurt and alone, trying not to imagine...

At last Thursday came. I wandered around the house all morning. I read the *Des Moines Register*, front to back. Sicily was conquered. Girls married soldiers to get the fifty dollars a month – they could live well on that. We were getting War Ration Book Four. The polio epidemic seemed to be easing. Drivers with "A" stickers who were caught pleasure driving wouldn't lose their gas rations any more. I looked at a picture of our troops landing in the Aleutians, and another of jitterbugging soldiers and their USO dates.

I tried to eat lunch, but I only nibbled. I was glad Mig was gone. Finally I heard Con's car pull into the garage. The wheelchair creaked as Con wheeled S.C. to the sunroom.

Going in, I felt sweat gather under my bangs. It ran down my back under my freshly ironed dress. I'd had my hair done the day before, and I looked as nice as I could manage to look when I was almost too full of guilt and fear to get lipstick on straight.

"Why come home early?" S.C. grumbled as Con braked the wheelchair by an open window. "What for? What's the mystery? The new press is on the blink, and we have to come home?"

"Fred's there – he'll get it going," Con said. "Miranda and I have something to tell you, and we wanted to be alone in the house when we talk about it."

"Talk about what?" S.C. reared back in his wheelchair to look at us. His eyeglasses glinted in the window light.

Con came to put his arm around me, and I held his other hand, so we were braced together before S.C.. "We want you to know," Con said, and hesitated. "Something wonderful. Miranda will have a baby next March. You're going to be a grandfather."

Pressed against the back of his wheelchair, S.C. sat without moving for a minute that seemed minutes long.

His big hands were gripping the arms of the chair, and as I watched they turned into fists.

Suddenly he leaned forward, spitting words at us as if he had a mouthful of bullets. "And who, may I ask, is the father?" he shouted. "Tell me that! It can't be Conrad Raymond Beale, can it?"

"No," Con said. I could feel him trembling a little against me.

"So you're going to raise some other man's child. Give him the Beale name?"

Once again S.C. dragged the unspeakable into that room and threw it before us as if he enjoyed it. This time I was the one he aimed at, and the room seemed to dim around me; I held on to Con, and he held on to me.

S.C. began to grin. "And Miranda here," he said, "raised in a parsonage? A minister's niece?" His grin vanished. "You'll get rid of her," he said to Con. "Get a divorce and don't give her a penny. She ought to be able to make money doing more of the same kind – "

"That's enough!" Con let me go and lunged for his father's shoulders, shook them and shook them until the old man's glasses spun off his face. "You've said your last word! You've made our life miserable for the last time!"

The two men glared into each other's eyes. "You're my father and I've tried for years to remember that!" Con shouted. "But do you think for one moment that I'll let you talk that way about my wife?"

S.C. groped for his glasses, but they slid down his leg to the floor and Con made no move to pick them up. "We're leaving," Con said. "Today. I've found a beautiful house for Miranda and the baby, and we're moving in. Mig can stay and take care of you. We'll find another housekeeper – "

"You'd better find another wife!" S.C. yelled. "If you don't, I'll tell everybody in town – "

"No," Con said in a cold voice. "You won't. Bring scandal into the family? Not if you're smart. Not if you want the grandchild you've always talked about. And if you say one word to anybody, you'll never see us again."

I couldn't take my eyes off Con – I hardly knew him, he was so angry.

"You've gone too far. I thought you would," he said to S.C. in the same cold voice. "So you'll need a new supervisor for the Beale Equipment Company, too. I'm not on your payroll any more." He said payroll in a scathing tone: he'd never been paid, only given an allowance like a ten-year-old. "But John Deere's going to put me on their payroll next month and I'll make more money than I ever made with you." He pulled me away with him to the sunroom door. "It'll be good to leave this house and its memories, but if you ever want to come and see your grandchild, you'll be welcome in our home."

Con shut the sunroom door behind us, and we went into our bedroom to stand for a while in each other's arms, too shaken to say a word. At last I said unsteadily, "You've really found a new job? And a new house?"

"I had a week to do it. Deere is up against it – they can't get good managers, and they were glad to get me. And I found a house I've bought furnished. It's even nice enough for you."

"Oh, Con," I said, "Con."

"I was afraid Dad would act that way, say those things." Con didn't add: *because they're true*, but the words seemed to hover between us. "Forget you ever heard him." He held out a key. "Come with me and unlock the door of your own home."

We passed the closed door of the sunroom. We went out S.C.'s front door. I looked back at that house that was full of cruel words, a voice on the telephone asking for "Wendy," a textbook with notes in the margin.

We went down the walk to the street. "Aren't we driving?" I asked.

"Don't need to," Con said.

"Then it's near here?" I looked around me, and felt that I was floating in sunshine, and yet I couldn't imagine that Con would buy a house without me. Didn't he care what I thought of it?

But he seemed so pleased, and he was Con, my loving Con. I smiled and pointed to houses as we passed them. "Is it this house? This one?"

"No," he said. "Not that one. No."

We crossed from one block to the next.

"That one," Con said, and stopped.

The house on the corner was no ranch house; it was the two-story house a banker had built in the roaring twenties: a big stone house of bay windows, sun porches, wide doors, wide eaves, set in a half-block of its own trees and its flowering garden.

I looked at Con, my mouth open. "*That* one?" I cried. "That beautiful house? You *know* I love it! You've heard me say so every time we walked past!"

"Come on," he said. "The Brandons moved out on Tuesday, delighted to sell it furnished. Brandon's been sent to another Deere plant, and they wanted him right away. It's all ours."

"You bought it before we'd even told S.C.."

"I thought he'd be nasty. I wanted you to forget him, have something new – and we need our own place, don't we? With a family coming?" Con said.

I walked up my own steps. I took my winding front walk for the first time. I climbed my broad stone steps to my wide and welcoming front door with my key in my hand, and turned it in the lock.

"Wait," Con said, and scooped me into his arms, then pushed the door wide with his shoulder, carrying me in.

The hall was a room in itself, with a winding stair coiled around a glittering chandelier.

He put me down gently. "You have a telephone," he said, picking up the one beside me. "And you have a real bedroom, and a bathroom without a claw-foot tub, and a kitchen, and furniture, and curtains, and rugs on the floor..."

He was remembering what I had told him about my first sight of the Letty parsonage.

"You're being given a house in Cedar Falls, Iowa," he said. "You're home."

27

We moved to our new house that same Thursday afternoon, loading Con's car while the door to S.C.'s sunroom stayed shut and no sound came from it. We hung our clothes in the big master bedroom upstairs at the front of our house, and our toothbrushes in its brand-new bathroom. "How about using the den for your study?" Con asked. "It's even got a fireplace, and French doors to the garden. The housekeeper's room and bath are off the kitchen. And we've certainly got enough bedrooms. Which one for the baby?"

My books filled shelves in the den. Con took a big room upstairs for his office. I packed a basket with the cold supper Mig had left for us, and laid S.C.'s ready for him on his dining-room table. We had our first meal in our own dining room, and toasted our new house with wine.

"Mig's having dinner with Joe and his parents," I said. "I'd better call her there, or she'll wonder where we've vanished to."

Mig came to the phone. Every sentence of hers was an astonished question: "What? You're living where? When? Come tomorrow?"

"She's mystified," I said when I'd told Mig goodbye. "I'll bet she comes here tonight."

She did. I opened the door and there she stood, and we threw our arms around each other while she kept saying that she couldn't believe it.

"Such a house!" she said, stepping into it as if it were made of eggshells. "The furniture! And all the rooms. Look at that kitchen. And you're moved in?"

"But we hope you'll stay with S.C. and take care of him until you marry– then we'll have to find someone else for him."

"How about you, though?" Mig said. "I've been thinking about what you'll do when I leave. My little sister's seventeen now, you know. Yvette. I've talked to her. She's a good cook. I don't suppose..."

"Yes!" I said. "We'll hire Yvette tomorrow, if you're sure she can make your chocolate cake, and your soufflé, and your baked chicken – "

"I've taught her," Mig said.

"Then here's Yvette's little suite," I said, showing her the room and bath off the kitchen, all ruffled chintz and garden view.

"She'll be so happy!" Mig said. "So happy! But what's going on? One minute you were living with S.C...".

"He was so cruel. Con couldn't stand it any longer."

"He's stood it long enough. Good for him."

"And Con's working at Deere now. And, most important of all: I'm having a baby in March."

"A baby!" Mig's dark eyes danced with pleasure. She turned to see Con in the doorway. "And here's the proud father-to-be!" she said. "Congratulations!"

It was Con's first facing of that lie. I suppose the awkward pause seemed like nothing but shyness to Mig. "About time!" she said.

I heard Con force a cordial tone into his voice. "Thanks," he said and smiled at her. "We're pleased."

I hurried Mig away to see the rest of the house. "I'll come tomorrow and help you clean," she said, running a sharp eye over dull glass and dusty corners.

We cleaned. We explored the closets and attic, admired the china, stocked cupboard shelves. I began to be at home in the big rooms, looking from windows I had seen for years from the outside.

I should have been perfectly happy: a perfectly happy, pregnant Mrs. Conrad Beale. In a week my fall classes would begin. I roamed my new house with its fine furniture, its new kitchen, its gardens blooming on every side.

But each night Con and I lay in our big new bedroom in our big new bed and talked kindly to each other about everything but the most important thing, and didn't do that most important thing.

And in a few days someone began to call my new number. "He wants somebody named 'Wendy,'" Yvette told me. "I tell him there's nobody here called that, but he keeps calling anyway."

The mute telephone on its stand in the hail seemed to hold Robert's voice in its black mouth: *I'll kill him. You think I don't know how to kill?*

I walked to my first day of classes. The same late August sun had shone on me my freshman year. WAVES and Army Air Corps cadets marched under yellowing campus elms. I wore the red plaid suit I'd worn then, a new bride attending her first college class, but now the waistband of the skirt was tight.

My first class, I'd discovered, would be in the same room I'd had for my first class the year before. This time I knew enough to come very early, and found the big room empty, except for a dark-haired man in a Marine uniform, alone with his bandaged face and pinned-up sleeve.

I gasped and stepped back into the hall. Robert hadn't seen me. Give up the class? Wait until the seats around him were all full?

I looked around the edge of the door. There he sat alone with one arm and half a face. He was waiting for the stares and the whispers.

What could I do but go in, sit in the paddle-armed chair by his bandaged face and missing arm and say, "How did you know I was in this section?"

I thought he wasn't going to look at me, wasn't going to keep the echo of our first class day going. But at last he said, just as he had joked when he was whole and handsome: "Bribed the registrar."

Coeds slowly found seats. Paddle-armed chairs scraped over the wooden floor. The professor stood at the same chalkboard. Nothing had changed but us. No one stared at Robert; they looked, then quickly looked away.

"Your same dress," Robert said.

"Yes."

"Your different house."

"Yes."

"Take out a sheet of paper," Professor Scott said. "Close your textbooks. Write your name on the paper and then put down any phrase, any line of Shakespeare that you can remember."

I looked at Robert. He looked at me. We'd read Shakespeare in high school and memorized lines from the sonnets and *Romeo and Juliet*. The room was full of busy pencils, but I knew Robert was remembering Spenser, and words that were secret messages.

No love words for me, then. Robert was writing, too. Then he covered his paper with his textbook.

Professor Scott went along the rows, reading each student's paper, telling what play it came from, what sonnet. Most of the students could only remember the obvious ones, and didn't always get them right: "To be or not to be," "A rose by another name would smell as sweet," "Romeo, O Romeo, where art thou, Romeo."

The class was a small one and we sat in the back row, so he came to the two of us last. He picked up my paper. "'Let me not to the marriage of true minds admit impediment,'" he read. "Good. Sonnet 116." He picked up Robert's paper. "'Love alters not with his brief days or weeks, but bears it out even to the edge of doom.' Same sonnet." He looked at Robert. "I believe, sir, that you've already been to the edge of doom."

"Yes, sir," Robert said.

"Now," Professor Scott said, walking back to his desk. "Every one of you knew at least a few words of Shakespeare. Why? And why would I know where to find those words, when the author has been dead for four hundred years?"

No one had heard what Robert and I were saying through Shakespeare's words, even though our sentences had been read aloud. But we knew what we'd said. Stony-faced, we sat in the back of a college classroom, two students listening to a professor.

That night I knew I should tell Con. We sat in our living room after supper, and I poured him a cup of coffee and said, "Robert's taking classes. He's in my Shakespeare class at nine." I kept my eyes on my cup of coffee, swirling it until it spilled into the saucer. "He's so angry. I sat beside him because everyone looks at him, and it's hard. And he feels as if he's...lost everything."

"Yes," Con said.

He said he'll kill you, I wanted to tell Con. *Bears it out even to the edge of doom.* "He hardly talks at all," I said.

But Robert could write notes with his good hand. As the class ended, he'd scribbled in my notebook and wouldn't let me close it until I read it: "Library, 4:00."

I had to go to him. I had to climb those same narrow stairs, my saddle shoes ringing on the metal, and find Robert there, grabbing me before I had left the top step, kissing me, cupping the back of my head with his one hand so I couldn't get my mouth away from his, kiss after hard kiss.

"I want to hold you," he said at last, sliding his hand down to press me against him. "I want to hold my baby. Tell me you love me."

"I'm your best friend. Didn't I sit beside you in class?"

"Didn't you sleep with me – didn't you? Didn't we make a child together – nobody else has done that with you! And you came to me. You wanted me. That's a love-child you're carrying, and it's mine."

I said nothing, there in his arms. Suddenly he pushed me away from him. "Christ!" he said. "He wants you, doesn't he? I was right!"

"He loves me – "

"He's going to keep *my child*!"

"He married me. You didn't."

"He's even bought you a new, fancy house! He's got a new, fancy job – "

"You had your chance – years of chances. Do you think I wouldn't have married you if you'd ever, once, asked me? If you'd ever noticed me? Con wanted me – the Lettys' hired girl!"

"Hup...two...three...four," chanted a sergeant below our small library window. The war reached us with that sound: me, bitter and angry, and Robert with his one arm, glaring with his one eye at me.

"I'll kill him," he said. "What's my life worth without you?" He looked down at me with a cold sort of satisfaction in his one eye. "He's nothing," he said. "Just the little groom on your wedding cake. Wasn't I your best man?"

I wouldn't answer. He clattered away down the metal stair.

He never came to class again. Each day I sat alone in the back row. I wouldn't look at him at church, and Con noticed it.

"Robert's not coming to class," I had to tell him one morning. "He's too angry."

We sat in our own breakfast nook where we could read the *Register* and plan the day, and didn't have to face S.C. spreading silence around him like cold fog.

"Robert's taken a job at Deere," Con said. "Came in yesterday to ask for it. He starts on Monday. We need every man we can find, and he can do the job with only one arm."

"Con!" I took his hands across the breakfast table. "Robert's – almost beside himself. He wants me and – "

"I know," Con said. "I didn't hire him – I let another man do it. I didn't even talk to him."

"He says you've got everything, and he's got nothing."

Con left the table and stared out the window. "He's right. If you stay with me, I've got everything."

"If?" I said in a furious whisper. "I'm here. The baby's here. We're going to stay here. He didn't care about me – not for years and years, not until you wanted me. I was so sorry for him...and look what I've done..." I remembered Joe crouched in the corner of his dark room.

"Don't worry. Not even for a minute," Con said. "Nothing will happen. He has a good job now to keep him busy."

But I worried. I took walks across the river, past the muddy banks where Robert and I had tramped, two barefooted children giggling at the sucking, belching sounds our steps made. Autumn trees above the water dropped splinters of reflected gold in the river-rush; leaves fell through deep woods: a constant, sad rain.

I found a perfect yellow leaf, a perfect orange leaf, a perfect scarlet, a deep bronze. Walking alone in the lonely woods, I looked at the four leaves and knew there were four people beside Con who could say, "Miranda Beale isn't having Con's baby": Robert, Robert's grandmother, S.C. and Adele Laird.

Robert's grandmother? She had almost drifted out of our world. S.C.? As time passed, Con and I had heard nothing from him. "He won't make trouble," Con said.

"Nobody hates tattle and gossip more than he does." If townsfolk chattered about Con's job in the top management of Deere, or about our new house, we never heard a word of it. Con was deferred: his job at Deere was "essential to the war effort," the draft board said.

Robert? He was the dangerous one, full of anger. He was the scarlet leaf in my hand.

And his mother?

I would have to tell her. She called me her best friend. Nearly every afternoon we smiled at each other across our cups of rationed coffee and sugar, sitting at her kitchen table before Robert came home from Deere. "Miranda!" she always said with delight when I opened her door. "Come in! I was just thinking about you!"

What would Robert's mother say? She'd say what S.C. had said – *Who, may I ask, is the father?*

I visited her. I didn't tell her. Robert wouldn't. Week by week I had to work beside her in the church kitchen and keep up my side of our friendly conversations.

So I was a coward. But Aunt Gertrude – why would she see anything to be cowardly about? Wasn't I a respectable married woman having a baby? One evening when Adele Laird and I were washing dishes in the church kitchen, Aunt Gertrude paused beside us at the sink, smiling, and said to Adele, "Have you heard our good news? Miranda's having a baby next March."

For a moment Robert's mother stood still, a plate half-wiped in her hand. Then she finished drying it and laid it on the pile. "That's nice," she said.

"Yes, isn't it?" Aunt Gertrude said cheerily.

Mrs. Newton beamed at me as she brought a pile of dirty dishes to the sink. "I'll bet Conrad is pleased."

"Yes," I said.

"And his father, too, I'm sure!" Then Mrs. Newton remembered Adele Laird was there, listening – she put the dishes down hurriedly and went away. So did Aunt

Gertrude. They left us in a silence so profound that I could hear the soap bubbles popping in the dishpan.

I dumped the dishwater out. Robert's mother took the last stack of plates into the dining room to put them away. When I looked in that room a few minutes later, she wasn't there. Her coat was missing from its peg in the hall.

"Where's Adele?" Aunt Gertrude asked, joining me. "She forgot her casserole and the rest of her flour."

"She must have gone home," I said.

"She didn't look very pleased at your news," my aunt said. "I've always thought she wanted you to marry Robert. 'It's so nice that Robert is dating Miranda,' she said to me once. And now you're settled, with a baby coming, and she's got Robert back so crippled. Poor woman."

Aunt Adele knew.

The next day at four I stayed home, trying to lose myself in homework.

At four the day after that I walked in the cold, wet woods.

A week went by, and still I hadn't opened the Lairds' kitchen door to find Aunt Adele waiting, tired after work, smiling to see me. I couldn't find words to tell Con. We were polite to each other, and kind, like good friends. We lay in our new bedroom side by side, like friends.

For another week I spent the hours before supper helping Aunt Gertrude and Betty harvest the last of the parsonage vegetable garden and clear the ground for winter. We were carrying squash down to the cellar the next Saturday when we heard a voice at the garden fence: Adele Laird's voice.

Aunt Gertrude picked her way through wilted spinach plants to the fence. "Adele. How are you?"

"Can't complain," Adele said politely. "And you're well? I saw Miranda come to the parsonage a while ago, and I stepped over to ask if she could come see me for a minute when she's through helping you." Then she saw me beyond the apple tree. "If you would," she said to me.

I'd have given anything to say No, but I said Yes, and followed Betty and my aunt down the cellar stairs, my dread so much heavier than my armful of squash.

"Adele's so thin now," Aunt Gertrude said, adding her squash to the rest. "She doesn't look well."

"No," I said.

"It's Robert," my aunt said. "No arm. One eye. Half a face. No wonder she looks so bad."

We went to the garden shed for another load of squash and then another, until there was a procession of them along the cellar wall. I put them down carefully but I hardly saw them. I would have to talk to Adele Laird.

The dark came earlier and earlier in October. When I knocked on the Lairds' kitchen door, it was almost night in the alley at my back. "Come in," Aunt Adele called.

She was at her new stove, her back to me. When she turned around, I saw how drawn her face was. "Won't you have some coffee?" she said. "Do take your coat off and sit down."

I put my coat on a chair in the corner. Every piece of china, every cupboard and saucepan in that room was familiar to me, but when Adele brought our coffee cups and we sat down, we looked at each other like strangers.

She passed me the cream.

She passed me the sugar.

She held out a plate of cookies and I took one in silence. When I looked up, I saw tears in her eyes.

"Oh, Miranda!" she said.

"Don't," I said. I took her hand. "Don't cry!"

"I'm so ashamed!" she said, pulling her hand away. "So ashamed. My own boy, to do such a terrible thing, and then not even be sorry! To talk about making you run away with him – talk about killing! I didn't know him! I came home from church just sick, because I had this feeling...that it might be him, you know. At least he didn't lie."

Tears were running down her face. I got up to put my arms around her.

And then Robert came through the kitchen door from the dark alley. He saw his mother sitting at the table crying, and me with my arms around her.

He slammed the door behind him. The half of his face I could see was white. His sleeve wasn't pinned up; it was filled with his new metal arm that had a glove for a hand. "What are you doing here?" he said, scowling at me.

"Your mother asked me to come," I said, keeping my arms around her.

"Why?" he said to his mother. "She doesn't want anything to do with us!" He came to pull me away from her, and held me at arm's length with his good hand. "Look at her. She's carrying my baby and she doesn't want me! *My baby*. She's going to give it to Con Beale!"

"No...no...no," his mother said, shaking her bowed head. "She was somebody else's! She belonged to your own cousin!"

"She loved me! She came – "

"She was sorry for you," his mother cried. "I know her! She's *Miranda*, she's not some...bone that Con and you can fight over like dogs! Con's not threatening to kill you, is he? He's got more sense."

"He's got more *everything*!" Robert shouted. "His father's given us charity all our lives – he's got the money! Con's got it – look at that diamond she's wearing – look at her house! He didn't fight in the war and get crippled like Joe and me – he stayed home safe, and made money! He's got a job that pays three times as much as mine. He's got her! He's going to have my baby because he can't make one himself! He's got more of everything than I'll ever have!"

I got away from him and sat down at the table, and Aunt Adele said, "How can you shout at her like that? You'll make her sick!" She took my coat from the chair. "You'd better go, dear," she said. "Try to be calm on the way home. Don't hurry. Lie down when you get there. I wish we had a car."

She looked so pale and old. I put my coat on and then took her hands. "Don't listen to him," I said. "It's your very own grandchild. And I'm having the baby for Robert because he was hurt, and I couldn't help him any other way."

"Pity!" Robert shouted. "Is that it? Nothing but – "

"And I'm having the baby for Con, because he can't have one. And because..." I couldn't look at either of them, "...because he loves me so much that he understands."

"You're mine!" Robert cried.

"No!" I yelled back at him. "I don't belong to anybody. I'm my own, and this is *my baby*. It's going to have the father I say it has."

"I'll kill him!" Robert said. "You give him my baby and I'll kill him!"

"Oh, no!" his mother wailed. "No!"

I stared right into Robert's one glaring eye. "If you kill Con, this baby will have no father – all it'll ever have is shame!" I grabbed his arms and felt the hard metal of his false arm through the cloth. "It will never, ever be yours – you won't see it or watch it grow up – you'll be in prison, or dead. And your mother will die of a broken heart."

I let him go, went out the kitchen door and slammed it behind me. I ran down the alley I'd taken that summer...I remembered...I had felt almost naked in my sandals and thin sundress, the hot breeze running over me.

It was October now. The cold went through my coat to my sweaty skin and made it colder yet. I almost turned in at S.C.'s house, wrapped as I was in the past. My own house waited on its corner, foursquare among bare trees.

28

Wedding dresses, bridesmaid dresses, honey-moons – I was in no mood to think of them, but Mig was. She had saved enough money for a simple wedding, and I gave her more. I was to be her matron of honor, and Yvette would be her bridesmaid. "You don't know what it means to my family," Mig said. "My own little house! A husband with such a good job! It's all your doing – we've been so lucky, you and me!"

Her happy words scared me: they were tempting fate. Every day Robert came to work at Deere and saw Con there.

Cold weather settled in, but it seemed to me that the baby kept me warm, and it was always company: a new person, growing.

One Saturday afternoon I walked to the grocery store in the cold wind. At the door I had to take a narrow path beside boxes of grocery orders; they half-filled a long aisle, each box with its list and bill clipped to it, waiting to be delivered by the store's delivery boy with his horse and cart. Mr. Ward behind his counter said, "Hello, Mrs. Beale. Cold weather. What can I get for you today?"

"Flour," I said. "Ten pounds." I pulled my shopping list and our ration books from my purse. "Thank heaven coffee isn't rationed any more."

"Some ladies saw the 'coffee' coupon in their ration books and came in here last week buying pounds of it," Mr. Ward said. "I had to tell them the government's promised not to ration it again. You want your usual two pounds?"

"Yes," I said. He went to get it, and when he came back, he said to someone behind me, "Hello, Robert."

"Hello," that voice said at my back. I had trouble finding my place on my shopping list.

"Two dozen eggs," I said, and Mr. Ward went off to get them.

I knew what I would see if I turned around. He stood close behind me, for the boxes to be delivered almost covered the floor.

Robert said nothing at all. Item by slow item, Mr. Ward piled my groceries on the counter to be brought to the house later, and I tore out the red stamps and blue stamps from our ration books. I paid him and said goodbye. Not looking back, I picked my way along the row of boxes, but a hand behind me opened the door for me. "Come have coffee," Robert said.

"All right," I said. I hadn't spoken to him since that afternoon with his mother, but we could talk, couldn't we, like rational people?

"At the drug store," Robert said.

We walked across College Street in the cold wind. The store was drug-scented and warm, and the soda fountain was empty; we found a table in a corner, and said nothing at all until the cups were before us, steaming.

"You're working at Deere," I said, watching a hand I knew so well pick up a spoon.

"I work at Deere," he said in a frigid voice. "I eat in the cafeteria. Yesterday some of the men gathered around Con, right there in front of me, slapping him on the back. Do you know what they said to him?" His hand trembled as he dropped his spoon on the table. "They said to Con: 'So you're going to be a father, hey?'"

"Robert – "

" 'You've made a hole in one, have you?' they said."

The male world, mocking and jostling, breathed cold on me from Robert's icy voice: " 'You hit the bull's-eye, did you?' they told Con. 'Good for you!' they said."

"I'm sorry."

"No. You're not."

"Sorry for Con." I left my half-finished coffee, stood up, and saw his eye travel down my body to where the baby was. "He can't have a child of his own, like you."

Robert jumped up as I walked away. "He can't lose one," he shouted. "Like me."

I left him there. I shouldn't have talked to him. He didn't follow me; I kept looking behind me to make sure.

I tried to forget him as I walked against the wind, tried to think how nine months were slowly passing, how every tree was bare now, except for oaks that would rustle all winter, catching snow on brown leaves. Leaf smoke had drifted in town streets for days, that sweet scent of a summer gone. I hurried, block after block, to Victoria's house.

"Miranda!" she said, and ushered me into the big room that was her place of business now. Her father rocked in a warm corner reading *The Woman's Home Companion*.

She sat down at "Minnie," her sewing machine. "Am I going to applique teddy bears or baby dolls on this collar?" She smiled her mischievous-monkey smile, and her little black eyes danced. She was making my maternity clothes.

"Both," I said. "Just to be safe."

"And a little of your mother's dresses in each one?"

"You still have some?" I asked, astonished.

"Bits and pieces. I had to be prepared, didn't I? After the wedding gown come the maternity dresses!" She laughed and I blushed. "I bet Conrad is so proud he's going to be a papa!"

Her doorbell rang. I opened the door and found Mig waiting, her cheeks pink with cold.

"You are beginning to round out," Mig said, looking me over as she came into Victoria's little front hall.

"A little," I said.

"And I'll be doing it, too, before long," Mig whispered. "It's lucky Joe and I are getting married pretty quick!"

"Oh, Mig!" I whispered back. "How wonderful! Isn't Joe happy?"

"He is! I love him so! But he says he never was this good at hitting targets in the war!" She giggled.

Mig's wedding dress hung from Victoria's sewing room doorway, trailing its veil along the carpet. My bridesmaid dress hung beside it, let out a bit at the waistline. When Mig was zipped into the white satin, she said to Victoria, "The waist seems a little tight," and gave me a big smile that Victoria, down on the carpet with pins in her mouth, couldn't see.

"'Zoot suiters in their drape shapes and pegs and knee-length key chains are like the college girls who wear slacks on campus against the college rules,'" Mr. Kline read in his monotonous voice.

"You're having the Lettys for Sunday dinner?" Victoria said to me.

"Yes, and we'll have a turkey."

"A big one," Mig said. "From my uncle's farm."

"But S.C. isn't coming," Victoria said.

"No. How is he?" I asked Mig.

"Quiet. Hardly says a word. Eats supper. Sits in the sunroom until bedtime. I make his breakfast and then he drives off with Howard Bremen to the Company. Tomorrow Effie Coring starts doing his housekeeping."

"She won't cook like Mig," I said to Victoria. "Mig's coming to help me tomorrow. It's my first big dinner in the new house."

Mig was there. By dinnertime my new house smelled of turkey and apple pie. "We're going to entertain," I'd told Con the week before. "At last. Just the way an up-and-coming young executive should. We'll start with the Lettys and practice on them – have the minister's family to dinner."

The fragrance of turkey and apples met the Lettys at the front door. I'd given them a tour of the house just after we'd moved in, but they were a little stiff in our living room, and took their seats in our dining room with hardly a word. They wore their "best clothes" – the ones I'd bought them. How long ago it seemed.

There was Con, standing at the head of the table to carve the turkey. He kept the conversation going, too. "At least we're fighting on Italian soil now," he said as the bird lost its drumsticks.

"It'll be a long, hard battle," Uncle Boyd said, unfolding his napkin.

My aunt and uncle had never asked why we moved, or why Con had left the Beale Equipment Company. They didn't ask why S.C. wasn't at our table.

Aunt Gertrude passed the gravy to Betty and said, "I wonder how we're expected to make up decent beds nowadays. You can't buy a sheet anywhere." Con asked Betty if she knew how to do the Lindy Hop, and she giggled and said she did. "What did you fellows think of the Yankees winning the World Series?" Con asked Ben and Bernard.

The dinner was going well. I sat opposite Con and didn't have to be hostess and keep conversation going, so I found I was watching Con more than I watched anyone else.

He'd been shy and awkward once. He'd sat listening to his father's cruel words, his shoulders sagging. Now – had I seen this so clearly before? – he stood straight and looked the Lettys in the eye. His place was at the head of the table; he fed us in his own house. He had already had a raise at John Deere. Men had slapped him on the back and said, "So you're going to be a father, hey?"

"Any names picked out for the baby yet?" Uncle Boyd asked Con.

Con grinned. "Not yet. We've only got as far as 'he' and 'she.' But we're taking suggestions."

Mig brought in the apple pie, and for a while we were silent to do it justice.

"It's nice that Robert's got his new arm," Aunt Gertrude said. "And he's working at Deere? Boyd knocks on the Lairds' door every now and then, but they never let him in – never have."

"Your house is so beautiful," Betty whispered to me as I passed the cream. "And the baby coming – aren't you excited? And Mig's wedding! What's her dress like?"

Mig's wedding. I dreaded it. But Mig was so happy; every day or two she came to tell me about Joe's job... her new house...the room they would use for the baby.

Her dress was as beautiful as Victoria could make it, and when her wedding day came, I helped her put it on in the church parlor.

She was a lovely bride. I spread her veil over the carpet and was ashamed to remember the heedless eighteen-year-old bride I'd been, waiting in that parlor to marry Con Beale for most of the wrong reasons. He'd watched me flirt and tease and show off, and loved me just the same.

We waited nervously in the chilly parlor as rain beat against the windows. I would be the first to go down the aisle; Yvette would follow, then Mig and her older brother. Listening for the first organ notes, I held my bouquet against my middle. The wedding march began. I took a deep breath with the first note and my first step.

There was the sheet-carpeted aisle lit with candles. There was Uncle Boyd in his minister's robe. There were the two tall Marines waiting. One of them was a blond man whose blue eyes were on Mig behind me. The other had a gloved hand and a bandaged face; his one eye watched me come.

Wasn't I your best man?

I had to pace toward him in my pale pink dress, step by slow step, with pink roses in my hair and pink roses in a spray held before me. I wore the groom's ring on my white-gloved finger, and an expression as cool and aloof as I could make it. Joe was smiling at his bride as she trailed her white veil down the aisle. Robert watched me come with one glittering eye.

Again Robert and I stood before that altar. A year and a half before he had been the man the women watched: a best man in a white tuxedo, my ring passing from his hand to Con's hand, from Con's hand to mine. Now the part of his face I could see was white gauze and tape; service ribbons gleamed on his coat. He gave the groom a ring for the bride; I gave the bride a ring for the groom. Once, as the groom kissed the bride, Robert looked at me.

There was nothing I could do about the receiving line. My uncle had given us our places at the rehearsal dinner: I had to stand between Robert and Con. The three of us shook the procession of hands and said, "So glad you could come" and "Nice to see you here." Sometimes Robert's sleeve brushed my bare arm. My baby had a father on either side, and they never looked at each other.

Con and I danced after we'd had punch and cake. Three old men played waltzes and foxtrots in the big basement room, and the couples revolved on the cement floor. Middle-aged couples danced, and women with women, women with children, and children with children, hopping to the music. The only young men there were Joe, Robert and Con.

"You're simply beautiful," Con murmured to me. I held my bouquet on his shoulder, and the sweet smell of roses breathed from it. I put my face close to it, and over the flowers I saw Robert watching us from the edge of the floor.

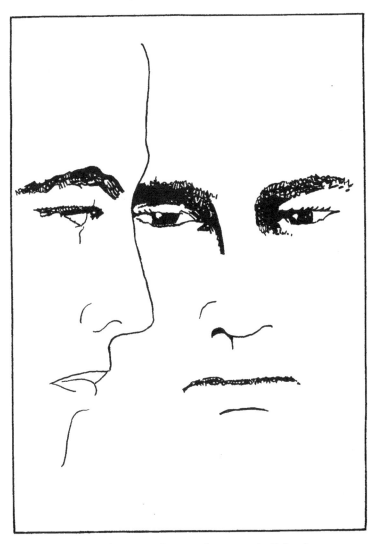

I saw – over my bouquet of roses – the venom in Robert's eye, and Con's answering hate.

"You're the most beautiful angel God ever made!" Con said; he laughed down at me and swung me around in the waltz. He was a good dancer now. How handsome he looked in his dark gray suit and red tie. He held me carefully with the baby between us –

"Cutting in," Robert said behind me.

Still in Con's arms, looking from him to Robert, I didn't hear the music; it seemed to stop. I saw– over my bouquet of roses– the venom in Robert's eye, and Con's answering hate.

Then Con said, "Of course" with such contempt that the half of Robert's face that wasn't bandaged turned red. But I stepped between them, put my bouquet on Robert's shoulder and took the glove that hung at his side in my other hand. Robert had to put his good arm around me and move away.

We danced under Con's steady gaze: he stood at the wall watching...what? His best man holding the matron of honor with their baby between them. *Their baby.*

"Let me go," I said in Robert's ear. We danced close to a door. "Oh, let me go – I'm sick – let me go!" I pushed against the medals on his chest and left him on a dance floor – again – and escaped to a dim Sunday school room to lean against children's drawings of lopsided jack-o'-lanterns stuck on a bulletin board.

Con was there in a second or two. "Are you all right?" His voice was shaky. He drew me out of my corner. "Are you all right? Should we go home?"

All I could say was Yes, Yes, so he took me to one of the pews in the empty sanctuary until he could bring my coat and scarf and gloves and boots. "I told Mig and your aunt that you were tired and I was taking you home," he said, coming back.

He knelt to take my pink slippers off and pull my furry boots on my feet. When he helped me into my coat and tied my scarf under my chin, I whispered, "Thank you," but he wouldn't look at me.

I watched him as he drove me home: the bashful man with the chocolates...the man who listened to his father's insults night after night and said nothing. Now he gripped the wheel of his car as if it were somebody's throat. I knew whose throat it might be, and some of my thoughts must have showed in my eyes when Con and I put our wraps away and stood in our front hall.

He saw it, and his brown eyes darkened; then we both smiled and went upstairs without a word. It was early in the evening; Yvette was still at the wedding dance. I snapped on the light in the smallest bedroom. It was pink and blue now, waiting for the baby; I put my arm around Con as we stood by the little crib.

"All ready?" Con said. I had finished the crib that day: folded the embroidered sheet over the baby blanket and tied the padded bumper around the four sides. The bright eyes of a small teddy bear watched us from a crib corner.

"So you've decided we're having a boy?" Con said, and put his big hands on either side of my head, careful not to crush my rose tiara. He looked into my eyes raised to his.

"Just like you," I said. "Whichever it is, it had better be just like you."

His eyes gleamed. "All right," he said. "As long as it has your heart."

We kissed as he turned the light off, and we kissed in the hall. Our bedroom was growing dark except for the faint glow of a streetlight through our trees. He was holding me so tight, kissing me so hard – I got my mouth away long enough to whisper, "Aunt Gertrude says we won't hurt the baby..." and felt him unzip my pink dress; I let it slither to the floor. His hands followed it down my body, then lifted again to slip the petticoat over my head. When I was bare under our sheet – except for my forgotten wreath of roses – I heard him shed his clothes and lock the door.

29

Christmas came, and 1944, and cold winter set in, but Con and I had our summertime love again in our big bed.

One January afternoon Con came from work to stamp his snowy feet on the back hall mat, slap the snow off his shoulders and arms, and tell me: "Old Mrs. Laird died in her sleep last night."

The day of the funeral was a bitterly cold day. I stood near Robert and Aunt Adele at the edge of a hole hacked in the frozen graveyard ground. Robert's eye gave me one look across his grandmother's grave; she had been our sleeping chaperon, swaddled in her sweaters even in June when Robert's bedroom had been so hot. Now she would have to lie in the winter ground.

My uncle prayed, but his voice was almost blown away in a rush of snowy air: the grave tent might have turned into a sail if two pallbearers hadn't rushed to the tent poles to hang on. Con kept himself between me and the wind, his arms around me.

"Adele doesn't look well, poor dear," Mrs. Valey whispered to me, holding her hat against the gale. "But her mother was a burden. She'll have time for herself now."

I didn't tell her that Robert's mother was quitting her job at Herbert's Grocery. "I'm just so tired these days," she'd told me the week before while we sat in her kitchen. "Robert says he can support us now and I should stay home and rest, bless his heart." She patted my hand beside hers on her kitchen table. "He's such a good son. You see him when he's upset, but he's so kind to me, and we're close. Neither of us has... " she hesitated, "...anybody else. Any relative, now, except you and Con, of course."

She came to my baby shower that the women of the church gave in February. We sat in the parlor: a wide circle of dressed-up, smiling women. I had gone to school with the younger ones and worked with the older ones for years of church dinners and suppers—I'd been the Lettys' orphan niece, who was so fortunate to be given a good home.

Now the seat of honor was mine. As I unwrapped presents, Mrs. Valey folded the wrapping paper and said, "My Burt tells me that the men at the plant are teasing Conrad's father about being a grandfather soon. He doesn't say much, but of course he's very pleased—a grandson to run the business someday, perhaps?" What could I say? I kept smiling at everyone until my smile was stiff and tired by the time the last gift was unwrapped and added to the pile beside me.

As the honored guest, I went to the tea table first. All afternoon I had known where Adele Laird was, just as I'd watched handsome Robert Laird once upon a time. She sat in the circle, her eyes on me, and she was at the tea table behind the coffeepot.

"Have you and Con chosen names for the baby?" Mrs. Palmer asked me just as Adele handed me my coffee.

"Yes," I said, trying to keep my voice and face as calm as if the question could not possibly wound anyone. "If it's a boy, we'll call him 'Raymond Conrad.' If it's a girl, Con wants to call her 'Miranda Alice,' but she'll be 'Alice' – that was my mother's name."

"How nice," Mrs. Valey said. "These lemon cookies – are they yours, Adele?"

"No," Adele Laird said softly. "Not mine."

The shower was over by ten. I went to the Lettys' for lunch, and we listed the gifts so I could write thank-you notes. It was one o'clock before I could cross to the Laird house and knock. Robert wouldn't be there –

Robert opened the door. I hadn't seen him since the funeral, except in church – and in my worst dreams, where he killed Con, or Con killed him. "Oh – I'm sorry," I said, backing away. "I didn't know – "

"Come in," he said. "I'm home to take Mother to the hospital."

"Hospital?" I said, following Robert to the living room. Aunt Adele lay on the couch with her eyes closed.

"She's had spells before, but this was the worst," Robert said. He knelt by the couch and took her hand, but she didn't open her eyes. Then we heard a motor on the street and Robert opened the front door.

In a moment the room seemed filled with men; they put Adele on a stretcher and carried her, blanket-covered, to the ambulance. Robert climbed in beside her without a single look at me, and they were gone.

I went back into the house. I sat at the kitchen table with the memory of long conversations with Aunt Adele in that room. She was as much a mother to me now as Victoria; I said a prayer for her in that quiet place.

It wasn't easy to get up from the chair; the baby was low and heavy. Lights in the house should be turned off, I supposed; a lamp beside Adele's bed was on, and another in Robert's room.

His bed was neatly made. I touched the pillow. Had the baby begun here, or in the house of the lost boys? *That's a love-child you're carrying and it's mine.*

The living room had no old lady asleep in it; her chair sat empty by the window. I washed the few dishes left in the sink, put them away, and walked to Sartori Hospital under a dark gray sky.

Mrs. Laird was very sick, they told me at the desk. "Is her son with her?" I asked.

"He had to go back to work," the woman said. "Are you a member of the family? Only family members can visit just now."

"She's my aunt," I said, and so they let me stay a few minutes by her bed.

Adele lay with her eyes closed. Her face looked as white as her pillowcase. "It's Miranda," I whispered.

Her eyes opened. "Miranda," she said. "Oh, my dear, there's something I wanted to give you for the baby, and I waited too long. It's in the top drawer of my dresser, wrapped in tissue – it's a little baby shirt Robert wore. I wonder...could your baby wear it at the christening? Underneath, you know? It's silly," she tried to smile, "but I wanted the baby to have something..."

"Of course," I said. "Don't worry – I'll go find it as soon as I can. I'm not due for a few weeks yet. And you have to get well so you can come see the baby christened."

"I'll try," she said faintly and closed her eyes when the nurse came to say, "Mrs. Laird needs to rest now."

The hospital air was an acrid mix of medicine and cleaners; I took deep breaths of winter cold as the door shut behind me. Robert was at work. The first flakes of snow touched my face and clung to my coat as I walked to the Laird house and opened the back door.

I was used to feeling like a thief there; I went past Robert's room to his mother's bedroom and opened the top drawer of her dresser. There was a tissue-papered package lying on top.

I opened it on her bed. The tiny shirt was fine hand-kerchief linen. Had she crocheted the lace, and embroidered the "B" among dozens of little roses with their centers of French knots? What had she been thinking as she worked seventeen years before? She had lost two babies. Surely she must have wondered: will I lose this one?

Snow was clotting the air with thick, clustered flakes now. The small bedroom grew dim: it was curtained away from the world by the snow, and silent with its silent fall. I put the little shirt in my purse.

The kitchen was dim and still, too. In a few hours Robert would come to this empty house where his mother had always had his supper waiting for him. He would try to find something to eat – try to cook with his one arm.

I knew that kitchen. It didn't take me long to find enough food to make a supper for Robert. The baby was so heavy that I propped that weight on the sink edge while I peeled potatoes.

And what if I weren't Miranda Beale, I thought, watching the knife slip under potato skin. What if I were Miranda Laird making supper in that old kitchen for Robert? We would eat at the kitchen table. We would listen to the radio in the living room. I would sleep with Robert where the walls were thin lath and the rough board floor creaked, and get breakfast in the morning while my baby crawled on kitchen linoleum that was worn gray to the edges.

I filled a plate and put it in the stove to keep warm by the pilot light. I slipped a note under the saltshaker on the table: "Your supper is in the oven." When I stepped into the alley, I left Miranda Laird behind, and Mandy Letty, too. It was Mrs. Conrad Beale who walked through the snow with her heavy baby and opened the parsonage door.

"Oh, my!" my aunt said when I told her. "In the hospital?"

"She's pretty sick. And Robert will be alone at his house," I said. "Do you suppose you could have him for supper sometimes? I'd invite him, but he'd have to walk that far when he's tired, and you're just across the street. He'll probably be at the hospital this evening and come home late, but I left a note and put a plate of supper to keep warm in the oven for him."

"Of course!" my aunt said. "I'll send one of the boys over with a note right now – put it with yours and invite him to have supper here tomorrow – breakfast, too, if he wants to come. Poor boy. He's only got Adele, and now... She hasn't looked well. Not for months. Sit down, dear, and I'll make you a cup of coffee. But you can't walk home in this weather – you might fall."

"I'll telephone Con. He'll pick me up when he comes from Deere."

Con had his own office and his own phone, but I never called him without a good reason. His voice had concern in it when he answered. "Miranda?"

"Adele Laird's in the hospital," I said. "She's not at all well, and they took her by ambulance at one-thirty – Robert was with her. I didn't go home after the baby shower, and now I'm at the parsonage. Could you pick me up when you're through?"

"I'll be there about five." Con had a distinctive voice, deep and full of feeling. "What about Robert? I'll get in touch with him, see if I can give him a lift to the hospital. The bus doesn't go very near it."

"Tell him I made supper for him at his house," I said. Aunt Gertrude was listening as she poured the coffee; what she couldn't hear in our words vibrated on the line between Con and me. "And the Lettys want him to take his meals here beginning tomorrow. Tell him that, too."

We said goodbye and I sat down heavily on the parlor sofa as Aunt Gertrude brought my coffee. She talked of the snowstorm, and circle meetings being canceled, and Bernard's newspaper route. I looked around the room. I'd bought new curtains, and a piano for Betty. The kitchen had a real refrigerator now. The boys had bunk beds. In the spring I'd replace the kitchen linoleum.

The parlor was chilly, as always. Such a shabby house – and I'd thought it would be paradise for my mother and me. I'd dreamed of it. I'd dreamed of being with Robert Laird in that house across the street; I could see it through the parlor window, small and dark in the falling snow. But Con Beale would come soon to take my baby and me to our beautiful home. I prayed a silent prayer of thanks in a room that had been full of prayers, and set my cup and saucer on the little shelf the baby made of my lap. Then I took it off quickly and laughed and said, "I'd better not put it there. He'll kick it right off!"

Aunt Gertrude laughed, too. "You don't have long to wait," she said.

"I'm so happy," I said. I was.

"It's worth anything," Aunt Gertrude said, looking at her rough hands in her lap. "To have your own baby."

I got up awkwardly from the sofa. "It's almost supper-time. Let me make myself useful."

Aunt Gertrude protested, but I helped her anyway. We were chattering together in the kitchen as we basted a chicken and cut up squash when Con came, stamping snow from his boots at the front door. "I'd better not walk on the rug," he called.

"Did Robert go with you to the hospital?" my aunt asked.

"I took him," Con said. "He said I should thank Miranda for his dinner tonight, and you folks for your standing invitation to eat here."

"Good," Aunt Gertrude said. "No – you mustn't put on those boots," she told me. "Sit down." I sat down and she pulled my boots on my feet that seemed a mile away, then brought my coat and scarf and mittens. "You two can take your basket of baby presents home with you," she said, and went to get it.

"Lots of booties and bonnets," I told Con. I kissed him in that little hall where Aunt Gertrude had found him on the doorstep with a box of chocolates, and I'd swept by my aunt to say, "Why, Mr. Beale! Do come in."

Con put the basket in the car and then came back for me. "I'll get her home safely," he told my aunt, hugging me close as we went down the snowy steps. My coat pocket rustled against him; another baby gift was hidden there: a baby shirt with roses embroidered on it, and a "B" for "Beale."

What had Con said to Robert, all the long way to the hospital? What had Robert said to him? Had they sat like two stone men without a word? I couldn't ask.

Con answered my silent question. "Robert said they don't have much hope for his mother."

"She's so sick?" I cried.

"It's her heart," Con said. "She may live a while, or go any time."

We watched the windshield wipers clear the glass: a regular rhythm like a heartbeat.

"What about S.C.?" I said. "He isn't well. He could die. He'd never know we really do want him as a father...a grandfather..."

Con was still; he watched snowflakes caught in the twin funnels of our headlights. They flattened their stars on the windshield, then were swept to slush by the wiper blades.

"He's there every night in his house, alone," I said. "He knows where we live. He must watch us go by. But he's hurt you so much – "

"You're the one who shouldn't forgive him," Con said.

"I'm through with not forgiving and getting even," I said. "Those kinds of feelings snake through your life if you let them – spoil the nicest times. Why should I carry anger around? I'd rather carry two buckets of rotten eggs everywhere I go."

Con grinned at me. "You do find just the right words."

"Maybe he doesn't want to carry his around, either. He's in so much pain. He must be lonely. He's lost you."

Con's smile was gone. "He knows why. Some things you can't forgive."

I watched his profile until at last he looked at me, anger and reflections of the snow glittering in his eyes. But I didn't glance away, so I saw his angry look turn thoughtful, turn ashamed, then twinkle with the snow-light. "Rotten eggs," he said.

Slow days. Slow nights. Aunt Adele was no better, no worse. I went to see her. We waited. One week. Two. Then the baby woke me in the middle of a cold, snowy March night: it kicked and pushed, hurting me. I only said, "Con?" once and he was wide awake, climbing out of bed, turning on lights; he played the part of a scared and nervous father perfectly.

Dressed and beside Con in our car, I looked at town streets going by and tried not to groan.

We were going to pass the parsonage. There it was. Across from it Robert was sleeping in his house; his bedroom window reflected our passing car for a second, then was dark.

My pains were coming more often. Con left the car at the curb and helped me up the hospital stairs.

"I'm Mrs. Beale," I said to a nurse at the desk as Con left to park the car. "Dr. Horton's patient. My baby's on the way."

"Ah, yes," the nurse said, and shuffled through papers. I held my breath, waiting for the next pain.

She asked question after question, writing each answer down precisely. I contributed the facts, suffering between breaths, and thought the baby must be coming out itself to hurry her up.

The nurse seemed satisfied at last. She arranged her papers in a neat pile, and then thought to ask how often I was having pains.

"All the time," I gasped, and she was suddenly interested in me, not papers, and started around the counter just as I turned and saw Con – and Robert – coming through the outside door.

I must have looked like a woman on the rack, to judge from both their faces: their expressions were so identically horrified and guilty that I would have laughed if I'd had breath enough.

Much good would either of them be to me. I turned my back on them and followed the nurse, who was, at last, moving briskly.

And then I was all alone, though people were talking around me. I felt hands taking off my clothes, hands lifting me to a high white surface, but I was as lonely as if I were dying.

Nobody was hurting but me. If voices came close, their ordinary, chatty tones were like an unfeeling sea where I floated, an island, crying. Someone was saying, "Push!" and kneading a heavy, hard stone into my abdomen, and someone was screaming – I wished they'd make her stop. But she screamed hour after hour, I thought.

And then, days later, it seemed to me, the heavy stone that hurt so much rolled away, and the screaming stopped, and the pain was gone. Voices were still talking around me, but there was another sound: a thin, furious small cry that said that somebody was as much at the end of a rope as I was.

I opened my eyes and there was that somebody, a boy so small and so furious, lying on my flat stomach and yelling at me. He was, literally, at the end of his rope, and bloody, and not giving up for one minute, no matter how many people stood around us.

"Never mind, Raymond Conrad Beale," I told him, and all at once he stopped crying, opened his amazing eyes and looked right at me.

"A bouncing baby boy," Doctor Horton said, smiling at his old cliche as if he couldn't see what a miracle we had there, those two small eyes and me.

Then they cleaned us up and wrapped us up, and I held him in my arms for the first time. He was a big baby, they said, and he wasn't a wrinkled little old man: his cheeks were plump and his dark hair lay neatly on his small head. He twitched and kicked just as he had inside me, but now he had the whole wide world to stretch his arms and legs in.

We looked at each other as they wheeled us away. He was learning my eyes, perhaps, as I was learning his, because eyes are the same when everything else changes. Far down a corridor, Con was running toward us. In a minute the baby had a new pair of eyes to study: Con was bending over us to kiss me again and again and murmur, "Miranda... Miranda... " They wheeled me into a hospital room and left us.

"Raymond Conrad Beale," I said softly. "Meet your daddy."

I'd never seen such a look on Con's face: so many feelings raced across it. "Hello, son," he whispered, and touched the baby's palm, and the little boy grabbed his big finger and hung on, and we laughed, and were relieved to laugh.

"You're all right?" Con asked me. "Tired."

"I'm wide awake!" I said. "I don't think I'll sleep for a week, I'm so happy."

"You certainly surprised us, going through it so fast."

"Fast?" I said.

"That's what the doctor says. Fast for a first baby."

A first baby. What ordinary words those were. People would say, "Miranda Beale's had her first baby."

"*For an only child*," I said.

Con looked into my eyes and heard the promise; I knew he had, because he paused and then said, with a logical, painful progression: "They called Robert in."

"His mother?"

"She's conscious yet, but it won't be long."

"Con," I said. "Could you possibly..."

I didn't have to finish. "You want to see her?" Con said, and then, in a lower tone, "you want her to see the baby."

"Will they let us?"

"We can try," Con said, and left. The window of my room was blue with dawn, and the baby was asleep now in his blanket cocoon.

A nurse came back with Con. "Your aunt's on the same floor," the nurse told me. "We can roll you right into her room, bed and all."

Two nurses wheeled my bed along the corridor; Con walked beside it. When they opened a door at the end, I saw Robert beside his mother's bed, holding her hand.

"We mustn't stay too long," a nurse said as they pushed my bed against Adele's. I heard the door close behind me, and when I looked, Con wasn't there.

Robert let his mother's hand go. He came slowly around the beds to me. He looked down at the sleeping baby.

"Robert?" His mother's voice was weak and quivery.

"Aunt Adele," I said, and reached to take her hand on the sheet. "I'm here. It's Miranda. And my baby's here with me – your new grandson."

Her hand tightened in mine. "The baby? A little boy?"

I sat up enough to lift the sleeping baby in his wrapped-close blanket. "Take him," I said to his father. "Let her see him."

Robert had only one arm to hold the small bundle. He managed to cradle it against him, then lifted the little boy enough to lay his unbandaged cheek against the small face. For a moment he stood there, and because he rocked himself a little, holding his baby, I began to cry.

In a little while he went around the beds and laid the baby in his mother's arms. "Here he is," Robert said in a choked voice.

Propped on her pillows, Adele looked at the little pink face and the pink fists; then she looked into Robert's face above her. I felt out of place in that room.

"He looks just like you did," Adele said to her son. "Just exactly." One of her hands rose to touch his bandaged face. "My beautiful boy."

"Oh, Mom!" Robert cried, laying his dark head on her breast, his good arm around the baby, his metal arm trailing its glove across the sheet.

For a moment they never moved; then a nurse opened the door, and another followed. The first one bent over Robert and Adele and said kindly, "We'll have to take the baby now."

Robert sank into a chair near the bed. The nurse lifted the baby from Adele's arms and brought him to me. "Such a good boy," she said. "Catching up on his sleep."

"Goodbye, Aunt Adele," I said. "I love you. I'll be praying for you."

Robert's eyes were on his mother, not me. There was no sound from the bed. The nurses wheeled the baby and me away. Far down at the end of the corridor I saw Con standing alone, looking through a window at the dawn.

30

Adele Laird died the next day, and I was still in the hospital when she was buried.

"Her second husband's grave is in Des Moines, but Robert wanted her to be in the Beale plot next to his father," Con said, sitting beside me in my hospital room he'd filled with flowers. "I told him that would be fine with us."

"But what about S.C.?"

"I talked to him about it first," Con said. "I had to. All Dad could say for a while was, 'Adele's gone...she's gone.'"

Con touched Ray's small face as the baby dozed in my arms. I tried to imagine S.C. grieving for anyone.

"And then he said, 'Bury me beside her, will you, when I go?'" Con said. "I promised I would."

"After all those years," I said. "Why wasn't he her best friend? He helped Robert – why couldn't he have made her life easier, watched over her?"

"Rotten eggs," Con said.

"Yes," I said. Ray stirred in my arms and opened his dark eyes wide. His fists bobbed this way and that until he managed to get one at his mouth to suck.

"After eight months Dad's found out he can't run the Company without me," Con said. "Maybe he's tired of carrying those rotten eggs around. He wants to see you and Ray."

"He does?" I cried.

"I think it's because I told him..." Con hesitated. He took my hand. "I told him I might enlist, and I depended on him to look after you and the baby."

Enlist.

"I want to talk to you about it," Con said. "I want you to understand how I feel. The baby was coming and I didn't want to upset you, but now ... "

I found I was holding Ray so tight that he wriggled in my arms.

"I've got a child now," Con said. "My son's going to have to explain, all his life, what I was doing while we fought a war."

"The draft board won't let you."

"There are ways to do it."

"When you're safe?" I cried. "When you're helping the country more than you ever could if you fought – "

"When I'm making so much money from it," Con said. "When other men are paying with their lives."

Perhaps the baby felt how horrified I was: he began to fuss. He wasn't satisfied with his fist any more; he was hungry. I opened my robe and felt him fasten on a nipple with a pull that darted to other parts of me like an electric shock; I was growing used to that.

"Robert told me he's going to clear his house out – won't rent it any more. He can't stand to live there, now that he's lost his mother. He's leaving Deere. He's leaving town, going to Chicago as soon as he can."

"Leaving?" I said. "What will he do, all by himself?"

"I don't know. I didn't think I should ask." Con kept his eyes on Ray, who was making his soft, satisfied little nursing suck-and-sigh.

Enlist. Enlist. That word hovered over us as we brought Ray home to his nursery and his crib with its teddy bear. Our house was a family home: it had a child in it.

But the father of the house was going to war.

The next Thursday we drove to S.C.'s house with Ray. When we came in the sunroom, S.C. didn't look up or speak. After seven months, how small and crumpled-up he seemed to me: an old man in a big wheelchair.

Memories stood around the four of us, as real as the wicker furniture in the sunshine.

"How are you, Dad?" Con asked.

"Not well." S.C. gave us one fierce look under his heavy eyebrows. "That's the baby, I suppose."

I glanced at Con, then went to hold Ray in S.C.'s lap where he could see him. Ray looked up at S.C. with fascination; it was the glasses that intrigued him, I suppose. He kicked his feet and waved his fists.

"Lively," S.C. said.

Just one word. Other grandfathers would have had dozens, but S.C.'s one was enough for us; it made conversation possible.

I carried Ray to a nearby chair and sat down, and Con sat down, too. "I've told Miranda I want to enlist," Con said. "She doesn't like it, but she understands how I feel."

"Tomfoolishness," S.C. said. "You ought to be running the Beale Company, not going off to get shot at."

"I'm not running the Beale Company," Con said. "Never have."

"Then who's going to run it, if you don't? Haven't got a single man down there who can do it – nincompoops, all of them. Behind in orders, don't get the steel –"

"If I came back to the Company I'd have to own it," Con said. "When the war's over. With you getting a share of the profits, of course."

S.C. stared at Con. "All right," he said. "But you can't go running off soldiering – there won't be a Beale Company to come back to."

"Profits are high. They'll go higher," Con said. "Italy's going to fall. We're bombing Berlin. We're going to land in France, you can bet, and go for German soil. That'll take every kind of armament we can send over there."

"And lives," S.C. said.

Con got up to stand beside Ray and me. "Yes. I may not come back, and that's what I want to settle now," he said to S.C.. "You never forgave Aunt Adele. Don't do it again with Miranda and Raymond. Take care of them for me if I die."

S.C. wouldn't answer.

Con waited. The clock ticked on the wall.

"Think twice," he said to silent S.C.. "Think twice before you tell me Miranda and the baby are no relatives of yours."

"Relatives?" S.C. said, glaring at me. "I don't think so."

"You said there was one Beale in the family you could be proud of," Con said. "But now he's a crippled man. Don't you pity him?"

"Of course," S.C. said in his sharp voice. "Wounded for his country? Of course I'm sorry."

I could hardly bear it: Con had to go on. "Miranda was sorry, too. She's so young. She pitied him." It sounded as if Con were pressing the words out of his throat, painfully. "So she's the mother of your brother's grand-child. She's giving him to me, not to anyone else who thinks he's entitled to him, because she loves me. I'll have my son. You'll have your grandchild – the one you thought you'd never have. He's Raymond Conrad Beale."

S.C.'s startled eyes went from Con to me, from me to the baby, and back to Con.

"Adele Laird's grandson," Con said.

Again it was so still in that room. Then Con said, "Remember that. Take care of Miranda and Ray. He's the only young Beale you and I will ever have, and it's Miranda who's given him to us. Promise me."

I saw S.C. take a deep breath. "All right," he said.

"Good," Con said, and took Raymond from my arms. "Then we'll be going home. We hope you'll come to our house often to watch your grandson grow."

As we turned away, S.C. said, "What about Robert? Does he know?"

Con turned back, his eyes dark and gleaming. "He knows Ray is his. He wants the baby, and Miranda."

"So he'll talk," S.C. said. "He'll fight." Suddenly his eyes were furious behind his glasses. "Took somebody else's wife – robbed us, didn't he, just like his father – "

"Miranda says I have a son. The whole town believes it." Con gave S.C. a stern look. "If Robert says the baby is his, who'll say Robert isn't lying – except you?"

Con shut the sunroom door softly behind us, and we went out to our car and drove home in silence. I hugged Ray and looked out the car window at town lawns growing green with spring, but I didn't see them. "I'm so sorry," I said softly at last. "I'm selfish. Stupid. Other people have to pay for it."

"No, you aren't," Con said, looking straight ahead. "You always want to help. Look what you've done for me."

There were tears in my eyes. "Do you have to go and fight? Even S.C. doesn't think you should. If you own your father's company, you can certainly – "

"No," Con said. "I can't."

"It's going to be an awful fight," I said. "We've got to drive Germany back, mile by mile, and the Japanese – they won't give up."

He looked at me, and then at the sleeping baby. "Don't ask me to stay. I can't."

For weeks Con worked overtime at Deere, training his successor. "Robert's leaving for Chicago on April twenty-ninth," he told me one night. "Going for good, he tells everyone." I thought I heard relief in Con's voice.

Certainly Robert must have seen our car in the Deere lot when he left work, night after night. He knew when Yvette had her afternoon off. He rang my doorbell on the day before he left town, a Thursday afternoon.

I saw him through the glass of the big door before he saw me. I was alone. The baby was asleep upstairs. I felt a little dart of fear, and yet there I was – look at me! – posing in the hall mirror a moment to see if my hair looked right, if my figure was as good as ever –

I met my own ashamed eyes in the mirror, then opened the door.

Robert's bandaged face wasn't smiling above a huge bouquet of roses. "Do you know," he said. "I've never given you a single flower?" His eye stared around him for a moment at the big hall and the rooms he could see through archways.

"Yes, you have," I said as I took the roses. "A carnation. And a paper rose."

"Carnation?" he said. I led the way into my living room, but he didn't follow; he stood in the hall, thinking.

"In the graveyard," I said. "After we graduated."

"Oh," he said with a kind of moan, and put his good hand on the unbandaged half of his face for a moment. "You weren't married yet. You stood by your mother's grave and said it was late and you had to go, and it was – it was so late – and all I wanted to say was, Stop before it's too late. Don't marry him. But what did I have to offer you, compared to him? All I could talk about was the Lost Boys' House, and you walked away."

The Lost Boys' House. The four words pressed us so close, there in my hall, that we might as well have been in each other's arms.

"And the paper rose?" he said. "You gave it back. You never came again."

"It was my fault. I shouldn't have been there at all."

"No?" he asked. "Then where would that little boy of ours be?"

He saw me take a step back and turn my face away. "It happened in the Lost Boys' House – where else would my lost boy begin? I can count nine month's worth of weeks as well as you can," he said. "Where is he? Upstairs?"

I nodded and left the roses on the hall table as I followed him to the second floor.

Sunlight laid a golden streak along the hall upstairs, but the baby's room was dim and cool. Robert leaned over the little crib to kiss sleeping Ray. "Goodbye, son," he whispered. "Your father loves you." He swung around to me. "Tell him that," he said. "If you ever dare tell him the truth."

"I've hurt enough people," I said.

"Me, to begin with." He pulled me into his arms beside the crib. "This will be his room," he said. "Remember that I kissed you in it."

He kissed me, then went into the hall. I followed him. "Is this 'the master bedroom,'" he asked, stopping at the door. He passed me to stand by the big, satin-covered four-poster.

"Yes."

"Then lie here and kiss me." He pushed me down on the bed. "I want you to remember me here, right here, every night."

"Robert!" I cried. "I'm so sorry! It was my fault, and now look at the damage..."

I stopped. He was furious; I could feel it. He wasn't even listening, and pinned me under him. His bandaged face snagged on the satin, and his hand slid under my dress. "Another baby?" he said. "Con can't make one. I can. Right here in the 'master bedroom' in the 'master's bed.' Then you can give him a second child of mine."

He couldn't keep me there, and somehow that was the most pitiful thing of all. He was strong, but I had two arms and two hands, and I got away. He was after me in a minute, holding me tight against him with his good arm. "Every room," he said. "I'm going to kiss you in every room of this house. For you to remember." He pulled me into another bedroom to kiss me, his hand in my hair, murmuring, "*So willingly she came into his arms.*"

"And what's this?" he said, going with me into Con's study. "Your study? No? Con's?" I nodded.

"Then we'll sit in his chair." Robert pulled me into his lap to kiss me – how smeared my lipstick was by then – and his good hand slid down the front of my dress. "Don't," I tried to say, but his kiss was holding my head

He pushed me down on the bed. He was furious, and pinned me under him. "Another baby?" he said. "Then you can give him a second child of mine."

against the back of the chair; I pulled his hand away and at last he let me go.

"Every room," he said, leading me downstairs. The mirror we passed showed me two people with red mouths and flushed faces. "Your study?" He pulled me inside and looked at my books, my typewriter, my view of the garden that was already yellow with daffodils.

"I'll come to the station tomorrow to say goodbye," I said, trying to calm him.

"Remember I love you – remember me here," he said against my cheek. "You made me *dream of loves and lustful play...Dame Pleasures toys –* "

The doorbell rang.

"Oh!" I cried, thinking of someone finding us alone, caught there. "Out the back door," I whispered. "Hurry."

In the second before I shut him out, we looked at each other. Our baby was in a crib upstairs.

No one was with me when I opened my door to Mrs. Newton and Mrs. Palmer from the church. I was a decent young matron who had scrubbed her face off in the kitchen sink on the way to the front door, and run her hands through her tangled hair. "Come in, come in," I said. "Sorry I'm in such a state, but I've been taking care of the baby," and indeed I had.

The women came in and stood primly in the hall. "We know Con's leaving for the war in a few days, and we thought maybe he'd like a little something sweet that he won't get in the army," Mrs. Palmer said, holding out a covered pie and a plate of cookies. "What beautiful roses."

Robert's roses on the hall table were tight buds yet, and scarlet as a fire. "Yes," I said. "I was about to take them to the church for Sunday service."

"You've got the baby to tend – we'll drop them off for you on our way home," Mrs. Newton said. "It's a lovely day for a walk."

So after I brought down sleepy Raymond to be admired, and served tea in my lovely living room on my lovely bone china, two middle-aged ladies carried away Robert's roses. Nothing was left of him in that house but Ray, and the memory of angry, wild kisses that would catch me sometimes – like a man with one arm – in a study, in a child's room, or on a four-poster bed.

31

R obert brought a dozen roses today," I told Con
    when he came home late that night. "I gave them
to Mrs. Newton and Mrs. Palmer when they brought over
pie and cookies – said they were for the altar on Sunday."

Con looked at me.

"He only came to see Ray for a last time, and say goodbye."

Still Con was silent. I could only hug him until his arms
at last went around me. That night, turning our bed down,
I saw how two bodies had wrinkled the satin spread.

The next morning was a cloudy late-April day; friends
gathered on the station platform to say goodbye to
Robert. Con shook his hand. S.C. said, "Good luck in
Chicago. Let us hear from you." Joe slapped him on the
back and told him he'd always be welcome at their house,
while Mig stood beside him with tears in her eyes, holding their new daughter. Robert's classmates and friends
from Deere were there, high school teachers, church
members, and the Letty family.

Once again Robert and I hardly looked at each other or
talked to each other, but this time we couldn't hide a
secret: it watched us from Con's eyes, and S.C.'s, and I
held Raymond in my arms.

The train came, and the group called, "Good luck!"
and "See you soon!" and "Come back to Cedar Falls!" as
Robert said goodbye. Just as he swung his suitcase up the
steps of the train with his one arm and then climbed
aboard, Robert looked back at Raymond and at me, a long
look from his one brown eye.

Robert's red roses hardly lasted through the final prayer on Sunday, though they were stabbed through and held at attention by green wire. Before the service I told Joe and Mig who had given the roses. Joe said, "Robert's going to Chicago to look for a job like he had at Deere. 'They'll hire a crippled veteran now,' he told me. 'They might not do it later,' and I suppose he's right. He said he couldn't stay here. Couldn't stand that house without his mother."

That Sunday was Con's last. After the service the congregation gathered around us to wish him God-speed. Tuesday he would be gone. Early Monday morning a florist knocked on our door, bringing bouquet after bouquet, plant after plant. There wasn't a single red rose, but he carried in dozens of pink and yellow and white ones, daisies and lilies, jonquils, tulips...every room in the house was full.

Yvette went home after supper, and when the three of us were alone, Con put on his white tuxedo and I wore my Empire Room dress – it was only a little tight. We put on records and danced through our big rooms, laughing and kissing and trying not to think of the next day. My blue net and satin rustled around me, and I remembered Con with my diamond in his pocket, asking, "Do you love me?" and I – I hadn't said Yes – to Con! To Con!

And I'd been so proud in that dress, waltzing at the Junior-Senior Prom with an orchid on my shoulder, leaving Robert – handsome Robert – standing alone among the dancers. For a moment I saw him with his bandaged face and metal arm, left alone now among all the dancers of the world.

"You didn't hear what Dad said yesterday at Raymond's christening," Con said; we were foxtrotting to *They're Either Too Young Or Too Old*. "He took the baby from me and looked down at him and said, 'Adele's grandchild...and my brother's.'"

"So he loves him," I said, "after all. I'll tell him about the little shirt Ray was wearing."

"Adele's blessing," Con said. "For you."

"I need her blessings," I said. "So does Robert, wherever he's gone. Ray needs them, too. His father and his grandfather know who he is."

Con said nothing; there wasn't any answer to that, or any way to make up for it. Dancing among the flowers in my blue satin and net, I wondered if hell might be the agony of watching your mistakes and cruelties happen over and over forever.

"The flowers," Con said when the record ended. "Let's put them in our bedroom. C'mon." We carried all the vases and flowerpots upstairs, and lit candles in every candlestick we could find. "A bower of bliss," I said. "I've always wanted to see a bower of bliss, haven't you?"

Ray woke just as we took off our fancy clothes. I changed him and brought him, not quite as naked as I was, to naked Con in our bed. The baby looked so little in Con's big hands; his small body was rosy in the candlelight. I nursed him while Con kissed me and made love to me, and we felt so delightfully wicked, but what did Ray care? Four arms around him were better than two, and nobody took his milk away, and it seemed to me that we were a true family: father, mother, child.

We hung over the crib watching him fall asleep. "He'll be so different when you come home," I whispered. "And you won't be the same. Nobody who goes to fight is ever the same again." I began to cry.

"Don't," Con said, putting his arms around me. He took me back in our bedroom and brought me to the alarm clock on our night table. "Do you see that clock?" he said, his dark eyes dancing with wickedness and candlelight. "I'm setting it for every hour all night long. Do you think I'm going to waste my last night with you sleeping?"

So we were a drowsy couple the next morning, but not drowsy enough. I tried not to cry. "You're my angel," Con said, and kissed me for the last time. "Remember that. And take care of Ray for me."

He swung himself up the steps of the train and was gone.

The war dragged on, dragged on, month after slow month.

D-Day in June took four thousand ships, three thousand planes, and more than four million Allied troops. Con wasn't in the Normandy invasion, but he lived through the Battle of the Bulge. He marched into liberated Paris. He was in Reims to see Eisenhower accept Germany's surrender.

In that long last year of the war, no one heard from Robert, not even Joe. Once I dreamed that Robert appeared at my door again with red roses and said, "Where is he? Upstairs?"

And then Con was home at last from the First Army in Germany. The war was over.

Now and then we talked about Robert – Con, S.C. and I. We'd looked in the Chicago phone book; Robert wasn't in it. If Con went to Chicago, where would he begin to look? And should he go?

"It looks to me as if Robert wants to start a new life," Con said. "We'd have heard if anything happened to him – we're the only relatives he has. So doesn't it seem to you that he's choosing to leave us behind?"

Yet Robert hadn't completely disappeared. There was Ray. And maybe Alibi Ritter had been right: something like a ghost of Robert was in my house. Sometimes the memory of a kiss caught me like a man's arm, or a breath of air like a rough bandage brushed my cheek.

But day after day dropped a slow rain of hours on me, year by year, constant as a ticking clock. Con had nightmares at first, and sometimes a look in his eyes that was like a shutter opening on unspeakable sights. Yet he was contented, I think; the habits of a good marriage surrounded us, warm as laughter at family jokes, or comfortable old clothes.

Once in a while Con and I talked of Robert living somewhere with a wife and children, and a good job. Sometimes, traveling with Con, I thought I saw Robert in New York, or London, or Athens – a tall man with thick, dark hair that would have grayed, like Con's. But when I saw the faces of those strangers, they were only that: strangers.

After Robert had been gone for a year, I walked out to "Mr. Calvinhorn's farm." I couldn't find it: bulldozers were there, widening the farm road to a highway, turning every view I remembered into tire-rutted earth. They roared, backing and filling in the woods where the underground house had been, making a bike path, and a park.

Joe and Mig had a second little girl, and then another. I graduated with my bachelor's degree. How quickly all of us forgot our fear that Hitler would take our country. We didn't want to remember the years when almost every young man was gone to fight, or was only a gold star in his family's window.

Cedar Falls became a little city, and our church grew to twice its size. But the church suppers still tasted the same, and there was always an angel saying, "Fear not, for behold I bring you good tidings" at our Christmas pageant.

Betty and Ben and Bernard and Bruce acquired wives and husbands, children and grandchildren. The graves of Aunt Gertrude and Uncle Boyd joined my mother's. Aunt Adele lies between the two brothers, Sam and Henry Beale.

I often walked by Robert's house. People with children lived there for years: there was a swing in the small front yard. Who would remember beautiful Adele Webster, or Robert, the Prince, the football captain?

Raymond grew to be as tall as Con, and he was a Beale; everybody said so – my one child, my dear joy – I understood Adele Laird, and Gold Star Mothers of a world war, and my mother, white-faced on a train to Iowa. When Ray graduated from college, he was a bomber pilot in Vietnam. In October 1966 we heard that 403 U.S. planes had been lost over North Vietnam.

But Ray was as lucky as Con had been: he came home, and was Con's second-in-command at the Beale Equipment Company, and married his childhood sweetheart, Joe and Mig's youngest daughter. But she died, and broke our hearts, and Ray lived alone for a long time, grieving.

Now he has a new wife, and my beloved four-year-old granddaughter, Margaret. Her name should be "Adele," for she looks like her great grandmother, but what child wants to be called "Adele" nowadays? And her great grandmother's name is the name of S.C.'s wife, isn't it, carved on a gravestone in the Beale plot: Lillian Marie McCutcheon Beale?

No. Sometimes Margaret and I visit the graves, and her real great grandmother, Adele Webster Beale Laird, lies between Sam and Henry Beale and hears Margaret's voice, I hope, and knows who she is, and where Robert is.

And Adele Laird is with us, after all, like Alibi Ritter's loving ghosts. One day when Raymond was almost in his teens, I heard S.C. telling him a story. I didn't mean to eavesdrop, and turned away from the sunroom door, but S.C.'s voice reached me: he said to his 'grandson,' "She called, 'Dad! Dad!' until she couldn't call any more. She tied a rope around her waist so she wouldn't get lost, and went as far as she could into that blizzard, calling him..."

And Margaret has her real great-great-grandfather's eyes: green eyes, "green as weeds." I told Con that; S.C. must have seen it.

But I hardly ever mentioned Robert, not for years. We moved to a new, bigger house when Ray was five, a house with no ghost of a man with one arm and one eye – not in any room, not on any bed.

32

Years, and more years. Each one left Robert farther behind, until he was only a distant figure holding a girl in his arms who had once been me.

Con and I grew old together: he had a fine office in the new Beale Equipment Company Building, and a son to share the work. I had my study, my big computer, and the novels I wrote year after year, until the copies of them in dozens of foreign languages filled a broad bookcase. Hadn't I always loved telling stories?

Hadn't I always loved Con? It seemed to me that I had. And then, early one May morning, Con and I woke and lay watching sunlight and the shadow of half-open leaves falling on our bed. Why did we start reminiscing in the sunlight there... an angel in cheesecloth, a box of chocolates, a diamond in Chicago, a man in a wheelchair, a baby in a dying woman's arms, a man with half a face and one arm?

"I love you," Con said, and I told him how much I loved him – why?

"I'll go get breakfast," I said. "The doctor told you to give your heart plenty of rest – go back to sleep for a little while."

I sang in my kitchen, I remember, where the sunshine of another spring dappled the plates and saucers and cups. When I went to call Con, that sunshine was in his face and his quiet eyes, watching me, watching me, watching me –

"Con!" I cried, and knew he was gone. I threw my arms around him – he was still warm! "I told you to go back to sleep, but only for a little while – a little while, Oh, Con!"

We buried Con at his mother's feet on the green hill, with space beside him for me.

For a year I didn't write a word. Summer, fall, winter – they all were the same to me. When another spring threw the shadow of new leaves on my bed, I hardly cared whether it was May in Iowa again. Every glossy leaf was new. Con was gone.

Raymond said, "You can't hole up in your house all day, Mother! Get out and see people! Start writing again!"

He was a loving son. He worried about me, alone in my house. He trapped me into babysitting my granddaughter one morning. Her mother had driven to Des Moines, and Ray was off to the Beale Equipment Company.

"What shall we do?" I asked four-year-old Margaret. She looked at me with her weed-green eyes. She had chocolate syrup down the front of her shirt; I washed the worst of it off with a wet washcloth and said, "Walk to the park? Go swimming at the pool?"

She was a modern child. "A movie!" she said, and ran to the ranks of them in her parents' entertainment center. "This is my shelf," she said, "and you've got to choose. Close your eyes! Pick one!"

I picked one, and she put it to work with the practiced ease of a four-year-old in the computer age. I settled down with a magazine from the coffee table. I was tired, so I appreciated television's story-in-a-box that could immobilize the body and voice of a small child for hours at a time. I hardly watched television, except when it tried to turn a book I loved into a picture book for grownups.

Disney cartoons filled the big living room with their mishmash of colors only a garden dares to mix, and frantic bleating in place of words. My magazine couldn't drown it out; I went off to the kitchen in search of tea, and sat in the color-rich garden in the shade for a while.

But I was supposed to be baby-sitting. I went in to find Margaret where I'd left her, staring at the screen where a little girl in a nightgown flew through the air.

I watched with Margaret until Raymond came home on an errand and looked in to see how we were. "Peter Pan?" he said.

I gave him an indignant look. "That's not Peter Pan," I said. "In the book, Peter Pan doesn't care about anyone but himself. He's mean! Wendy's the loving one, and she ends up old – that's so awful – don't you remember?"

"I remember," Raymond said. "You read it to me, and I've got the book here somewhere. Here it is."

He handed the old book to me. I knew it so well; I opened it to one of the last pages and read Wendy's words to her daughter Jane: "I liked the home under the ground best of all ... "

"Yes," Margaret yelled, pointing to the screen. "See? There's Peter and the Lost Boys in it."

I read: "The last thing Peter Pan ever said to me was, 'Just always be waiting for me, and then some night you will hear me ... " I stopped and shut the book.

"You ought to read it to Margaret," Ray said. "She'd love it." He smiled and left. I watched the busy little cartoon boys slide into their underground house. Suddenly I was appalled: I couldn't remember the feel of Robert Laird – he'd flown out of my memory, disembodied as a ghost. What had he been like to kiss? To make love to? How had his voice sounded, murmuring, *Dame Pleasures toys?*

When I left Raymond's house, I went home to my study.

Where was a picture of Robert? I got down on my knees and rummaged at the back of a closet for a dusty box. And there was Robert in my high school yearbooks, a handsome boy in his teens with two dark eyes and two arms, throwing a pass as football captain, giving a speech as class president. The back of one book broke as I opened it.

Under the last yearbook was my freshman humanities textbook, waiting for me with notes scribbled in the margins: *In your secret place at the library. I'm here. You'll have to pay up.* Halfway through the worn book was *The Faerie Queene.* I had marked the lines from Robert's letters in red: *Her grace to have which of all earthly things he most did crave ...* and my cruel choice in blue: *In vaine he seekes that having cannot hold.* And his answer: *Let me not die in languor and long tears.*

No shoestring in that box. No paper rose. But as I sat on the closet floor looking at Robert's picture, my memory woke – that hoarder of feelings, tastes, smells, sounds – a camera that never loses the thing it sees.

I put the books away, crawled to my feet, went out to my car, and drove down the new highway to what had been Mr. Calvinhorn's farm.

The fields were green with June-high corn and soybeans. I parked my car near where the old barn had stood, I thought, and looked at the park across the road, and the parking lot where the cornfield had been. But a wood still crowned the slope with its dense June leaves, rustling beyond picnic tables and trashcans. A part of the woodland I remembered was still left. When I reached the shade of the trees, they breathed out the scent of damp forest floor.

Sunlight fingered through branches just as it always had. It shone on a space between trees: rough ground, heaped with earth the bulldozers had shoved there fifty years before.

Was that where the Lost Boys' House had been? The heap of earth was overgrown; I waded into bushes on that pile and saw nothing beneath them but dead leaves.

Fifty years.

Burrs from the bushes had fastened themselves on my jeans; I walked away trying to pick them off, but they stuck fast, bristling with stubborn spines, and went home with me.

I stopped when I got to the faint path and looked back. Had that been the place where Robert had moaned, "Christ! Christ!" under the ground?

The little park was pretty. I brought Margaret there that summer, but she was soon bored with the swings and slide and explored the woods beyond, running back along narrow deer paths to show me her "treasures": cushions of moss, acorn saucers, a dead moth.

We went there in autumn, too, when the leaves were masses of red, russet and gold. Margaret ran through the woods to collect handfuls of them, each one the most beautiful of all, and I sat on a stone in the sun and picked four leaves from her pile for memory's sake. "Can I have these?"

"Why?" Margaret came to look at them.

"This one is for an old lady, Grandma Laird, and this one is for your great-aunt, Adele. And this one is for your great-grandfather, Sam Beale. And this red one is for your grand...your grand-cousin, Robert Laird."

"I don't know any of them," Margaret said. She looked up. "That tree hasn't got any nice leaves."

I looked where she pointed. A huge oak had died. Its few crumpled brown leaves hung in the brilliant maple canopy like skeletons at a feast.

I stared at the oak. It stared back at me, I thought. A memory brought me the look of a familiar trunk and spreading branches, with a deep hollow...

I left my leaves on the stone and went to put my hand in that hollow. Once it had been too high for me to reach. Once young hands had crept over that bark to find the mason jar still hidden there.

"What's that?" Margaret cried. She grabbed the jar. "It's got a paper in it! It's got a flower, too! Is it a secret? Open it – what does it say?" She jumped up and down in her delight.

The lid wasn't rusted shut; it opened easily. The afternoon wind ruffled my hair as I read the paper's few lines to myself.

"What does it say?" Margaret pulled my hand down to peer at it.

"It says..." I looked at the paper as if I were reading it, though the letters were swimming before my eyes. "It says: 'Once upon a time a prince and princess came here when they were young, and made a secret house, and left their notes to each other in a bottle in a tall oak tree. If you find this, you will know that they grew up and fell in love, and lived happily ever after, and you are their royal child."

"Really?" Margaret said. "It really says that, really?

"Really," I said. "See for yourself."

Her young hand took the paper, and for a moment she held it under her green eyes, squinting. "But I can't read!"

"And," I said, "that's not all. It tells whoever finds the paper and rose to tear the paper in many, many pieces and throw them in the air, and bury the rose twenty feet from the dead oak tree in the middle of the circle."

"We have to do it," Margaret said in a hushed voice. "It's me that has to do it – I'm their child. You're old."

So she took the paper with a serious look on her face, sat down in drifts of dry leaves, and slowly, carefully tore the note into small pieces, then into smaller pieces yet, stuffing them in her pockets. At last the paper was only confetti.

"Is it in many, many pieces?" she asked.

"It certainly is."

"Then I throw it in the air!" She tossed the paper bits above her head. In a few seconds they were lost in the forest floor's deep grass.

"Now the rose," she said. "Is it a rose? It's just paper."

"It was red once," I said.

"It isn't any more. And I've got to bury it. How much is twenty feet from the oak tree?" She looked around her at the open space.

"The note said, 'in the middle of the circle,'" I told her. "So this clearing must be the circle, and the center's in that high, piled-up place."

"Shoosh," Margaret said, climbing the sloping ground and wading into the bushes. "Stuff is sticking to my jeans."

"Cockleburs," I said.

"I'll bury it quick," she said, and rummaged in dead leaves under the bushes. "There. It's gone."

"And we'd better be gone, too," I said. "It's almost time for supper."

"Just wait till I tell them!" Margaret cried as we both picked cockleburs from her jeans. "Wait till they hear what I found!" Then she scowled. "But they won't believe me, will they? About the prince and princess and the rose and all?"

"Maybe we can find some pieces of the note," I said.

We hunted, and we found two. Margaret closed them tight in her hand. "But where are your leaves?" she said as we passed the stone.

"The wind's blown them away. They're lost with all the others."

"Hurry!" Margaret said. "I want to tell everybody!"

She did. She told her story and showed her bits of paper. "It happened!" I heard her say on her way to bed. "Grandma knows!"

Raymond and I were left on the living-room couch together. "Margaret's had a wonderful day," he said. "She's convinced that a prince and a princess really did build a house in the park and leave a note to say she's 'a royal child.'"

I put a hand on his cheek. He was still good-looking, even though he was over fifty – the dark eyes, the dark hair silvering with gray.

"That was your doing, wasn't it?" he said. "You're responsible for that note in the tree, and the rose."

"Yes," I said. "I'm afraid I am."

"You made up stories for me, remember?"

"I was good at that," I said, and suddenly I began to cry – sobbing and shaking while Raymond put his arms around me and whispered, "Go ahead. Cry. I know, I know, you miss Dad."

So I sat there in his arms and cried for his father, and heard rain striking a window nearby. Rain was blurring ink on bits of paper among dark, dead leaves:

I brought you roses yesterday. Today, grenades
I brought home from a war are my way
of flying out of a world I can't face.
If you find this, leave me here
in the house we made.
We mixed our blood. You promised never to tell.
I want to be in the Lost Boys' House like the others
who never came back from the war,
here with your pictures, near you.
Take care of my lost boy for me.
How much I love you no one knows.

THE END

She tossed the paper bits above her head. In a few seconds
they were lost in the forest's deep grass.

CRITICS PRAISE NANCY PRICE'S NOVELS:

A NATURAL DEATH
by Nancy Price

This novel of the Carolinas in pre-Civil War days is beautiful, terrible, heart-breaking – A powerful evocation of what it meant to be black and a slave.   *-Publishers Weekly*

A rich first novel with a large cast of characters that movingly dramatizes culture and life in the South Carolina of the 1840s…quite remarkable.   *-Kirkus*

The author is a poet; her first novel is a rich and realistic account of vividly recalled times past.   *-Chicago Tribune*

A brilliant first novel by poet Nancy Price, deserving of respect for unerring detail, realistic treatment, and accurate reporting of rhythm and idiom. The Carolina rice-growing country in the 1850s becomes so real under Ms. Price's hand that the smells and sounds remain long after the pages are closed…A sensitive and humane writer of merit.   *-Houston Post*

An authentic and fascinating evocation of the past.
                                                            - Shirley Ann Grau
                                                            Washington Post

Mesmerizing prose…frightening, absorbing and enlightening reading.
                                                            -Cleveland Press

From the standpoint of a historian, it is a novel I could not put down, for the detail is as fascinating as it was accurate and compelling.   *-Carl Degler*

I felt as though I had been living in the terrifying world of a South Carolina slave plantation…A fascinating novel: vivid, poetic, very moving.   *-Ann Petry, author of* The Street

My God, what film it would make...There is nobility in these characters–and absolutely no sentimentalization. It's not just fiction: it's Literature.   *-Mary Carter, author of* La Maestra

The novel draws the reader...we read as things happen, not as if they once happened...as if we are watching a film. This is a sensitive, sympathetic and historically accurate novel. And it is by far one of the best about the antebellum South.   *-Providence Journal*

An authentic and fascinating evocation of the past.
                                                        -Washington Post

Price's portrayal of both sides of the slave society is both persuasive and saddening.   *-New York Times Book Review*

The book is saturated with that inimitable atmosphere that is South Carolina...[a] long and absorbing novel.
                                                        -Chattanooga Times

A splendid, strengthening addition to the literary voice of the South.   *-News and Observer, Raleigh, N.C.*

AN ACCOMPLISHED WOMAN
By Nancy Price

A seductive, almost hypnotic book...so much of its intensity and success derive from the manner of its telling ...a language...that avoids difficulty and unreadability. I found myself racing...excited by all its elements and by the way Price has managed to put them in sophisticated and engaging relation to each other.   *-Chicago Tribune*

Elegant detail.   *-New Yorker*

Nancy Price is a very talented writer and her characters are unique, her story line is inventive and unusual. This is a moving, even terrifying novel with rare richness, subtlety and depth.
                                                        -Publishers Weekly

Strikingly illustrates the extent to which we are all products of our own and others' imagination. -*New Republic*

Price can create the essence of a scene with a few vivid words...Intense and deeply moving...a touching love story that reveals things all women should know about themselves.

-*Los Angeles Times*

Catherine Buckingham was reared...as a thoroughly liberalized female in an unliberalized age. Her struggles to adjust create a stunning yet tender odyssey...Readability issues effortlessly from Ms. Price's fine prose. -*Cleveland Press*

Heady and powerful. -*Booklist*

Ms. Price tells her story quietly, allowing points of understanding to make themselves unobtrusively and, therefore, indelibly...It's altogether a very neat piece of writing, and Ms. Price is a valuable artist.

-*Philadelphia Bulletin*

A young girl's coming of age, coming to terms, coming to grips. Prices's understatement, her very tentativeness, makes for a story that can only be described as innocently passionate and achingly erotic.

-*Detroit News*

A sheer pleasure to read. -*Chattanooga Times*

Finely written, whole chunks of this second novel are dedicated warmly to the proposition of indefatigable character–and that's very nourishing. -*Kirkus Reviews*

A heady, powerful novel. -*Advance Booklist*

What would happen if a girl were allowed complete freedom [in 1920-30] to explore, to experiment with life?...Nancy Price has written a fascinating novel, a brilliant and deeply disturbing study of what it means to be a woman. -*Charlotte N.C. News*

Nancy Price, novelist and poet, has blended a keen feminist sensibility with a fine poetic style in this strangely haunting story…a meaningful statement about…the unrealized potential of generations of women and the lifelong impact of an ideal love affair.

-Cleveland Plain Dealer

What unfolds *is* a kind of "love affair that never existed"…Price's stunning diction, human compassion and intellectual rigor not only portray "An Accomplished Woman"–but how women are "accomplished."

-Des Moines Register

After I'd read the last page I could only lay the book down and stare at nothing for a long time, my cheeks wet with tears…Read this book, it will change your heart, not your head.

-Sacramento Bee

To describe more of the story is to take away from the sheer pleasure that it is to read the whole novel. Rarely does one come across a love story such as this told with so much sensitivity.

-Chattanooga Times

Compelling and poignant…More than just an accomplished novel; it is a work of art.

-Houston Chronicle

SLEEPING WITH THE ENEMY
By Nancy Price
(filmed by Twentieth Century Fox and starring Julia Roberts)

A sensitive and humane writer of merit.

-The Houston Post

Powerful, moving and well-controlled thriller…chilling scenes of observation and pursuit, and the author…brings the novel to a triumphant conclusion.

-Publishers Weekly

Rich characterizations, an ability to move the reader emotionally, and a lovely sense of atmosphere…right on the money.

-San Francisco Chronicle

Absorbing...sensual...the reader roots for Sara/Laura all the way.
-West Coast Review of Books

The plot [is] every woman's nightmare...mesmerizing...You won't be able to put it down. *-Houston Chronicle*

A tense, tightly woven novel...Price has managed in the writing to be absolutely faithful to the villains as well as the victims...The characters and events are so vivid that one is troubled, longs to know what becomes of these people. *-Louise Erdrich,*
Minneapolis Star and Tribune

Terror grips like the coils of an anaconda. *-London Observer*

NIGHT WOMAN
By Nancy Price

The tension rises almost unbearably.
-Express-News (San Antonio)

NIGHT WOMAN is a brilliantly disturbing study in co-dependency, but it is also a story of courage...Price is masterful in her characterizations: the characters are frighteningly real...Much as you might want to, you won't be able to put it down until you've read the last page. *-Houston Chronicle*

Following up on her novel SLEEPING WITH THE ENEMY, Price returns with a terrific suspenser...Don't even wait for the movie. *-Kirkus Reviews*

Highly recommended. *-Library Journal*

Well-written and engaging...an intriguing situation. The book pulls its punches until the very last chapters...gritty, wry characterization, chilling images of insanity...long, ultimately satisfying...will keep readers flipping pages. *-Publishers Weekly*

photo credit:
John Thompson

Nancy Price was born in Sioux Falls, South Dakota and spent her childhood in Detroit, Michigan. She graduated from Cornell College, received her M.A. from the University of Northern Iowa and studied at the University of Iowa Writers' Workshop. Nancy was given a National Endowment for the Arts fellowship, and awarded residencies at the Karolyi Foundation in France, the Tyrone Guthrie Center in Ireland and the Rockefeller Foundation Center in Italy.

Poems and short stories by Nancy Price have appeared in numerous magazines, newspapers and books, and she is a member of the Authors Guild. Her novels have been best sellers, translated into fifteen foreign languages; a Twentieth Century Fox film was made of her novel *SLEEPING WITH THE ENEMY*. She has three children, is a professor of English at U.N.I. in Cedar Falls, Iowa, and spends her winters near Orlando, Florida.

Malmarie Press
4387 Rummell Road
St. Cloud, Florida 34769
E-mail address:nancypricebooks@aol.com
Fax: 407-891-9001

To order copies of NO ONE KNOWS by Nancy Price

FAX ORDERS: 407-891-9001

TELEPHONE ORDERS: 800-509-4905

E-MAIL ORDERS: nancypricebooks@aol.com

Please make your checks payable to Malmarie Inc..

CREDIT CARD: (A note to credit card users: your credit card will be charged to "Instant Ancestors, Inc., Kissimmee, Florida.")

❑Visa   ❑MasterCard   ❑American Express
❑Discover   ❑Diners Club   ❑Carte Blanche

Card number _____

Name on card _____Exp. date_____/_____

Signature _____
                                (signature and expiration date required)

Malmarie Press
4387 Rummell Road, Suite IA
St. Cloud, Florida 34769

Please send me _____copies of NO ONE KNOWS by Nancy Price. I am enclosing $27.95 for each book, plus $3.95 shipping for the first book, and $1.95 for each additional book.
Florida residents please add applicable sales tax.

Name _____

Street address _____

City _____State_____ Zip_____

(Kindly allow 1-2 weeks for delivery)